Also by Maureen Freely

Mother's Helper

The Life of the Party

My Year with the Stork Club

My Year with THE STORK CLUB

Maureen Freely

Alfred A. Knopf New York 1993

This Is a Borzoi Book
Published by Alfred A. Knopf, Inc.

 Published in the United States by Alfred A. Knopf, Inc., New York. Distributed by Random House, Inc., New York.

Originally published in Great Britain by Bloomsbury Publishing, Ltd., London, in 1992.

Library of Congress Cataloging-in-Publication Data
Freely, Maureen [date]
My year with the stork club : a novel / by Maureen Freely. — 1st American ed.
p. cm.
ISBN 0-679-41154-2
I. Title.
PS3556.R3836S76 1993
813'.54—dc20 92-54788
CIP

Manufactured in the United States of America

First American Edition

To Matthew, Emma, Kimber, Rachel and Helen

Sometimes

Chapter 1

Sometimes, when I am sitting at my desk and gazing out the window, and watching, as I am at this very moment, a new wave of fog engulf the sky, leaving me with nothing to look at but a suffocating white light, I think I hear a child crying behind a closed door—or you in the bedroom, laughing on the phone.

And for a moment I think I still have a family. Then the truth comes back with all the stinging surprise of a slap across the face. I remember you are gone and what I did to make you go. And I tell myself this is my penance, to be left for dead in this tomb of an apartment, mocked by my own last wishes and condemned by my will.

Everywhere I look, I see things the way I always wanted them. The toys are in their baskets, the shoes in pairs, the pens with their caps on, and without toothmarks. There is not a single monster face on the memo pad next to the phone. Even the bookshelves are perfect: no longer will you find the *Aeneid* standing between *Dare to Discipline* and *101 Decorating Ideas for Playrooms,* or *Children: The Challenge* wedged in upside down behind *Remembrance of Things Past*. Books are arranged first according to subject and then alphabetically, and when I look at them I ache as if it is my own heart I have violated, my own heart I have slashed, cubed and brutally rearranged alphabetically and according to subject along that shelf.

There is no way to reverse the damage, no way either to breathe life and disorder back into the bulletin board, where messages and reminders obey the symmetry of an obituary page. Where are they now, the five-year-old birthday invitations, the three-year-old babysitting co-op lists, the extinct coupons for extinct toxic-shock-causing tampons, the introductory offers for brain-damage-linked soya formula, the frayed napkins with phone numbers on them but no names? Where are the paper-plate doilies, the warped brown-and-purple watercolors, the canceled checks decorated with flowers and stick figures, the castles with eyes for windows and fangs for gates? What grandiose notion compelled me to take them down?

Did I really think they would improve my life, the things I have tacked up there instead—the cramped little lists of hospital-corner errands to run on Monday, the anal-compulsive bills to pay on Tuesday, the let's-play-Monopoly telephone messages? Look on my work, ye Mighty, and despair.

As I sit here in my tomb with nothing to look at but the sky and expensive furniture, and nothing to think about but the colossal wreck that is my life, I ask myself, what is the use of an education? Or rather, why did I learn so little from mine?

When did I lose you?

It is thirty-seven days now since I said goodbye to you in that garden, and still I don't understand what was going on behind those eyes, still I am haunted by the smile you gave me before you turned your back on me, before you returned your attention to the roses. Were you happy that you were still able to hurt me? Laura—can you have any idea what it's like to watch your own children run into the arms of another man?

Most of the time I can convince myself that I have salvaged something. But then I'll wake up and remember what's beyond my reach, and in another man's arms, forever. That was the point I reached yesterday. I didn't see the point in trying anymore. I spent the afternoon playing games with the medicine cabinet, and lying on the couch taunting myself for not having enough courage to walk out onto the balcony and throw myself over. I had gone so far as to work it out mathematically. I knew I could do it in under four seconds, and maybe I would have if your friends hadn't decided to check up on me—although I certainly was not happy to have them turn up like that. There is nothing more annoying than having to get up in the middle of a suicide fantasy to answer the door.

The apartment, with its open bottle of Halcion on the mantelpiece, its garbage bags filled with tax records and old correspondence, and its collection of wine bottles on the kitchen counter, spoke for itself. But they knew better than to allude to the obvious. They pretended it was a social visit. And so I did the same. As we sat at the dining table sipping our Camparis, I calculated the time difference, imagined you in your four-poster bed eating breakfast with that man who is pretending to be my children's father, that man who is pretending to love you more than I do, but then the pain subsided, the vision died, and, when I looked in the direction of the kitchen, I could almost see you smiling at me from the doorway.

A breeze was coming in from the balcony, playing on the back of my neck and rustling the leaves of the yucca tree.

"It's warm tonight, isn't it?" I remember Charlotte saying.

"Yes," I said. "That's why I made us Camparis."

Ophelia said she didn't see the connection, and so I explained to her that Camparis reminded me of summer.

"But it *is* summer," she said.

I had to spell it out. "I meant it reminded me of summer in the Aegean."

All three of them nodded, even though two of them had never been there. They all knew it was time to change the subject.

Ophelia pointed at the old map I bought at that store you told me about on my last night in Athens. I had just gotten it back from the framers. "That's new, isn't it?"

I said yes, in a manner of speaking.

And Becky said, "What happened to the picture you used to have there?" I told her that the wall had been bare for years, but she said, "Exactly. I mean the picture you had there before it went bare. That statue. What was its name again?"

"The *Diadoumenos,*" I said.

"That's right." She squinted as if trying to see it beyond the map. "Why don't you put it back up again? It might cheer things up."

When I said that I couldn't, because I had destroyed it years ago, they looked up at me as if they expected me to explain. I told them not even to ask. My voice came out sounding sharper than I had intended. After an uneasy silence, I apologized. "I'm not really in the mood for polite conversation."

"That's fine," said Charlotte. "You just sit here then and relax while we fix dinner."

I told them I didn't need dinner. I lied and said I was going out.

"Too bad then," said Becky. "You'll have to cancel. After all, how often is it these days that you can have all three of us at your service?"

This was too close to the bone for me, but it made them laugh. As I watched them, I asked myself why, when I thought of them, they were always so grim and reproving, casting shadows that were larger than life.

When here they were, so small and so cheerful. Their laughter, inappropriate as it was, made the apartment feel lived in. And so I decided not to fight it. As I settled into my armchair, I had occasion to think, yet again, what an oddly matched group they were. If it weren't for the fact that they had all had their first children at the same time, they would never have made friends.

Or was I wrong? As they bustled around the apartment, gathering up the garbage bags and getting supper started in the kitchen, what I noticed most was how different all three of them were from me. And how easily, and mysteriously, they communicated.

Their conversation was full of jumps I couldn't account for, gaps I couldn't fill. They seemed to be talking about a man one of them was involved with. He lived in Chicago, or was it Washington? He was married to a ballbreaker, or was it an airhead? He was longing to get away from her, except that he couldn't, because of the children? Because he was afraid of change? Because he had a pretty good deal already and didn't want to make sacrifices? Because, even though he was a nice person, the fact remained he was a man?

Or was he two men? Or three? It was hard to tell. By the time they joined me in the living room, they had moved on to subjects that they didn't mind my overhearing. Charlotte had some damning gossip about her former head of department; Becky claimed that a bank manager had refused to give her a loan because she had failed to use the right male code words; Ophelia had a new set of atrocity stories about a surgeon at the hospital whom she called, yes, you guessed it, the Missing Chromosome. Apparently he could not bear to operate in the same theater with any female colleague who happened to be taller than he was. What was wrong with him? they wanted to know. I *didn't* want to know, and so I was thousands of miles away when Becky pounced on me.

"So," she said. "What's going on here?"

She was standing right over me, so close that all I could see was a pocket on her Chinese brocade jacket.

"I don't know what you're talking about," I said.

"I'm talking about the garbage bags."

"What about them? Maybe I'm spring cleaning," I said.

And she said, "I'm also talking about the substance abuse."

"I'll drink what I want to drink," I shouted.

To which she said, in a low and menacing voice, "That doesn't explain the pills."

"It doesn't *have* to explain the pills," I said. "And neither do I."

For a few moments, we glared at each other. Then she said, "Don't do it, Mike."

"Oh fuck off," I said. I lit up a cigarette just to annoy her.

Here Ophelia moved in. *Doctor* Ophelia. Leaning forward, she said, "Seriously."

"I'll smoke if I want to," I told her.

"That's not the issue we're concerned with at the moment," she said.

"Seriously, Mike, my dear," echoed Charlotte. She leaned forward, took hold of my arm and pulled me toward her. "Seriously, darling. What's the point?"

I'm afraid I broke down here. They gathered around me to hold my hand, pat my back, squeeze my shoulders. I thought I was going to suffocate, but at the same time I couldn't control myself. It all came out. I asked them, what reason was there for living if I had lost my family?

And Charlotte said, "Listen, Mike. What makes you think you're different from the rest of us? We've all lost our families if that's how you want to look at it." And of course she was right.

And—equally of course—you could write the script for the ultra-earnest conversation that followed. All the old history got dragged out, complete with their updated statements on what they had learned from our mistakes. Then came the advice.

I defended myself as best I could, but they knew me too well, and so I was finally forced to agree with them: my life followed a repeating pattern because I had grown up in a dysfunctional family. When they went on to assure me that it was not too late to take charge of my life, all I could think was, God, if only it were.

They forced a string of promises out of me. I would call them if I was upset. I would call them if I was lonely. I would come out for a movie, a meal, a cup of coffee, a run, a swim, a walk. I would not let this latest setback get me down. There was still hope. In the meantime I had to take steps to cure myself of codependency. They had even brought books to get me started.

Ophelia's last move was to take my Halcion pills and throw them down the Disposall. I was glad when they left.

I spent a long time on the balcony that night, one of the few this summer without fog. I watched planes come in for landings. I watched others take off and disappear. I watched the cars travel across the Bay Bridge, down Columbus, around Washington Square, up Telegraph Hill, down the Crooked Street. I watched the ferries disappear behind Coit Tower and then emerge on the other side. I watched the lights go on and off in the Pyramid Building. And I thought how smooth it all looked, this passage of ferries and planes and cars. How expected. How graceful and inevitable this changing of lights.

And yet that cleaner of the ninth floor of the Pyramid Building probably didn't know if she could live another day before the loan shark got to her. And the driver in the middle lane of the Bay Bridge probably had a heart condition, had a pain in his chest, did not know if he could make it as far as the exit for Treasure Island. The car inching its way up Union was being driven by a thief, by an illegal alien, by a fallen rock star on his way to the kind of humiliating gig where people talked through your songs, so what was the point, he was probably thinking, why even get upset that there wasn't a single fucking parking space in all of North Beach, why not dump the car on a double yellow line (since he wasn't going to be able to keep up the payments anyway) and split for Yelapa? And all the while he kept on moving at twenty-four miles per hour, while beyond his field of vision another ferry crossed behind Coit Tower on its way to Tiburon, steady, on course, sparkling with lights even though the woman who was standing at the rail was probably thinking of throwing herself into the bay because she had lost, again, and badly, in the futures market, because her last baby had left for college, because she was in love with her best friend's wife. What should she do? Was it possible, at her age, to break away and start a new life?

All these problems, all fresh starts, the world didn't have room for them, because there were only so many roads and bridges and ferry routes, only so many lights. I remembered something you had said once, about the Herculean effort people put into being predictable. It was as true of us as it was of anyone. After all the contortions we had put ourselves through—what had we done? The same thing millions of other people had done, for the same reasons, with the same results. It made you wonder why we had bothered.

But then I told myself, that wasn't the whole story. That was when I remembered those other summer evenings I had spent on this balcony, had spent with you. When you were there, right there, in the shadows, when I could tell exactly where you were and what your expression was even though I couldn't see you. When it was the two of us against the world, when we could still use our imaginations to escape the maze, when we knew how to make each other happy no matter how bad things were, when I could still convince myself, if the stars were bright enough, that I was married to a woman and not a committee.

When you look back now—don't you think it was a mistake to give your friends so much power over us?

Chapter 2

Not that either of us had any idea what you were letting yourself in for. In the beginning, I could hardly tell them apart. All the women in that birth class looked the same to me, with their pert seminar smiles, their pastel overalls, their karate slippers and their basketball stomachs, their Barbie-goes-to-college hairstyles and their unconvincing Ken-doll husbands, with their sure-I-used-to-go-on-marches-but-shit-what-did-the-Cambodians-ever-do-for-me-I've-got-a-family-to-support-now smiles. If they took on separate identities as the weeks dragged on, it was not as Charlotte, Becky and Ophelia, but as Charlotte-and-Trey, Becky-and-Mitchell, Ophelia-and-Kiki.

Ophelia-and-Kiki who were both-family-practitioners, who were going-to-be-lucky-enough-to-share-the-childcare-fifty-fifty, who were going to have the nursery in the office so that Ophelia could "totally" breast-feed. I remember the importance she gave to the word "totally." I remember laughing with you about it afterward.

Just as I remember laughing with you about Becky-and-Mitchell. Becky-and-Mitchell, who were three renovated houses away from the counterculture, and two haircuts away from the middle class. I remember Mitchell leaning forward and saying, "How many of you people are planning to confine your children inside the bars of a crib?"

And I remember that before anyone could answer, Becky had added, "The real issue, of course, is the underlying concept of bedtime."

"Total bedtime," I remember saying. Everyone (except you) nodded eagerly. Just as everyone nodded when Charlotte-and-Trey presented *their* game plan. I remember Charlotte tossing her famous golden tresses, slapping her husband in the face with them as usual and as usual not noticing, and saying, "We've pretty much come to terms with the fact that my work is more important to my self-esteem than Trey's work is to his. That's why we're going to try him out as primary caretaker." And then pausing, wondering why Trey had missed his cue (it was because he was still taking hair out of his mouth), and saying, with an edge to her voice, "Isn't that so, Trey?"

They all talked about the future as if it were a cabinet they had ordered from a master carpenter. Even I, in my ignorance, knew what a shock they were in for. But I did not want to be there to watch. I had nothing to learn from them, and I didn't think you did either.

I thought we were going to do things our way. And didn't we, for a while? Didn't I hold your hand for all thirteen hours of labor? Didn't I draw you your focal point? Didn't I remind you how to breathe when you forgot? Wasn't I there telling you what a good job you were doing, when everyone, including the doctor, was shouting at you for not pushing hard enough? Didn't I burst into tears when I found out it was a boy? Didn't I make sure they gave you Jesse right away so you could put him on your breast? Didn't I cry again when I got to hold him myself? Didn't I take three weeks off work?

Didn't I get up in the night when I heard him crying? Didn't I do all the shopping and the cooking and the birth announcements and the washing? Didn't I tell you, the day I had to go back to work, that I dreaded leaving you? Didn't I give you that bracelet, that one with the three interlocked gold bangles, and tell you it stood for our family? Didn't I cry, later on, when we had to hock it?

Even when I did go back to work, I was still the one who walked up and down with him at night, who sponged him when he had fevers, who looked into his face and told him, even when he was too little to understand me, about all the places you and I would take him when I had made enough money to buy us out of San Francisco. It was the nights and weekends I lived for, Laura. The happiest moment of my day was when I left work. Every evening, when I changed buses in Washington Square, I would stop and look up the hill at our building and imagine you standing at the window waiting for me with Jesse in your arms.

The Jesse in my imagination was always the Jesse I came home to, the Jesse who had learned to crawl, who had his two bottom teeth now, and now his two top teeth, who had learned how to say "Mama" and "Papa" and called our downstairs neighbor a dog. But the woman who was holding him was always the Laura in the hospital, the tired but radiant Laura pressing her newborn baby against her breast. And that was why I dismissed Charlotte, Becky and Ophelia as diversions. The first time I came home and found them strewn all over the living room, I was surprised. How had it happened? What on earth had you found to talk about?

Then I found out you had actually invited them, that the four of you had organized a playgroup. What? I thought. But then I thought: She's lonely. I'm gone for nine, ten hours at a stretch. She has to talk to someone.

Then these words, these alien words, started seeping into your vocabulary. Words like "parenting." Expressions like "childcare option" and "ego disintegration" and "setting limits." Things we had once laughed about. Together.

Then you started signing up for things. Because you found life at home "depressing." (Depressing? With our Jesse?) It was Diaper Gym, and Little Flippers, and Child Observation Class. And twice a week now for that cooperative playgroup, so that you could take turns getting away from the children. (Away? From perfect Jesse?) You started coming home with weird ideas about food, which you insisted on calling nutrition, and you would only tell me about them when I did something wrong—for example, if I offered Jesse pear for the first time without waiting sixty hours before we could establish that he was not allergic to banana. If I suggested, after Jesse fed apple sauce to his cheeks, his chin, his ears, his hair, and his nose, but not even once to his mouth, that perhaps we should feed him with a spoon. If I brought home bread that was not made of rice flour. Then you would tell me what Becky or Charlotte or Ophelia had told you about wheat or bananas or the evils of spoon-feeding. If I complained about the price of sodium-free rice crackers, if I said that soya milk tasted like potato juice, you would go into a sulk.

And then this obsession with equipment. Every week it was something else we couldn't afford that you couldn't live without. A mechanical swing. A Johnny Jump Up. A portable restaurant seat. A safer, hundred-dollar car seat. A hundred-and-fifty-dollar stroller, designed by the same people who brought us Concordes. A high chair made of real wood instead of the plastic-and-steel one my mother got for us. Half a dozen safety gates to replace the confining and repressive playpen. An indoor climbing frame. Bars for the windows so that he didn't fall out of them when he was climbing on the indoor climbing frame. A two-hundred-dollar Cuisinart, not because it mashed up food any better than the blender, but because Charlotte swore by it, Becky already had it and Ophelia was going to order it from a catalogue.

Then you even started to look like them. I remember, with horror, the day I came home to find you wearing those shoes. I can't remember what you called them. Familias? They were brown and grotesque and had thick, rippling, rubber soles, the kind that said just try and get a hard-on now you've seen me, just try and tell yourself that these feet belong to a woman. I remember how insulted you were when I told you this.

But didn't we still manage to have a good time together? Even when you wore those shoes? Remember all those trips we took, just you and me and Jesse, to Eureka and Yosemite and Yelapa and the Yucatán? All those Sundays we spent in Napa and Half Moon Bay? It was easy, when there were still only three of us, to dismiss the Stork Club as a weekday annoyance, and to believe that our real life, that one that counted, was the life we three shared on weekends. It was Maria who tipped the balance.

I am not trying to say, now that she exists, that I regret our decision to have her. Wasn't I there, right next to you, all through the ill-starred labor? Wasn't I the one who saw the danger signs on the graph on the fetal monitor? Wasn't I the one who insisted that Ophelia call Kiki in for a second opinion? Wouldn't Maria have died or been severely brain-damaged if Kiki hadn't done an emergency cesarean?

If I was closer to Maria than you were, Laura, it is because I watched her being born. I can't tell you what it did to me to watch them slash you open, and to see your blood splatter over Kiki's shoes. I don't know if anyone ever told you this but she had the cord around her neck. She was blue when they put her into the incubator. But I was there, right next to her. I watched her turn red. I heard her first cry. I was the first to pick her up and hold her, right there in the operating room.

There are still unanswered questions. I still find it strange that you and Becky *and* Charlotte all gave birth to your second children within seven weeks of one another.

What I resented most at the time was the way they took over the birth room. Remember how upset they were about the "intrusive" fetal monitor (without which Maria's distress would have gone undetected)—and that awful Peruvian folk music Becky brought in to soothe your nerves? (Ha!) And that acupuncturist! The toddlers in the hallway! The least they could have done was clear out when I brought Maria in to you. But they didn't. They stayed to watch you bond. I began to see that I belonged to a much bigger family than I had bargained for.

That night they even had the childcare angle covered. Jesse was to eat at Charlotte's, would be moved to Ophelia's for the night, would be driven to playschool at Becky's in the morning. Deprived of responsibilities, I was left to my own very dangerous devices.

That is why I went out drinking with Mitchell—because my judgment, after watching that cesarean, after watching a long unwanted and suddenly loved baby almost die, and then recover in my very arms—my judgment, after having that same infant whipped away from me, was impaired.

I had been keeping Mitchell at arm's length for going on two years by then. I didn't see why we had to be friends just because we happened to have gone to the same college. But with you in the hospital and Becky due to deliver within the month, we were back in the same boat. Or should I say stud farm? We didn't even have to say it—we both needed to break away. And so off we went to Specs, where we forged a spurious alliance based on drink, accidental fatherhood, and parallel memories of Harvard Yard.

I don't remember what story I told you about what happened that night. My own memories are disjointed. The Game, if I remember correctly, was a big item in our conversation. So was Elsie's. So was Tommy's Lunch. But most of all, we talked about the strike. He went on and on about the scars it had left him with, and so, I'm afraid, did I. It didn't take too many shots of tequila before we were agreeing how bad it felt when we looked at how our aspirations had dropped since graduation, and telling each other how much we wanted to opt out of the system. (We actually called it that! That's how drunk we were!)

I ought to have realized he was leading me up to something, but I didn't. And so, foolishly, I told him that I was saving up for a house in Greece, so at least we could have our summers the way we wanted them. That was when he told me—in a careful, persuasive voice I have since come to know all too well—about the great real-estate bargains to be had South of Market.

He told me about one (as it turned out, fictitious) building that was going for nothing. He wanted to buy it, sit on it for two, three years ("Fuck improvements, just rent it out as it is"), and then, when the neighborhood came up, sell it and make a thousand percent profit. All he needed was a partner with some capital. "So how about it?" he said. "Why not make your money work for you? Think it over. Have another drink." Unfortunately, I did. And then, when I said it was a deal, he put me through what he claimed was the authentic Black Panther handshake.

We ended the night by taking some women I can't remember to the Hot Tubs on Van Ness. It was (if you exclude the final year) one of only two occasions when I was unfaithful to you. The other time was a month later, when Becky was in the hospital with Paloma. Mitchell and I did a repeat performance with yet another forgettable woman. We picked her up at one of those fern bars on Union. By then we had already begun our doomed partnership.

It wasn't just work that was getting me down by then. It was the way you were treating me. From the moment you brought Maria home from the hospital, you seemed to hate me. You seemed to think I had all the freedom you had lost. No matter how much I did around the house, it was never enough. If I so much as picked up a newspaper I was taking advantage of you, I was treating you like a slave. The fact that I was the only one bringing in the money was unimportant. I had no right to expect any free time unless I was willing to give you free time, too. If I went out for an evening, even if it was for business, that meant you deserved an evening out with your friends. If I questioned your logic, I was treated like a caveman. I had to put up with telephonic postmortems which would always end with your friends reminding you that I was doomed by gender because of my deficient Y chromosome.

The day arrived when I felt as if I had no chromosomes left at all. When I found out they had talked you into signing up for that wretched bar exam—even though it was clear you did not have the time to prepare for it—I didn't dare say a thing, and I can't tell you what that enforced silence did to me.

Still, I wanted you to pass. I can't tell you how bad I felt when I came home that day to see you crying over that stupid letter, blaming yourself when it wasn't your fault. When I took you in my arms that night and apologized to you for giving you such a miserable life, I was not trying to reassert paternalistic authority. I was just trying to cheer you up. And later, when I told you I wanted to get out of that business, and take you back to Europe, I was trying to cheer myself up. I didn't begin to hope it might be possible. I had long since lost hope of extracting myself from the temple of doom that was my office.

Chapter 3

You were smiling when I brought you in your coffee the next morning. When I asked you why, you said you had been thinking of the Palatia—although now that I think about it you didn't mention it by name. You just said you were thinking of the marble arch standing all alone on the island at the far end of Naxos harbor, and that the thing you liked most about it was that it was going nowhere.

You said that, whenever you felt upset, all you had to do was imagine you were back there. You told me how clear the shoreline became in the late afternoon, how the sea and the sky were the same translucent blue, how the slanting sun rays cut through the blanket of dust on the mountains and made the whitewashed houses look as if they were radiating light instead of reflecting it. You said your memory of that view was so detailed that you could even see the seaweed swaying in the rockpools, and the sea urchins rocking back and forth, and the shellfish. I remember asking you which shellfish. You said you didn't remember their name, even though you could tell me exactly how they tasted.

"So," I said, "they belong to the famous Thing Category, do they?"

You said you guessed they did.

And I said, "God, that mother of yours really knocked herself out educating you."

You said there was no reason for your mother to have known the names for everything in the Mediterranean when she herself had grown up on the North Atlantic.

And I said, "That still doesn't account for the rest of the Thing Category. When I met you the only kitchen utensil you knew by name was a corkscrew."

You wrinkled your nose the way you always did when you mistook a joke for a criticism, and then told me that in the end you thanked her for not telling you the name of every single thing you set your eyes on.

You said that was what you enjoyed most about the rockpool—seeing things instead of names. It was not as important to know which sea urchins were poisonous—the black ones or the blue ones—as it was to watch them sway in the waves, as it was to be able to remember them, and to remember them perfectly.

You were interrupted here by Charlotte, who was calling to remind you that it was your floater day for the car pool. So we never had a chance to finish our conversation. But I would like to think that you were about to say you wanted to take the children to Greece for the summer, so that you could show them the Palatia and the marble archway going nowhere.

Do you remember how I dressed the children in their sleep while you made their lunches? Do you remember how they were still asleep when we strapped them into their car seats? Do you remember how they looked up at us with their eyes still fogged as they sipped their box drinks?

In your mind's eye, can you still see yourself rolling the window down and reaching out to stroke the side of my face?

I would like to think you meant it when you said you didn't know what you would do without me.

And I would like to think that the picture I am about to paint of your friends as I imagine them that morning (lying in wait for you as you proceed, unsuspecting, on your circuitous route) is, if not accurate in every detail, at least reasonably familiar to you.

Chapter 4

I'll begin, then, with Charlotte's house, Charlotte's narrow, yellow-shingled Victorian modestly clinging to its neighbors on its steep incline. At half past eight on the 28th of May I imagine . . . that its light-blue shutters are closed (except, perhaps, for the one in the rafters), while its front door—its dark-blue front door with the street number hand-painted off-center in bold, calligraphic black—is inexplicably ajar.

Inside, the hallway leading to the back of the house is dark and cluttered. Along one wall are the coat hooks for adults. Along the other are lower ones for children. Each hook holds more than it was designed for: piled on top of one another, the jackets and robes and sweaters fan out like petticoats over the shoes and the boots, the kites, umbrellas, tennis rackets, golf clubs, beach balls, flippers and snorkeling masks stacked beneath them.

The kitchen is bright, almost too bright. The shafts of sunlight coming in through the bay window enclose the dining table like a tent. At one end sits Charlotte, looking solid and fit in her UC Berkeley tracksuit. Her large blue eyes are clear, almost luminous; her long, honey-colored hair is still damp from her early-morning swim. Her broad, handsome face looks composed but tense. This may have something to do with the cartoon sound track that is wafting in from the den next door and blending infelicitously with the muted Mozart concerto on the kitchen stereo.

Look at how she clutches the handle of her coffee mug. Look at the To Do list beneath it—at how the carefully curved handwriting of the top items: "Discuss P. with L. 2:45—Toothpaste—Nectarines," turns into the frantically large additions at the bottom: READ BOOKS! LETTERS! REARRANGE OFFICE HOURS! REMEMBER HAMLET! Notice how some items are underlined while others are starred, and how she has crossed out each completed chore at least three times.

How can you tell she's a teacher? From the loud, professionally affable way she calls her children in from the den for breakfast. How can you tell she teaches at the college level as opposed to primary or secondary? The words she uses have too many syllables. She is trying a new kind of "initiative," she tells Patten and Dottie as they climb into their chairs. This is because she is entering a "bottleneck" and so finds herself "hugely overextended." She is due to give a paper at a symposium—in fact, *this* paper (she waves the draft at them). She needs some peace and quiet right now, in exchange for which she is offering them what would normally be "forbidden substances." She points at a selection pack of cereals, but already the children are tugging at it, tearing away at the cellophane and fighting over the Cocoa Puffs. With a patient and excessively intent smile, Charlotte sets out to talk them both into "experimenting with other products." It is clear, from the careful way she discusses their options with them, and from her adamant refusal to favor one child over the other, that she is not just talking about cereal boxes, but about the larger (and largely gender-related) issues lurking inside them. This is a woman who could find a gender-related issue in a nail clipper.

Finally she talks her daughter into Frosted Flakes and her son into Rice Krispies. They rip open the boxes, play tug-of-war with the milk carton, watch jealously as Charlotte takes possession of it, and protest, each of them, that she has given more milk to the other. There is an edge to her voice as she threatens to make them eat Muesli instead. But they don't even listen. When she sits down at her place again, it is clear, from the blank way she stares at her lists, that she has lost her train of thought. From the way she jumps up and pulls the Mozart cassette out of the stereo and riffles through the piles of cassettes on the table behind it for a replacement, it is clear that the metaphor "train of thought" has reminded her of something. Clear also, from the first strains of "Blue Train," that she has managed to preserve her sanity—yet again!—by escaping into the past.

So much of which took place right here in this kitchen. The reminders are everywhere—starting with the very table where she and her children are now eating breakfast. It is, with its blue-and-purple legs, and its little evil eyes inlaid at the corners, the most telltale survivor of the Days of the Commune. Although if you take a close look at the rest of the kitchen, you can see other traces: the rust marks on the tiles where the older, larger, *circa* 1948 stove used to be, and that wall between the kitchen and what used to be Trey's and his (then) girlfriend's bedroom (and is now the den). This wall is white but you can see that it, too, was once blue-and-purple.

And that collection of pinpricks fanning out from a virgin circle in the center of the same wall—that is the legacy of the famous dart board that played such an important part in the disintegration of the commune. Thinking about the episode now, Charlotte has a hard time understanding how eight highly educated people could have allowed things to get so crazy—how they could have allowed a man on mescaline—and not just a man, but a political science major, a *political science major who had returned from an Alaskan hiking trip saying that mathematics was the Answer*—how they could have allowed a man who was probably certifiable even when he *wasn't* on mescaline put an apple on Trey's (then) girlfriend's head and line it up with the bull's-eye! When, in addition to everything else, he wasn't even wearing his glasses! Charlotte can only conclude that Trey's (then) girlfriend must have been doing mescaline herself.

It is hard to believe that it could have happened here. How to describe the kitchen's present incarnation in the language of the commune? Looking around her, at the children's toys and drawings, at the earnest, well-meaning, unheeded and yellowing labels on the cabinets and flowerpots and household appliances, Charlotte decides they would have (snidely) dismissed it as a temple to early education. Except that it isn't. No, not quite.

Because it has never been done over, this kitchen. It has been touched up and added on to as necessary. The telephone answering machine is on top of the stereo is on top of the refrigerator. The speakers are on the counter propping up the cookbooks which are obscured from view by the juice squeezer, the Cuisinart, the yogurt maker and the toaster oven. There are wires everywhere. The drying rack is piled high with upended pots. There is a trolley full of unfiled letters in front of the toy cabinet, which served briefly during the Last Days of the Commune, and without Charlotte's prior knowledge or consent, as an arms cache, and was, in fact, the main reason why she began to have doubts about her (then) boyfriend, although in the end it was he who abandoned *her* for that waitress. Or to be fair, ex-waitress. Although to be honest, ultimate airhead. Charlotte doesn't know how Rick of all people put up with her, or how, for that matter, he can be content working in a bank. Rick, in a bank! Such an about-face! Charlotte cannot understand how he can pretend a whole section of his life never happened.

And yet she wonders if he might be on to something. There is, after all, a lot to be said for the complete overhaul. Imagine being able to look at your geranium pots without remembering that they used to be for marijuana plants. To use a breadboard without recalling that it used to be for cutting coke. To go into the attic and not come across letters to her (then) boyfriend from the airhead waitress (long before she was officially an item), plus photographs of Trey and *his* (then) girlfriend naked and on acid, not to mention a collection of wax hands (from other, long-forgotten acid trips), and a nargile, and a list of demands from the Symbionese Liberation Army, and, last but not least, a *very* embarrassing pair of platform shoes that brought to mind Minnie Mouse . . . How tall would she have been with those on? Charlotte now asks herself. (Talk about a slave of fashion!)

But there you are. And here *she* is, for better or for worse, feeding her kids breakfast at the same table where she made her first tabbouleh, read the opening pages of *Fear of Flying,* designed invitations to her last orgy. No wonder she feels overwhelmed!

"Snap crackle pop SMASH," she hears her son saying. "Snap crackle pop SMASH . . ."

"Do you have to do that, darling?"

"Yes," says Patten.

She is almost afraid to ask why. Perplexed by the eternal mystery that is the male psyche, she looks away from him and out the (unwashed) plate-glass window at the (untended) garden. And asks herself, but what if it isn't nature after all, but nurture? Had she weaned him wrong? Did she have two bad breasts? Had she perhaps overwhelmed him with erotic attention? There is a book she read recently (in the original French) in conjunction with this paper she's about to give—"Women and Language: the European Perspective"—about the Jocasta complex, which blamed just about everything on the mother (yet again!), but to be honest she did see bits of herself in the construct. And just to think of Jocasta now upsets her, and that is why she turns away from her own unknowable problems . . .

To the crisis at 2238 Hyde.

Poor Laura, she thinks. It is terrible, just terrible, that you have failed your bar exam. It is essential, absolutely essential, that your overbearing husband not be permitted to use this failure to his advantage.

You, Laura, will do just about anything to avoid responsibility for your actions—a common syndrome in adult children of alcoholics.

Charlotte is well read on this subject as she herself is the adult child of alcoholics. Trey is an adult child of alcoholics, too, and this is probably why she was initially attracted to him. Which is sad, although how can she regret any chain of events that resulted in two such adorable children? When she thinks of her friends who put off families and now cannot conceive . . .

Although Charlotte thinks that you, Laura, are weak because you had children too early. If you had had a chance to use your law degree productively before you had children, it would have been OK. You would have developed some backbone. But because you went straight out of law school into motherhood, and *I* went straight out of law school into that practice—and what's more, the wrong kind of practice for my temperament (of all the people to go into corporate bonds!)—our paths diverged. Our relationship went off balance. I, Mike, was unable to understand the problems you, Laura, were facing at home, while you were unable to anticipate or handle my troubles at work. This left me free to overdevelop my worst character traits, one of which was a tendency toward delusions of grandeur.

This idea that I was born to privileges instead of having to earn them. This anger I felt when things didn't come my way just because I snapped my fingers. This desire to live like a gentleman—it is all very, very familiar to Charlotte because I bear an uncanny resemblance to this former boyfriend of hers, Rick. Like me, Rick had been the poor boy in a school full of rich kids. They had unbalanced him and given him false values. She thinks that this is my problem too. No money in the family, but growing up abroad in all those consulates and embassies, all those private schools in Italy and Switzerland. All those servants—it had given me a warped idea of my place in the world.

Then there was my inability to call any one place in the world my home. This was Rick to a T (or, to be more accurate, Rick to a T before the waitress). I was a Drifter. This was why I felt so threatened now that my wife wanted to put down roots. A stronger woman would have anticipated these negative feelings and incorporated them into something constructive, but you had not been able to do this because you had this impossibly idealized view of me as a father figure.

Hard to believe that anyone could mistake *me*, Mike, for a father figure. Which is not to say she didn't *like* me or find me attractive. After all, she had a soft spot for bad boys. (That was why she was more tolerant of me than, say, Becky or Ophelia.) But! I was so *difficult!* So hard to *control!* Always out prowling! . . . no wonder you, Laura, had not had the chance to grow. You hadn't had the time!

All this stood to change once your law career was back on track. This terrible setback was not the end of the world. Charlotte would be there to make sure you kept sight of your long-term goals. She would be standing on the sidelines, supportive, ever tactful, holding back any comments, any advice that didn't refer back to the principle of equality within difference.

Which is Charlotte's working goal. The key word being (for lack of a better term) androgyny. Although that is a long way off. What we have to seek in our everyday lives, she says to herself as she darts about the kitchen adjusting picture frames, is balance. As she is always saying to her students, the future is male *and* female.

She looks at the clock. It is twenty to nine: the time you are due to come pick up the children. Thank God you are a few minutes late! She gets out the cookies she was up half the night baking for the school bake sale, puts them next to the door so she won't forget them. Then she looks at the nursery-school calendar to see if there is anything she has forgotten. There is! Oh no! Tuesday is T-shirt day! She runs upstairs to retrieve her son's T-shirt from his chest of drawers. Having established that it's not there, she runs down to the kitchen again and opens the dryer, only to find the T-shirt is still wet!

Why can't Trey ever remember to check the cycle when it's over? And what was he thinking, anyway? The machine is stuffed—he must have squeezed two loads in here! She takes all the other wet clothes out of the dryer, throws the wet Creative Learning Center T-shirt back in, puts the machine on high, and then rushes over to the counter where the lunchboxes should be, except that they're *not* there. They're on the floor with the leftovers of yesterday's lunch still in them.

Another count against Trey! she tells herself, as she rushes to clean them out. She reads, with passing annoyance, the note her son's teacher has inserted into his lunchbox. "Dear Mommy, Help! I know peanut butter–and–honey sandwiches are healthy, but can't I have something else tomorrow? I need variety! Please find enclosed a list of other nutritious foods that have proven popular with my classmates." Etc. Etc. It is, of course, in the teacher's handwriting. God, she hates that school sometimes. If it weren't such a superlative program educationally speaking . . . She goes over to the refrigerator to get the sandwiches Trey is supposed to have made the night before while she was teaching class, and surprise, surprise, they're not there!

Now she is getting angry. As she slaps together two peanut butter–and–honey sandwiches on stale, no, worse, rock-hard, bread, she hears you pulling into the driveway. As she retrieves two box drinks—without their straws, but fuck it—from the refrigerator, she hears you honk the horn. She picks up the first two apples she can get her hands on. As she is washing their bruises, she hears you honk the horn again.

"Kids! Coats!" she yells. Then she remembers the T-shirt. It's not dry yet, but so what. She is not going to risk any more demerits. "Take this," she tells Patten. "If you hang it on your hook it'll dry by lunchtime." She pushes both children toward the door at just the same time as you ring the bell.

"Here, take them. Take them," she says. "I'm sorry for holding you up."

"Don't worry," you say. "I'm not in a rush."

This is when she notices you're looking happy. How strange! This can't mean you don't care about the bar results anymore, can it? This couldn't mean . . . she walks down the driveway, phrasing her questions step by step.

Just as she reaches the car, her son says, "Mom! We forgot Hamlet!"

Oh God! Hamlet! She should have taken him back yesterday, and last night she didn't even check to see if Trey had remembered to feed him! She goes back inside to find the canary's cage lying open and on its side in the den. "This is the fucking limit. What is *with* this guy?"

Chapter 5

What is with this guy is that he is a failure. Or is that just what he tells himself? Look at him as he lies on the floor in his long gray box room of an attic office. His long blue eyes are watery slits. His square WASP jaw looks wired shut. His shoulders are hunched; his turned-in toes make him look smaller than he really is—and this has always been his problem. This is the price he has had to pay for growing up in a family that was larger than life.

Imagine what it must have been like for him when he was a boy, with his B-movie father, his Queen of Santa Barbara stepmother, his sister careening in and out of screen magazines with her succession of legendary car wrecks. Imagine poor Trey, normal leave-it-to-Beaver teenager, arms flapping, braces glistening, as he stands in the driveway, saying, "Listen, guys, you just can't do this. Drunk driving is immoral." No wonder he gave up too soon. No wonder he hasn't seen his father since his sister's funeral. No wonder also that breaking ties with him was not enough.

Because even his failures compare unfavorably to the disasters that made his family so famous. *They* ran through fortunes, staged ugly scenes at White House receptions, used Oscar ceremonies to further vendettas and shot rejecting lovers in the back. While this Trey we see lying on the office floor here—all he ever wanted was to be a regular guy with a house and a station wagon and a steady job. And he can't even do that.

It is a good five years now since he left his beloved desk at the IRS and during this time he has (he counts the mediocre ways) failed as (1) a househusband, (2) an organizer of corporate wilderness expeditions and (3) a cut-rate accountant. He is too honest, says Charlotte. He is also (permit me to interject) too literal-minded, too inaccurate and too slow: it is thanks to him that Mitchell and I almost went under in 1983.

A number of other friends—Charlotte's friends, he himself doesn't have any—used him, too, and took similar beatings with the taxman. All Trey's major clients are gone now. The only ones who still use him are the ones who never pay. As he lies on his study floor, listening to his wife crash about the kitchen, yelling, "What is *with* this guy?" he asks himself how long he has before she serves his balls with nachos and turns him back into a househusband.

He looks at the far wall—at the photo of the kitten he had when he was a freshman in college, at that kitten's induction notice, at the dunning letter the kitten once received from *The New York Times*. He looks at his first baseball glove and his lucky Frisbee hanging like mistletoe over the door. He looks at the poster from *Citizen Kane* on the near wall ("Everybody's Talking About It! It's Terrific!") and then he looks at his three-thousand-dollar computer.

He has to get out of here! He picks up his shoes. Heart pounding, he creeps down the back stairs.

He does it so quietly he can hear the mail dropping through the letter box. He pauses, shoes in hand. And then he thinks: Oh my God! What if the Visa bill arrived today? He has got to get to it before she does. He rushes for the door, but when he rounds the corner she is already standing there, taking the Visa bill out of its envelope.

He backs into the kitchen. She follows him, never taking her eyes off the bill. From time to time her eyebrows lift. Then she looks up and says, "Sit down, Trey. It's time we had a talk."

"I'm sure I can explain," he warbles.

"Then do. Tell me why I can't even trust you with a canary."

A canary? What canary? Then he sees Hamlet lying on the windowsill. "Oh God. I'm sorry. I didn't . . ."

"You can bury it with the kids this evening, but first I want you to get a new one. Take the carcass along to the store. If you can get an identical bird, the school need never know. In the meantime, tell me about this new piece of bodybuilding equipment I see you bought. Two hundred and nine dollars?"

She proceeds to question him, in the same tone of voice, about the eighty-five-dollar Tower Records charge, the hundred-and-eleven-dollar L. L. Bean charge, the hundred-and-forty-eight-dollar home-ski apparatus. With every pointed question, she gains in stature. The unspoken reproaches linger in the air and metamorphose. Why didn't you check the clothes in the dryer becomes, Why is your dick so small. Why didn't you give me the phone message becomes, Why can't you make me come. Next time if you don't clean out the lunchboxes I'm going to make you buy new ones out of your account becomes, Next time I see my friends I'm going to tell them you want to fuck your mother. Another wave of hysteria overtakes him. I didn't do it! Honest!

He goes into ultra defense mode. No answer using two words if one will do. Deny everything. Lie. And if that doesn't work, deflect.

"By the way . . ." A lame effort, even he realizes.

"Yes?" Charlotte says in her teacher voice.

"Yeah, did, um." He still doesn't know what he's going to say. Then, in a flash, he remembers The Crisis. "Did, um, Laura . . ."

"Oh God, how could I forget? What time is it?" Charlotte jumps to her feet. "Which of these clocks is correct, do you happen to know?"

Charlotte picks up the phone, half dials Becky's number, and then pauses. "Or does she go to Ophelia's next on Tuesdays? I can't remember. Let me check."

As she goes over to the bulletin board, she mutters, "This car pool is so goddamn *complicated.* It's getting to the point where we need to hire a traffic controller." She doesn't seem to realize she is talking to the wall.

She picks up the phone, dials what she thinks is Ophelia's number, then realizes she has dialed Becky's number by mistake. Starts all over again, dials what she thinks is Ophelia's number, and gets the answering machine at a Japanese restaurant. Slams down the phone. Reaches out for the phone book, but it's not there.

Neither is Trey. Typical. She looks up at the ceiling, taps her foot and counts to ten and then dials information. Then remembers that Ophelia's number is unlisted. Pours herself a cup of coffee, sits down, tries to concentrate. How can she forget a number she has been dialing three times a day for five years? She turns on the stereo for inspiration.

Chapter 6

While she sits there, giving another run-through to "Blue Train"—

And while you make your way down Van Ness, with four children in the backseat all mouthing the words to "The Ewoks Join the Fight"—

I imagine the miniature Big Ben clock in the front hallway of the Mendoza home chiming the quarter hour. It makes a hollow echo: there is no clutter here to absorb the sound. You could be walking into an office. The signs on the doors to either side contribute to this false impression. "Dr. Christopher Mendoza" says one. "Dr. Ophelia Mendoza" says the other. If you glimpse inside, you'll see identical heavy oak desks, as well as matching swivel chairs, answering machines, executive toys, and photographs framed in cushioned velvet of the same emaciated four-year-old boy.

Neither desk contains any sign of work in progress. These are not rooms any sane person would want to sit in. This is partly to do with incongruous "human touches"—the doll's house, the umbrella stand in the shape of the Chiquita Banana lady, the collection of blue glass vases, the large oil paintings of autumnal forests and storms at sea in Ophelia's office, and, in Kiki's office, the tiger throw rugs and the trophy heads of endangered species, all of which turn out, on closer inspection, to be fakes.

In fact, there is only one display in the entire Filbert Street apartment that says anything revealing about our friends Kiki and Ophelia: this is the double frame on the corporate-type sideboard in the breakfast room. The photo on the left is of Kiki with his parents and his sisters and their husbands and children. It was taken in the studio of a chain department store in El Paso. You can tell from the parents' stiffness that they are manual workers in their Sunday clothes, from the sisters' frilly blouses, big hairstyles and sleek high heels that they are the type of upwardly mobile Chicanas who hate ethnic politics and insist on calling themselves Mexican-Americans. Their husbands are all dressed in expensive suits, while Kiki is wearing jeans and a T-shirt and Reeboks. You can tell from his central position in the photograph that he is the family's great hope, while the emaciated smiling boy in Oshkoshs on his lap is the trophy he has brought home to bear witness to his progress in homogenized America. (Although the boy, it has to be said, looks a lot less American than his El Paso cousins.)

The photo on the right is a far more stylish affair. It is of Ophelia on the eve of her "Fifteen" and it bears the embossed gold stamp of a Havana studio that relocated to Miami in 1962. Ophelia, who is seated on a velvet stool, is wearing pearls and a canary evening gown. Her black hair is long and wavy and swept back in the manner of a forties actress to reveal the full charms of her long, slender neck. Her parents stand behind her. The elegant, slightly balding father is holding her hand and gazing at it admiringly. The mother, who has her blond hair tied tightly back and is wearing a busy floral print that almost overpowers her garish emerald necklace, is smiling directly, and somewhat belligerently, into the camera. She has her hand on Ophelia's shoulder. It almost seems as if she is trying to press Ophelia down: this serves to heighten the impression these two photographs give in tandem. Humble Kiki is on his way up in the world, while grand Ophelia is on her way down. The breakfast room where they both now sit, compressed into an uneasy equality, has the atmosphere of an elevator stuck between two floors.

The real Kiki—the one at the breakfast table—is wearing sunglasses. They give him the bland look of a man who is trying to avoid the attention of muggers. The real Ophelia looks shorn and cranky. She is yawning, her short black hair is tousled. She is still wearing her stethoscope. She is shuffling through a pile of real-estate listings and eating a bowl of Alta-Dena yogurt.

Son Seb has a bowl of Alta-Dena yogurt, too, but he's not eating it, he's dragging a spoon through it. From time to time he asks a question. What's an echo? Is a strep culture the same thing as a drug culture? If you fill a bottle of milk and put some berries in it and put it into the freezer, will it taste like ice cream? Do the missing children on the milk carton know each other? Do robots have brothers? Each time the answer is the same: Maybe, darling, but I'm not sure.

He asks a more daring question: Can I have a spoon of chocolate syrup? When no one answers, he glances up over the counter that opens into the kitchen. His look is first hopeful, then distressed, because he can't make eye contact with his grandmother, who is in the kitchen chopping vegetables while humming along to the easy-listening station. He can only see her torso.

His father, meanwhile, is pretending to read the paper, except that Ophelia knows he can't be, because he's wearing his non-prescription sunglasses.

His eyes are closed—she knows this because, when she waves her hand right in front of him, and then gives him the finger, she gets no reaction. But he's not asleep, because when the phone rings he startles. It's the office line. She asks, "Why isn't the service picking this up?"

"Picking what up, hon?"

"This call."

"What call?"

"Forget it." She picks up the phone and says, "This is a recorded message. The office is closed until 9:00 a.m. All patients requiring appointments should call after that time. Patients requiring emergency treatment should . . ." Hearing the patient hang up, she finishes the sentence the unofficial way. "Should try and see if they can find an emergency room all by their little baby selves."

She replaces the receiver. The phone starts ringing again. She picks it up and begins to simulate the same recorded message, except that the patient hangs up after the first sentence. No sooner has she replaced the receiver than it starts to ring again.

"This is ridiculous. I'm just going to turn the sound off. Mom?" she shouts into the kitchen. "Could you turn the sound off?"

"Sure thing!" says Mom, and she picks up the phone in the kitchen. "Oh hello! Hello! Sure thing!" She pokes her head into the breakfast room.

"It's for *joo*," she says, even though she's perfectly capable of saying "you" if she wants to.

"I wish you wouldn't talk like that," Ophelia tells her.

And Mom says, "No, hon, honest. It really is for *joo*. It's Tcharlotte."

Ophelia reaches behind her and takes the phone off the wall. "Charlotte, was that you just now?"

Charlotte says yes.

"Why were you using the office number?"

Before Charlotte can explain, they are interrupted by the click on the line.

"Could you hold?" Charlotte asks Ophelia.

"Sure," says Ophelia. "*I'll* hold."

Ten seconds pass. Fifteen. Twenty. Twenty-five. "This is fun," she says. "This is *really* fun. Don't you love call-waiting?"

No reaction from any of the living persons in the room. She puts the receiver in front of her and talks to it as if it were Charlotte in the flesh. "Could you get your act together?" When she puts the receiver back to her ear, Charlotte is on the line again, but only to say she has a suicidal student on her other line and will have to call back.

Restoring the receiver to its home on the wall, Ophelia says, "That was typical." No reaction from Kiki. Or her mother, or even her own son, who is staring into his yogurt bowl like it's a crystal ball. "Kiki. *Kiki*. Look at me. I'm talking to you."

Kiki looks up, his vacant expression emphasized by the sunglasses.

"I can't believe it. You're doing it again," says Ophelia. "It's like Friday all over again."

"What happened on Friday?" he asks.

"The counseling."

"Oh right." He clears his throat. "So what did I just do that I did there?"

"Went to sleep on me."

"But I'm awake!"

"Oh really? You're awake, are you? Then tell me what I was talking about."

A pause. "Counseling?"

"Before that."

"Before that . . . before that you were . . . before that you were . . . oh God, Filly, I don't know. You took a call from a patient even though you should have let the service handle it. Is that what you want me to say?"

"Actually, it was Charlotte on that line."

"Well, great. Can I go back to my paper now?"

"Sure. If that's all you have to say, then fine."

"Christ, Filly. What do you expect me to say?"

"Something slightly more relational. You know, show some interest in the important experiences that make up my life."

"Oh right. OK then. Tell me, Filly. How *is* your dear friend Charlotte this morning?"

"A mess. Like she always is."

"Oh really? I didn't realize that."

"What is *with* you this morning?"

"I'm just tired, is all."

"*You're* tired. What about me? I mean, *I* was the one who was at the hospital all night. With *your* patient."

"She's not *my* patient, Filly. She's *our* patient."

"She's an elderly primigravida."

"I thought you didn't like that term."

"I don't like someone yawning in my face when I'm the one who's been up all night either."

"Then for God's sake, Filly, go to bed."

"I can't. I have that conference."

"It can't be as important as your health."

"No, of course not," says Ophelia. "It's only about fertility."

"Honey . . ."

"If it were about testosterone, on the other hand, it would be very important. Right? Or golf. Or the ethics of playing squash with neurosurgeons. Or the stockholders' meeting at Coors. Right?"

"Honey, I really didn't . . ."

From the kitchen, Mom calls out, "*Cálmate, muchacha.*"

"I'm so sick of this whole thing, I really am."

"Then keep it to *joorself,* eh? We have had enough too."

Here follows a staring match between Ophelia and her mother. Even when it breaks off, no one speaks. While an orchestral version of "Feelings" plays on the easy-listening station, Ophelia tries to calm herself down by telling herself that this hellish living arrangement isn't forever.

On the surface, things look great. As Charlotte says, every working woman needs a wife. Well, that's what Mom has been, all right.

Just about all the women doctors Ophelia knows have had to cut way back to make time for their kids—go part-time, enter specialties that don't put you on call every other night. Not so Ophelia. She puts in every bit as much time as Kiki. She has always been able to follow her interests, and look—she has the sex-education program to show for it, and now the fertility program. She can go off on conferences, accept speaking engagements . . . and if she has any doubt as to who made that possible, all she has to do is think about that first year when she tried to go it alone, and the hospital bed where she ended up, and the muscle-bound, bejeweled blonde who bailed her out.

They would never have gotten through Seb's early years without her. The thing is, the early years are over now. Seb is in school six hours a day. Time for Mom to think of herself a little, and less about them. Time for Mom to take herself and her blond wigs into an apartment.

Time for Ophelia to have a house of her own.

Ophelia has strong ideas about this soon-to-become-a-reality dream house. They are all negative. Unlike this breakfast room her mother decorated for them without bothering to consult them, *Ophelia's* kitchen will not have any cutesy-pie decorative plates with bas-relief kittens on them, or potholders with sentimental poems on them about hearths and helping hands, or dried flowers sticking out of pink-and-yellow horns of plenty, or china stewardesses, or ashtrays from the Madonna Inn. She wants wood tables and counters. No Formica like here. She wants the radio set—eternally—on the classical station. She wants it to self-destruct if anyone turns it to the easy-listening station. She wants cookbooks, so that they don't have to eat rice and black beans every day of the year. And she wants blinds instead of these frilly curtains printed with rows of Little Bo-peeps and curds and whey. She doesn't care if it's extra work, because as soon as she has her kitchen done she's going to get to work on the ground floor, which is where she's going to put her new, superefficient, flextime clinic.

The guiding principle of this new clinic is, again, a negative one: there will be no room for Kiki in it. This is going to be a clinic staffed entirely by women who have children. Instead of having to accommodate Kiki and his unilateral decisions and his obstructive action with regard to her sex-education program, his lack of interest in her fertility clinic, his inability to take in any information she gives him about any patient even with regard to drug dosages, his refusal to see the importance of nutrition in a balanced preventive-medicine program; instead of having to spend all day attending to details he is too busy and important to attend to, only to find that, when they get home, Mom treats *him* like the breadwinner, and *her* like some upstart who talks too loud—well there's no place for any of this junk in her new clinic. She and her hypothetical, like-minded, like-suffering female colleagues are going to build a routine around their *own* needs, their *own* . . .

The phone rings.

"It's for *joo.*"

Chapter 7

Ophelia goes into the next room to take the call. God, just look at her, Kiki thinks. Forget feminine. This woman hardly even looks human anymore, she looks like she's running on batteries, she looks like she needs oiling, and a new set of ball bearings with a fuse box thrown in. What would that counselor woman think of Ophelia if she saw her now?

What he would really like to say to this counselor is, Look. The problem isn't that my wife and I don't communicate enough. The problem is we are communicating all the goddamn day.

He imagines himself drawing the curtains, flicking the remote control and taking the counselor through a video demonstration of a typical day. Try this one for size, he imagines telling her:

> 9:00 a.m. Film of Kiki backing the car out of the garage. Filly is sitting in the passenger seat. She says something like, *I really think we should walk.*
>
> He says something noncommittal, like, Maybe tomorrow. Then, all the way to the office, he has to listen to a blow-by-blow account of last night's birth management. He does not give his opinion, since any criticism would be construed as the S word.
>
> 9:10. As he struggles with the office lock: I really think we should consider changing the lock. Weren't you going to call someone on Friday? Why not?
>
> As she looks over the appointment book: That's strange. Why is Mrs. Hernandez coming in? Why does Mrs. Caliban have a double appointment? And oh, I see you have Mrs. Howard today too. Listen, if she tries to get any tranquilizers out of you . . .
>
> 9:20. After they have both taken their first patients. He is working up the courage to tell a Mrs. Karl that her unborn child might have spina bifida, when the door flies open. *Could I speak to you alone?*
>
> He steps out. What is it?

I have a bad feeling about that baby.

But I thought you said everything went A-OK.

Maybe I should have insisted on an episiotomy.

But I thought you were against episiotomies.

YOU aren't, though.

So?

So, I sense your disapproval.

What is there to disapprove of, Filly? Look, when I do my rounds, I'll check and see. OK?

Sob. *Thanks.*

10:05. As he is about to leave. He knocks on the door of Examination Room A. *Just a minute.*

I have to run. Can I call you from the car?

No. I want to speak to you in person.

He steps into Examination Room A. Filly has a Mrs. Let-her-go-nameless in stirrups. He exits quickly, waits outside.

I can't believe the way you think you can just barge in on me without asking.

10:10. He heads for the hospital, where he spends twenty minutes on his own patients, twice that time with Mrs. Dodd, who had no episiotomy but is about to have a nervous breakdown, with Mrs. de Groot, who is in a coma in intensive care.

12:00. Stops off and gets two sandwiches on his way back to the office.

12:20. *You can't seem to buy a sandwich that doesn't contain at least three carcinogens.*

Eat it anyway, bitch. (He thinks but doesn't say.)

They sit together in his office. She keeps putting her Tab on his desk, leaving unsightly wet marks. She talks at length about the fertility program. His mind wanders.

So. What do you think?

Think about what, hon?

Why don't you ever listen to me anymore?

No comment.

We're supposed to be running this program together. But you really don't care about it one iota. Cracked voice. *If you would just come out and say it, I could accept it. But you continually say you WILL refer your patients. You continually say you WILL come to the seminars and conferences and read the books. But then do you?*

Oh Filly, stop exaggerating things.

I can't help it. I'm so tired.

Why don't you go home, then.

No. Going home would be unprofessional.

1:10. When they are back with their patients again: *Could you come out here a.s.a.p.?*

He steps out. What is it this time?

Why didn't you tell me about Mrs. de Groot?

What was there to tell about her?

She's dead. She's dead and I didn't get a chance to alert her family. I let her down. Shuddering sobs.

You can't take everything so personally, Filly.

She's not a thing, for God's sake. She's a person. Why are all men so COLD *about these things? Why don't they* CARE?

1:25. Finally convinces Filly to go home.

1:30–5:30. Breaks his back seeing his patients and her patients.

6:00. Arrives home aching all over. Finds Filly watching TV. God. Could I use a Coors.

Well, don't expect ME *to get it for you. Don't expect* ME *to wait on the Master of the Universe hand and foot. Don't expect* ME *to . . .*

A shadow falls across her face. The film in his head cuts off. To be replaced by the real Ophelia, standing with a telephone in her hand in the next room. Asking him, "Why are you staring at me like that?"

What if she knows?

His sunglasses are about to slide off his face. He takes them off, wipes his nose with a Kleenex. "Are you trying to eavesdrop on me?" she asks.

He shrugs his shoulders.

She kicks the door closed with her foot.

Breathing normally again now, he returns to the sports page. And what do you know? There's an article about his home baseball team—his very own team! It must be an omen. He shows the picture to his son. "You see that stadium? I used to go there with my dad when I was a kid." He is telling his son that the two of them should go down there one time (at this time of year, too, because that is when Texas is at its best) when Mom comes up to the table and interrupts him, to say that Seb has done a good job on his "breakfast for goats" and now deserves to come into the kitchen for a "little treat."

Why does she have to use those same words? He breaks out into a sweat. When she has taken Seb into the kitchen, when the knot in his stomach loosens, he tells himself, hey, buddy boy, quit while you're ahead.

Crisis management, he tells himself. It's what even Ophelia admits he's best at. He has got to get his hands steady. He goes over to the window, takes a few deep breaths, and what do you know!

There she is. Wonder Woman. Coming out of her apartment across the street. As she turns around to lock her door, he watches with grateful pleasure as her long auburn hair sweeps across her perfect ass. He looks at his watch: 8:52. Right on target. Hey, babe! He tries to will her to look up at him, wills her to develop an urgent need for a family practitioner who will take care of everything for her. He is half-done putting her through a mental striptease, half-done imagining her lolling on his examination table, begging him, begging him to attend to her every need, when who should appear around the far corner but the Amazon from Number 54321! 54321 blast-off! Because she is wearing that see-through blouse again! He can see her nipples all the way from here! He can see them so well he can almost taste them. He is half-way through sending her a telepathic message to cross the street so he can poke his head out the window and bite them, when—who should appear walking in the opposite direction but the Ultimate Twelve-Year-Old! With her mother! And they both look like they need it! He imagines himself attending to their every need, both at the same time. He imagines the threesome becoming a foursome and a fivesome. He imagines them lying in adjoining waiting rooms, waiting for their turn, begging for it. For a few blissful seconds, four naked women writhe before his eyes, but then the film in his head goes off—clunk—when Mom appears behind him.

She puts her hand on his shoulder and gives him a proprietorial smile. He tries to look confident, unaffected. "Hey, little buddy," he says to his son. "What's that chocolate on your face?" Hey, big buddy, he says to himself, you are in deep, deep shit.

Which is why, when Kiki takes Seb out to you (with his bake-sale cookies, and his freshly pressed T-shirt, and his scrubbed and overloaded lunchbox, and his string of pathetic little pipsqueak questions that no one ever has the time to answer ["Is it illegal for grown-ups to drink lemonade? Can children smoke in France?"]), when Kiki looks up at the window to see Mom watching him, Mom remembering with obvious satisfaction the unthinkable, he decides to beat it.

He asks you, "Are you off to Becky's next?"

As the Ewoks are just rejoining the fight, you can't hear what he's saying. You nod out of politeness and are taken aback when he jumps into the car.

From her place at the window, Mom looks surprised, too. She taps on the glass. "Tell her I have another breakfast meeting with Mitchell," Kiki snaps. Again, he has to shout to make himself heard over the Ewoks. "Tell her it's about those investment possibilities." Again, you do as he asks.

Mom nods and closes the window.

"Do you really?" you ask Kiki as he pulls away from the curb. "Have a breakfast meeting with Mitchell?"

"More, or less," Kiki says. Then he tells you about the investment group he's joined. Five neurosurgeons, two radiologists, one podiatrist and himself. "We've been looking for up-and-coming ventures."

"Well, this might be the day," you say. "Because Mitchell is going to be looking for a new partner."

Have I guessed right? Whatever you said, I'm sure you had no idea what you were giving away.

By now, Kiki has been gone for five minutes. Ophelia is still on the phone to Charlotte.

They have just come to the conclusion that everything, absolutely everything, boils down to economics. Which means that everyone, absolutely everyone, must have a solid economic base. They are going to have to make sure you know this. They arrange to visit you together in the late afternoon.

"I'll try to get Becky to come, too," says Ophelia. Before she does, she glances into the breakfast room to find out why it's so quiet. Mom explains that Kiki has gone to talk to Mitchell about making an investment.

"But he can't do that without consulting me. That's our money, not just his! The fucking bastard, he's just trying to block me on the house again!"

"*Joo* shouldn't talk like that about *joor* husband."

"Like hell I won't."

Ophelia picks up the phone.

Chapter 8

Five blocks away, in Becky and Mitchell's recently deshingled and repainted blue Victorian, eight telephones ring together but remain unanswered. Where is Becky? She must be in the kitchen, on the other side of that powder-blue door that matches the oriental runner carpet in the hallway. While Mitchell . . . I imagine that, if you went up the front stairs, if you let your eyes follow the powder-blue running silhouettes Becky has painted on the skirting boards . . . I imagine you would find Mitchell standing on the top landing in his shorts.

He looks tanned and fit but underrested. His thick brown hair is tousled. His birdlike face shows signs of a headache, he winces with every ring of the phone, but he is wearing the pain the same way he wears everything—stylishly. "What the hell," he says as he walks back down the corridor. He appears to be looking for something, but it is not on the back of his bedroom door . . . or on the back of the first bathroom door . . . or on the back of the second bathroom door . . . When he finally tracks his bathrobe down in the closet in the baby's room, he shouts out, "God damn it, Becky!" Look at him as he walks back down the hallway. From the way that he smiles and shakes his head as he starts down the stairs, you would almost think he was back in his ad exec father's place in Westchester County, drinking his first Sunday morning shot of vodka with his hungover mother on the lawn, watching Becky do some kind of trick dive into the lima bean–shaped swimming pool. *God damn it, Becky! You spilled my drink!* Tit for tat. Tit for tat. Man errs. Woman gets angry, looks cute, and retaliates. This is Mitchell's mind-set. The moment of truth always comes the morning after.

Leave him on the landing, struggling with the antennae on the portable phone. Go through the powder-blue door to find Becky standing in the middle of the kitchen trying to get Baby Roo comfortable inside the African shawl and having the usual problem with that last knot around her waist.

She is looking far too alert for nine in the morning. Her shoulder-length hennaed brown hair swings back and forth like a sheet of silk. Her severely short bangs make her gray eyes look more feline, and her lips fuller—or is it the scarlet lipstick? She is wearing a tie-dyed T-shirt over purple leggings that make the most of her dancer's legs—and match the purple in the African shawl, which is not quite like anything you've seen before—like everything else in this kitchen. The upside-down plaster feet that serve as shoe racks, the lazy susan flower boxes, the pieces of painted driftwood that serve as doorstops—they are all stridently unique. This is a room invented by a woman who has to prove over and over that she is smart and creative and discerning and sophisticated even though she didn't go to college.

The phone is still ringing when she finishes with the shawl. She flicks on the intercom. It's Ophelia. "Can I speak to you for a minute?"

"Not really. I'll have to call you back."

"OK," says Ophelia. "But in the meantime do me a favor and tell my asshole husband to call me."

"How am I supposed to do that?"

"You mean he isn't *there?*"

"Not as far as I know."

"He's supposed to be talking to Mitchell."

"Well, maybe he is."

"Could you check for me? It's important."

"I can't," says Becky. "We're not communicating."

"Oh right."

"It would be easier if you just tried him yourself on the other number," Becky says.

But Becky is wrong. Mitchell is already on the other line. When Ophelia interrupts this call and asks, "Is my asshole husband there?" he doesn't miss a beat.

"Hold on," he says, and returns to his first caller.

He is standing now in what he hopes will not be the study for very much longer, talking to someone he hopes will soon become an investor in one of the many sidelines he hopes I, his long-suffering partner, won't ever find out about. This one has to do with a share in a marina-cum-condo complex.

He has a towel wrapped around his middle, and he is leaning against another sideline, this one really but really on the back burner: a screenplay some ex-plumber–cum–carpenter friend of his wants him to read and, if you can believe it, market. There are other piles lined up along the wall for other sidelines, but there are no longer any chairs in this office, not even at the table where he had his in and out trays, which is now, mysteriously, the home for his wife's sewing machine. Material for a child's dress is lying on the floor over the proofs for his publicity material for the Hunter's Point conversion. There is a child's educational program on the computer screen.

Meanwhile, here he is talking to this potential investor, trying to sound like he's sitting in an executive suite—a challenge.

Easier, though, than confronting his wife about the chairs. Or anything. How many days has it been since he (quote unquote) condescended to her?

God, he hates that word. Whatever he does, that's the word she throws back at him. And the irony is, he really does want to help her.

Take this most recent six-day war. All he had wanted to do was get her the backing she needed to start a legitimate children's art center.

Or, if we're going to be totally honest about this: all he had wanted was to get her out of this downward spiral of misdirected philanthropy that had started with her father's death. This Catholic relief organization she had become involved with—there was nothing wrong with it per se. But why she thought it was a way of working through her guilt—and why she felt any guilt in the first place—was beyond him.

How many times had he told her, it wasn't her fault her father had died the way he did. It was *admirable* that she had wanted to reach out to other people with the same problem. But she ought to have known that she would have a hard time dealing with the realities of AIDS counseling when she was already overemotional on account of being pregnant with Baby Roo. Which was not to say she hadn't acted like a trooper. Few people could have coped with a client who was supposed to die quietly after being taken off a respirator but instead sat up and screamed.

She ought to have taken time off then, at least for the duration of the pregnancy. But no, there was no taming Joan of Arc. Now she had to come to terms not just with her father's secret life and public death but also the relative stranger on the respirator.

Why this meant she had to throw herself into raising funds for a relief organization that ran a Salvadoran refugee camp on the Guatemalan border he didn't quite know: the Catholic imagination was a closed book to him. Why it had to be the San Rafael branch was another mystery he dared not look into for fear of being branded a rockjaw WASP.

Once or twice he had tried to introduce the idea of analysis as a possible option. Had she ever barked at him. He had backed off. And surprise, surprise, she had run herself into the ground. He had hoped this would mean the end of the San Rafael connection, but no, unfortunately not. She had made her mark on these people. San Rafael had started coming to *her*. Her whole last trimester, the house was knee-deep in priests and nuns. The fact that they didn't wear clerical habits didn't make them any more palatable.

He had told himself not to jump to conclusions. They were here to help, not to convert. And so he had put up with these priests with bicycle clips on their pants making supper for him, these nuns with baby voices and hairy legs reading Guatemalan fairy tales to his children. He was so busy overcompensating for his prejudices that he had actually been shocked when he discovered that they had, indeed, been putting pressure on Becky to "renew her faith."

Fortunately he had kept his mouth (mostly) shut at this juncture, because, as it turned out, the problem took care of itself. When she tried out the neighborhood church, the priest gave an antiabortion sermon in which he cited as an example a pregnant woman who had been raped and stabbed in the stomach, but whose assailant could not be prosecuted because the victim, the unborn child, was not officially alive. Becky found this deeply offensive, and said so to the nuns. This led to a series of tearful evenings during which she had battled with her conscience while Mitchell had (mostly) avoided saying what he thought. This was: Get out of the Middle Ages and go work through your feelings about your dad with an analyst.

Then the baby was born, and because it was born on Becky's father's birthday, somehow the baby became the replacement for him even though it was a girl and swoosh! the mourning period was over. Suddenly she was her old self again and complaining about the demands San Rafael was making on her, and saying she needed to center herself. That's why he had come up with this idea of legitimizing this playgroup she was already doing for peanuts. He had even set up an interview for her at the bank. That was last . . . Wednesday?

He had taken the morning off so that he could hold the baby

during the interview. He was annoyed when she insisted on taking the baby in with her, and livid when she informed him afterward that the baby had thrown up all over the banker's desk, because God, this guy was an important contact of his! Didn't she understand anything about professionalism?

That was what he asked her on the drive home.

And that was when she said it to him: "Do you know how condescending that sounds?"

He hadn't had time to explore this with her, because at about this point the car had started making noises. This was the Peugeot, i.e., her car, which, it emerged, she hadn't had serviced for 15,000 miles. If it hadn't been tense in the car already, he might have said something to her about her negligence, but he had decided, oh what the hell, she's forgetful because Baby Roo is keeping her up all night, and so when they got back to the house he just went ahead and made a service appointment for Monday, only to find out that *she* was planning to go to San Rafael on Monday. And so he said well in that case he guessed she was going to have to wait until Tuesday, at which point she said that she was a grown woman and would therefore make that decision herself.

He had asked her if she realized that the car could break down at any minute and was she willing to take the consequences, and she had asked him, for the second time that day, if he knew how condescending that sounded.

He was still managing to keep his temper at this stage. Except then, when she asked for help in untying the ridiculous double sheet masquerading as an African shawl that she had Baby Roo swaddled in, and he was rummaging through the kitchen drawers for a skewer to loosen the knot, he came across her new Conran credit card, which she hadn't even bothered to sign.

He had given her a lecture about how foolish this was, and asked her to sign it, at which point she had said, "Absolutely not."

He had asked her why.

She had said, "Because you're condescending to me."

He had said, "Well, in that case, excuse me, but you don't even deserve a credit card. I'm going to cut it up."

And she had said, "If you cut it up then *I* am going to shred your American Express Gold Card."

And Mitchell had said, "You wouldn't do that, it's our meal

ticket." At which point Becky had grabbed his wallet and taken out all his credit cards and hidden them all over the house.

The whole time he was hunting for them, she kept taunting him, but he was not about to let her know how upset he was. So he pretended it was a big joke, while all the time the tensions inside him were piling up.

What happened finally was that he was going through the books on her bedside table to see if his gold card was hiding in one of them. And he just happened to look at the title of the one on the top of the pile. It was *Christian Faith and Practice.*

Christian Faith and Practice??? His physical repulsion to this book was so automatic, and so great, that he had, without thinking, screeched, ugh, cooties! and dropped it onto the floor.

He had apologized immediately, but somehow that gesture had focused her. Her last words had been, "You miserable, asshole rockjaw." She had said it several times, as if practicing intonations: "You miserable, asshole *rockjaw*. You *miserable,* asshole rockjaw. You miserable, *asshole* rockjaw." She had not spoken to him . . .

For how many days now? As he stands in his mahogany-free office talking to this potential investor whose name he can't even remember, his hardsell voice weakens now as he tries not to count. Over and above the sound of his daughters' high-pitched squealing, over and above the din of his own forced optimism, he listens to his wife click-click-clicking back and forth across the kitchen. The cash register that is his brain goes haywire. Oh my God, he thinks, another new pair of shoes. A hundred dollars if he's lucky. What was it that his mother used to tell him about Catholics and money sense?

He gauges Becky's mood from her expensive new footsteps and decides it's springy, which means happy maybe even jubilant. The energy contained in each step brings to mind a vacuum cleaner running amok, a bulldozer on angel dust. Nancy Reagan operating a wrecking ball. If Mitchell ever finds the courage to walk into the kitchen, the kitchen he has, incidentally, busted his balls for, will he even recognize it, that is the question. Already the office, the bedroom, even the staircase, are disaster areas.

And this morning in the bathroom! There he was, all lathered up. He looks into his shaving mirror and sees—nothing. His shaving mirror is gone, split, *finito* without a trace. And where does it turn up? On her makeup table. Her new, three-hundred-dollar makeup table! Which has a mirror already built into it! But for some reason she's decided she needs his shaving mirror too!

What she has done with his razor only The Shadow knows. Ditto for the Quaaludes he was hiding in that old penicillin bottle. His robe has grown feet. No matter where he puts it, it walks back into the spare bedroom all by itself. And his kids have taken to sleepwalking in the opposite direction. Or does she herself get up in the middle of the night and carry them into the big bed for company? Oh yes, he gets the message. Too bad, then, that he isn't sure how he's supposed to read it.

She is angry at him . . . for taking her seriously? For thoughtlessly throwing a book on the floor while operating under intolerable pressure? For trying to teach her how to treat her car and her credit cards? For being a Protestant even though he was—at most—only half Protestant? Even though the last time he went to church was four years ago at Easter?

He has no idea what he's supposed to be apologizing for.

Chapter 9

What he's supposed to be apologizing for is his attitude problem. It is not his anticlerical hysteria that bothers Becky. It's his failure to understand the spirit of the thing. He may look like a twentieth-century Cambridge, Massachusetts, liberal but it's a paint job. This is a man whose ancestors burned witches.

She knows you never really outgrow the prejudices you learn on your mother's knee. So she can put up with a certain amount of puritan claptrap. What she will not tolerate are these subtle little hints he has been making since her father died, about *unfinished business* and *acting out unresolved conflicts* and *the therapeutic effect of insights* and *the benefits of exploring deep-seated patterns in the therapeutic context as opposed to seeking solace in the teachings of a culture-bound church.*

The gall of this man, who thought all her problems could be traced back to one basic insight that she had not had. Who thought that all a woman had to do to get her act together was lie on a couch until she admitted out loud that she had wanted to fuck her father.

That was what made her want to kill this guy—that and the implication that we had a very wonderful shrink to thank for the Mitchell we enjoyed today.

As she darts about the children's end of her L-shaped kitchen, she tells herself that at least some good has come out of the argument—six days of peace during which she has had a positive surge of creative energy. She has been able to get all sorts of new art projects going for the playgroup. The ideas don't come from a book—they come from her head. She is developing her own educational method, which is why she has decided the hell with Mitchell's condescending, cost-cutting initiatives. She is *not* going to charge her friends more per hour. She is *not* going to use newsprint instead of art paper, or enlarge the class size, or advertise, or draw up plans for expansion. She knows the *real* reason why he criticizes the way she runs her playgroups. It's the same reason why he throws her father's books on the floor and says they have cooties: to undermine her confidence, and thus limit and control her. But she is holding her ground. In the six days since she has not been speaking to the Salem Rockjaw, she has done everything she has always been longing to do to the kitchen, and now she has it just how she likes it.

She pauses now to look at it, this kitchen that has the angry edges of a dream come true. The new light fixtures: they are the brass and not the cheapo plastic ones Mitchell wanted. And the white tiles, which she has speckled down with the same pewter-blue as the dish racks—she had a real and not a hippie carpenter in to do them, and what do you know? No hard-luck stories! No smelly hiking boots in the middle of the kitchen floor for eighteen weeks! No psychotic ex-girlfriends pointing guns at her and accusing her of selling out! No proto-yuppie, disgusted daughters saving up pennies (Becky's pennies) for med school and revenge! No more maudlin reminiscing about how good *AM Radio* used to be! No—just eight hours of George Michael and Madonna and they're done! And if Mitchell thinks they can't afford it, then fuck him. Because she has his number now. She knows how he controls things—by engineering one crisis after another so that his needs and his business's needs come first, so that any money *she* might need for the house or the children or, God forbid, herself, becomes an impossible extra. Well, she's taken a long time getting here, but she's wise to his tricks. The only way to stump him is to follow her instincts.

And just look at the results. Her kitchen has *coherence*. The aluminum fridge and cabinets match the restaurant stove. The counter and tiles give the room definition, the blue blinds drama, and the boxes of geraniums warmth. That is not all; she likes the way her girls look this morning. Fuck hand-me-downs. She wants them in matching outfits. And she likes what she is wearing too. She is glad to have rediscovered makeup. It reminds her that she was the one who took the money out of her trust fund to help Mitchell start that business. Not to mention the down payment on this house! No matter how Mitchell tries to distort them, she knows the facts.

She recites them to herself as she returns to the kid corner to set out the paint sets. Just as she decides she has her life under control, the phone rings at the exact same time as the doorbell rings and all hell breaks loose.

It is Ophelia again. Flicking on the intercom, Becky says, "Hold on a sec." She goes to the door to find Kiki standing there with Maria and Dottie. Looking past them she sees you sitting in the Volvo with the other children. She calls for her eldest. "Time to go! The car pool's here!"

She lets Kiki in, and at the same time, Mitchell jumps out of the study in his towel, while over the intercom, Ophelia says, "Is my fucking husband there yet?"

Kiki looks as if he is about to die.

"Sure thing!" says Becky. She ushers him into the kitchen and leaves him to it. Then she takes her eldest out to our car.

From the driveway she and you can hear Ophelia and Kiki's raised voices. "So what's wrong with the Equal Partners this morning?" Becky asks.

You shrug your shoulders. "It's a mystery to me."

"A severe imbalance seems to have occurred," says Becky. "Looks like today it's not 50–50 but 49–51."

You both snigger. Then Becky says, "I shouldn't talk, though. I'm cleaning up over here."

"Oh really?" you say. "What's your score?"

"98–2 and rising."

You laugh hypocritically.

"Well, anyway, you look more cheerful today," Becky says as she belts her eldest daughter into her seat in the far back. "But that doesn't mean you can let your standards slip! You hear? I'm not going to ask, but I'm assuming that you have had these seat belts back here ergonomically tested. And that both your children are wearing regulation underpants." She turns to the children. "Everyone remember it's T-shirt day at Hitler Youth Camp?"

"Yes," say the children in a chorus.

"Well, good. And I hope you are also making good progress with the Canadian friendship cake, and have remembered to include along with your blanket and crib sheet and set of fresh clothes clear and easily verifiable proof of Aryan descent."

"We have all that," you tell her.

"Well, good then. Great. Go get there! And listen, give Eva Braun my love, will you?"

You laugh again, and pull out of the driveway. As you pause in the middle of the street to turn on "The Ewoks Join the Fight" again ("or the flickering flame . . . of freedom . . . would die . . .") Becky returns to the kitchen to start the little ones on their art project.

Kiki is off the phone by now. When she offers him a cup of coffee, he thanks her in a stiff, exaggeratedly Latin voice. She almost feels sorry for the guy.

Because Ophelia is really going too far, she thinks. There is nothing to be gained from humiliating a man in public. If she has learned anything during the past five years, it is that words get you nowhere. Action is the only thing men understand. That is why, when Mitchell comes into the kitchen still wearing a towel, and dares to address her directly, asking her obsequiously for a shirt, she points, without speaking, to the ironing basket.

The fucking bitch, Mitchell screams internally. What is she trying to *do* to him? Why has she invited Kiki over? And how, since she is still refusing to speak to him, is he going to find out without making an asshole of himself, without having to say something like, Hey, Keeks, what can I do for you this morning?

Which is more or less what he ends up having to say. Only to become even more mystified. So! Kiki's here to discuss investment opportunities! Hey! Terrific! So what else is new? Here Mitchell has an hour to get downtown for an appointment with the banker his baby daughter threw up over only days ago. He doesn't even have his shirt ironed. And now here's Kiki, standing in his kitchen at his wife's invitation. Why did she set it up for breakfast? And why a playgroup morning? How is he supposed to sell this guy anything while she's supervising a bunch of three-year-olds in the same fucking room? Why does she have to humiliate him further by making him iron his own fucking shirt?

He is going to ask her point-blank. Tonight at the latest. In the meantime, he has got to think professional. Think bank. Pull himself together. Rise to this totally laughable occasion. So here goes: a cup of coffee. And then, if that doesn't work, a joint. After all, he's not the only one. This Kiki doesn't live in a bed of roses either. Maybe what is in order is a little male bonding.

So when the phone rings again, and it turns out to be Ophelia, wanting to speak to Becky in private this time, Mitchell is almost glad that Becky asks *Kiki* to ask *him* to keep an eye on the little ones while she goes into the next room. "Fine with me," says Mitchell, although to whom exactly he could not say.

He decides that the best way to play it is to pretend that the whole scenario is normal. So he picks up a shirt out of the basket, spreads it out on the ironing board, and starts ironing—forcefully, as if he is branding cattle.

"So. How's it going?" he asks Kiki.

"Great," says Kiki.

"Everything OK on the home front?"

And Kiki says, "Couldn't be better."

"Oh right. The same old story, huh?"

Kiki just looks at him. And so Mitchell tries again. "Women," he says, "you can't live with them, you can't live without them."

"Actually, I live with two," says Kiki.

Mitchell thinks: Huh? But he still keeps trying. "I live with four," he says. "And you know what? One of them has multiple personalities."

"I'm happy with two," says Kiki in the same hostile voice. "It can be rough at times but at least I don't have to do my own ironing."

Can you believe this guy? Mitchell feels like asking the three-year-olds. He has to remind himself that this guy has what he needs, a lot of money. So he says, "Oh I don't mind. Because you know what? I do it better than she does. I'll tell you what I resent, though. And I'm sure you find this too. It's her attitude.

"You know what the magic word is in this household?" Mitchell continues. "It's 'condescending.' She can get me to do anything she wants if she can get me to believe I'm condescending to her.

"Take these shirts," he continues. "Her attitude toward these shirts is a perfect example. She won't touch them, and all because of this one thing I said to her once which made her decide I was condescending to her. God, I want to nuke entire continents when I hear that word.

"I mean," he says, "I'm not all that bad. I get up with the kids every other morning. I do the goddamn dishes every third night. And as you see, I iron my own shirts. And you want to know why? Because once, a couple of years ago, I asked her to go over one of the ones she had ironed because it still had some wrinkles in it. You know what I'm saying? We're talking a white dress shirt. You can't have a white dress shirt with wrinkles in it. It defeats the purpose, right? Anyway, she flipped, and I am talking three hundred and sixty degrees. You know? She said if I didn't like the way she ironed shirts, then I'd have to iron them myself. And so here I am, ironing my own shirt when I have to be in the Embarcadero Center ten minutes ago. You know? I mean, does Ophelia give you this kind of crap? I mean, in your case it's different, because . . ."

Kiki says, "I wear permapress."

"You wear . . ."

"Yeah, permapress."

Oh boy, says Mitchell to himself.

Kiki looks at his watch. "Speaking of which, you have exactly three minutes to tell me why I should get my venture group to come into that building with you."

"What building?"

"You tell *me* what building. You now have two minutes and forty seconds. I can't give you more than that. I'm a busy man."

And *he's* not? And he's fucking not? When Becky walks into the kitchen, he feels like saying to her, Hey, babes, next time you want to humiliate me, why stop at one asshole? Why not sell tickets?

Of course he doesn't dare say this to her, because they're not communicating.

Or . . . is he about to witness a miracle? Is she . . . ?

Yes, she is. She is about to talk to him.

She says, "Would you mind if I asked Kiki here a question?"

"No, of course not. Go right ahead."

"Thanks," she says.

His wife has said thanks to him?

"When you were talking to Laura this morning," she says, turning to Kiki, "did she say anything out of the ordinary?"

"No, not really. No, she seemed fine. She was talking a lot about that trip they're taking after Mike gets himself out of real estate. Which is why I thought you might be looking for new backing."

"What the hell . . . ?" says Mitchell.

And Becky says, "I *knew* it. I knew he was going to do something to sabotage her career! The lengths some people will go to . . ." Looking Mitchell directly in the eyes for the first time in six days, she says, "Will you take care of this guy when you see him today? Will you tell him to leave his wife alone and cut out this shit?"

"I certainly will," he says. But he has something else in mind, and so does Kiki. There is no need for either of them to put it into words. They are communicating perfectly.

Chapter 10

"Are you sure?" I remember asking him. We were sitting in our old Potrero office. It was early afternoon. I had just broached the vacation idea to him. He had said would I prefer to dissolve the partnership altogether? His eyes were too alert, his voice too flower child. I ought to have asked myself why.

And the terms he suggested—they were so favorable as to be ridiculous. Twenty thousand now, five percent of the profits for the next ten years, full inspection rights, full protection . . . offering to take the "company car" off my hands . . . I thought our troubles were over. I thought our real life, the one we had always longed for but never been able to afford, this real life of ours was about to begin.

No more creative financing, I thought. No more selling Dalí prints and coin collections to make the rent. No more long shots in the Kentucky Derby, or dented Volvos, or foggy summers cooped up in the apartment. No more dingy South of Market office buildings with winos hanging out in the doorways. No more tenants or maintenance contracts, no more potential investors with bald spots instead of conversation, no more ulcers about up-and-coming neighborhoods that went down-and-out instead. No more unpaid bills and unanswered letters from collection agencies, no more S and M sessions with bankers, no more secretaries with dyslexia or hallucinating messenger boys, but, most important, no more Mitchell. No more Mitchell! Can you imagine how it felt, Laura, to know that I never had to do this guy's homework ever again? That from now on it would be someone else's problem if he overinvested or fiddled the books or made commitments that we couldn't have honored even if we had both had kagemusha? Think how I felt, Laura, as I coasted down Potrero Hill.

I have never had less trouble arranging a vacation. (That alone should have warned me.) I did not go into that travel agency with any firm idea about where to go. But when the agent showed me Molivos in the brochure, and I saw that picture of the villa we had always longed for, it seemed fated. *That* was where we would begin our new life. You must try and understand that I was in a trance.

Normally something would have happened to shatter my happiness before I got home. As you know, it does not take much. But amazingly, and perhaps tragically, that afternoon nothing did, even though the odds were as always against me.

I left the car unattended, with the engine running, in front of City Lights, while I ran across to Specs to give Rob my good news. And then, after doing the exact same thing in front of Coit Liquors, I drove the wrong way down a one-way street to get to Flower Power before it closed. I double-parked in front of the Oakville Grocery—but did I have to rush out of the store halfway through and plead with a policeman? No. As I said, everything went my way.

There were no convenient parking spaces when I got home. So I pulled up into the heart patient's driveway to offload the champagne—and for once the old fart didn't see me. And who should be there to hold the door for me but Mrs. Last-resort Smith? I told her the good news, and that was when she offered to babysit so we could go out to celebrate.

Together we loaded up the elevator, which she then offered to hold for me while I parked the car. I don't know if you remember, but they were filming that day at the top of the Crooked Street. I was sure I was going to have to drive halfway to North Beach. But no sooner had I turned the key in the ignition than a space opened up. You know, that space that is technically on the yellow line but that in my opinion shouldn't be?

I could not believe my luck.

I don't know how I managed to make it up to the seventh floor and into the apartment without something happening to diminish my euphoria. Without the elevator gates crashing and compacting my shoulders, as they have done on so many other occasions. Without dropping the case of champagne on my feet, or having to hold the flowers in my teeth as I fumbled for the keys, and dropping either them or the flowers into the crack between the elevator and the landing. Somehow, miraculously (and uniquely), everything was where I wanted it when I needed it.

And of course I had Gabe with me in the elevator. When I came back from parking the car, there he was. He was carrying his toolbox and was wearing that worshiping smile that had me fooled for so long . . .

"So, you gave Mitchell what for, huh?"

I told him yes without pausing to think how he knew.

When we got to the seventh floor, he held the door for me while I carried out the champagne and the flowers and fumbled for my keys. Then he gave me the thumbs up. "Give 'em hell," he said, and again, I didn't pause to think what he meant.

As I sit here now in my tomb of an apartment, with nothing to listen to but the low rumble of the refrigerator, I think back with unspeakable longing to the noises that greeted me when I pushed open the door.

I remember a baby crying. A toddler talking nonsense. A group of four-year-olds pretending to be spaceships, and beyond them, the plinking of the *Sesame Street* theme song; the death throes of Dr. Seuss as he recited *Green Eggs and Ham* on a tape recorder that was crying out for batteries; a single desperate and unheeded request for juice.

I must have had to do a certain amount of carting cases and bags between the door and the kitchen. But all I remember is standing there with the champagne weightless in my hands, and the flowers suspended in midair, and looking into the bedroom, above and beyond the TV screen.

From which the sickly music of *Mister Rogers' Neighborhood* now emanated. For once I did not wonder about his secret sex life. I was able to look above and beyond him, and through the window without even thinking how badly we needed a window cleaner.

The sun was low in the sky. Shafts of light were pouring through the windowpane and a swirling pattern of children's fingerprints. Looking beyond them, I could see the slate-gray silhouettes of the pine trees on the far side of Russian Hill Park and the black outline of the Golden Gate Bridge rising above them. Looking over my other shoulder, moving my eyes quickly over the *Star War* figures, the huddled children and the gaping diaper bags, I could see the city spread out before me, the city and the bay and the bridge and even Contra Costa County at my feet.

I have since, in my solitude, tried to relive that moment, which is how I know I have invented it. There is no one spot from which you can see all the things I saw on that late afternoon or was it early evening when I came home with the tickets. I remember gasping for breath, as if I had climbed all seven flights of stairs, as if I had been climbing stairs for seven years. I remember looking first over one shoulder and then over the other, at the Bay Bridge and then the Golden Gate Bridge, at the children on our bedroom floor and Mister Rogers condescending to Chef Brockett and then back to the bay and the Pyramid Building and the pastel houses of Telegraph Hill and Coit Tower standing perfectly centered in the middle bay window of our living room, and then at Jesse, with his Superman underwear and his Superman cape, standing on the armrest of the leather couch, surrounded by his friends in their Spider-Man and He-Man and Incredible Hulk underwear . . .

He was preparing for flight. He was standing on the armrest poised for takeoff and waiting for his friends to stop talking so that they could give him their full attention. I watched him will them into silence without even raising his hand. I noticed but did not mind that he was wearing his shoes. I watched him brush back his golden curls and poise his perfect athlete's body and then—as his puny, ugly, round-shouldered friends looked helplessly on—I watched him bend his knees with a kind of grace that can never be taught and rise off the couch leaving scuffmarks I forgive him a thousand times over, to go sailing through the air in a perfect arc, to land on his feet with his hands still straight, his knees bent, his cape still half suspended behind him. My son! I thought.

And then, as if she had read my thoughts and decided to rebuke me, there, suddenly, was Maria, smiling at me through the window of her Wendy house.

She looked so . . . so . . . I hate to say it, but it's true. I didn't buy that doll for her, you did. (I didn't give her doll that name either.) She was sitting at the window of the Wendy house, rocking Baby Jesus in her arms and pretending to breast-feed it, and she looked . . . as I said, I hate to say it, but I'll say it anyway. She looked feminine.

And so did you when you stepped out of the service elevator with that basket of laundry so beautifully poised on your shoulder. I hate to say it, but . . . no, I don't hate to say it, because it's true.

You were barefoot. You were wearing your oldest sweatshirt. Your jeans were streaked with flour, but you looked feminine, and if I had to choose a moment to freeze forever on a vase it would be that one. You, stopping short at the sight of me and sucking in your breath, me, half kneeling over the flowers and champagne and looking up at the ringlets that had escaped from your ponytail to make a halo for your face. Following the curves of your slender arms, of your long fingers draped so gracefully around the edge of the laundry basket, and remembering all the sorrow you had had to carry over the past ten years, all the disappointments I had made you bear. And just reaching out to take the basket from you, to regain my full height, take you in my arms, and show you the tickets, the brochure with our villa in it . . .

Why didn't you realize how much this moment meant to me? Why didn't you send them away?

Chapter 11

I remember standing in the kitchen with my back to them, looking at the toaster, trying not to listen to them asking you if you were sure this was what you wanted.

I remember pushing aside their things to clear a space on the counter, a modest space just big enough for me to butter the toast and spread out the salmon and cut the flowers and get the glasses ready while they continued to query our plans.

"Are you sure you've given yourself enough time to think this through?" they asked.

I remember pushing aside their keys and their handbags and their children's juice cups, pushing them aside as gently as if they were living things while at the same time fighting the urge to send them flying, and then looking around for the knife, and finding it under a pile of Becky's baby's teethers, and being overcome by an urge to mash up every last one into the Disposall, and longing for the sound of crunching plastic, longing to lose control and run amok slashing furniture—

As I cravenly washed the knife. Retrieved the lemon. Cut it into wedges, and listened to you disappear into a vapor of weak apologies:

"No, he didn't consult me but it will be nice for the children . . . Why? Oh just because . . . Come again? No, I like surprises . . . No, really, he has my best interests at heart."

What right did they have?

It was all I could do to serve them their champagne in a civilized manner. If this manner was also somewhat cold, it was because I was preoccupied with my hands. In other words, it was only extreme vigilance that kept me from uncorking the champagne bottle in the direction of Charlotte's head when she reminded us that Chandon was not champagne but sparkling wine, or clipping Ophelia with the hors d'oeuvres tray when she gave her lecture about eighty percent of the salmon in Puget Sound having cancer, or giving Becky the finger when she proposed that sarcastic toast about the road to Damascus.

You may remember I gave you a look, but you didn't respond to it, or in any event didn't make a move to get rid of them so that we could enjoy the imitation champagne and cancerous salmon and make our Bohemian plans in private. It was to keep myself from yelling, If you disapprove of me that much, then why are you accepting my hospitality? that I went into the bedroom to watch the evening news.

I thought they would be happy to see the end of me. I had no idea they would take my withdrawal as an additional offense. When you came into the bedroom after seeing them off, I actually thought you were going to apologize to me for *their* behavior. I was shocked, therefore, when you asked me why *I* had been so rude to *them*.

No need now to go into the details of our argument. All I'd like to say is that, if I acted vicious, it was because it hurt so much to hear you say that maybe your friends were right about me.

I regretted my harsh words almost as soon as I said them. It was horrible to see you so upset on a day that should have been such a happy one for both of us. My intentions were honorable when I said I would do whatever you wanted in order to make things up to you.

But when you said, "I want to share our celebration, I want them all to come out to dinner with us tonight," I nearly spat.

Share our celebration? *Share?* The hated word cut me like a knife. Of course I was going to look glum while you called them up. Of course I was going to let you take the initiative with babysitters and reservations.

But believe me. As far as the dishes were concerned—I *was* planning to go back to the kitchen and clean the whole thing up. How was I supposed to know that by then you would have already "taken the hint" and cleaned up by yourself? (And let's keep our sense of proportion here. We are talking five glasses and three plates.)

I'm sorry, though, about abdicating bathtime. I also ought to have read to the children so as to give you more time to get dressed. I ought not to have sat there looking impatiently at my watch as you rushed to throw your clothes on in under three minutes.

And when we left for the restaurant, I shouldn't have pulled away from the curb before you had a chance to put on your seat belt. I was distracted by the effort of keeping my feelings to myself. Because I did mean to keep up my end of the bargain, if only to show you the lengths to which I was willing to go to degrade myself in your behalf.

But let me tell you.

I have never felt so desperate as I did that night at the Hayes Street Grill.

So let me say it again: I have never felt so desperate as I did that night at the Hayes Street Grill. Never have I felt so acutely that I was an alien in my own country. All I wanted was to take your hand in mine and talk to you about Greece. But you were six people, three vases and thirty-nine stultifying conversations away from me.

You were at the head of the table, obscured from my view, over-entertained by Mitchell and Kiki. I was at the foot of the table, hemmed in by your unfriendly friends and wedged into a space that had never been intended to accommodate a chair. Every time I moved my elbow, I knocked over the bread basket on the table behind me. Every time I exhaled, I jostled the wineglasses on same. I could hear every hushed word that passed between the people whose wineglasses and bread basket I was jostling. Every single word was about me.

They thought I might be in violation of the fire code. If somebody had told them I was also the host, they probably would have fainted.

Ditto for the waiters. Even when I was the one to order the wine, they would take it to some other man to taste. Every last thing they served me was cold.

From time to time, if I moved my head far enough to one side to see beyond the towering vase, I could catch a glimpse of your shoulders, of the outer reaches of your hair, of your arm waving or your hand reaching out for a glass. From time to time your laughter floated down to me through the monstrous tangle of petals and stems. Instead of lifting my spirits, it only made me angry at the men who were monopolizing you. It only served as a reminder of the evening we could have had if we had gone out by ourselves.

I did try to keep up my end of the bargain. But your friends were not any happier about the seating arrangement than I was. They acted as if I were there just to keep them from discussing me.

Imagine Charlotte and Ophelia to either side of me, toying with their first courses, fixing me with Stonehenge glares. And now imagine me, trying to interest them in the following subjects:

> Art. Literature. Music. Dance. Politics—both local and national. Foreign policy. Nuclear disarmament.

> The Siege of Troy. The Greek War of Independence. Byron. Shelley. The Hellenic Age. The lessons to be learned from Prometheus. The tragedy of Iphigenia. The persistence of matriarchy on the island of Skopelos.

Here is the one topic they responded to:

> The persistence of matriarchy on the island of Skopelos.
>
> And this was only Charlotte, to tell me it was not the entire island of Skopelos, but a single coastal village.

"So what?" I said. "It's still a matriarchy."

"Not necessarily, if you look at the overall kinship structure," was her response.

At which point she turned away and started up a conversation with Ophelia that was so unspeakably boring I felt like taking my fork and stabbing my chest.

Here are some of the things I found out that night from Charlotte and Ophelia, as you sat beyond my reach, separated from me by three impenetrable tiers of Stork Club:

1. It takes under two minutes to freeze-dry a pre-cancer, if it's somewhere accessible, like, say, your nose.
2. Wheat, like cow's milk, is mucus-forming.
3. While we may have a woman on the Supreme Court, women in general still have a long way to go.
4. Women bankers do not tend to get promoted as far as their male colleagues because they tend not to play golf.
5. This is grossly unfair.
6. Things are not going to improve until corporations are run by men AND women (that's how they always said it: men AND women, men AND women) who have firsthand experience of childcare.
7. It is not clear if the nursery schools that emphasize fantasy prepare children better or worse than nursery schools that emphasize practical life.

It was when they got onto the monolithic and stultifyingly important subject of kindergarten admissions that my eyes began to roll around like panic-stricken eight balls in their sockets. I didn't care to know which kindergarten best served the whole child. I didn't care to know how many kindergartens the wise parent applied to, or what I had to do to keep on the good side of the directress of the Creative Learning Center, or when their next rummage sale was taking place, or why the hell the wise parent of the whole child was well advised not only to attend but to participate in these functions. I remember thinking: Paint a bull's-eye on my head. I was dropping three hundred bucks for this?

I was already feeling persecuted, in other words, when Ophelia turned on me.

"You *are* intending to get the children back in time for the new school year, aren't you?"

When I answered, "Not if I have anything to do with it," I was being sarcastic, but they both took me seriously.

"That's a mite presumptuous of you," said Charlotte. She used the same voice I remembered her using that time years ago at the playground when she thought she needed to teach me how to tie my own child's shoelaces. "You didn't happen to tell your wife about this part of your plan, did you?"

"Not yet, but I will next time you permit me a few seconds alone with her."

"And you think she'll go along with it?"

"I don't think," I said. "I know. You may not realize this, but actually we're very close."

"So close that you know what she needs better than she does? So close that you know you are doing her a favor by depriving her of a career?"

"You got it," I said. "That's how close we are."

"You really are the limit," said Ophelia.

And I retorted, "You really are the pits."

"There's no need to get personal," said Charlotte—to me, even though Ophelia had been just as personal. "There's a serious issue at stake here. You *do* realize how important the final year of nursery school is? You *do* realize how hard it is these days to get a child into kindergarten?"

"Yes," I said, "and I think it's sick."

"Well, you may be on to something there, but it's what we have to work with. What's the alternative?"

"The alternative is to split."

"By which you mean?"

"By which I mean move my family to a country where they have a normal educational system."

"And which far-flung planet of our solar system would that be?"

"The one where no one would ever dream of discussing kindergartens in public. Or cancer. Or dentistry. Or women's rights."

They stared at me, stunned by my rudeness.

"You weren't born this way, I'm sure of it," I said. "It's San Francisco that's done this to you. But do you have any idea how fucking boring you've become?"

They caught their breath and exchanged looks.

"It's not even worth responding to," said Ophelia.

Charlotte nodded. "So let's just eat."

My gratitude at their silence was short-lived. Because I had a chance to listen to Becky, who was sitting next to Charlotte. Or rather, I had a chance to listen to the noise she was making.

Like everyone else at the table, Becky had left her personality at home that evening. She had brought Baby instead. And if she wasn't slapping Baby on to her right breast, she was pulling Baby off her left breast. Slap. Pop. Slap. Pop. I failed to see the point of a new breast every ten seconds. But I soon discovered why she had to struggle to keep her eyes from closing. It was because she was listening to Trey, who was sitting next to Ophelia.

Now talk about torture. Charlotte and Ophelia were like Monegasque socialites compared to this guy. Here are some fascinating tidbits he passed on to me over the course of the next half hour, whenever my eyes, dancing frantically from head to head in search of relief from the growing panic of boredom, accidentally locked with his:

1. BMWs are cheaper if you buy them in Germany.
2. Mercedes Benzes, which you can also buy in Germany on a similar export plan, are better value dollar for dollar.
3. There is a big market out there for remote-control videocassette recorders.
4. Golf carts do not make much noise because they are propelled by electricity.
5. L. L. Bean is the best catalogue for mountaineering gear.
6. Microwave ovens come in several sizes.

* * *

Extra! Extra! Read all about it! I remember thinking, throw me into a Siberian tidal pool. Anything, anything, but having to sit there nodding while Trey Phillips, the Ripley of the eighties, reveals the amazing truths of modern living. I'd rather discuss cancer and allergies until the Second Coming if that's what it took to keep this guy away from me. I would even do a doctorate in mucus formation.

Things took a turn for the worse with the arrival of the main course. By now he had run through his repertoire of consumer tips and moved on to his A Thousand and One Tales of IRS Tedium.

I tried to protect myself by keeping my eyes on my (cold) fish. But he just wouldn't get the hint. He kept saying things like, "There was this guy once who . . ." or, "One of the most interesting cases I ever had was once when . . ."

My efforts to silence him became more and more desperate. "Did you say you wanted some more wine?" I kept shouting. I'd pour him some, I'd pour myself some. I'd look down the table and pretend to lift my glass to you, pretend not to hear the tail end of whatever mangled anecdote my so-called partner and so-called doctor were telling you at my expense—doubly at my expense . . .

And then wham, there he was again, drawing me into another endless monologue about the joys of taxation: "I'll tell you what people always forget to figure in when they're calculating their expenses and that's property tax. Even Prop 13 did not alleviate the drone drone drone. I knew a guy once and he drone drone drone . . ."

I tried to feign tolerance. A look of interest being beyond my range. But then—it was at about the same time as they passed out the dessert menus—my patience snapped and I made a number of uncalled-for comments.

When I asked him, "How many people you audited had cancer?" he took my question at face value.

"Gosh, you know? I don't think I ever even . . ."

My sadism encouraged by his witlessness, I continued. "How many were allergic to milk?"

"Gosh," he said. "I don't think I even . . ."

"How many had cancer AND milk allergies? And of those, what percent were in nursery school?"

"That's easy. None of them. I only audited adults."

"But are you more or less likely to have your property assessed if you have a nursery-school education?"

"I'm afraid I can't help you there," said Trey.

"*That's* for sure," I said.

This was when Becky saw fit to intervene. "Would you stop this nonsense? It's not even funny."

"I wasn't *trying* to be funny," Trey said.

"I wasn't talking to you. I was talking to Mike."

"Why?"

"Because he's making fun of you."

"Why is he doing that?"

"It may have something to do with his emotional age."

Trey turned to me. His face was starting to flush. "Why were you making fun of me?"

"Because I found your conversation boring."

"That's really great," he said. "If it's not entertaining then it's not worth talking about—is that what our country's come to?"

"That's what people say. If it's boring, forget it."

"That's really great," Trey said again.

"But don't worry, dear," said Charlotte. "You're not the only one. Apparently we're all boring this evening. Apparently it's what happens to people who settle in San Francisco."

"Oh, he's not on *that* kick again," said Becky. "Complaining about all the people in this city who think they're interesting because they *used* to read? Telling you exactly how many bookstores there ought to be here and how many there are in actual fact? Yeah, I've heard all that before. But tell me, did he get around to saying I was an autodidact because I didn't go to college?"

"Fuck off," I said. "Don't put words in my mouth."

And she said, "Fuck you and all you stand for."

As you know, I had always had a harder time with Becky than I did with the others. Because there were times when we got along, times when I had even confided in her. Times when she, too, got fed up with all things West Coast and talked to me like a fellow-sufferer. But then, for no good reason and usually with no advance notice, she would turn on me, use my own words against me, and whenever she did, I felt doubly betrayed. Also—there is something horrible about a woman who manages to give you the finger while also managing to keep an infant feeding at her breast.

By the time the desserts arrived, no one at my end of the table was talking. We were all five of us like pinless hand grenades waiting to be pushed over the edge. This meant that we had zero patience for, but no way of not listening to, Mitchell and Kiki as they updated each other on their two favorite topics:

Restaurants:

1. The Hayes Street Grill was a really good restaurant.
2. The original Mai's was also a really good restaurant.
3. The *calamari* at Caffè Sport were out of this world, especially if you got them with spinach pasta.
4. The nut loaf at Green's was definitely worth a try, and so was the pasta. But it was still a better deal for lunch. ("Especially since they go slow on salt.")
5. There was a new place in Oakville that was worth a detour. ("They oversalt things, though.")
6. The new North Indian place on Van Ness gave good value for money. ("And surprisingly enough . . .")
7. Alice Waters grew her own vegetables, but her portions were too small. ("But at least she goes slow on salt.")
8. The Hunan did not use MSG. ("You should see how they pour on the soy sauce though.")
9. If you wanted Cajun food, the place to go was still that one up on Fillmore. ("Although that is one place where they go positively apeshit with the saltshaker.")

The World of Finance:

1. The man to talk to at Crocker Bank was Joe Blow-job. ("Yeah, I've heard of him," said Kiki. "He plays golf.")
2. The man who knew everything there was to know about windfarms was Paul Preposterous. ("Right. I've heard of him. We have a mutual tennis partner.")
3. If you ever wanted to go into corporate bonds, however, the firm to contact was Boredom & Boredom. ("Sure, I know them. They handled a deal for my cousin's brother-in-law.")
4. If, however, you wanted the lowdown on the mini-storage racket, the man to talk to was Bob Even More Boring. ("But what a backhand!")

* * *

It was while I was sitting through the above competing monologues (and smoking openly) that my sense of desolation at our wasted evening turned into rage. Why were you putting me through this? Why had you stranded me at this end of the table? Why weren't you defending me? Why were you allowing Mitchell and Kiki to be so boring?

I wasn't the only one. Trey was shredding his napkin. Becky's breast-feeding manner was going from peremptory to dangerously rough. Charlotte and Ophelia were communicating their dissatisfaction with distended nostrils. It was a question of who would snap first. It turned out to be Trey—just as Kiki was giving us the name of the man to contact at City Hall if we had too many parking tickets.

"I guess you think breaking the law is funny," was Trey's opening comment. His face was scarlet. "I'm sure you won't believe it could happen here, in a democratic stronghold, but did you know there were people in this city—and I'm talking reputable businessmen and -women—who think they can get away with claiming parking tickets as legitimate expenses?"

Silence. Everyone stared at him glumly. Particularly Kiki, who, I later discovered, had been doing this for years.

"Oh, I don't know," Mitchell said. "I don't do crazy stuff like deducting parking tickets . . ."

"You just don't pay them," snapped his wife.

"OK, but so what? What I am trying to say is, I think the best thing is to take the cowboy approach. Get liquidity *today*. Even if it means balloon payments. And you know? The same holds true for Uncle Sam. I mean, why should I go by the book if I can play the game?"

"Mitchell."

"What, hon?"

"Mitchell, I shouldn't have to tell you this, but now is not the time to talk about taxes."

"Why not, hon?"

"We're in a bad mood down at this end of the table here, that's why. We're in a bad mood about taxes, particularly property taxes."

"But I wasn't talking about property taxes."

"No, and don't," Becky said, but still he didn't get the hint.

"Oh, so you mean you've already told them what *I* did."

"No, I didn't."

"Did *you* hear what I did?" Mitchell asked Kiki. "No? Well, what happened is I made friends with the assessor."

"Mitchell, this is the last time I'm going to warn you." Becky's voice was shrill now.

"Warn me about what? What's going on here?"

"They're laughing at me," Trey told him. "They think I'm funny because I'm an idealist."

"Well, ha ha ha," said Mitchell. "Is that what you wanted me to say? So anyway, there was this assessor. When he came in I could tell where he was coming from even though he looked real straight. So I sat him down with a glass of Chardonnay, asked him where he was from . . ." Slap went Becky as she threw Baby on to Breast One. ". . . and I asked him where he went to college, and before you know it we're sitting there sharing a joint and rapping about Bolinas . . ."

Pop. As she was pulled off Breast One, Baby let out a yell that was smothered—smack—by Breast Two.

". . . and it turned out that he has a friend who knows the ex-lady of a friend of mine . . . and then he tells me he's just bought this farm outside Santa Rosa . . . but that the guy who did the plumbing fucked up . . ."

Pop. Yell. Slap.

". . . and so I say, listen, man. Let's do a deal. There's someone who owes me one and he lives in Sebastopol. He's really a sculptor but what he does for a living is . . . you guessed it, plumbing."

Pop. Yell. "So how about this?" Slap. Silence. "I tell this guy, let me give this sculptor plumber friend of mine a call and . . ." Pop.

". . . and ask him . . ." Slap. "Let's ask him to do your plumbing for free. And in return you'll let me tell *you* what this here house looked like before we poured all that money into it, and you can . . ."

This was when Trey interrupted him.

"You know," he said. "You should be careful what you say to other people about your shady dealings. Especially someone who has put his name to your tax returns and staked his reputation on their contents."

Slap! Slap! Slap! Becky had totally lost it. And now it was my turn. I vaguely remember standing up and telling her not to use Baby like a club. I also remember telling Mitchell to shut up before he landed himself in jail. I remember pointing at Trey and making the cuckoo sign. I remember saying something to Kiki that made him look as if I had slapped him across the face, although I do not remember it being anything that anyone could construe as a racial slur. And I remember telling you, or rather the giant lilies that I thought obscured you, that we had all suffered enough now: it was time for the bill.

I remember panicking when I discovered you weren't there. I ought to have assumed you were in the bathroom, but somehow I got it into my head—it must have been because the other women were away from their seats at this point too—that your friends were abducting you. I do not remember the lecture I apparently gave them (and everyone else at that end of the restaurant) when you all returned to your assigned places. I particularly do not remember telling them that it was a woman's lot to follow—or that it was a man's privilege to wear the pants.

Chapter 12

When I woke up I was lying behind our living-room sofa. The room was dark except for a shaft of light coming in from the dining alcove. I tried to remember the chain of events that had brought me to this strange position. I couldn't remember anything after the restaurant, and what I could remember about the restaurant was so bad that I hesitated before getting up to join you in bed.

Did I want you to be next to me when I woke up in the morning? Could I bear to listen to the list of all the horrible things I had done, before I had a chance for a cup of coffee? Better, perhaps, to stay out here, maybe go out early and get some things for breakfast, face you after I had already made an appeasing gesture.

Why did I always do this to myself? It was while I was lying there, lacerating myself with reproaches, that I heard you clearing your throat in the dining alcove. There was the sound of a can being opened. Then I heard you saying, "Thanks."

Then a man cleared his throat and said, "What I think is . . . well, I don't think much, so it doesn't matter."

It was Gabe.

What was *he* doing here? And what were you doing giggling at his halfhearted joke in such a throaty, brazen manner? Since when had you and Gabe been so close? What had been going on behind my back? Nothing you said to this guy over the next half hour had you ever said to me. It was like listening to a stranger, except that no, it was much worse, because up until now I had thought I knew you. But as I lay there behind the couch and listened to you play up to this other man, I realized I didn't have a clue. My wife was a stranger. The woman I loved did not exist.

"The only time I feel like an adult is when I'm with you," I heard you say to him.

"*What* do you mean by *that?*" Gabe asked.

"Oh, I don't know," you said. "I guess you make me feel as if I've learned something. You're just so young, Gabe!"

"I don't know if I like your attitude," said Gabe.

"Well, take *your* attitude to the future. You consider your options as if they were empty houses that will stay on the market indefinitely while you make up your mind."

"Why rush?" he said.

And you said, "Well, exactly. If you did, you wouldn't be so cute. And I like listening to what you say about Audrey. That's cute, too."

"Why?" he asked.

"Because you don't even know each other. You've never argued over a utility bill, you've never sat on a plane together, never had a joint account. The only things you've ever shared are beds and tables."

"Then why can't I stop thinking about her?"

This made you laugh.

"You can't stop thinking about her because you're both playing hardball and she's winning. And you know what? I feel for you, of course, but you deserve it. You weren't so nice to her, were you? You know, it's not enough just to love someone. But you seem to think that it's how you feel that counts in life, and not what you do."

"You're a hard woman," said Gabe.

"That's what Mike used to say."

"Poor guy."

"Don't I know it." Here you paused. "Did I ever tell you he had hair longer than yours once? It's hard to believe now, but he was adorable."

"Like me," said Gabe.

"That's right, like you. He was always changing his mind like you, too. In one breath he would say he wanted to join the fight against Pinochet, and in the next breath he'd say he wanted to travel around the world in a yacht. And you know, the stupid thing was, I used to hate him for it. I didn't want ideas, I didn't want contradictions. I wanted results. But what was the hurry? Now that I know what growing up is really like, I wish I had put it off."

"You have to put up with more than most," he said.

"Oh, don't worry about it. It was just one bad night."

"How often is he like this?"

"Well, he doesn't usually try to throw himself off the balcony, and he doesn't always hide Mrs. Smith's teeth in the freezer, but I do often have to liberate his car keys."

"How do you manage all this and stay so cheerful?"

"Oh, you're making too much of it."

"Don't you feel trapped?"

"The way I look at it, I made a choice. I had a chance to live differently and I didn't take it. He still hasn't given up, though."

"Who hasn't given up?"

"This person I almost married. He still calls me up. I don't tell Mike because it's not important. His name is Stavros. And to tell you the truth, I don't know why he *hasn't* given up. I mean, it's nice to get flowers, but as far as I'm concerned that's not love."

"It sounds sort of crazy," said Gabe.

And you said, "As far as I'm concerned, you don't really love someone until after he's betrayed you."

What? (I nearly shouted.)

"You build on the ashes," you went on. "Because that's all you have left when you get married and have children."

To my unspeakable horror, you then went on to explain what it was like to be at home with a baby, on the day after the day you found out the full implications of men not being able to breast-feed. What it felt like to watch a man get up rested at nine in the morning when you had been up since four, what it felt like to watch him take a shower, read a paper, and know that it was all forbidden to you—the eight-hour rest, the shower, the newspaper, the outside world. That you were never going to be able to do anything again that you couldn't combine with holding a baby.

"What about babysitters?" he asked.

You tried to explain about babysitters, not very successfully in my view. He protested common sense. You conceded that eventually it eased up. Eventually there were babysitters. But they didn't make up for the horror of knowing you had walked into a trap under false pretenses.

"What trap?"

"The family trap."

"What false pretenses?"

"That it has become possible for men and women to be equal."

"That was the breaking point for me," you told him. But what mattered was what you did next. "You have a baby who is interested in nothing but putting a teether into his mouth. How do you find a way to pass the afternoon so you can both enjoy yourselves? You have a husband who comes home so late that you can hardly look him in the eye. What do you do to salvage the evening?" This was why it was so important for you to spend time with Becky and Charlotte and Ophelia. "We all felt the same. It was up to us to make something out of nothing and we did."

You explained how exhilarating it had been to take four screaming infants to a dim sum restaurant and see the meal through to the end. To meet at a designated corner with your strollers and walk east one afternoon, and west the next. To take them to museums that were beyond them, to beaches where it didn't matter that it was too cold to swim. To sit down on the cold and windy beach and say to Ophelia, "Do you know what he said to me this morning?" and find out that Kiki or Mitchell had said exactly the same thing. You told him about the Christmas morning when you had dragged yourself and Jesse up to Lafayette Park, thinking that fight you had just gone through was going to bring the world to an end, and watched three other stooped figures pushing strollers up to the playground. It was hard not to laugh, you said, because if the same thing was happening in all four houses, that meant it wasn't any one person's fault but a pattern. And, when you knew that, you could go home again and find the strength to keep going and that was love.

"But you're living on crumbs!" Gabe cried.

But you're living on crumbs!

Those were the words that kept jumping out at me the next day no matter how hard I tried to push them away. And your response:

—I suppose you're right.

How could you say that?

And how could I, knowing that you had said that, bring myself to apologize to you for my own bad behavior, when I knew that I had at least acted openly, while you . . .

How could I get up and start making plans for this trip you were only pretending to want to take with me?

I realize now I ought to have told you what I was so upset about. I can see that without this information my behavior must have made no sense. I only hope that now you can understand why I refused to apologize for the restaurant fiasco, why I offered to cash in your ticket so that you could liberate yourself while I took the children on vacation by myself, why I said so many nasty things about your friends, why I called Gabe up to fix the sink and then left the house and came barging back in five minutes later, and acted as if he were an intruder, and cross-examined you as to why you were talking with him in the kitchen, how well you knew him, why you gave such an airhead the time of day, and why I made such a fuss about a letter from Stavros that I had discovered after a long and determined search.

Why had you never told me you were in touch?

Why did you prefer Gabe's company to mine?

Why did this trip we had dreamed of together suddenly mean so little to you?

Why did you think you were living on crumbs?

These were the thoughts that were still plaguing me on the day of our scheduled departure.

AND

Chapter 13

It is four in the afternoon. We are sitting in our bedroom, or rather I am sitting in our bedroom, watching a Giants game on TV. I am having a hard time hearing the commentary, because the children have dragged the Fisher-Price slide right next to the sofa and are fighting over who gets to sit at the top. I am trying to reason with them without raising my voice.

You are rushing back and forth with armloads of toys and toilet articles. It is clear to me that you are trying to pack too much, and I have decided not to say anything, because I don't want to have a fight.

At the same time I am fucking annoyed at you because you have left so much until the last minute. For ten days now I have been transferring funds, buying luggage, tying up loose ends at work, and what have you been doing? Slouching around in one of your low-grade depressions, and I'm fed up with it. Fed up with all this staring at the ceiling, this pausing at the window to frown at the view, this whispering on the phone. Why do you always slam down the receiver the moment I walk into the room? Why can't you say to me what you say to them? And why is food suddenly no longer your responsibility? Ever since I came home with the tickets, you haven't gotten it together to cook a decent meal. It has been hamburgers or Chinese take-out every goddamn night. If you had given up on cooking in order to devote your time to organizing the house, it would have been different. But with two hours to go before we are to leave for the airport, the apartment—which I consider to be your responsibility—is a wreck. Unpacked toys, unpacked clothes, unpacked books, unpacked toilet articles . . . piles of dirty sheets all over the place . . . is this what it has come to? With your fine mind, with your exceptional abilities, are you finally incapable even of taking the sheets down to the basement and throwing them into the machine?

It pains me now to remember how I sat there thinking ill of you. I mean, talk about out of touch. What kind of balloon was I floating around in? God, when I think about the way I just sat there on the sofa with my can of beer and my Giants game, feeling so superior, so sure of my unilateral decisions, so unaware of the ways in which I was taking you for granted. I cannot believe the way I sat there and said to myself, When is this woman going to get it together? How is it that a woman with a 4.0 grade-point average can have left so much until so late?

God! How could I have failed to see it? The proof was standing right there in front of me, and I didn't see it. Or rather, I didn't see what the luggage meant, how the way in which the bags were divided among us was significant.

Nine matching Le Sportsacs, standing in a smug little row.

For the baby bears, two teeny tiny Le Sportsacs.

For the mama bear, a medium-sized Le Sportsac carry-on bag and a twenty-eight-inch Le Sportsac suitcase.

For the papa bear, a forty-two-inch Le Sportsac suitcase, a twenty-eight-inch Le Sportsac suitcase, a Le Sportsac garment bag, a Le Sportsac duffel bag for the snorkling equipment, and another one for books. Plus a typewriter and a camera case.

How the sight of them, neatly packed and ready to go, must have galled you as you tried to squeeze your own and the children's belongings into bags too small to hold them.

If you only knew how much I regret saying, "No, absolutely not," when you asked me if you could pack some of your reading material in my book bag. More to the point: I do not know how I felt justified in objecting to your putting two of your dresses into my garment bag.

Technically, I was right. You can only put so much into a garment bag. If you have three suits AND two dresses in a garment bag, everything is going to get wrinkled. Which defeats the purpose of the bag. The question is, Why did I think my suits were more important than your dresses? Why had I not thought to buy you a garment bag of your own? The answer is, I wasn't thinking.

Looking back, I can see why you got so angry when I told you that there had to be enough room in your carry-on bag for the children's toys. But still, even with hindsight, I am shaken at the memory of the hatred in your face when you hurled the carry-on bag at my chest and screamed, "I hate you, I hate you," over and over again, and then launched into that merciless list of all the things I had ever done wrong. I mean, I just couldn't fucking believe it.

It was the attention to detail that got me—then as now. The fact that you could remember exactly what I had said to you on the 9th of October two years ago, and exactly what time I had or had not gotten out of bed for the past eight weekends. Had you written it down or what? I also couldn't understand why you had chosen this particular moment to share this information with me, or why you had to do so in front of the children.

Looking back, that is what I regret most—that the children witnessed your transformation from a sweet, giving, pleasantly absent-minded woman into an ogress. I cannot even begin to imagine what it did to them to see you savagely attack my garment bag and drag it brutally down the corridor, shouting vicious curses. As for the way you took it out on to the landing and dumped the contents down the stairwell—tell me. Was that really necessary? Couldn't you have waited until the children were asleep?

I realize that I should be the last person to criticize you, after the way I acted at the airport. But I am trying to be honest, in the same way I hope you will be with me one day. What I want to do is explain how I came to do what I did. To explain—not to justify. Because I am not at all proud of what I did in front of the metal detector.

Chapter 14

I know. I was out of control. But I could not accept this portrait you had painted of me, of this bear . . . this bull who stood between you and the world, blocking your way. Who treated you like a toddler. And you, who had never had an ounce of viciousness in your body, I could not believe you had painted this portrait single-handed. No, I could detect the heavy-handed influence of the Stork Club.

That is why it really bugged me to have to stand there in the airport lobby watching your farewells. From the looks your friends were giving me, you would have thought I was extraditing you to the Third World for an unfair trial. They kept saying things to you like, "You know where I am if you need anything," and, "If it gets too much for you, just give a shout." You kept sobbing, and blowing your nose, and saying, "I'll be all right. I really will be." You would have thought I was standing over you with a whip. I kept saying to myself, All right already. Let's get the show on the road.

I mean, when you look back on that day—if, in fact, you ever think back—don't you agree it was going too far to have all three of them come out to the airport? I was already reeling from our fight over the garment bag. And on top of that, to have your friends glaring at me as if I were abducting you to Bhopal . . . it was too much. I didn't really see a tow truck take away the car that was parked next to Becky's BMW. I just made it up to get rid of them.

I hope this goes some way toward explaining my behavior in front of the metal detector.

Chapter 15

Again, let me stress that I am not trying to justify myself. But by the time we got to the metal detector, I had long ceased behaving rationally. I was too upset about what happened at the check-in desk.

I don't know if you remember, but the "flight attendant" was a Grade A bitch. She had no good reason to refuse to check Maria's car seat through. I mean when you think of the number of times we've carted that thing on and off planes . . . I tried to tell her that she had it all wrong. But she was the expert. "I'm sorry, sir, but according to our regulations . . ." I can still hear her whiny little reject-cheerleader voice. "I'm sorry, sir, but . . . I'm sorry, sir . . ."

You may remember that I lost my temper. You may also remember that you tried to calm me down. But by reprimanding me in front of the baboon attendant, by treating ME like a toddler, you had the opposite effect on me than the one you intended.

There's something else I should mention. I try to keep it to myself, but I hate car seats. I hate putting children into them. I hate groping between their legs for the buckle. I hate seeing my children sitting there like trussed turkeys on their way to market. But most of all, I hate weaving through crowded departure lounges carrying two bags in each hand and balancing an upside-down car seat on my head. Because everywhere I look I see airport employees laughing at me.

That's why I kicked Maria's car seat off the scales, and why it was so satisfying. OK, bitch, see if I care, was what I was saying. To the flight attendant. Not to you. So. I was appalled when you went back and insisted on carrying it yourself. I was also furious at the sanctimonious harpy manning the metal detector because of her idiotic insistence that I take Maria up out of her stroller. So when the stroller slipped backward, and the camera bag crashed to the floor, and all the lenses and attachments went spewing out onto the floor . . . well, who wouldn't flip out?

That said, I am sorry about the way I turned on you. I should never have "congratulated" you, or said that thanks to your expert packing the four hundred dollars I had just spent on the zoom lens was down the drain. I knew only too well that the camera case had not been designed to hold a zoom lens. Sooner or later, it was going to fall out.

If you only knew how sorry I am about the way I acted when you said you weren't going to go through the metal detector until I apologized. I acted like a child, and traumatized the children when I grabbed them like that. I should never have told you to go fuck yourself in front of all those people. It was wrong of me to push you away and wrench the children from you.

I know I have no right to have felt the way I did, but when the children ran back to you screaming "Mama! Mama!" I felt betrayed. I thought you had turned them against me. That's why I said, "*Adiós* forever."

But I'd like to take this opportunity to point out that when I said, "You know where to find me, if you change your mind," I did not mean Greece. I meant the plane.

I know I can't prove it, but I did wait until the last possible moment to board the plane. I stood there at the gate, clutching the boarding passes, craning my neck to catch some glimpse of you and the children hurrying down the corridor. It didn't even occur to me that you needed those very passes to get past the metal detector.

Then finally I thought: Fuck it. If she wants to play games she can go ahead and play them but not with me. So I got on the plane, and five minutes later I was in the air. And then, suddenly, as if by magic—

Chapter 16

No more baby seats or strollers. No more whining children or disapproving wife. Just me and nine matching suitcases flying fast forward toward the Atlantic. No changing planes in St. Louis. No sleeping on second cousins' couches in New York. No boat trains across the English Channel, or camping on the outskirts of Amsterdam, or backtracking to Brussels for the cheapest charter. Just one flight, without a single stopover, to Athens—

And once in Athens, no need to wait in the scorching sun for the bus. Just hop into a taxi with the nine matching suitcases and sweep into the city down the same sun-baked avenues where you and I had once struggled with string bags of groceries under the cruel midday sun. Brush past the narrow winding side street where we used to live, past the soulless office building where we taught for wages even a slave would laugh at, and past the Parthenon, the Palace Gardens, the House of Parliament and the bench in Syntagma where I had once put my head in your lap and wept. Ignore the street that leads to the icy doors of American Express, where we had failed to receive so many important letters, where urgently cabled money could just sit, undetected, in a secretary's desk drawer for months. Where they never apologized to anyone in jeans, where they treated you like shit, and assumed you were there for the air-conditioning, if your hair came within six inches of your collar.

Remember all this and then look away and smile as the taxi pulls to a stop in front of the hotel we had passed so many times with our string bags, never dreaming that one day we would be able to afford it. Watch the doorman approaching, watch the bellboy dart back and forth with the nine matching suitcases. Proceed to the desk. "Ah, yes, sir," says the clerk. "You wish for a suite?"

Step into the well-appointed elevator. Press the top button and step back to make room for the porter. Step out into the plush corridor for tips, smiling bellboys, and respectfully closed doors. Look at the antique chairs in the sitting room. Look through the French windows at the Acropolis. Look at the beds. Flop onto the largest for an undisturbed and unresented nap.

Wake up to darkness and the hum of the air conditioner. The room seems to be swaying and for a moment I think I'm on a boat.

I am not on a boat but my head is swimming. Slowly I remember that I am in the Grande Bretagne, that my name is Mike and that I'm married to a bitch. I remember I have money. I remember I'm alone. I can do whatever I want. I am free, but I am also lying upside down and on a diagonal on a different bed from where I started.

I am also not sure I can still use my arms. To sit up and reach out and turn on the light—it may be impossible.

Quick. Up.

Out with the suitcase with the summer clothes. Into a short-sleeved shirt before I notice that there's no one there to notice. Out into the evening. Feel the warm air hit my face as I push open the lobby doors. Off to Zonar's. No need this evening to go to the cheap place next door. Take a seat outside, at a table in the back row. Sit back with a Campari and soda and look beyond the empty chairs around your table, look instead at the Greek gentlemen in their gray, short-sleeved shirts reading their papers, the foreigners writing postcards and flipping through guidebooks, the cars rushing past every time the light turns to green.

Remember my coming here when I was in high school, the lengths to which I went so as to not look American.

Remember that time when I was wearing my father's sunglasses, and drinking a Pernod, and reading the *New Statesman,* and trying not to choke on my cigarette, and those demonstrators went past, anti-American demonstrators—and remember how I tried to act as if they were just another battalion of taxis trying to beat the lights. Tried to remind myself I was a sympathizer. I had nothing in common with my father.

I don't want to think about my father, as I have no intention of looking him up. I want to enjoy my freedom and my new capacity to pay for it. And so bring me the check, please. Keep the change. Thank you, sir. It's nothing. In fact, it's a pleasure. Make a path between the tables. Step off the curb and hail a taxi. Watch him nod knowingly when I say L'Abreuvoir—as if there were nothing strange in going to a French restaurant for my first meal in Greece. Speed along more avenues up through Kolonaki and sit at the same table where you and I sat on our first anniversary and ordered the cheapest things on the menu.

No need for that tonight. I order seafood crepes, and fillet of beef and peach melba and expensive wine. When I'm through, I'm still hungry, so I start all over again. I have a couple of brandies with my coffee, and then I'm off to the Stagecoach—the *Stagecoach,* on my first night in Europe—for a "number" of margaritas. I sit, undisturbed, on the edge of a loud U.S. Embassy conversation which brings back other, more difficult memories—not of the years when you and I were living here together, but of those earlier years when I belonged to the diplomats.

Because they haven't changed, these people. The women are still talking about the drape allowance, the latest scandal at the community school, the problems with maids, and what so and so saw an NCO's Vietnamese wife do at the Commissary. The men are talking American sports and American politics—in confidential whispers even though their every word spells obedience. I almost wish my father were here to needle them.

Then I look down the bar and see that he *is* here. He is sitting at the last stool doing a crossword puzzle. His hair is white, but he looks younger than I remember him, and neater—he brings to mind a schoolboy actor who has made himself up to play an old man.

He looks up and sees me. "Well I'll be damned."

He gets up and comes over and hugs me. Stands back, chuckles, hugs me again. "Well, I'll be damned."

He makes me sit down, buys me a drink, tells the bartender who I am and how many years it has been since we last saw each other. "But he sure knew where to find me, didn't he, Gus?"

He asks after you and the children. Neither of us mentions Mom. He says my sister has kept him posted about my various achievements. Wonders if I have any photographs of his grandchildren but nods too readily when I say I don't. "Oh well."

"Maybe I could send you some," I say.

"That would be great. Here. Let me give you my address before I forget." He writes it out on a napkin and as he does I notice how shaky his hand is. "In fact, you could come back and stay with me. I have a spare room. I'm sure the GB is costing you something terrible."

I lie and tell him it's expense account. I explain I'm here on business. He accepts my excuse although I can tell he sees through it. I ask him how he spends his time these days, and so he talks for a while about his various little research projects, and the tutoring he does, just for the human contact. "And then someone comes through from the old days and I get to go out on their yacht."

He goes on to say that he has run into your parents recently, and that they haven't changed. "I can't remember which cruise line they were working for, but it was in Lindos. I was there with the Gilliots—you remember, he used to be the commercial attaché—and suddenly this ship appears and unloads two hundred Middle American idiots who thought they had landed on the moon. And Laura's father was their tour guide. Going crazy with the questions the idiots were asking him but they loved him to death. I don't think I could do it."

"But you're happy doing what you're doing," I say.

"Yes, and why aren't you?"

This takes me by surprise.

"You aren't in trouble, are you?" he asks.

"What makes you think I am?"

He takes me by the arm and says, "I know my boy."

This is unbearable. I stare into my drink so as to avoid looking at him. He tightens his grip and says, "Junior. Look at me. Look into my eyes." Against my will, I obey him, but it's horrible, horrible.

"Junior. I know I let you down. But you ought to know by now that these things happen. Men take jobs and then lose faith in them. They find out they're working for an outfit of crooks but they have a family to support. And then the marriage goes sour and they want out but then they'll never see their kids again. So they start compromising. You know all that by now, don't you? Even in California, people get stuck, don't they?"

"Yes, but they don't all keep a bunch of fascist colonels in power while they're at it."

"I lost my job, didn't I? Isn't that enough for you?"

He looked at me with that same horrible mixture of hurt and affection. It made me want to kick him.

"Look," he finally says. "It happens all the time. If you divide your life into compartments, one day one of them takes over. You forget who you are. Until one day you get a jolt—like the one you gave me. Don't you know what you did to me that day when you walked in on me? When I tried to put things right, it was for you."

"That's really great. You walked out on Mom because you were trying to put things right."

"I still supported her. And supported her well."

"If you had supported her well, she wouldn't have ended up the way she did."

He slammed his drink down on the bar. "For crying out loud. Don't you understand yet that it was the best I could do? Don't you know that yet—that if you do one thing right that late in the day it means doing everything else wrong?"

"I thought they fired you because you drank too much."

"That, too, my boy. That, too." He knocks back his drink, looks for a long time at the bottom of a glass, and then he says, "I've waited fifteen years to tell you that." And then he gives me the same look he gave me the day I walked in on him. *Please,* it says. *I'm a bastard and I know it—I just didn't want you to know.*

And I do the same thing I did then: I walk out. For the same reason. I can't take it. I hail a taxi and as we pass the Embassy I look up and try to remember which pinhole was his office, and I ask myself why my father has settled so close to the place where his life came apart.

When I return to the hotel there is no one to ask me if I know what time it is. When I wake up groggy the next afternoon, there is no one to blame for having missed the morning flight to Mitilini. I treat myself to room service. I eat my toasted cheese sandwich in the tub. Then it's more accommodating bellboys, deferential doormen, exorbitant tips and lightning taxis to the airport for a thirty-five-minute flight over an Aegean it used to take us fourteen hours to cross deck-class on a ferry.

Once in Mitilini there is—again—no need to kill time waiting for the bus. I fling my nine matching suitcases into the back of yet another gray Mercedes. I doze in the backseat as we speed past the olive groves, through salt flats and over mountains. We reach the north coast just as the sun disappears into the sea. We pass Petra, round the promontory . . . and there it is! Molivos, just as we left it. The hill of stone and pastel-colored houses crowned by the castle. The claw of land extending out to sea, curling itself around the harbor. The curving beach, the olive-oil factory, the fishing boats in the bay . . .

I go straight to the house I still cannot believe we have the good fortune to be renting. The view takes my breath away. I exchange smiling nods with the owners, take my bags inside, and off I go into town.

The same vines hang over the main walking street. The same grocers are selling the same boxes of Tide and cans of California squid. The hardware store has the same display of flippers and beach toys. The one-eyed butcher is still hacking away at the same side of beef, and his cronies in the café opposite are still engaged in the same game of backgammon, while younger men stare darkly at the television on the wall. The only thing that has changed is Costa's taverna. It has doubled in size and seems to have a roof garden, but in the kitchen Costa is still frying *keftedes*. His mother is still washing dishes, his wife is still drying them. His father is lingering over a Henniger at the table next to the jukebox and his father-in-law is still hunched over a bowl of water, peeling potatoes.

Costa gives me a quick, appraising look when I walk into the kitchen. "Yes?"

"Yes and no," I reply—the way I always did. It doesn't seem to ring any bells with Costa.

"What can I do for you?" he asks.

"What you can do for me," I said—because I have decided he's pulling my leg—"what you can do for me is wipe that half-assed expression off your face and tell me what you've been up to all these years."

He peers at me with raised eyebrows, takes a drag from his cigarette and puts it into the ashtray next to his elbow. "So," he says, "you want me to tell you what I have been doing all these years. There's only one problem."

He beams at me. "I don't know who you are."

"You're joking," I say. "You're trying to get even with me for not writing, aren't you?"

"Tell me your name," Costa says.

I tell him.

He thinks for a moment and then shakes his head.

"You can't be serious!" I say.

He shrugs his shoulders. "What can I say? It happens all the time."

The awful thing was, I could tell he was trying. After he closed the kitchen that night, he came over to my table with two Hennigers, one for me and one for him, just like the old days, and listened with baffled interest as I supplied him with details of the three summers you and I had spent in Molivos. I described you, said you spoke Greek, mentioned that we had both been working on books. ("You think that makes you different?" He laughed. He gestured at the other tables. "You all bloody write books, didn't you know that?") I tried another tack.

I pointed out landmarks. That was the table where he had served us lobster on the evening of his daughter's christening—we had been the only foreigners to be included. And that was the table where he had served us rotten squid one night when he was angry at us. I mentioned friends' names—George, Ellen, Barbara, Cynthia, Rod, Chris. None of them meant a thing to him.

And so I dragged out the scandals. These he remembered. The Athenian musician and his American wife flipping their Volvo on the road to Eftalou. "She was a drug addict," Costa recalled. "She wore long sleeves on hot days." The Canadian poet whose wife ran off with the English Buddhist: "He would sit on the beach all day"—he pronounced it "bitch"—"but he was always saying he was bloody writing a book." From time to time he would look at me and say, "And you were here *that* summer?"

By now I was beginning to get upset. When he offered me a cigarette, therefore, I accepted one. I told him how old he was, how many years he had spent in Australia—even how long his wife had been in labor with his eldest daughter.

"What are you anyway?" Costa laughed. "Some kind of bloody computer?" He called over his family, explained the problem to them in loud, laughing Greek. They looked me over. For a moment his wife thought she saw something familiar. "Your wife has short blond hair?" Costa asked.

"No," I replied.

"Then my wife must be thinking of someone else."

I wake up the next morning with a hacking cough. I am distressed by the disorder—balled-up socks in one corner, shoes and underpants in the other, pants draped over the wardrobe door, tweed jacket draped over the foot of my bed, keys and coins strewn over the floor and the bedside table.

I am slipping into bad habits. I must exert my will. I am not going to allow myself a swim until the house is in perfect order. I unpack my clothes, arrange them neatly in the wardrobe. I give the only hanger to the tweed jacket—

Of which more later—

And then I take the toilet articles into the bathroom, put the shampoos and shaving equipment on the ledge, the shower caps on the hook behind the door, the aspirins and Band-Aids in the medicine cabinet. I find a cup for the toothbrushes. I put away the children's clothes, arrange their shoes underneath their beds, their books on the bedside tables, their stuffed animals on their pillows. At first I am going to leave your clothes for you to take care of—why should I put myself out?—but then I relent and give you the best shelves in the wardrobe. I even double up two of my suits so that I can hang up your good dress.

I go into town to stock up on necessities. I have to fight my way through hordes of bronzed German lesbians and sunburned Scandinavian families, fat Canadians, morose Frenchwomen, jocular Italian students, pensive English students, half-nude, middle-aged German couples . . . They are swarming into Costa's taverna. Wave after wave of them packing into it as if it were a train at rush hour . . .

Costa gives me a friendly wave. He has decided he likes me. He invites me in for a beer, but what's the point of having a conversation with him if he's only going to forget it? I opt, as I will continue to opt, to go back to my villa, where I make myself a sardine sandwich and look down at the beach onto which wave after wave of newcomers is spilling. With their beach balls, their flippers, their pails and shovels, their tubes, mattresses and children . . .

The one o'clock bus arrives. I'm just about positive you'll be on it. I consider starting down to the beach and meeting you halfway, but then I think: No, why lose points by looking eager. Let her come to me.

Ten minutes pass. Fifteen. Twenty. Twenty-five. Maybe you've decided to spend a night in Athens. Maybe you'll be on tomorrow's bus.

But you're not.

I make some halfhearted attempts to get in touch with you in San Francisco. I try our number, but it's disconnected. I try the office and get the answering machine, which cuts off before I can leave a message. I consider calling your friends, but I don't have their numbers, and the operator is unhelpful. Becky and Ophelia are unlisted, and there is no number at all for Charlotte under either her professional or her married name. I try leaving a message at Kiki and Ophelia's office, but I keep getting through to some other doctor on call.

I am still convinced that you are on your way. On Day Two, at one in the afternoon and then again at six, I watch the bus come and disgorge swarms of bronzed and sunburned tourists—but never you. My hopes diffuse to include taxis on Day Three. As I sit on my veranda with my breakfast, my lunch, my cocktail and then my supper, I crane my neck as cars round the point at the far end of the bay.

I call up the airline. They cannot find you on any of their passenger lists. I take this to mean you have already traveled. So where are you? I lower my standards and call up the Consulate. They tell me you are neither in jail nor in the hospital. I tell myself you've given yourself a few days on another island, just to teach me a lesson.

But the deadline keeps extending itself.

Are you still in San Francisco? I leave a message on my office answering machine—it works this time—asking Mitchell to tell you to cable me at poste restante. I pay two visits daily to the post office. No reply. I leave a message with the receptionist at Ophelia's office, and when I still hear nothing, I tell myself you must be in Greece.

I decide you will only come if I'm out at the beach, and so on the fourth day I stop waiting for the one o'clock bus. I leave a message tacked to the door for you, but it's always there, untouched, when I return. I think that maybe I should go back to Athens and station myself at the airport, but what if our paths cross? I have no option but to sit here and wait, and, while I do, I have to stop dwelling on my memories.

I take my spearfishing equipment down to the beach. I fight my way through the mothers, children, Germans, lesbians, husbands, wives, students, Englishmen, Frenchmen, Canadians and Italians to get to the water, and then I fight my way through the buckets, shovels, beach balls, tubes and air mattresses to the place where the sand floor ends and the rocks begin. I submerge myself and drown out the rock music from the beach taverna jukebox. I listen to my own breath bubbling up to the surface and swim toward the harbor.

I run into a school of fish. I corner a big one, aim and pull the trigger. But I have lost my underwater judgment: the fish is nowhere near where it should be.

I try again. It's as if they are taunting me, magnifying themselves and then defying the laws of optics and gravity, shrinking to the left if I have made allowances for the left, to the right if I've made allowances for the right. One second they are eyeball to eyeball with me, and the next moment, when I release my spear, they are gone, and wherever they were is a moss-covered boulder that bends my spear and pushes it bent and pathetic back into my face.

I throw it down to the seafloor. Quickly regretting this gesture, I dive down to retrieve it. When I look up at the surface, I see an army of hulls and rudders mashing up the sea, and no way out. I stay underwater until my lungs are about to burst. I come up in the middle of a fishing fleet. The boats zoom past me, oblivious of my bobbing head.

So much for spearfishing.

I go back to the villa to take a nap. When I wake up I go into the kitchen to make myself a drink. The refrigerator is larger than I remember it, the soda bottle smaller, and the Campari bottle almost too high up to reach. The ice cubes slip too easily from the tray. The knife hits the side of the lemon with the thud of rubber. A wedge of lemon falls with a slap onto the undulating floor.

Something—there must be some mark we made here. But, when I wander up to our old neighborhood, it, too, seems distorted. The children have faces that are enlarged and elongated versions of the ones I remember. And the house . . .

Do you remember how we used to look down at the courtyard from our studies and see the landlord standing there with his head cocked to one side staring at the walls? How could he stand there so long? we would think. And why waste the time? I understand why now.

I go into the landlord's garden and knock on his door. In a garbled mixture of English and pidgin Greek, I try to explain that you and I once lived in his other house. I point up to the door on the second floor leading nowhere, the door with the screen in it, the screen I made. I mime us sitting at our typewriters. Tak tak tak, I say. He lets out a howl of recognition. He hobbles into his house and returns with a box.

It contains: your old Olivetti portable; four plates; three sets of knives and forks; six glasses; two coffee cups; a saltshaker; two inflatable armchairs; one dented pot; one bent frying pan; a set of watercolors; two chapters of my thriller; a hundred and four pages of your romance; a pair of flippers; two masks; one snorkel; and my old safari jacket.

I put away the kitchen things. I can't bear to have them there on the table, mocking all the meals we made with them—the chicken soups that had to stretch for days, the ever simpler spaghetti sauces as we could no longer afford meat, onions, canned tomatoes . . . I inflated the armchairs, and sat down in them, and remembered that last fall, the cold cold days without heating, the long long days without even enough money to spare for a chicken if we bought coffee, for coffee if we bought chicken. Running out of paper, running out of ideas. Getting rejection letters from offices five, six, seven thousand miles away. I reread the thriller—puerile. I reread the romance—halfhearted.

I opened the Olivetti case and it was like taking the lid off a coffin. Ten-year-old Correctotapes came flying out. They fluttered to the floor. I picked them up and examined them. "Friend" and "lymph nodes" said one. Another said "would you please," and "in response."

I took the typewriter out of the case. This time it was a postcard that fell out. It floated to the floor.

It was a postcard of the *Diadoumenos*.

Let me try and describe what it was like to be sitting alone in that villa and to find that postcard of the *Diadoumenos*. It was like walking across that empty room again and bumping into that statue and then standing back to examine the pose, and wondering where the arms would have been on this statue if they hadn't been chopped off, and backing into someone, and turning around, and seeing you.

Seeing you and remembering how you looked that day, and what you had said: "There *is* an answer. There is only one place where the arms could have been. All you have to do is find the center of gravity."

And watching you put your arms out in the same pose as the *Diadoumenos*, and saying, "See? He was tying a band around his head."

And knowing, just like that. Feeling a sting on my cheeks, as if you had slapped me. Losing my balance. And then watching you break the pose and offer me your arms.

Feeling your hands on my shoulder. Hearing you say, "Are you all right?" And knowing I would always be all right, so long as I could put my arms around you.

That was when I knew what I'd come back for, and what I'd lost, what your goddamn friends had taken away from me. I began to cry and in my mind I screamed at them. Bitches!

I had another drink and a few more cigarettes. (By now I was chain-smoking.) When my Bic ran out of lighter fluid, I went inside to look for some matches. I went through the shirts hanging in the wardrobe. Finding nothing, I fished into my tweed jacket, which was hanging at the back. In the inside pocket, I found your passports.

I opened up the children's passports, looked at their little faces, cried as I remembered the day the pictures were taken. I opened your passport, looked at your picture. Memories rolled out of me like dead stones down a hill.

It was some time before I realized that if I had your passports, that meant you did not. That meant . . .

I walked out onto the veranda and looked out into the night. No moon. No stars. Just a few strings of lights.

I stared into the blackness and thought of you as I last saw you, on the other side of that metal detector. Clutching two children, crouching between an overturned stroller and an upside-down car seat. Trying to tell me something. Calling my name. Your face deformed by desperation as you cry, "Mike! Don't go without . . ."

Don't go without . . .

I stared into the blackness and then I walked with slow, reluctant steps into the bedroom. I opened the wardrobe. Took out my tweed jacket. Reached into the breast pocket and brought out the tickets. My tickets—

And your tickets.

I walked over to the bedside table. There, with the piles of loose Greek and American change, were the keys to 2238 Hyde. My set. And your set. I looked at my watch.

How many days had passed since I had left you and the children stranded in front of the metal detector? Without passports. Without tickets or boarding passes. Without keys to the apartment. Without a car. Without even a . . .

I subjected my tweed jacket to a second search. Well, that's one thing, I thought. At least she has her checkbook. Then I remembered there wasn't any money in the joint account. It had all gone into money-market funds, which were in my name only, and into traveler's checks, which were not only in my name but in my pocket.

Chapter 17

Never in my life had I tried harder, and with less success, to make a call than I did on my last morning in Molivos. As I sat in that stuffy purgatory of a telephone office, I kept thinking of you crouching in front of that metal detector. I knew it was only in my mind's eye that you were standing stricken and abandoned, hungry, disheveled and penniless in the middle of a departure lounge. But if, in real life, you were OK, then who was this harpy I kept getting through to, who kept screaming *"La Señora no está"* at me and then slamming down the phone?

In retrospect, yes, right. She was the babysitter. But how was I supposed to know? I had twenty words of Spanish, none of which I had used since my freshman year in college, and I was desperately trying to string them together to ask for some news of my family. And this honking bitch you had hired kept hanging up on me. It made me want to tear the phone out of the wall. Although I assure you. I didn't.

I think it was when I tried to reach you from Hellenikon Airport (and got Eluisa) that I first heard the children moaning in the background.

I can't tell you what that did to me.

Twice (in Fiumicino Airport and then later that same afternoon at Heathrow) I tried to ask to speak to them. She wouldn't let me.

Never has a journey halfway across the world seemed longer.

When I called you from JFK, it was 7:00 p.m. your time. You were still not home. I could hear a monster movie in the background. Thank God I couldn't tell which one.

When I tried to reach you from St. Louis, a man answered. "*¿Bueno?*" he drawled. "*¿Bueno?*" I was sure I had dialed the wrong number, so I hung up and dialed again. The same man answered. "*¿Ricardo, eres tú?*" he asked. I could hear salsa music in the background.

When I finally staggered through the front door of 2238 Hyde at four o'clock the following afternoon (and again, I'll spare you the details of my fiasco-ridden passage from coast to coast, suffice it to say that I was bumped off more flights in a day than most people are in a lifetime) . . . when I finally dragged our bags into the downstairs lobby, I could hear the same music floating down the stairwell.

I could not quite bring myself to accept that it was coming from our apartment. But the closer the elevator drew to the seventh floor, the more audible it became. It turned out that the apartment door was open. The man on the couch did not notice me walk in.

Let me describe this man for you. He was young, black-haired, and wearing boxer shorts. He also had earphones on. He was lying on his back with his feet propped on the far armrest and one arm distended above an overflowing ashtray.

"Hey. You!" I yelled. I got no reaction, so I tried again. *"Hola. ¡Usted!"* Again, nothing. I was about to yank him to his feet when I caught sight of Maria.

Maria was on the balcony.

That's right. On the balcony. She was not simply "on" the balcony either. She was on a chair on the balcony. The chair had been pushed right up to the edge of the railing. She was not actually standing on the chair. She was kneeling on it, i.e., she was not in immediate danger. She did, however, have half a plastic Easter egg in her mouth.

I didn't lose my cool. I moved swiftly but silently to lock my arms around her. She was glad to see me. Until I took the plastic Easter egg out of her mouth.

Her screaming stunned me. I staggered inside. It took me a few seconds to remember Jesse. Where was he?

Clutching Maria close to my chest, even though she was trying to bite me, I raced through the apartment, calling Jesse's name. He was not in the kitchen or the spare bathroom, or the children's bedroom.

The door to our bedroom was closed. I pushed it open with my foot. Peering through the billowing smoke, I caught my first glimpse of Eluisa.

During the three days I had been communicating, or rather, failing to communicate with this woman on the phone, I had developed a nightmare vision of her. But let me tell you, her actual face was ten thousand times worse.

She had her hair in curlers and a hairnet wrapped tightly around them. There was an incongruous pink bow on top of the hairnet that made you even more aware of the tautness with which her yellow skin was stretched across her skull. She was wearing a quilted aquamarine dressing gown whose stitching had begun to unravel. She had her feet in that footbath thing my mother gave you for Christmas. She was smoking a cigarette.

Correction: cigarillo. Another overflowing ashtray sat beside her, precariously balanced on the cushion next to her. And I don't need to tell you about that sofa being made of the same highly flammable material as the furniture in that hotel in Las Vegas. The one that burned to the ground? In which most of the deaths were attributed not to the fire but to the poisonous fumes from burning furniture?

Teetering on the edge of the armrest was a bowl of peanuts. Yes, you heard me: peanuts. She had knocked it over a few times, too, because there were peanuts all over the carpet. I don't need to tell you that just one of those peanuts lodged in Maria's throat could have killed her.

That was not the worst of it. The worst of it was, she was watching a video. A horror video. Yes, you guessed it. That's the one. I did not pause to identify it right then, though. I went straight to the TV and turned it off. Eluisa looked at me and screamed.

I myself kept my cool. "*¡Estoy el señor en la casa!*" I informed her. This news made her scream even louder. So I said it again. "*¡Estoy el señor en la casa!*"

She lifted her hand to her mouth. "Aggghhhh!"

"*¿Dónde muchacho?*" I demanded.

Eluisa jumped to her feet. Babbling and gesticulating, she went careening toward the bathroom. I followed her. She pointed at the bath. It was filled to the brim with water. And bubbles. And toys. But not Jesse.

"Hesse! Hesse!" she called. No answer.

She tossed her cigarillo into the toilet bowl and began to dredge the bath with her arm.

"JESUS CHRIST!" I yelled. I practically threw Maria on the floor. I plunged both my arms into the water. I can still remember how cold the water was, and my horrible relief when my arms did not brush against Jesse's corpse.

I turned to Eluisa. "*No está,*" I informed her.

She scurried out of the bathroom and opened up the walk-in

closet. "Hesse!" she shrieked. "Hesse!" Her hairnet was coming off now, her curlers were askew. She gesticulated at a large pile of plastic dry-cleaning bags.

"JESUS CHARIST!" I yelled.

But Jesse wasn't lying suffocated in a plastic dry-cleaning bag. Nor was he spread-eagled on the asphalt driveway seven stories below our balcony. He was playing Dr. Who, in the service elevator.

That's right. The service elevator. The service elevator, that is, as far as we can make out, the same make as the service elevator that toddler walked into a few years ago? Only to find it wasn't there? Remember? It was on the news? The parents were both lawyers? They had a Spanish-speaking babysitter? The child died?

Even today I still cringe when I look at the service elevator door. I remember my sinking stomach as I listened to the service elevator ascend the shaft, going click-click-click as it passed each floor, bringing Jesse's voice closer to us; bringing him within hearing range first of Eluisa's cackle and then my beseeching whisper. As it passed us again on its way down, giving me only the briefest glimpse of my son in his helmet. In his cape. In a fantasy world so impenetrable that he hardly seemed to register I was back when, after what seemed like hours of desperate tapping at the elevator window every time he passed, he came to a stop at our floor, and I opened the door, and the "safety" gates, and tried to take him in my arms.

Only to have him prod me with his laser sword and shout out, "Halt, intruder!"

"*¡Gloria a Dios!*" was Eluisa's reaction. As far I was concerned, that did it. I eighty-sixed her.

But if I thought I could erase her from our lives as easily as that, I was mistaken. Because the witch had left her poison behind.

I am referring, of course, to the soup.

I did not notice it right away. As I darted breathless and frantic around the apartment, emptying baths, picking up peanuts and setting up safety gates, as I tried to erase all trace of her, I could smell something acrid, something halfway between smoke and steam, fill the upper reaches of each room, but I thought I was imagining it. Because if you had to come up with a smell that could convey the full extent of my horror every time I opened up a drawer or looked under a bed, it was that one.

Here are some of the things I discovered that the children said belonged to Eluisa: six pairs of silver lamé ballet shoes; one pair of filthy stiletto gold lamé sandals; five false eyelashes; one jock strap; a plastic bag full of half-used candles; another plastic bag full of cat food and condensed milk; sixty-four prayer cards, all but one in Spanish; a makeup bag filled with old lipsticks and eleven pairs of nail scissors; and a pile of magazines that had almost all the people's faces cut out of it. This was the woman you later told me was an evangelist????

"What do you think?" Jesse asked me at one point. "Was she from outer space?"

I didn't know what to tell him—or what to make of his sunny California smile. He had the same smile for everything. Halt, intruder, I'm pretending to be Dr. Who. That's why I'm smiling. Oh, hi, Dad. It's you. Same smile. Same smile again for Eluisa as Dad hounds her and Joe Bolivia out the door. Gosh. That was quick! I thought she was going to be a babysitter for a long time. Well, guess I was wrong! Too bad. She gave us lots of treats. And she was teaching us the numbers in Spanish. Oh well. Maybe one day I'll see her on *Sesame Street*. Same smile.

So, Dad, he says to me as he follows me, smiling, around the apartment. How did you like it on that planet?

What did you say? Who told you I was on another planet?

Mom, of course.

Still smiling: Won't you ever give us peanuts, Dad? Not even a teeny weeny one if I stop eating with my mouth open? Not even after I'm six? Look, Dad, you missed one. No, three more peanuts over there. Look. *Uno, dos, tres*. Can you count to three in Spanish? Still smiling. Why not?

Didn't your mother teach you how to say *manzana* and *plátano*? She didn't? That's awesome.

It's so easy, though. Look, Dad, here. I'm closing the door. That's *cerrada*. Repeat after me. *Cerrada*. Now I'm opening it up again. That's *abierta*. That's good, Dad. Now you know four words you can share with Eluisa. Oh yes, you do. You know *plátano*, *manzana, abierta* and *cerrada*. You don't think she's coming back? It doesn't matter. You can say it to the new one. All babysitters speak Spanish.

Same smile. Do you still have all that money inside your head? Mom said all that money went to your head. It *didn't??* You *don't?* Oh good. Same smile.

Fathers came and went. Mothers metamorphosed and went up in

smoke. Spanish-speaking babysitters came, ate peanuts, ran unattended baths, and split so fast they didn't even bother to change out of their disgusting bathrobes. Sisters howled. About everything. It was all in a normal day. I kept looking at Jesse, at his bright white California smile and his large phosphorescent-blue videoscreen eyes, and thought: Where is the infant I held in the delivery room? What had we done to our perfect child?

Nothing fazed him. Nothing was real. "Oh, I know that cry," he said when Maria bit my arm and screamed. "She wants her bottle."

Bottle? I thought. I thought we had gotten rid of bottles years ago.

"Oh, I know that cry. She is probably angry because you threw away those God cards. She liked to play with them. Eluisa used to read them to her, but you didn't mind, did you, Maria?

"Oh, I know that cry. She's hungry, the poor thing. She wants to eat."

"I don't want to go out until your mother comes home," I told him.

"Oh, we don't have to go out," Jesse said. "We can have some of Eluisa's *caldo.*" He looked at me and smiled. "Can't you smell it?"

The soup was in our biggest Le Creuset pot. You know, the one you never saw again, because I threw it away.

It was bubbling away on the back burner.

It was grotesque.

It had whole, unscraped carrots sticking up out of it like icebergs, and the fat bubbling on the surface was two inches thick. It had a greenish tint to it. Not from parsley but from mold. But that was not the worst of it. It was full of bones. Jagged chicken bones that looked like strands of meat until they stabbed you in the throat.

This was what our children had been "living" on? "I'm sorry," I said to Jesse. "But I cannot let you or any other human being eat that poison."

"Eluisa made us *poison* for *caldo?*"

"Yes," I said.

He looked impressed.

I said, "Let's see if we can find something else."

We were looking through the stinking nightmare of the refrigerator when Jesse had an idea.

"Something better," he informed me. "Something delicious. Something so delicious when you see it you'll be happy Eluisa's one of the people in your neighborhood.

"The nice thing about Eluisa," he continued, "is that she brings us special treats to make us happy." He went into the foyer and came back with a canvas bag that I had somehow missed. He reached in and brought out a mason jar stuffed with chocolate éclairs.

Yes, you heard me right. I said chocolate éclairs. After all your ranting and raving about nutrition and health foods, you had left your children in the care of someone who fed them chocolate éclairs. And they weren't even fresh. The cream was yellow. Naturally I couldn't let the children eat them. Naturally the children were upset. Especially Maria.

It was Jesse who thought of a way to calm her down.

"I think we could cheer her up with a very special treat." He smiled at me. "Watch this," he said.

He took Maria's hand. "Maria?" he said, mimicking the falsetto of a condescending adult. "Would you like me to give you something very special? Something . . . pink?" Maria sniffed. "Something nice and round and pink that tastes like candy?" She bared her teeth. "OK, then. I'll get you some. But only if you're quiet. Hear?"

I watched, aghast, as he returned to the canvas bag and fished out a bottle of aspirin. Yes, aspirin. Not Tylenol. Not acetaminophen. But aspirin. The substance that gives your children Reye's syndrome if they happen to have the flu. I watched in disbelief as Jesse walked over to Maria and asked her, "How old are you now?"

"Three," Maria said.

"Three? You're three already? I remember when you were a teeny tiny little baby. You were only *this* big. I never thought you would grow up to be such a *lovely, big, beautiful* girl. Did I?"

"I'm big," she said. "I'm three."

"That's right," he said. "And you know what *that* means, don't you? *That* means you can have *three* lovely little fat pink aspirins! So put out your hand then. Put out your hand, you little rascalette."

I honestly didn't expect him to be able to open the bottle. After all, it had a childproof cap. But whoever had used it last had not closed it right. Because Jesse was able to open it without any trouble. "That's the thing that's so nice about Eluisa," he told me. "She always gives us aspirin for dessert."

Chapter 18

How I wish you had come home then. But you did not even call. I was left alone with the children for six more hours, with no real information on your whereabouts and a growing pile of evidence that things, in my absence, had gone irreparably wrong.

I could read it in the children's eyes that night as they lay in their beds staring at me and the ceiling, with their covers pulled up to their chins and their hair spread out like sunrays on their pillows, in beds that hardly had room for them, because of the dolls and the doll's clothes, the stuffed walruses, tigers, dogs and kangaroos, the tape recorders and Walkmans, the cassettes, the pop-up books, the crayons, the Magic Markers, the crumpled drawings that offered no explanation, no relief for the frightened shadows in their ravaged eyes. They had their memories.

Here are some of the things Jesse told me about you as we lay together in his bed:

1. He said one night you had "forgotten" to come home.
2. He said another night you had come home with an illegal alien.
3. He said you were almost always in a bad mood.
4. He said you had started wearing eye shadow and lipstick. And alien clothes.
5. He said Maria had gotten a rash because you had let her use your deodorant on her cheeks. Apparently you were in bed, trying to sleep off a hangover. Or at least that was what I assumed—
6. Because he said the night before that you had come home drunk, fallen flat on your face and called Jesse an asshole.
7. He said he couldn't remember the name of the place, but that he thought you were working in a bar.

* * *

Naturally I was alarmed. And not just by what Jesse told me.

Here are some of the conversations I had with Maria as I was putting her to bed:

ME (to Maria, after reading to her for twenty-five minutes): So. That's the end of Eloise. I think it's bedtime now, don't you?
MARIA (in a spoiled voice): No! I'm not sleepy!
ME: But it's seven-thirty already. It's Jesse's turn to have a story.
MARIA (in a staccato shriek): No! It's *not* Jesse's turn! It's *my* turn!
JESSE (giving up in his usual gentlemanly way): Oh, I don't mind. Read her another story.
ME (giving in, out of guilt): OK. Just this once. What would you like, darling?
MARIA (Screws up her face and says nothing.)
JESSE: I think she'd probably like a Dick Bruna.
(NOTA BENE: I hope you can see how hard I'm trying to be even-handed and patient.)
ME (after taking a handful of Dick Bruna books off the bookshelf): So, Maria. You're getting one more story and then it's bedtime. Which one do you think you'd like? *THE KING?*
(She shakes her head.)
THE FISH?
(She shakes her head.)
THE CIRCUS?
(She shakes her head.)
(I come close to losing my patience.)
ME: You don't want *THE KING*. You don't want *THE CIRCUS*. You don't want *THE FISH*. Which one *do* you want?
MARIA: *THE PENIS*.

And later, after I have finished reading to Jesse, a similar exchange, while I'm lying down with Maria:

MARIA: I'm three and a half now, aren't I?
ME: That's right, Maria, you're three and a half.
MARIA: On my birthday I'll be four.
ME: That's right, Maria. You'll be four.
MARIA: All the childrens at school going to coming to my party. All the childrens except Heywood. Heywood's an asshole.

ME: Little girls shouldn't say words like that, Maria.
JESSE (with his typical fairness): Little boys shouldn't either.
ME: That's right, Jesse. Boys and girls shouldn't say words like that. Only grown-ups, and even then only at certain times.
JESSE: Mommy says asshole all the time.
MARIA: Mommy has a vagina.

And still later, when, for some insane reason, we have wandered back to the subject of birthdays:

ME: What do you want for a present on your birthday, Maria?
MARIA (Silence. Followed by deranged laughter.)
ME: Would you like a . . . tricycle?
MARIA (Shakes her head and laughs.)
ME: Do you want a (I think I said "dress" but if I did I really meant "outfit.")
(Whatever. Does it really matter?)
MARIA (Shakes her head and laughs.)
ME: Do you want a . . . huge enormous ice cream cone?
MARIA (Again, shakes her head and laughs.)
ME: What DO you want, then?
MARIA: A penis.

Again, a penis.

Why?

What had been going on in this house during my absence?

Why did they stiffen when I brushed the hair from their foreheads? Was it simply because I had scared them by venting my rage on the aspirin? And if so, if they were scared of me, why were they so scared when I got up to go?

Here are some of the things Jesse told me he was scared of as we lay together in his bed:

1. He was scared there was an illegal alien in the closet.
2. He was scared that there was a small, but growing, illegal alien in his chest. *In his chest?*
3. He was scared that I was just pretending to be his father, when I really was an illegal alien from outer space.
4. He was scared that his sister was an illegal alien reject from a defective planet.

5. He was scared that his real mother had been killed by an illegal alien and replaced by an identical robot.

And so was I, Laura. And so was I.

What bar were you at tonight?

The nightmare scene, the nightmare scene I had pushed out of my mind for so long, came back. I was back in that bar again. I was pushing my way through the crowd to get to my wife. I was seeing her with her elbows on the bar, talking to a big guy with a ponytail. I was seeing her laugh and then stop laughing when she caught sight of me.

This is Trooper.

Here we go again, I thought. The same nightmare I went through with Mona, except this time involving children. Then I turned on the VCR and found out it was a thousand times worse.

At first I couldn't make sense of the scene. It seemed to be an operating room, an operating room in a spaceship, I decided, because conditions were cramped, and the doctors were dressed in metallic outfits. They were struggling with a patient on the operating table. He, too, was dressed in uniform. What was wrong with him?

I watched, aghast, as a mechanical monster exploded through his chest.

I stopped the video, stared at the still of metal and exploding flesh. I stifled a silent scream. Then I backtracked. Watched the mechanical monster explode out of the spaceman's chest again. Backtracked to the beginning of the movie. Watched the whole goddamn thing.

And so there you have it. American culture in a nutshell. I was appalled by that movie, Laura. Both artistically and because of what it had done to my children. But at the same time I could not resist it. I watched it all the way through.

The more I watched it, the more mesmerized I was. And the more I watched it, the more it summed up for me all the influences, all the ideas that I had always wanted to keep away from my kids. The more I realized how little you, with your fairy tales of virtuous careers and supportive friends, could see. It was neither here nor there if you had spent your evening in a bar or a bar-review course. Wherever you were, you were in trouble. We were all in trouble. Any country that could produce a movie like *Alien,* any country that could expose its children to a movie like *Alien,* any country that condoned parents leaving children in the care of illegal aliens in order that they might alienate themselves at bars and bar-review courses, any country that could let these things happen was fucked.

It was not until after I had watched the movie (and had a few more drinks) that Ophelia called to have it out with me about my alleged abusive treatment of Eluisa.

Apparently Eluisa had turned up at her door in hysterics, telling all sorts of lies about me, which Ophelia, of course, believed. I do realize that it would have been better for all of us if I had been civil to Ophelia. But her timing could not have been worse.

Her sign-off was ominous. "You know," she said, in a trembling voice, "you're sitting there mouthing off like the king of the castle, but I don't know if you even have a right to be there. You'd better find some way to cool off, and quick, or you're going to be very sorry."

Then she hung up on me. I decided, disastrously, to take her advice.

Chapter 19

I had not been in the shower long before someone—Jesse, I assumed—came into the bathroom to take a piss.

BAM. Could that be *Jesse* kicking up the toilet seat?

Before I could answer that question, I saw the answer, unequivocally, through the mist.

A man. A man who now rapped his fist on the glass.

"Knock, knock!" he said. "Anybody home? Hurry up, babes. Dinner's on the table."

It was Gabe.

Our handyman Gabe.

What was Gabe doing in my bathroom?

Talking to you about dinner? Addressing you as "babes"?

This was the fucking limit. The time had come to draw the line. There was only one problem.

I couldn't breathe.

I watched the shadow of Gabe washing his hands. "I don't know, babes," he was saying, "Mitchell did you any favors selling you that car. It's not a *lemon,* babes. It's a fucking *citrus grove*. I did my best, but if you ask me . . . hey, Laura? You OK in there, babes?"

He opened the shower door.

"Oh. Hi," he said, adding in a croak, "You're back!"

"What the fuck are you doing in my bathroom?" I asked.

"Well," he said. "Um, I mean, well . . . you see . . ." Now *he* was having trouble breathing. "Um, there's this guy I know. Who does services real cheap."

"Services," I repeated.

"Car services." He cleared his throat. "And since I was going there. Anyway. I offered to . . ." He slapped his pockets. "Oh man, don't tell me I left it downstairs!"

"Left what downstairs?"

"The service booklet. I'll go get it now, before I forget." And baboom, he was off. "Back in a sec!" he shouted from the service elevator. I threw on a towel and tried to catch up with him. Slam. Clonk. He was gone.

I got dressed and went into the kitchen. I caught sight of some car keys sitting on the counter, on top of a service booklet for a 1980 Pontiac Phoenix.

A 1980 Pontiac Phoenix?

My wife had bought a Pontiac Phoenix? A Pontiac Phoenix with (as I discovered upon examining the service booklet) 85,000 miles on it?

Again, it took me a while to take this information in. It wasn't until eleven-thirty or so that I was able to propel myself to the bookshelves in search of *Consumer Reports*. I think that even under normal circumstances I would have found the information it contained disturbing. But after the day I had had, it was the last straw.

I had some questions to ask Mitchell—if he was the one who had sold you this car. I had some questions to ask you. But first I had some questions I wanted to ask Gabe. And if he was too cowardly to come to me . . .

I assure you, however, that before I took the service elevator down to the basement, I did check the children, and they were sound asleep.

As you are well aware, there was no answer, but a lot of incriminating noise, when I knocked on Gabe's door.

I did, however, call his name three times before I kicked in the door.

I really wish you could have seen him cowering behind those drums, with his teeth chattering, and his left arm raised as if to fend off a blow. He didn't look too impressive.

I suppose there is no point in reproducing our conversation here. Suffice it to say that I would have behaved differently had I known you were hiding underneath the bed.

When I took the elevator back up to the seventh floor, I couldn't get in. My key didn't work. I went back down to the basement. This time, as you may remember, the door to Gabe's room was bolted. "They're on the washing machine," he whispered hoarsely through the keyhole.

"What are?" I asked.

"The keys. For the new locks."

For the new locks.

This guy had the keys for the new locks? And I didn't?

This guy had the keys for my home and I didn't.

This was the thought that was running through my mind as I let myself back into the apartment.

This was the thought that was running through my mind when I punched a hole in the bathroom door.

This was the sound that woke up the children.

I had not managed to stop their howling before the phone rang.

It was Becky.

Sounding very strange.

"I thought you would like to know," she said. "Laura's not coming home today. She's staying here with us."

Needless to say, I did not take this news well. I should not have cross-examined her. But I knew there was something fishy going on. That's why I decided to drive over to Becky's and get you.

The children were the ones who, once I had bundled them up and taken them out into the street, pointed out your abomination of a Pontiac Phoenix.

Even in my drunken state, I could not believe my eyes. I mean, didn't you *look* at the goddamn thing before you bought it? Couldn't you *see* that the chassis was bent? Couldn't you tell from the sound it made that the transmission was fucked? And the muffler gone? Totally? I know I was wrong to drive in that condition. But Laura. It wasn't me who drove into that telephone pole. It was your 1980 Pontiac Phoenix.

Chapter 20

The fog had not yet lifted when the nurse pushed my wheelchair out into the street the next morning. Set against the dead white sky, the row of houses across the street from the hospital looked like gravestones. The only sign of life was the litter swirling down the sidewalk.

I remember feeling chilly as I stood there in my robe while you cleared the maps, receipts and wrappers off the passenger seat of Becky's aging BMW. I did not warm up on the drive home.

The apartment had that damp, after-breakfast look—pajama tops on the floor, trails of cereal on the table, a towel draped over the filing cabinet in the hallway . . .

"Where do you want me to set you up?" you asked.

"Set me up for what?"

"For the afternoon," was what you said. "I'm going out." You went on to explain why in your usual roundabout manner. Thus I found out about the sale on attaché cases in Mill Valley, and the woman car dealer near Tiburon, before I found out that you were starting work the next morning in Mitchell's new office on Jackson.

You? Starting work? With Mitchell? In his new office on Jackson? The idea was too bizarre for me to take in.

The next thing you told me about was, significantly, the dishwasher. I was not to worry about it even though it was broken because the landlord hadn't been able to find a replacement handyman yet. That's how I found out that Gabe was no longer with us. It was no accident that you chose to tell me this while you were putting away groceries. That way you didn't have to look me in the eyes.

Ditto for the way you dropped the bombshell. You were putting on your coat and had just finished telling me about the videos I could watch, and the baseball game I might not realize was on this afternoon, when you added (with your back to me), "And oh, if the babysitter calls . . ."

I think you can understand now why I raised my voice when I said, "THE BABYSITTER? WHAT BABYSITTER?" And why I reacted so strangely when you explained you had had to hire a new one.

I don't know if you remember what you said next, but I do. You said, "Well, honestly, what did you expect? I could hardly keep Eluisa on after what you did to her."

What *I* did to *her?*

"I was lucky that she even agreed to recommend someone else."

I assume that you will also be able to understand now why there was a crack in my voice when I said, "You're telling me you're hiring another Salvadoran evangelist?" And why, when you replied, "Well, it's either that or a boat person," I said, "Oh God, oh help me, God, I can't be hearing this."

Once again, you misunderstood: "I mean, really—what *did* you expect?" was what you said now. "My friends all think I'm crazy to let you back at all. And if you want to know how *I* feel—if you weren't an invalid . . ."

"Is that my new classification? Invalid?"

Again, you did not seem to hear the panic in my voice, because what you said next was, "Where I come from, you look after sick relatives, no matter what."

That was when it hit me that I wasn't the man of the house anymore but a pathetic drunk driver who was here at your sufferance.

Where did that leave the children? Who was going to protect them from this new evangelist nightmare?

You may remember I voiced some weak objections. Why had you hired someone without consulting me? What if I wanted to look after them myself?

It was now that you made first use of your new, assertive voice. You said, "You're trying to tell me I was supposed to consult you when you were in a coma? Or on a beach in Greece?" You also said, "I mean, what was I supposed to do? How was I supposed to know what you wanted to do this week, or, for that matter, any week? Or that I would even necessarily trust you to look after them? Last time I talked to you, you . . .

"I mean," you said, "when *was* the last time we talked?" I suggested that we sit down right then and there and make up for lost time, but you said you had to go. "Just relax," I remember you saying.

(Hah!) "We have plenty of time to discuss all this. First you have to get better."

But already, as I paced, or rather, limped, in front of the baseball game, my mind was racing. It was the third inning: I had until the ninth to come up with a plan of action.

I looked at my watch.

Chapter 21

What time is it?

I imagine that it is . . . going on four in the afternoon. All over the city, hundreds of thousands of sets are tuned in to this same game. Hundreds of thousands of neon-green baseball diamonds, hundreds of thousands of tiny video pitchers and batters and outfielders all doing the same thing.

Trey (who has had a slow start today—he hasn't even made his first coffee) is watching the game on two sets simultaneously. The one in the den has the better picture, but he can't afford to sit down in there until he has the coffee machine under control. So he has his new (and disappointingly indistinct) mini transistor TV set up over the message machine. This means he can watch the game and descale the coffee machine at the same time (and just run into the den for replays).

He puts his glasses on. They're still fogged up. He takes them off, wipes them, and at the exact same millisecond both TV sets start howling. He looks up at the transistor TV, and wow, amazing, even though he's standing at the other end of the kitchen, he can see everything! Which means that it is his eyes that are defective, and not his new purchase.

As for the house, it is better blurry. There are more crayon marks on the walls this afternoon than he remembers being there yesterday. The den looks like someone had taken all the toy trays and upended them. There is a trail of Lego on the stairs—he nearly crippled himself on his way down from his study by stepping on what turned out to be the support stem for a Lego satellite dish. He had almost not been able to open the door into the kitchen for all the piles of laundry on the floor—when his glasses are off they resemble the Sierra Madre Mountain Range.

As he picks his way across the Sierra Madres to pour the rinse water into the coffee machine, he remembers—that's strange—wasn't he supposed to have been looking after the children this afternoon?

Well, he thinks, Charlotte must have changed her plans. Funny she didn't leave him a note. He picks up a part of the paper—it, too, is strewn all over the floor—reaches into his shirt pocket, puts on his glasses, and that is when he sees them.

First he sees the Post-it on the pressure cooker: "Wash AND put away." Then he sees the one on the message machine: "Before erasing other people's messages, see to it that ALL relevant details, INCLUDING TIME OF DAY, have been notated on the pad on the lower right-hand corner of the bulletin board." Looking at the pad on the bulletin board, he sees a Post-it that says: "Where is the pen that used to be in this holder?" and an arrow pointing to the empty holder. He can tell from the handwriting that she has written this note in a fury.

About what? He reviews the events of the previous day but can find no clues. Things had been tense, yes, but then when weren't they? They had spent most of the day avoiding each other, but again, what was new in that? They had gone through the motions of a family Saturday: in the evening, they had even watched *Being There* together. So what is she upset about? The laundry?

Because the pile of clothes on the kitchen floor seems to be trying to tell him something. It doesn't have a Post-it on it, but everything about it says "Do me." So well, fine, he thinks. He is happy to help her. What he minds is the way she has decided to ask. There was no need to throw the clothes all over the floor so that he couldn't even get to the coffeemaker without tripping over them. He doesn't mind doing laundry. He is a reasonable guy. All she had to do was leave him a note.

Then he sees that she has. It is on the lid of the washing machine. It says: "This time, when you add the bleach, why don't you make sure you're not pouring it directly onto a valuable garment—for example, the thing you ruined last week, *id est* the dress that cost me eighty dollars at a SALE at Betsey Johnson's."

Oh for crying out loud, he thinks. There was no need to take that tone. All week long she has been taking that tone with him, and what irks him most is that it wasn't his fault.

I, Mike, was the culprit. It was the fact that I, Mike, was once again getting away with murder that he, Trey, was in the doghouse.

So you, Laura, had not heeded Charlotte's warnings. You had taken your unilateral-plan-making, drunk-driving husband back into your home when you would have been fully justified in never letting him back through the door again. So what does it have to do with him?

God, Trey hates the way his wife extrapolates generalities from other people's weaknesses. The fact that you are a pushover does not mean that all men are sneaks and ruthless manipulators, does not mean that Trey ruthlessly manipulates Charlotte's weaknesses and then serves his own selfish interests behind closed doors.

God, how he wishes sometimes that someone had run over Simone de Beauvoir in a truck in 1953. It is all her fault. Or so he thinks until he takes his (very scaly-tasting) coffee up to his office.

Oh no! He left the computer on from last night! There is Donkey Kong, still on the screen. Also on the screen is another yellow Post-it: "Is this what you fucking call building a fucking accounting business from the home????"

Strewn all over the desk are the other discs, for Autochess, Scrabble, Dungeons and Dragons, you name it. She even found Pacman, which means that she has been through the filing cabinet, which means there is a fair chance she has been through his correspondence. He feels a hot flush rising as he walks back down the stairs. Well, he says to himself upon returning to the kitchen, that explains the laundry! Not to mention the tone of the note! What does she have planned for him next?

He can see her standing over him, cataloguing not only her towering accomplishments but also the sacrifices she has had to make in order to find the time to do them, "while YOU sat in that room up there and played Donkey Kong." And then the inevitable gender aspersions, "God, I don't know what it is with you men, I really don't."

The thing is, he doesn't either.

He takes the note off the washing machine, picks up the Betsy Johnson dress lying next to it, looks at the bleach marks, and again, yes, she is right.

He sees himself standing outside his house, watching suitcases come flying through the windows, wondering if he dares take the car, wondering if transient hotels take credit cards.

It is useful, when you are standing in the middle of your kitchen saying: What am I going to do? What am I going to do? over and over in your head, to have a lot of Post-its all around you answering that very question. He feels just that bit better after he has washed the pressure cooker and found the pen for the bulletin board and put all the spice jars back onto the designated lazy susan and unloaded the dishwasher before adding his coffee mug. But some instructions are easier to follow than others.

For example, the Post-it on the window: "Does this look clean to you?" (Did she mean the window? The ledge? The yard?) And the one in the middle of the table: "All markers without tops must go." (Which ones? Where?) And the two on the refrigerator, one of which says: "Do NOT touch the marinade." (Which marinade?) And the other of which says: "I am not going to call you up for once and remind you. I'm expecting you to remember to feed them lunch." (Feed whom lunch? The birds?) It is this note more than any other that makes him aware of the fact that he is not dealing with a rational woman.

It is while he is putting the first load of laundry (the whites) into the dryer that he notices that somehow he has gotten toothpaste on his feet, that in fact he has left little white marks all over the tile floor. Then he notices that there is a trail of toothpaste going all along the bottom edge of the washing machine, in fact all along the counter standing next to it, not to mention the skirting boards. Now he notices that the trail leads to the door to the garage, and that that door is in fact open, and that when he stands in the doorway he can hear a car running in the garage.

His car running? Hurling himself down the back stairs, kicking open the garage door, he finds it is. There is his son in the driver's seat. There is his daughter sitting next to him wearing her mother's hat.

His first thought is: Why didn't she leave him a note?

For a moment he just stands there, staring at the car, while over the hill, in the Richmond, Mitchell does the same thing.

Chapter 22

Mitchell is watching his wife pack Lara and Paloma into the back seat of the station wagon. How sweet they look in their Sunday best. So what if they turned out to be Catholics, did he really think he had something better to give them? He feels strangely proud of their yellow ribbons, their shiny, neatly cut chestnut hair, their black patent-leather shoes and their matching white dresses with the daisy belts he doesn't know how their mother managed to make for them. In her own way, she's a genius.

She closes the station wagon door with her foot. Then she looks up at Mitchell, quizzically, as if she's still in shock from his offer to stay at home with Baby Roo. He likes the shape of her face when it's upturned like that—the sharpness of the chin, the fullness of the pouting lips. And her eyes, how large they look. You'd never know she had a six-month-old baby, to look at those legs.

He tells himself, as her eyes slip upward, that he really doesn't deserve this look of adoration that has come over her face, until he realizes she's not looking at him but at Baby Roo, who is on his back in the African shawl. She calls up something. He can't hear so he opens the window—not an easy feat when you have a six-month-old in what seems to him to be an awfully loose-fitting carrier. (How does she do it?) He feels Baby Roo shifting dangerously, has to compensate abruptly so that she doesn't go flying out the window.

"Do you remember how to take it off?" she asks.

"EVERYTHING'S GOING TO BE OK!"

She gives him the thumbs up, then jumps into the car. She does her usual kamikaze backing-up job, misses a motorcycle by that much—although her vision may have been blocked. There were a lot of things he can see that she can't see at street level.

When she's gone, he turns around (slowly, to avoid swinging Baby Roo), and surveys his office, which (as usual) doesn't look like one: there is material draped on every single table, stack of papers and machine. Becky has been on a sewing binge this summer, and not just for herself and the girls. The material that's actually under the sewing-machine needle—that blue plaid flannel—that's for a shirt for him.

It's not the pattern he would have chosen. As he looks at it hanging so trustingly from the edge of his desk, he imagines Becky agonizing over fabrics, trying to choose the one that will make him happiest, tragically selecting the wrong one, bringing it home and hiding it, staying up late to get it done, straining her eyes over buttonholes, while he . . .

His mind goes into panic mode as he reviews the new commitments he has crash-landed into—that new building, those new partners, the shaky loan, that shady banker (like hell he was Kiki's cousin's ex-brother-in-law). There is only one word that describes his behavior since I left the business, and that word is spree. He has committed himself up to his eyeballs, and now, unless he does some very fancy footwork . . .

What the hell is he going to do with you, Laura, when you turn up in the office tomorrow? What misguided Samaritan impulse prompted him to hire you? How is he going to be able to use you productively if he has to hide the truth from you? What if you find out anyway? What if you feel obligated to tell not just your husband but your good friend Becky?

What will Becky do if she discovers that the paper he had her sign last week makes her the guarantor of every last shaky loan he's put his name to?

The thing that kills him is, she's been so *nice* to him lately. Take last night. He woke up at 3:00 a.m. to a strange chirping noise. His first thought was that it was a burglar, his second that it was a bird, his third that it was a bird underneath their bed. And so he had looked, but the only thing he could see down there was a blue, low-heeled sandal. He had waited for the chirp to repeat itself. Typically, it didn't until he was back in bed and drifting off.

It was at this point that he began to wonder if the chirping noise was coming from inside his head. He had spent the next hour or so trying but not quite succeeding to face this possibility. Every time he heard it, he marveled despairingly at its authenticity. He found himself thinking of his freshman roommate, who had also heard voices during those months before they had to commit him. Was this how real they had sounded to the poor guy?

It was past four when Mitchell went downstairs to roll a joint and just happened to pass underneath the smoke detector at the same time it chirped. Oh, his relief when he realized its batteries were running low!

But the anxiety had taken its toll. He had almost broken his neck while putting the new ones in. The hastily set up stepladder wobbled dangerously when he was standing on the top step—if he had not compensated for it abruptly, it would have sent him flying over the banister. Sleep was out of the question after this. So he had rolled the joint and turned on the TV and tried to mellow out, but as luck would have it the only thing he could find in English was a talk show about credit-card abusers. Their grim faces would have depressed him at the best of times: combined with his already stressed state of mind and the sinsemilla it sent him tumbling into an extreme attack of earthquake phobia.

It went along classic lines. First he thought the house was shaking. Then he went down to the cellar to check to see if the foundations were still anchored. They were. Then he went back into the kitchen and sat down and looked at the pots and pans hanging on the rack over the sink and wondered what would become of them in a 4.9, a 6.7, a thirty-second 8.2. If it happened now, where would he go? Under the table, upstairs to the girls' room? Would there be a fire, did they have emergency supplies on hand as detailed in the front of the phone book? If it happened when he was at work, how would he make contact with his family? What if his kids were in their nursery school in the Marina and the landfill liquefied? What if he was under a high-rise when the plate glass started popping out? What if Becky was driving across a bridge?

More to the point, what would have become of him if Becky hadn't come downstairs when she did? His hands were so shaky by then that he couldn't even turn the TV off—which was lucky, because it was the TV that had woken her up. Not that she was at all annoyed—and that was what killed him, the fact that she didn't have a single thought for herself as she sat there next to him holding his hand. Why was she so easy to fool? He had almost broken down and confessed, but praise the gods! he had held himself back.

Now, as he abandons the office–cum–sewing room for the kitchen with Baby Roo on his back, he tells himself he still has a chance.

Successful people are people who take setbacks and complications and turn them into advantages. Maybe he'll be able to find some way to turn this new building around fast enough to pay back that loan fast enough to make the balloon payment on the house fast enough to make sure Becky never finds out he conned her into signing a very serious and binding document without explaining to her what it meant.

He conjures up her trusting, concerned face. As he aims the remote control at the TV, he vows to become worthy of it.

He finds the baseball game. He sits down on the couch and remembers at the last moment that he can't sit back because if he did it would mean squashing Baby Roo, who is—how could he have forgotten?—hanging off his back in that flimsy African shawl. And so he sits forward to give her room to breathe, but she doesn't really like it even if he sits forward; in fact, she whimpers and squirms and digs her little feet into his kidneys. So he gets up, and tries to watch the game while pacing the floor, but then she starts crying so loud he can't even hear the commentary. He decides she must be thirsty. He goes over to the counter where Becky has left a bottle of breast milk. It is only half defrosted. Ugh.

He is ashamed of his disgust at its appearance. Especially when Baby Roo begins to wail again. That is why his thoughts become muddled, that is why he puts the bottle into the microwave without checking first to see if the bottle is microwave-safe.

Oh no! He braces himself for an explosion that doesn't happen. He takes the bottle out with shaking hands and tries to pass it to Baby Roo first over his shoulder, then under his arm. He drops it, then picks it up with great difficulty, and then tries passing it over his shoulder right into Baby's hand, except that this time it falls into the shawl.

A wetness starts spreading. By now Baby Roo is hysterical, her little fists pummeling at his back. He has to get her out of there, but how? If he unties her here in the kitchen, she'll just fall to the floor. He can't risk that, so he runs—too fast, sending her into even more frantic wailing—up to the bedroom, where he tries to untie the shawl while lying sideways, except that he can't undo the knot with one hand. The next thing he tries is to encourage Baby Roo to climb out of the shawl of her own accord while he is lying on the bed on his stomach.

But she doesn't climb out. Instead she starts choking and spluttering. The wetness spreads across his back. She sounds like she's suffocating. He sits up to give her air. She screams. He stands up. She is gnawing at his shoulder blade between frantic wails. He has to find a way of getting this bottle to her!

At last he hits on a solution: by standing between the two mirrors in the master bedroom, he is able to (a) locate and (b) fish out the milk bottle and (c) get it into Baby Roo's little hands. The crying comes to an end. He is able to go downstairs. And even watch the baseball game, which is somewhat amazing to him. Except that he can't stop worrying about the little bundle on his back. She's not drinking the milk properly, she's gulping down the air which promises all sorts of trouble, in addition to which she is, as he knows from the upstairs mirrors, all tangled up in this ridiculous shawl thing by now. How can he pay attention to this baseball game knowing that his daughter could be suffocating?

He hits on a new idea. If he puts the TV on the far end of the counter, he can sit at this near end, or rather half sit on the stool with the rest of his weight distributed on the counter. And if, at the same time, he can have his shaving mirror propped up on the stove, he can also see over his shoulder, and make sure Baby Roo is alive even when she isn't kicking. It's precarious, and uncomfortable, but it's the best he can do.

Chapter 23

Kiki, meanwhile, is the picture of hard-earned Sunday-afternoon indolence. Stretched out on the waterbed, watching the baseball game between his splayed stockinged feet, his eyes half shut . . . but look at his hand, look at the grip he has on the channel changer. Why does he have the sound turned so high? Why does he not even register a reaction when Mom walks into the room in her baby-pink terry-cloth robe?

She pauses in front of the TV set, blocking his view. "Kiki," she says, "Kiki." He won't say a thing. He won't even look at her. "Oh, forget it," she says in her heavily accented English. She goes into the bathroom. Kiki exhales as she turns the lock.

He takes a swig of his beer.

"How are we doing in there?" Ophelia calls from the kitchen.

"Great," he says. "Do you have any more?"

"Sure do," she says. She brings him in another plate of nachos. Actually brings it in herself! "They're good, aren't they?" she comments.

"They're great. You should cook more often."

"Well," she says. "Does it come with a kitchen?"

"The Tahoe place? Sure. It's got to."

She pinches his nose and makes to turn around.

"Wait," he says. "There's something else." He pinches her thigh.

"Stop it!" she giggles.

As she saunters down the hallway, he has déjà vu: for a moment she looks exactly like she did the first time he ever saw her, at that bar near the medical tape library in West El Paso. What was it called? Lloyd's? At that redneck bar, where, when he saw her that first time, playing pool, he had thought she was a biker.

God, had he been knocked for a loop when he saw her at the tape library the next day! A *girl* who had a brain *and* looks *and* liked to shoot pool? A medical student who doodled and passed notes to friends while listening to lectures on endocrinology?

A. Long. Time. Ago.

She has Charlotte in the kitchen with her. Charlotte is in the middle of a long horror story about her male colleagues. Ophelia is leaning over the counter and doodling while she listens. Her nods are heavy and convincing, but then she gives Kiki a glance down the hallway and rolls her eyes.

He turns down the sound on the TV to catch what Charlotte's saying.

"So then the third woman applicant came in. A nice, attractive-looking woman, sort of on the young side but with a good CV, and giving out totally the right professional signals. My co-interviewers acted their enlightened best while she was in the room. But the moment she walked out, they started saying things like, Did you get a load of those nipples? And, I could sink my teeth into that ass. I wanted to let them know I was hearing them. So when we had our next applicant, a man, what I did right after he left was say to them, 'You know, guys? I bet he could stretch to a good thirteen inches.' That caught them off guard for exactly two seconds, and then one of them turned to the other and said, 'Sounds like he has one of those stretchy ones.' They thought I was truly joining in!"

Ophelia shrugs her shoulders. "Maybe they were paying you the ultimate compliment. Maybe the ones to watch out for are the ones who pay lip service."

"But that's so depressing!" Charlotte picks up a nacho and looks at it as if it has hurt her feelings. "Because you see . . ."

Her voice is drowned out by the sound of Mom sobbing in the Jacuzzi. He turns the TV volume up and so misses Becky's arrival.

"I've just been with Laura," Becky announces as she takes off her cardigan.

"How was she?" Ophelia asks.

"I'm not sure," Becky says. "She *sounded* positive. But she *looked* dejected."

"Did she say why she took him back?"

"No, and I didn't want to press it," Becky says. "But there *is* something I want to tell you."

The other two lean forward. "Yes?"

"Well," says Becky. "You remember I told you I met Mike's ex-wife in Nevada City last summer?"

"Oh right, at that party. Her name was Mona?"

"Right. And you remember we really hit it off? Well, she called me up last night because she's thinking of moving to Santa Rosa. Anyway we got to talking and naturally Mike came up and so I told her the latest."

"Was she surprised?"

"Not a bit. She said that during the three years they were together he totaled three cars." Becky picks up a nacho. "She also said that he was the one who turned her into a feminist."

"She's pretty way out there, too, you said."

"Basically, whatever she does, she's an extremist. Like she feeds her kid nothing but bananas."

"Oh no, not another one."

"But she's a really good artist," Becky adds. "She says that the reason they split up was that he resented her work. He told her everything she had ever done was crap. He was real down on himself then, and she thinks that he took it out on her."

"So you're saying it's a pattern," says Ophelia.

Becky says, "Is there any evidence he's learned?"

"Do they ever?" Charlotte says.

Before anyone can think of an answer, Mom pushes open the door and stalks through to the breakfast room. She settles herself down with her manicure equipment. She says something to Ophelia in Spanish.

Chapter 24

Here follows an argument between Mom and Ophelia. The Spanish is too fast for Charlotte to follow, but she gathers that Mom is angry because Kiki and Ophelia are not taking her with them to Tahoe. Which is unreasonable on Mom's part, Charlotte thinks—except then Ophelia loses a hundred points by writing out a prescription and pinning it to the bulletin board: "Mom. Go to hell twice daily."

After which Ophelia blithely suggests a walk to the park. Charlotte follows her friends downstairs, but her conscience does not let her go a step farther. She tells them she has left her jacket in the utility room. Which is technically true. But already as she heads up the back stairs to the apartment, she is telling herself that this is her chance to nip back into the kitchen and remove the offending prescription before it does any harm.

It is while she is in the breakfast room that she hears Mom sobbing an incomprehensible lament. Then she hears Kiki say in loud, emphatic English, "Then how about this? What happened between us does not constitute a . . ."

The end of his sentence is muffled by a crash. Looking over his shoulder, Charlotte sees Mom running down the corridor with her robe flapping open.

Did this constitute conscious prurience on Charlotte's part or was it involuntary voyeurism? An hour later, as she sits with her family eating chick-pea soup and chick-pea salad, she is still asking herself this question, still terribly upset by the memory of this proud, sixty-year-old woman crying like a girl, and of the spectacle . . .

Is she going to admit that her first thought was not about Mom's feelings but her body? That this first thought was: Ugh, is that how *I'm* going to look in twenty years?

What did that say about the sincerity of her humanism?

She wonders if Mom saw her, if Kiki heard her, what he'll do if he did hear her. Should she talk to him?

She runs through the various options that are open to her: all are farcical, all betray at least two people.

She gives up, tries to return her attention to the neat kitchen, the meek children, the ingratiating husband, the nice though monotonous meal.

What happened here while she was gone?

What is Trey trying to put over on her? That he's been in a business slump. Oh really? she says, barely able to keep the contempt out of her voice, and why is that? Because certain clients who ought to have known better were liers and cheats. How unfortunate, she says, and then she has to listen to him talk about his big insight about the source of his passivity, and his new resolve, and this big push he's going to make to put things right . . . does he honestly think that after this many years she is going to take him seriously?

"Oh Trey," she blurts out. "You're never going to get it right, are you?"

He stops talking. She blunders on. "I'm sorry, but I can't believe in these new initiatives anymore. Not a single one of them has ever happened."

Except that . . . she looks at him sitting there, wounded and uncomprehending, and thinks: Well, at least . . . he means well . . . he tries . . . he's not . . . he's not playing Russian roulette with her emotions . . . he would never . . . no, he wouldn't because . . .

He's decent. And the best she can hope for.

Chapter 25

I imagine Charlotte walking to the window and looking across Polk Gulch to Russian Hill, and wondering how we are. Would she have been surprised at the ambitious meal I had cooked? Would she have laughed or cried at the impassioned plea I made to you over dessert?

I remember you sitting with your back to the window. Fingers of fog were sweeping across the sky, now erasing Coit Tower, now restoring it, now pouring down Columbus to strangle the high rises, now rolling under the Bay Bridge, while on your face moods came and went just as suddenly. You didn't know what to make of my ardent promise to devote the rest of my life to acting out of character.

I remember your muted objections to my plan: *But are you sure you really want this? You've never wanted to babysit long enough for me to even go to an exercise class, how are you going to look after them full-time?* How strange I must have looked as I so desperately overacted my sincerity.

I am not sure, looking back, that I actually convinced you. But I do remember it didn't take long to get you to give in—so you must have believed at least some of the things I told you about Eluisa.

Do you remember how happy we all were after you gave in? How we did the dishes together, and the baths together, and how, instead of watching television, we sat all four of us on the couch going through the pictures and postcards I had brought back with me from Greece? Do you remember when I told the children the story behind the *Diadoumenos?*

I remember: looking into their eyes, which were as blank and faraway as the eyes of the Apollo, and thinking (hah!) that all I had to do to teach them to look at the world the way I did was to feed them my memories, imprint them with my ideas of truth and beauty, beauty and truth.

The things I said to them that night! I went on and on about

Apollo's missing arms. I said things like, It's not important where the arms were in the beginning, or what became of them when they fell off. What's important is to complete the statue with your imagination. That was what the imagination was there for, I told them: to complete the broken statue and make it whole again, to see the past inside the present, to look at a half-built house, a half-lived life and see what it could become. I recited "Kubla Khan" at them. I told them about the daffodil and the nightingale and the urn and Ozymandias. To complete the lunacy, I even dredged up that Rilke book and read them the sonnet about the torso of Apollo—*in German!* And said to them, Listen to the sound of the words before I tell you what they mean: "Du muss dein Leben andern." To a three-year-old and a four-and-a-half-year-old! How I expected them to understand immanence I do not know.

That night I dreamed we were all in Molivos, or rather we were all just outside Molivos, on our way to the beach. But every time we rounded a bend in the Eftalou road, the season would change, or the time of day. Buildings would spring up out of nowhere—hotels, monasteries, department stores, tavernas—the children would run into them and disappear and when we found them they would be different ages from before. There was a marble archway we wanted to get to that kept receding like a rainbow, always a headland away. And as we ran from cove to cove to catch it, we were suddenly not in Greece anymore but in San Francisco. Suddenly I was alone inside a sea of luggage. I dragged it up the hill to our apartment house, I dragged it up the stairs, kicked open our door . . . and there you were, making supper. There the children were at our dining table.

I looked out the window. There, instead of Telegraph Hill, was Molivos. And there, in the place of Fisherman's Wharf, was Eftalou. There was the Parthenon on Treasure Island. Mingling with the flock of sailboats on the bay were red and blue caïques casting their nets. There were monasteries and terraced olive groves in the hills above Berkeley and Oakland.

Molivos faded, Telegraph Hill reappeared and then itself faded to make way again for Molivos. One moment the Parthenon radiated so much light you would think the sun was rising behind it, other times you could see through it to the barracks of the naval base. One moment the water was battleship-gray; the next it was as blue as the Aegean. But even when the bay had nothing on it but a flock of white sailboats, I could almost see the blue and red caïques hiding behind them, just as I could see the olive groves and monasteries hiding behind the blank windows of the modern houses perched on the hills above Berkeley and Oakland.

I turned around to call you to the window. When you came up to me, at first I didn't know you. You looked as if someone had erased ten years of memories from your face. But then, as I stood there watching you, the years and the memories came back. Your face grew older again. Except that now, when I looked into your real face, I could see your other, younger face hiding behind it.

I could even see it after I woke up. While I watched you sleeping next to me, I told myself how wrong I had been to think I would recover anything in Molivos.

BUT

Chapter 26

The past was always with us. I had to learn to trust what I could not see. This is what I told myself as I kissed you goodbye after breakfast the next morning. I had to let you go, even though it felt like dropping you into darkness. I couldn't begin to imagine you in an office with Mitchell.

I managed to keep my spirits unnaturally levitated during the morning, but after lunch I made the mistake of taking the children to the Palace of Fine Arts. It was here it hit me that something was wrong, that somehow I had messed things up, that I had had a shot but failed, that we ought to have been in Greece.

I tried to fight it. I tried to put myself back into the afternoon. I tried to enjoy watching the children get so much pleasure out of feeding stale bread to the ducks, tried to see the Palace of Fine Arts for what it was—a concrete imitation of a ruin sitting on the edge of a man-made duck pond—instead of what it ought to be. I tried not to fault the columns for their fake orange tinge, tried not to compare it to the sparkling white of weatherbeaten marble, tried not to think of the Aegean when I looked at the dull green linoleum floor of a pond, tried not to think of the gliding caïques I could be looking at instead of these predatory geese. I tried to accept the bed of grass instead of longing for a stark and rocky mountain slope, and a bright-blue Aegean, and a smooth white marble ruin and everything else that made Greece what it was for me, and this place what it was not and never would be.

I told myself that one day it would be this I'd miss, the luxury of an afternoon with two children who adored me and who thought I was as happy as they were to be feeding stale bread to the ducks. But the bad taste remained.

Not that I had much time to sulk. It was not an easy summer, after all. I couldn't drive, remember. I was in constant pain. I had trouble breathing, and, until I threw it into the bay, I had that neck brace. I was up to my eyeballs in medical bills, and cryptic computer printouts from our fucking useless insurance company. Do you remember how much I ended up having to pay out of my own pocket? We might as well have had no coverage at all.

And then there were the—excuse me for saying so—fucking useless counseling sessions, not to mention the driver's-ed course they were forcing me to attend, not to mention the legal complications and the visits to expensive and condescending robots who gave few indications of having once looked almost human when we were at law school together.

And the children—I know I tried to protect you, but didn't you ever stop and ask yourself what had come over them in my absence? You would never have known how many thousands of hours we had spent reading books to them—or that they had ever set eyes on an educational toy. All they wanted to do was slouch in front of the TV on the sofa watching cartoons with their fingers in their noses.

They refused to touch anything I cooked them. They kept asking for chocolate éclairs. When I explained why they couldn't have any, they would burst into tears. The nights were the worst. I have never heard such shrieking.

God only knows what was upsetting Maria. All I had to go on were the questions she asked. Why did I have a penis? Why didn't she? I was never able to give her a satisfactory answer.

Jesse was easier. I knew what was troubling *him*. It was Eluisa's taste in movies, it was the alien bursting out of the spaceman's chest. That didn't mean I could stop him from sleepwalking or worrying about the contents of the radiator. No matter how many times I told him the alien wasn't real, I couldn't get through to the boy. Of course the alien wasn't real, he would tell me. It was UNreal.

And because it was UNreal, he couldn't afford to let me out of his sight for a second. This put a strain on my patience. There was a moment halfway through the first week, when I went into the bathroom to take a piss, and both children came in with me—Jesse to make sure I didn't get attacked by the alien and Maria to watch me drop my pants—when I despaired of ever erasing Eluisa's influence.

Then, in six short weeks, I turned them around. Didn't I?

I remember looking at them at breakfast on that Sunday before school began and saying to myself, Who would have known even a month ago that I would have them sitting here with their hair so neat, their faces so clean, their eyes so bright? Saying please when they asked for more cereal, thank you when I gave it to them. Asking intelligent questions. Laughing at each other's knock-knock jokes. Trusting me to return if I darted into the kitchen for milk or another cup of coffee. No longer asking me to check behind the door/under the table/behind the couch for aliens, no longer attributing supernatural powers to the pictures on the walls, no more mumbled prayers in Spanish . . . I looked at them and said, *I* did this. What does it matter if I am the only one to give myself credit?

Because the truth is, a little praise from you would have gone a long way. The better the children did, the more I yearned for it. And yet . . . there was something to be said for virtue going unremarked and unrewarded, for you being the thoughtless, selfish one, and me the martyr.

No matter how callously you behaved, I was determined not to sink to your level. Had you neglected to thank us for the birthday cards we had made for you? Had you gone off to work without them? Were the children devastated? Did I tell you? No, I bit my tongue, reminded myself you had a job to do. A lousy job, granted. A job for which you were grossly overqualified. But before you could realize this, you had to regain your confidence. I was determined to do everything in my power to help that process along.

And so I did. Didn't I? I remember taking you your breakfast on that ill-fated Sunday before school began, and watching you emerge from the shower and saying to myself, Could this flushed and vibrant woman be timid, frail, insecure Laura? Could this be the woman who couldn't walk up two flights of stairs without gasping, or take three words of criticism without bursting into tears, who would drive fifty miles out of her way to avoid an expressway, go without water, electricity, heat or even food if getting any of these things involved talking on the phone to a stranger?

I took full credit. If you were thinner and healthier, it was because of the food I cooked for you. If you were fit, it was thanks to the health club I had found for you. If you were rested, it was because I let you sleep in on weekends. It was because I brought you breakfast in bed.

Of course I couldn't tell you how much I was doing for you. It would have undermined your confidence. But it is hard to go on making sacrifices, day in day out, if no one even realizes you are making them. If the person you are devoting your life to becomes cold and distant, and never asks you how your day has been, and never even touches you, not even in bed, having lost all apparent interest in sex, you begin to wonder. You begin to nurture resentments, especially in the middle of the night, when you have just been rejected sexually. Certainly this was the case for me.

It was when I was suffering from blueballs that the doubts raised by your housekeeping would surface most dramatically.

I don't know if you remember now, but at the beginning of that August I reorganized the apartment. In the process, I made some very disturbing discoveries.

Here, for example, is what I found in the kitchen cabinets, behind a deceptive façade of china canisters:

a. A mason jar full of kidney beans that had little green shoots growing out of them.
b. Four half-spilled packages of spaghetti, one of which had spilled all over, and another of which was infested with weird-looking bugs I thought were termites.
c. A half-used jar of mayonnaise.
d. A box of cereal—open—that we bought before Jesse was born.
e. A piece of petrified chocolate cake from Maria's first birthday, with a fork from our good set sticking out of it.
f. A swollen can of Texas-style chili. It obviously contained botulism. My first thought when I saw it was: What if Eluisa had served it to the children? What if she had eaten it herself? What would we have done if an illegal alien had expired on our kitchen floor? As the owner of a law degree, do you have any idea of the ramifications?

As for the bookshelves—I mean, do you remember what condition they were in? How could you claim to have an organized mind, how could you expect me not to entertain severe doubts about you, if you were in the habit of cramming Asterix upside down next to Tacitus? Leaving half-eaten cookies on top of Proust? Putting all of John Coltrane's albums into one sleeve? I couldn't even begin to tell you how many irreplaceable LPs I had to throw away. I could fill a book with a list of broken, incomplete and dangerous toys I found behind their chest of drawers, and ten volumes with what I found under their beds. How were you ever going to organize your day at work if this was your attitude to detail?

I was also disturbed by the photo albums. They stopped at Jesse's second birthday. They contained no pictures of Maria. Going through the mountain of unsorted photographs, I found twenty-nine pictures of ceiling corners and brake pedals. They were held together by a rubber band and shoved to the back of the cabinet. This indicated to me that you had forgotten, at least twenty-nine times, that the zero setting on our camera was actually the first frame on the roll, and also that you did not want me to know you had forgotten. In other words, you were not just sloppy, but devious.

Our August Visa bill confirmed my suspicions.

I'll tell you the truth. I didn't think much of these clothes you'd been buying. They were too young, and too suggestive, and bound to give people the wrong impression. But since you assured me they were as cheap as they looked, I said to myself, What the hell. Let her find herself.

Naturally, my attitude changed when I found out what those clingy little dresses and pointy little witch shoes *really* cost.

I felt I had to impress upon you the fact that your salary did not come close to supporting us.

Although you took my lecture quietly, you must have been raging underneath. You must have gone out that same day and bought that number that made you look like an off-duty Jell-O wrestler. Did you think I was going to be fooled just because you hid it in the linen closet for a week before daring to wear it? As I remember saying to you, if you expect to sneak something past me, it has got to be something subtler than neon pink.

Your response alarmed me. "Oh, for God's sake. I'm a working woman now. Don't I have the right to a little privacy?"

Privacy for what? I asked myself.

It was at this point that I began to take an interest in your diaphragm. To see it sitting in our bathroom drawer on nights when you were held up at work was, I must admit, a comfort to me. That is why I was so unnerved by what happened after the Lifestyle Christening.

Chapter 27

Before I go any further, I feel I must point out that I do not approve of double baptisms. Nobody can be Catholic *and* Protestant at the same time.

And nobody should make their friends and relatives go to two churches in one morning, as they made us do on that Sunday before school began.

With specific regard to the Protestant christening—what hole did they dig that minister out of? Or rather, what closet? The guy had not been near a church in years. I know that the rest of you thought his irreverent little jokes were hilarious. But if he didn't know the service, and if he was of two minds about the Episcopalian church, why then was he doing it at all? Why were we watching him?

Don't tell me it was for the sake of the grandparents. Remember: I am one of the few people who actually talked to Mitchell's parents. And his father isn't even Protestant. He's Jewish. While his mother, who *is* a Protestant, is *not* an Episcopalian. She's a Methodist.

What about Becky's mother? She really *is* religious. What did the poor woman make of the show you and your friends put on for us at the Catholic church? The idea of having two sets of godparents—who thought that one up? I liked it even less for the fact that you were one of the godmothers. As for the misunderstanding over the communion! The sight of all six of you saying no thanks to the bowl of communion wafers and passing it down the row like a dip at a cocktail party—that was bad. And I mean real bad.

You should have seen yourselves: six grown people collapsing into giggles in the front aisle, while that poor mother of Becky's stood behind you trying to keep what was left of her dignity. How could you collude in such a thing? I remember looking at you at the reception afterward, or rather I remember looking at your new loud makeup and geometric haircut and your scoopnecked clinging neon-pink excuse for a dress and your pointy black witch shoes and suddenly being overcome by a wave of fear. Who was this woman? Perhaps I was too much under the children's influence—this was my first time in adult company since getting out of the hospital—but you looked UNreal to me.

The feeling was mutual. You made no secret of wanting to have zero to do with me. This made things worse, as it allowed my paranoia to expand to the other guests at the reception and eventually, as I will explain, the house.

I am sure, looking back, that you had no designs on that braying restaurant radical you talked to for more than an hour. It must have been embarrassing, therefore, to have me hovering on the edge of the conversation, too far away to join in, but close enough to impose the full weight of my disapproval. Likewise, I can see now that you were just being polite when you laughed at the Santa Rosa plumber's jokes. There was no need for me to insult him.

I also had no right to ask you why you were taking down that balding lawyer's number. But please try and understand. This was the first time I had been out with you in public since my return from Greece. It was one thing to congratulate myself at home on the strides you were making. It was quite another to see where these strides had taken you.

As I think back on that disastrous afternoon, I have a picture in my mind of you and your friends standing together in front of the plate-glass window that looked out from the kitchen into the backyard. You and Becky were leaning against the glass: she had a green-neon number that matched your pink-neon number. Ophelia was looking unusually Cuban, with a loud flowery shirt and white tight pants and gold chains everywhere, while Charlotte was wearing a tired posthippie floral print. Behind you in the garden, Lara and Paloma were going wild in the sprinkler and trying to coax our two to join, while Seb looked on dubiously and Dottie wailed. You didn't pay them any attention. You were all laughing about some book idea Becky had about treating husbands like babies. You were thinking up chapter headings: Breast Is Best, From Walking to Crawling, His First Day at Work. I did not think it was very funny.

Who's been looking after YOUR kids all afternoon? I wanted to ask them. Who was it kept the girls from shoveling sand onto the newly christened baby's face? Who kept the boys from trying to fly like Superman out of the kitchen window? It was me, both times.

Hadn't they noticed? If they had, then why did Becky keep coming up to me and asking if I was completely a hundred percent sure I had everything I needed for school the next day? Why did Ophelia interrogate me about how I planned to get the children to and fro without a car? Why did Charlotte keep blabbing about the dangers of isolation and the importance of support systems? Why did she keep dragging me over to the barbecue to talk to her gruesome husband?

"Remember," she told me, "he was once a stay-at-home himself. Try and get him to open up."

Thanks but no thanks, I felt like telling her. I would rather die. He didn't want to have anything to do with me either. Whenever I happened to bump into him by accident (next to the beer cooler, usually) he acted like I was some kind of insect he had spent his entire summer trying to eliminate from his garden.

Kiki was not much better. If I happened to stray near whatever group of people he happened to be boring, he would stop talking, break out in a slow, not particularly friendly grin, point his finger at me like a gun and say, "OK now. You've got five seconds. George Brett's batting average in the '81 World Series." Or, "Who's the Tex-Mex guy who plays for the Dodgers?" When I wouldn't answer he would go, "Pow. You're dead. Better luck next life." And then turn his back.

This is how Mitchell introduced me to his brother: "This is Mike—my frontwoman's househusband. We used to be partners. Now Mike spends all day fooling around with au pairs on the playground while his wife and I do the work."

"Jesus, Mitchell! When are you going to learn some goddamn tact?"

At which point he threw up his arms and said, "OK, Mom, no offense, Mom! I didn't mean it, honest." For the rest of the afternoon, whenever he came near me, he addressed me as Mom. I can't tell you how close I came to popping him.

It is humiliating when people you have always looked down on begin to make fun of you. It is even more humiliating, though, when you get stuck in the corner talking to stultifyingly dull strangers and see that *they* are the ones who are desperately searching for an excuse to break away. I thought I knew why, too: it was because I had had the courage to change my life and put my beliefs to the test. Was this what I had to pay, though, for my integrity? Was social leprosy my reward?

I tried these ideas out on a dental hygienist who claimed to be a distant relation of Becky's. I found a sympathetic listener in her, but this only sent me further in the wrong direction. Just as the restaurateur and the plumber had borne the brunt of my fears about losing you to the outside world, now all the guests who wouldn't talk to me came to stand for California. Look at these people, I said to this poor, well-meaning dental hygienist. Just about every faction of the middle class was represented. We disagreed vehemently about almost everything—except for the importance of false cheer at social gatherings. How did we create this false cheer? By deliberately making ourselves shallow. I told her we needed to come out of hiding, and fight our differences out, and that was when I lost her.

Then some poor unsuspecting corporate lawyer struck up a conversation with me. He began by asking me point-blank who I was. I told him I was an alien from outer space and then asked him a number of questions about his planet. Were all humans hypocrites? Did they all use religious rituals like interchangeable floor shows? Did they all like to fill the cracks and contradictions of their lives with conspicuous consumption? How long had he known Mitchell and Becky? One couch long? Two couches long? Three? Four?

"What do you mean?" he asked, shrinking away.

"I have never seen the same couch in this living room twice."

"Maybe the other ones are upstairs somewhere," he suggested.

"I'll bet you a hundred bucks they are not."

"I don't like bets," the lawyer said.

"I'll go up and prove it to you anyway." I then proceeded to do so. I couldn't find a single thing that could be older than six months—or anything that didn't have a duplicate. In the new baby's room were two Aprica strollers, two bassinets, two changing tables, two two two. I went down to find the corporate lawyer so that I could show him this disgusting waste. He was talking to the dental hygienist. They both looked through me.

I went into the kitchen. There you were on the window ledge with Becky, two Day-Glo spectaculars. Both of you were looking right through me with squints in your eyes, as if I were a pane of glass and there was a shape right behind me that you couldn't quite make out. I didn't intend to eavesdrop, but then I heard Becky say to you, "Well, thank goodness it was a false alarm."

Then Becky asked you, "Does he suspect anything?"

I watched in disbelief as you shook your head and said, "On some level he must. Even though I've always been extremely careful. We only ever meet at lunch."

"They always sense it, though," Becky said.

"I know," you said. "Because every time, *every* time I'm about to leave, he calls up."

"The famous male intuition," Becky said.

You laughed and mumbled something about the missing chromosome. This made both of you laugh. Still stunned, but made ambulatory by the force of your contempt, I headed back for the stairs, coming to a stop on the first landing. Gazing into what I took to be a mirror, because what I saw was a room identical to the one behind me, I tried to stop your words from reverberating in my head.

Who was "he"? What did I sense but not know? Who *had* you been meeting secretly for lunch?

Had you been lying to me about Gabe? Was he back from Mexico? *Had he never gone?* Had you been screwing him at lunchtime, when I thought you were safe at work?

No, you could not have been screwing him, I said to myself as I gazed at the glass table, the oriental carpet, the parquet floor and blue walls in what I took to be a mirror. You could not have been screwing him if your diaphragm was safe at home with me. Thank God I had been checking up on it. Or had there been days when I hadn't?

Hoping to rid myself of the specter of the diaphragm, I stared into the room in the mirror.

It was at this point that I noticed there was something wrong with the image.

I wasn't in it.

At any other time, it would have taken me two seconds to figure out that I was looking into the next house. I might even have remembered you telling me about the computer people who lived there, who were so unsure of their own taste that they actually did copy what they saw in Becky and Mitchell's house. Normally I would have seen the funny side about mistaking a window for a mirror. But today it was the confirmation of my worst fears. The forces of California had turned against me. I had been erased.

That is why I was a little brusque with you when I barged into the kitchen and told you I needed to go home.

Not that this did any good. Would you come home with me? Not on your life. You acted as if I were some throwback Victorian explorer who was trying to catch you with a net.

Yet another indication of how little weight my word carried now that we had switched places.

Chapter 28

I remember walking back into our newly reorganized apartment and thinking how pathetic it looked. Not even the sight of the diaphragm sitting safely in its drawer reassured me. And believe me, I checked.

The children were angry at me for having dragged them away from the party early. They had wanted to play with their friends, whom they informed me they had missed. "If you missed them why didn't you tell me?" I asked. But I couldn't get a straight answer from them, in Maria's case because she had come back from the party talking baby talk.

Terrific! I thought. A day back with her friends and a whole summer's work is undone. It was the same with Jesse. The fears I had worked so hard to chase away were back. It wasn't just that he wouldn't sit in a room without me. He wouldn't even sit in a chair alone. And having glued himself to my side, he couldn't sit still. This made it very hard to lose myself in the paper. (By now, this was the only thing I could think of doing to stop the fantasies that had begun to crowd my brain—about what you might be getting up to with Gabe, Mitchell and/or any number of people, including bikers.) My patience was short, and so there was an edge to my voice when I asked Jesse if he didn't have to go to the bathroom.

I am sure this is why he lied to me and said no.

"You do have to go," I said. "But you think the alien is hiding in the toilet. Right?"

He looked at me with a trembling lower lip.

I tried a gentler approach. "Believe me. The alien does not exist." I went into my stock explanation, a difficult feat at the best of times, made more difficult now by Maria's interference.

She was playing waitress. Not a game I usually permitted. After what I went through in my first marriage, waitressing was not something I was able to have much of a sense of humor about. But I did not have the energy to stop it today. So while I was talking Jesse out of his fantasies, and fighting a losing battle against my own, Maria was taking our orders and setting the table—i.e., filling plastic plates with shredded paper towels.

Imagine what it was like. I had no control over my thoughts. In my mind you were banging sometimes Gabe, sometimes Mitchell, and sometimes a battalion of Hell's Angels. You were writhing, spreading your legs and biting his/their necks. And what was I doing? Sitting at the dining table, singing "Happy Birthday" to Maria's dolls, and pretending to eat and enjoy the shredded paper towels.

It seemed an eternity before I could ask for the check.

I knew there were any number of things I ought to have been doing to get the kids ready for school the next morning. But I couldn't, so I went back to my paper. I was halfway through a movie review when Jesse climbed onto my lap again, making it impossible for me to breathe.

"What's wrong now?" I asked.

Pointing up at the poster on the wall, he said, "The *Diadoumenos.*"

"What about it?" I asked.

"I think it might have special powers."

"Oh, for God's sake, Jesse," I said. "It does not. It's just a statue. Lay off."

"I just saw them, though," he said.

"Saw what?"

"The arms."

"But it doesn't have any arms."

"It does now," he said in a trembling voice. He looked out the window and said in a stage whisper, "They're back."

"What do you mean, they're back?"

"They're over there," he said, pointing out the window. "I just saw them."

"Listen," I said to Jesse. "You didn't see them. It was just your imagination. The *Diadoumenos* lost its arms thousands of years ago. They're not coming back."

"Where are they then?"

"Somewhere far away," I said. "In a ditch in Greece."

"Why, though?"

"I don't know," I said. "Maybe some barbarians chopped them off. Or maybe they fell off in a storm."

"Is that why people aren't made of stone anymore?"

"People were never made of stone," I told him.

"Then why is the *Diadoumenos* made of stone?"

"Because the *Diadoumenos* is a statue."

"But you said the *Diadoumenos* was a man."

I tried to explain. "Technically, yes, it's a man. But it is supposed to be a statue of a god. It's a statue of Apollo, the god of love."

"Is that why it has no arms?" he asked.

"No."

"Why does it look like a man, then?"

"Because the ancient Greeks believed that gods looked like men."

"So what happened to the rest of them?"

"The rest of what?" I asked, my patience wearing thin.

"The rest of the gods," he said. He paused to give me a significant look. "There's only one left now. Remember?"

He gave me a nudge. I didn't know what to say. "I'll tell you what *I* think," he continued. "*I* think they turned into alien robots."

Not aliens. Not again!!! I wanted to hurl myself out the window. "Listen, Jesse," I said. "The Greek gods did not go anywhere. They never really existed. They were figments of the ancient Greek imagination, just like the alien is a figment of yours."

"You mean Apollo never existed?"

"Right."

"So then how can there be a statue of him?"

"Because—as I already told you—it is not a statue of Apollo. It is a statue of a man who *looked* like Apollo."

"But how did they know what Apollo looked like? If he didn't exist?"

"They didn't know," I admitted. "They guessed."

"But I thought you said this statue was real."

"It *is* real."

"But *you* said it didn't exist!!"

By now even I was getting mixed up. "Look," I said. "Let me explain how this statue came into being. There used to be a man who looked like this statue."

"Did he have arms?"

"Yes, as far as we know, the man who looked like this statue had arms."

"But you're not sure," Jesse said.

"No, I can't be a hundred percent sure because I never met him. He died thousands of years before I was born."

"If you never met him, how can you be sure his name was Apollo?"

"His name was NOT Apollo. Apollo is the name of the god the SCULPTOR thought he looked like. God!"

"Which god?" Jesse asked.

"No, no, no," I said. "Listen carefully this time. We don't know what the real guy's name was. And we don't know what the name of the sculptor was. All we know is that he sculpted this statue and that he based it on a real human."

"How can you be sure, though?"

"I *can't* be a hundred percent sure. But I am almost positive. There has to have been a man once upon a time who looked like this simply because this statue looks so much like a man."

"It doesn't look like a man to *me.*"

"Why the hell not?"

"Because. It doesn't have any arms."

"But it *did* have arms, God damn it. It did. IT DID! Until that storm came along, or until those barbarians whoever they were hacked them off, it had arms. OK? Got that straight? Can I read my paper now?"

But the paper had become a lost cause. Jesse had eroded my faith in what I saw. I looked at the *Diadoumenos* and said to myself, he's right. What scanty evidence we base our conclusions on. How could we be sure the model for the *Diadoumenos* had arms? The answer was, we couldn't. We took it all on faith. And because of what had happened, I began to think how much I took on faith in my own life.

The return of my paranoid fantasies made it hard for me to stay at Jesse's level. This is why, when he asked me what barbarians were, I did not give him the full answer he deserved. I was sarcastic. I said they were people who hated art. When he asked me if they still existed I said yes but now they made Hollywood movies. When he said maybe that's what was in his radiator, I said yes, it was probably a Hollywood director. For the first time since I had taken the children over, I did not want to talk to them. I just wanted them to leave me alone. That is why I did not object when Maria, influenced by the travesty she had witnessed earlier, began to play Church.

I remember looking up from the paper and seeing her pushing

the baby stroller with one hand and with the other hand holding open a Golden Book as if it were a hymnal, and singing something ghostly in the upper registers.

The next thing I knew she was asking me to get some money ready. "Time for collection," she said.

I didn't pay any attention to her.

The next thing I knew, she had shoved your diaphragm into my face.

She had already put some quarters into it.

I don't think I have ever been so horrified by a contraceptive device.

"Where did you get that?" I screamed. I grabbed the diaphragm. The quarters went flying. "This is not a toy. If anything happened to this it could be very dangerous."

"Give it to me!" Maria shrieked. "It's for Church!"

"No, it's not. It's for Mom," I said. I took it back to the bathroom where it belonged. I opened up the drawer and found . . . your diaphragm case. I opened the case and found . . . your diaphragm.

Once again, I nearly had a heart attack. I turned to Maria. "Who gave you this?"

She looked at me, her sullen expression an alarming replica of yours. "Mom gave it to me. For Church."

"Where did you find it?" I'm afraid I took her by the arms and shook her. "Show me!"

Still pouting, she took me to your jewelry case and lifted out the bottom. To reveal not one, not two, but three more diaphragms.

No need now to go into the hysterical accusations I leveled against you when you finally came home. As for the things you said back to me, I can't tell you how they stung me. *I* was threatened by your rapid progress? *I*, who had done everything in my power to bring it about? *I* was smothering you? *I* was forcing myself on you sexually? *I* condescended to you? *I* couldn't understand how you could have a friendship with a man that wasn't based on sex?

"I'll give you something not to trust me about," you said in your new, assertive snarl. "I always wanted to hear his band anyway. So why not now? And why go unprotected?"

I can't tell you what it did to me, watching you throw all five diaphragms into your bag—or what the children's crying did to me after you had slammed the door on us. Then, to have to sit there waiting for you to come home . . .

What time did you finally roll in? Ten, eleven o'clock? I may have been pretending to sleep in that armchair, but let me tell you, I have never been more fucking awake. I could smell the stale cigarette smoke on you. I could see your hair was tousled, and on your disheveled clothes I could imagine the hands of other men. When I got into bed next to you, I could smell the men—not just Gabe and Gabe's band, but my partners, and the balding lawyer who had given you his card, and the Santa Rosa plumber, and the restaurant radical, and the faceless hordes of bikers, twenty-three-year-old junior lawyers, Mitchell . . . When I couldn't bear it any longer, I put my clothes back on and went out.

I really needed to see my old friend Rob. I hadn't seen him since before Greece. I found him at Specs. He had just gotten off his taxi shift and was drinking Miller's with tequila chasers and sitting with a woman who turned out to be a stripper from one of those places on Broadway.

She had silvery blond hair and a loud voice and she chewed gum. She had glitter eye shadow and a brain the size of a pasty. She kept poking Rob playfully near the groin. Every other word she said was "fuck." He pretended not to notice but then suddenly he jerked around and in a low and menacing voice said, "Cool it." And presto! Magic! She did, even though she didn't want to. When was the last time I had seen that?

She lit up a cigarette and squirmed around in her chair, while Rob droned on about a recent deep-sea fishing expedition and his plans to hit Guanajuato that winter.

"Hey, fuckhead," she said. "Maybe I'll come with you."

"Like hell you will," said Rob.

He turned his back to her and started telling me how his writing was going. "I think all those porno books fucked up my style."

"You're fucking right they did," his companion said.

"Amy Jean?" Rob showed no signs of being ruffled. "I've just about had enough of your backtalk. I feel this urge growing inside me to knock you clear off that stool. So why don't you take a walk down to the other end of the bar while I talk to my friend?"

"If you say so," was her meek response. She slouched away to talk to a gaunt, desperate-looking woman at the other end of the bar.

Rob and I watched them light each other's cigarettes, and then he snorted and said, "Women!" He took a long drag out of his cigarette. "So," he said, exhaling. "What's up with you?"

There was no way I could tell him. No way!

I had lied to Rob before. But this time I went at it in a new way. There was no relation between me and the macho miracle I described for him. I did not mention you or your job or my accident or my decision to stay at home with the children. Instead I talked travel and fictitious one-night stands and business conquests. Rob was not particularly impressed, but as I was telling him what he expected to hear, I guess he believed me.

I was the one who needed convincing. That is why I ended up going back to Amy Jean's friend's place. I thought she would be easy.

Just when I was working myself up to a climax, she stopped me and said, "Wait. Before you finish. You have to know who I am. You have to accept me." She turned on the light. Looking down at the body underneath me, I saw it had one breast missing. In its place was a scar. "This is me," she said, almost proudly. "This is the real Samantha. I used to be ashamed, but not anymore. I've come to terms with it and I want you to do the same."

There was no way I could get it up again after that. I guessed I deserved the abuse she gave me. When I got home, I couldn't bear the thought of lying next to you, so I poured myself another drink and settled into an armchair. I lit myself the cigarette that would end up burning a hole in the leather. My last memory is of looking up at the *Diadoumenos,* looking up at his blank eyes and his stumps and almost catching them move, then closing my eyes to trick them, opening them fast, and seeing the last trace of a disrespectful gesture. I must have been very drunk.

I fell asleep and dreamed I was defending a bunker. I was surrounded by an army of bikers, handymen and twenty-three-year-old junior lawyers. They were trying to close in on me. I was spinning around and around with my submachine gun, spraying them with bullets. But I couldn't kill them for longer than two seconds. They would get up laughing when I wasn't looking and move in on you, and you let them. While I was spraying them with bullets, other intruders would sneak up behind me. This nightmare was still playing itself out when the alarm rang at seven in the morning. I was still under its influence as I went through the motions of breakfast. I think that is why I did such a bad job—that and the fact that the children were wired up anyway on account of it being the first day of school.

For Maria it really *was* the first day of school, ever. She must have been awake for hours when I went in to get her. When I took off her covers she was already dressed—inside out and backward. I am sure if I had had enough sleep I could have managed to get her dressed properly without injuring her pride and therefore causing a scene. But because I wasn't thinking, I was too direct.

"Take those off," I said. "Let me put them outside out for you." She refused to obey me.

I was stupid enough to issue an ultimatum. "You can't have breakfast until you're dressed right," I said. She refused to budge. I had to undress her by force. Furious, she refused to eat her cereal. So I insulted her, told her she wasn't acting like a three-and-a-half-year-old. My heart aches when I remember the horrible things I said to her, that I really ought to have been saying to you.

How could I have done that to a child that age on such an important day? Even Jesse couldn't take it. When I did Maria's ponytail, and she screamed, and I threw the brush across the room, he pleaded with me to be nice to her. And what did I do? I just told him it was a fine time to become her ally since he was the one who had revved her up. Glossing over my own deficiencies, I reminded him of all the things *he* had done to annoy me over breakfast.

This made him even more upset. "I'm sorry!" he yelled. "I can't help it! It's not me!"

"Then who the fuck is it?"

"It's the alien inside me," Jesse said. "The alien inside me made me do it."

I'm afraid I shook him.

"How many times am I going to have to tell you this. There is not an alien inside you. Now eat your cereal. There's no school until you do."

Obediently, he chewed for me. But he continued to cry and eventually food started spilling out between his quivering lips.

"What's wrong now?" I asked.

"It's moving again."

"What's moving again?"

"The *Diadoumenos.*"

"Oh it is, is it? Well, let me assure you. It is never going to fucking move again." And that is when I tore it off the wall and stamped on it.

I then proceeded to tear it into little bits. "That good enough for you?" I asked Jesse. Looking up at him, I was shocked to see that he had stopped crying.

"Oh Dad," he said. "Oh Dad!"

He was still clinging to my leg and sobbing when you walked into the dining alcove.

You took a look at the shredded photograph and broken glass on the floor. You walked over to Maria's high chair, examined her cereal, and fished out a shard of glass three inches long. You gave me a prize look.

While I got out the broom, you made a big show of calming the children down. You, who had done nothing at home for weeks except lounge in bed. You, who had gone God only knew where the night before with all five diaphragms. Suddenly you were playing the martyr again. Suddenly you were the one whose patience was again being tested by a man with a missing chromosome.

The last straw was when you said, "Let me show you the right way to make a ponytail."

You show *me* the right way to make a ponytail? ME, who had worn a ponytail for five fucking years of my life? When you turned to me with that supercilious smile and said, "Next time try and sweep the hair up from underneath, like this," well, naturally I was going to flip.

I don't remember exactly what I said, but whatever it was, it couldn't have been bad enough to warrant the malice in your response. "OK," you said, "you think you're so smart. You think you can take over my job and do it better than me without my advice. Go right ahead. But don't expect to cry on my shoulder when you run into trouble."

"What the hell are you talking about?" I asked.

"You'll find out soon enough."

Chapter 29

It was with this threat in mind that I set off for school. The children were still shaking from our argument. Just outside the Creative Learning Center, I sat them down on the low garden wall.

I told them that, no matter what happened, I would always be their father, and that meant I would take care of them, and protect them from all that was bad in the world, and help them grow strong. We were a team. I remember how they looked at me, with never-to-be-duplicated respect.

I remember how soft Maria's features were under her uplifted ponytail. I remember the pink cardigan and the gold locket. I remember that Jesse was wearing a red jacket, that it was only zipped halfway up. I remember also just how the curls in his hair fell over his forehead and his ears. I remember pressing both children against my chest and looking through the front window of the Creative Learning Center, at the bright little chairs and table, and the clever little partitions, and the charts, and the bookcases, and the mobiles of geometric shapes in primary colors. And the children, now milling around, now allowing themselves to be herded into a circle by the young woman I would come to refer to as Fatso. I remember she was dressed that morning in a baby-blue tracksuit.

I watched her while I patted my sobbing children on their backs. I did not attach much importance to what I saw, but I do remember being impressed, in a distant, idle sort of way, by the smoothness of her operation. Now she was leaning over, talking to a few of her charges. Now she was standing up and issuing them an instruction. One sentence, that was all it took for her to get all thirty, forty children to arrange themselves on the floor in a circle. Now she raised her hand, and it was like clockwork. She had the children singing. She had the children return to silence with a single clap and now she was pointing to them one at a time and getting them to recite something. Now she was standing up. She was pointing at a large calendar and asking a question and getting a flurry of answers. She was reprimanding the overeager children. She was getting one of them to answer her question correctly. She was writing something on the board I couldn't see, and pulling down a picture from a roller.

It was, as I discovered when we approached the door, an illustration of an aviary. The word she had written on the board was "SEPTEMBER." The book she was holding up for the children was called *Chickens Aren't the Only Ones*. Lying on the table next to her was an assortment of eggs of various sizes and colors, and a brown plastic apparatus I would later find out was an incubator.

"Can anyone tell me why chickens have to sit on eggs?" This was the question she was asking as I took our children's jackets off. She did not get an answer because all of the children had turned to stare at us.

It was, according to the big red clock on the wall, 8:48. I was three minutes late.

Not such a good way to start the school year, perhaps, but not such a bad one either. And anyway, they were late because I hadn't wanted to send them into school crying. Now they were calm. So I had done the right thing, although you wouldn't have known it from the look Fatso gave me.

It was the kind of look you'd expect to get if you ran into a one-night stand months after the event and said, Don't I know you from somewhere? Except that no, it was even worse than that. It was the kind of look you'd expect if you knocked someone up, ran off to join the Navy, and came back four years later expecting dinner on the table. Reproachful does not even come close to describing it, and because I had never, to my knowledge, set eyes on her before, it both confused me and put me on the defensive, so that at the same time as I was thinking: What did I do wrong, I was also sure I had indeed done something wrong, which sin I had then compounded by forgetting all about it.

Now, I know you are going to say that I was reading things into the situation that were not there. She was simply trying to do her job, I can hear you saying, and this is a school that takes promptness seriously.

But all Fatso had to say was, "Go into the cloakroom so that Vampyra can do the checklist. These kids are not allowed into my Circle until Vampyra gives me the OK."

Did Fatso say this? No. First she had to get even with me for belonging to the same sex as all the dates who had made her feel worthless for being fat. She kept me standing there with my arms flapping while she (a) greeted Jesse with controlled effusion, and then (b) asked him to introduce Maria, and then (c) asked him, with controlled sternness, if he had forgotten some important things, and then, when he couldn't remember, (d) opened the discussion to the floor. Could the other children tell Jesse what they had done before joining Circle? Slowly, painfully, the story emerged: they had had to go into the cloakroom one by one to be processed. "Otherwise, what would this room look like? It would be covered with coats and shoes and lunchboxes and all sorts of *other* personal effects, wouldn't it? And then we couldn't play, could we? How could we teach our new friend Maria how to play sleeping lions *then?*"

"We couldn't," said one little horror with a piping voice. "We would have to scrunch up like underprivileged children."

"That's not a very nice thing to say," said Fatso. "Does anybody know why?"

A flock of hands shot up. The last thing I heard as Jesse led me out of the room was, "So, Donner. Why aren't we supposed to say bad things about kids whose moms and dads don't have as much money as *our* moms and dads have?"

Vampyra was waiting for us in the cloakroom. The moment I saw her I thought: Oh my God. I've walked into a Kafka novel. Because again, I had the strong impression that I had done something wrong and that I was never going to be able to make up for it because she was never going to tell me what it was.

Now I know you all think Vampyra is a really nice woman. Well, not to men she isn't. Despite her standard-issue nursery-school teacher appearance, there was something about the way she flinched at extraneous noise, and something about the wild fear that would flick in her eyes that made me wonder if she hadn't spent the previous night on a stretcher South of Market being whipped.

In the beginning, she, too, refused to look me in the eyes, although in this case there was more nervousness in her behavior than disapproval. It was as if she were afraid of being recognized. Every time she turned to Jesse to ask him a question, she would take a big breath first, as if it were a tremendous effort to do her day job properly after whatever it was she had been up to during the night.

I don't know what was more horrifying—her interrogation or the fact that Jesse understood it. When she asked him if I was his primary caretaker this year, he didn't blink an eye. He just said yes, his mother had become the breadwinner. *Breadwinner.* How old was I when I started using that word? Eighteen? Twenty-five? I was also alarmed by how comfortable he was with a term I had always found clinical—namely, sibling. His sibling's name was Maria, he told Vampyra. She was three years old, the same as Ken's sibling. When I asked him, "Why can't you just say sister?" he said, "Because it's sexist."

He then went on to tell me—with Vampyra's prompting—that from now on I would have to be punctual. Tardy children were only allowed in "at half-hour increments." He actually knew that word—increment. I could hardly have been less shocked than if he had turned around and said to me, By the way, Dad. While you were in the shower last night I joined the Freemasons. Because that's what this school was beginning to look like to me—a secret society in which I was branded as an outsider because I didn't have the right handshake.

Or the right number of chromosomes.

This first intimation that my son belonged to a world I knew nothing about—it was like getting an electric shock. But I had no time to think what it really meant, and again, this set the pattern for the rest of the week.

Because now, after having ignored me completely, Vampyra turned to me and said, "So. Let's get down to brass tacks. Could you please provide me with two crib sheets plus two changes of clothing which you have clearly marked in a plastic bag and two passport-size photographs of the children for their Personal Effects Boxes?"

"Come again?" I said.

She came again.

"Could you please provide me with two crib sheets plus two changes of clothing which you have clearly marked in a plastic bag plus two passport-size photographs of the children for their Personal Effects Boxes?"

I told her I didn't know I was supposed to bring in any of those things. She stared at me as if I had told her I had a mistress and two illegitimate children in rural Thailand.

"But if you had read the fine print in the contract," she said, "you would have known about these requirements."

"I think my wife must have signed the contract because I never saw it."

Now she looked at me as if I had just admitted to buying a Guatemalan baby on the black market.

"But that's terrible!" she yelped. "Because if you are the primary caretaker from now on, there are all sorts of things in there you should have at your fingertips! For one thing, it makes it extremely clear that in order to successfully process your child on the first day of school you must provide all the items I mentioned. I honestly don't know if I can let your children in today, as distressing as that would be for all of us."

"How about if I go home now and bring back all the things you need by lunchtime?"

She looked at me as if I had said, Why don't you throw off all your clothes and do the cancan on the table?

"I'll have to check with Eva on that," she said dubiously, "i.e., our directress. But first let me check the lunchboxes because we want to make sure we're all clear on the other requirements before we disturb her. As you can imagine, we're up to here today." She gave me the kind of crazed smile you'd expect from a Baptist spinster who had just accepted a thimble glass of low-alcohol sherry.

Then she opened Jesse's lunchbox.

She gasped, with the mixture of surprise, pleasure and dismay you would have expected if I had crawled under the table when she wasn't looking and put my tongue into her cunt.

"OOOOOOH," she said. "OOOOOOH. You have some fruit roll-ups in here! That is a no-no! As is white bread, I'm afraid!" Again, her tone of voice was inappropriate. It was as if she were saying, Under normal circumstances I would love to, but I'm afraid I can't because you're not wearing a condom.

And then, when I said, "It may be white bread, but it's good, it's from a French bakery," her eyes bulged as if I had assured her not only was I wearing a condom, but it was ribbed.

"This has never happened before!" she exclaimed. "I don't know what to say. I simply cannot admit them myself if they are carrying inappropriate lunches. I'll have to talk it over with Eva."

She knocked on the door marked "Directress." A pert little voice that seemed horrifyingly familiar to me asked her to enter. She entered. She shut the door behind her. A muffled conversation ensued. It was punctuated by the slamming of a filing cabinet. The door opened. Out staggered Vampyra. She was pale and out of breath.

"I don't know how to tell you this," she said. "But there has been a serious oversight. We can't find Maria's contract."

"Maybe my wife forgot to send it in," I said.

"That may be so, but it puts us all into an impossible position, because no child can be admitted without a signed contract."

"How about if I sign a new one now?"

"I'm afraid you'll have to take that up with Eva yourself."

I headed for the door with Jesse and Maria, but she held me back. "No. The children had better stay with me." She shepherded them back to the far end of the cloakroom. Giving me a significant look, she said, "Don't forget to knock."

As I followed her instructions, I asked myself, Where have I heard that before? *Don't forget to knock*. Then, as I heard the crisp command to enter, I remembered. I had heard that voice every day of my long and miserable childhood.

I opened the door and there she was, a nightmare vision of my sister Jane. The pointed chin, the electrified hair, the glinting eyes, the taunting smile, the way she pushed out her breasts, daring you to look at them so that she could say in front of all her smirking friends, "Why are you staring at my underwear, you little twerp?"

All Eva had to say to me was, "Come sit down," and I was five years old again. Five years old and afraid for my life because Mom was out shopping and Jane and her friends had decided to play house. For which read torture chamber, with me as sacrificial victim. Ball-shriveling memories, many of them buried for thirty years, began to spin about my head as I watched this woman shuffle papers.

I told myself to calm down. This was not my big sister. She was not about to strap me to a table and singe my toenails, or blindfold me or prick the soles of my feet, or make me put on women's underwear and force me to parade in front of all her taunting friends. No. This was the director of my children's nursery school. All she wanted was to get me to sign some papers.

Only to discover that she *was* like Jane. She *was* playing house. I *was* her victim. But she had given up singeing toes and pricking feet. She had learned how to torture her victims with red tape.

She let me watch her shuffle papers for two or three minutes. Then she looked up. "I've processed Jesse," she informed me. "He can join his peers as soon as you correct his lunch. Maria is another question. I'm afraid we don't have anything here for her except the initial deposit."

She passed me a mimeographed form. "This is a warning. The warning system is explained in the contract which I'll give you in a moment. Basically, the warning states that you are tardy with your monthly payment. As the contract explains, you have two days to settle. After that, you will receive another warning. This second warning will state that you have incurred a penalty for late payment. This will give you another two working days to comply. If you do not comply, the child in question is suspended." She smirked at me. "So far so good?"

"Listen," I said. "Money is not the issue here. If you didn't receive payment this was an oversight on the part of my wife. I don't think my daughter should suffer because my wife forgot to do something. Especially since I have my checkbook right here and can pay you whatever we owe you right now. Maria's been so excited about coming here. I don't want to have to take her home like this on her first day of school."

"You say you have your checkbook with you," she said.

Assuming a check would make it possible for Maria to stay for the day, I wrote one out and gave it to this woman.

She wrote me out a receipt.

Then she collected a pile of forms. "I would advise you to read everything I'm giving you carefully," she said. "Most of our problems here stem from parents overlooking the fine print. You'll find, if you do read it, that it spells everything out. Our childcare philosophy. Our nutritional policy. Our parent education and participation program. And so on. You may find you have questions. I would be happy to answer them for you when you come in with the completed forms tomorrow."

"But I *can* leave Maria here today, can't I?"

"I think there might be some chance of letting your daughter join her peers tomorrow."

"Why not today?" I asked. She ignored the question.

"I can see you to process your signed forms at 8:15 tomorrow morning."

"Listen," I said to her. "Let me fill out the forms right now."

"I can probably squeeze you in at 7:55 if 8:15 is no good for you," was her response.

"Listen. I want to get her in now. I can't wait until 8:15 tomorrow."

"In that case," she said, "I'll see you tomorrow at 7:55."

"How about if I can get all the paperwork done this morning? Can she stay this afternoon?"

She shut her diary. "As you'll discover when you've had a chance to read our contract, we do not permit admission after half-past ten."

"But that's like Nazi Germany!" I protested.

She smiled to herself, proudly, as if I had said, But you've managed to keep a spotless house even though you have a full-time job!

"We'll discuss that tomorrow," she said.

Chapter 30

What I wanted to do was to take the lunchboxes, shove them up Vampyra's ass, take both kids and get them out of there. Go to the bank, cancel the check I had just written out to that New Age Nazi, take out all the money, and run.

Unfortunately Becky was standing in the cloakroom. When I started venting my rage on the technically undeserving Vampyra, she intervened.

I remember she was heavily made up, but dressed as if for a bicycle race. Nevertheless, her voice was at its most maternal and condescending. "Let's just calm down here." She turned to me. "What did Eva say about Jesse?"

"Jesse's not the problem. The problem is . . ."

"Did she say Jesse could be admitted today?"

"Yes, she'll let Jesse in so long as I (quote unquote) correct his fucking lunch, but I'll be damned if I . . ."

She held her hand up. "*Silencio.* I said we had to get the story straight. I'm right in thinking that as far as Eva is concerned, Jesse can go in so long as he gets his lunch, right?"

"I don't care what that bitch says."

"Don't be sexist, Dad," said Jesse.

"Let's find out what *Jesse* wants," she interrupted. She knelt down. "Jesse? Do you want to stay in school today? Or do you want to go home with your sister and your dad?"

He looked at us all and burst into tears. "I want to join my peers," he sobbed. "I haven't seen them for the whole summer."

Becky embraced him maternally. "You poor little thing! There really is nothing to cry about, you know!" Looking over Jesse's shoulder with a take-charge look, she asked Vampyra, "Anything at all left in Jesse's lunchbox?" Vampyra opened it up to reveal a carrot and an apple. "*No hay problema* in that case," Becky said. "I gave mine extra." Drawing back from Jesse, she looked him in the eyes and said, "I'll tell you what. When it comes to lunchtime, hon, you ask my kids to share their sandwiches with you, because I made them more than they can eat. OK?"

"OK," he said, and with that Vampyra took him off to the corner next to the window.

Here she examined his hair: I did not realize what for. "Well! That's OK at least!" she said, beaming at us. Then she took Jesse into the classroom.

Maria tried to follow them. When I told her she couldn't go, she began to howl. I can't tell you what that did to me. Again, I think my instincts were right when, with Maria in my arms, I kicked open Eva Braun's door to let her see what her Brave New Creative Learning Center had done to my child. "Is this your idea of an education?" I remember yelling. "To punish a child because her mother is too goddamn lazy to pay her bills? Why are the rest of us supposed to pay because *she* didn't tell me how much we owed or what you people won't permit in a lunchbox? Huh?" I stand by what I said then, although I wish I hadn't said it, because all it did was confirm their suspicions about me being a man. This lost me the argument and allowed Becky to take charge.

She was full of sympathy, which she administered with what she meant to be friendly (and what I took to be emasculating) pats on the back. She was full of advice about how to handle the school, which she referred to as Hitler Youth Camp. She made sure she got through to me by fixing me with long, unblinking stares every time she made an important point. She could understand my predicament, and your predicament, and our collective predicament. "Trying to bring up children these days, it's mission impossible, it really is," she kept saying. Every time she said it, she closed her eyes and shook her head.

Which would have been fine had we been sitting in her kitchen. But we weren't. We were driving down California. Maria and Baby Roo, at least, were strapped up in the back, but my seat belt was defective, and I was sitting in the death seat.

Not only did she forget to look over her shoulder when she backed out of the driveway, thereby missing a minibus by that much, but when she got out on California, she kept straying into the oncoming traffic. She kept forgetting to brake for red lights, but if a light turned yellow when she was practically underneath, she would slam what felt like both her feet on them. Not only did she take her hands off the wheel for the back pattings and hand squeezings, but also to adjust her ponytail and/or unwrap another stick of gum. She ran through red lights at 5 m.p.h., just to make it a little more dangerous. She swore and shook her fist at drivers who looked armed, kept changing her mind about what route to take, forgot when she had left her handbrake on and left her choke out from start to finish. That is why, when she said, "We're all in this together," I did not take it in the way she had intended. I thought: Dear Lord, have mercy. I've been caught by the enemy and the enemy doesn't know how to drive.

It was out of terror that I agreed to understand why the school had to be strict about regulations. I was further compromised by the doubles of everything she lavished on me after she had corralled me into her house. Crib sheets, changes of clothing, toothbrushes, you name it. The very thing I had disapproved of the day before at her party! It was several hours before I got my bearings back. Before I was able to ask myself what had actually happened this morning. Assuming that what Becky had said was right, assuming that this was the way schools had to operate these days, assuming that I had misinterpreted the characters and intentions of the teachers, assuming that this KGB questionnaire I had before me was actually in the best interest of the "whole" child, assuming that you *did* need a more structured and protected environment these days in order to nurture the "whole" child. If I bought all that, then what had gone wrong this morning?

I recalled the argument you and I had had after the ponytail. I recalled in particular the sting in your voice when you told me I would find out for myself how much I needed your help. That was when I saw it.

You had set me up.

You had deliberately arranged things so that I would self-destruct in public.

You were jealous of the bond I had forged with the children, because it left you out.

You wanted to destroy me.

You wanted them back.

Well, I decided. It wasn't going to be so easy.

If the only way to hold on to my kids was to go by the book, that was how I would play it then.

As you may remember, I didn't talk to you at all that night, not even when you tried to say sorry.

Instead, I read and reread every fascist bit of small print in that contract until I knew it by heart. I signed every last permission form. I put up the calendar, and suspended my disbelief. I went through the mess of papers in your files, retrieved Maria's medical certificates. I packed obedient lunches, laid out obedient clothes. I went to bed early. I got up on time and ran through the breakfast routine without a hitch. And at 7:55 the next morning, I was sitting in Eva Braun's office with an abject apology already to my credit. She was running over the basic points of the contract with me again, and cracking the metaphorical whip over me with every sentence. And I submitted to it, priding myself all along at how cleverly I was outwitting her.

Did I realize what I was going to have to pay in the way of penalties if I brought the kids in late again? she asked me. Ouch, yes. Anything you say, Madame X! Fine, then, that was settled, she said, and then she went, crack, did I understand the nutritional program I had undertaken to support? Yes, ouch, yes! And the bake-sale regulations! Yes, ouch, aaagh, aaagh, I can even recite them for you, aaagh, aaagh, ouch! "Fine, then," she continued. "You understand that as a new primary caretaker you will be expected to attend all parent seminars. In addition to which there will, of course, be an orientation night next Tuesday for those primary caretakers such as yourself who will be starting to look at kindergartens for their five-year-olds. I'll explain this in full that night, but since you're new I think I should explain that your child—this is Jesse I'm talking about now, you understand—will be assessed in the upcoming weeks by the school psychologist."

"Listen," I said. "I told you already. I'll agree to anything. And more. I really want to prove to you that I'm sorry about what I said yesterday."

"Fine, then," said Eva. With a pursed smile, she handed me back Maria's medical records. "We'll be able to receive her just as soon as we have the results from her TB test."

"Her what test?"

"Her TB test. As we state very clearly in this medical information sheet," and then she handed it to me, "no child can be allowed on school premises without a TB test. I am already stretching things by letting her into the cloakroom."

"But that's insane," I said.

And she said, "It also happens to be state law."

And so I found myself, for the second day in a row, standing outside the Brave New Creative Learning Center with my sobbing, now doubly traumatized daughter. Once again, I was unable to calm her down. Once again, Becky was lying in wait. But I was damned if I was going to let her risk my life again like she had the day before. I told her I would find my own way to the doctor's office. I grabbed Maria by the hand and walked her off. I hadn't gone two blocks before a Volvo station wagon pulled up alongside me.

It was Charlotte. She was all blond hair and empathy.

"I can't let you walk all the way to Ophelia's. It's too far. Get in. I'll drive you."

"Thanks but no thanks," I told her. But she wouldn't take no for an answer.

When I finally got in, I let her have it. "Why can't you people just leave me alone? I know how to take care of my kids without your help."

"We know that," she said. "We also know you need support." She patted me on the back. "OK, good soldier?"

"Dear Lord, help me," I said, covering my face with my hands. This got interpreted as a breakdown, and earned me more unwanted pats on the back.

"Listen," she said. "Don't be ashamed. We all have our breaking points. I mean, I couldn't count all the breakdowns I've had the past five years on the fingers of both hands."

That's right, I felt like telling her. That's why your kids are so fucked up. But there I was sitting in her car, so instead I said, "I am not having a breakdown."

"Oh pooh," she said. "You can't fool me, my young fellow, so don't even try. I know what horrible stress you're under at home right now." Oh great, I felt like saying. "And I know better than anyone what a taskmaster Eva can be until she thinks you're broken in. So let me help you out a little. OK?" She gave me a Mrs. Walton smile. "I am going to take you to Ophelia's office. I am then going to go do my chores. Then I'll pick you up in an hour or so, and take you home. And then this afternoon, I'll bring your son home. I know Becky thinks she's going to do this, but frankly you're not the only one who doesn't like her driving."

She then went into a complicated explanation of the car pool arrangements for the rest of the day. It involved after-school art, swimming and gymnastic lessons. Which ones was Jesse attending? I had no idea. "You let me handle it," said Charlotte, reading my mind. "You just sit at home and enjoy your time with Maria. We'll get Jesse back to you in time for supper." She pulled up in front of the doctor's office. Stunned once again into obedience, I got Maria out.

I think back often to that office and the way it looked that day, and I am disturbed by the fact that I saw nothing out of the ordinary. Kiki, Ophelia and Mom responded to the crisis like a team: there were no indications that in real life they were no longer talking to each other.

Of course, Maria was just what they needed. Nothing like a traumatized three-year-old in the care of a distracted and mistrusted father to bring out all their fondest illusions about their caring instincts.

There, to get things started, was Mom. Refusing to stand on ceremony, and being pretty loud about it, too. Coming out from behind the reception desk to embrace poor little Maria. Cooing at her in Spanish, making a big show of bejeweled affection in the waiting room, which was, of course, so child-centered as to not be believed. Oh, what wonderful toys! And wouldn't Maria like to play with them and wouldn't she like Mom to help? How about if Maria helped Mom make a fire station with the blocks? She refused to allow Maria to put a single block where she, Mom, didn't want it. Having achieved the kind of fire station you would expect from a fifty-eight-year-old Cuban woman, she then pulled Maria back into the reception area. Here she set her to drawing. Again, she insisted on holding Maria's arm so that she drew exactly what Mom thought she should draw. When Maria objected, she said, "Don't *joo* be a silly little crybaby." When I tried to get Maria out of her clutches by saying there was no need for Mom to lavish such attention on the girl, Mom just pushed me away, saying, "*Joo* let me do what I know best, OK, mister?"

And now here was Ophelia herself. "I heard what happened," she said to me, revealing that the grapevine had been buzzing. "Don't you worry, though, we'll get working on a rehab right away."

She rang for the nurse, who took Maria off into an examination room. "Now you know how these things work," Ophelia half said, half asked me. She handed me a card. "On, let's see, Friday at about this time, you can check Maria's arm and analyze what you see. Notate it on this card and send it to us. Or if you really want her in school by the beginning of next week, maybe you should bring her by on Friday and I can give you the form Eva needs from you then and there."

"On Friday? Why do I have to wait till Friday? We can't wait till Friday! This is insane!" I shouted.

She put up her hand. "Let me see what I can do." She went into her office and came out again two minutes later. "OK, I've got you clearance. She is going to make an exception just this once. She does make exceptions, you know, if you state your case reasonably." She gave me a look, indicating that she knew everything I had said to everybody we both knew during the past twenty-four hours. "And by the way. Her name is not actually Eva Braun, even though Becky likes to call her that. It's Eva Prout. She runs an A-1 program. You're lucky to have your kids in it."

This was when the nurse stepped in. They consulted in whispers. The nurse looked concerned, the way nurses look concerned in soap operas. Ophelia scratched her nose and said, "Oh dear. Here we go again."

She whispered something to the nurse, who then went into Kiki's office. She went in and closed the door behind her. Soon she came back to confer with Ophelia. Then she led Maria into the reception area, ostensibly to get a sticker that said "I am a great kid." After she had put it on Maria's shirt, the nurse leaned over and whispered something to Mom, who put her hand to her mouth and gasped. "Ay, *pobrecita,*" she murmured.

Now Kiki's door had opened, and Kiki had come out. Did I notice a cloud of stale air coming with him, the smell of socks? Probably not. I was too busy wondering why this man was wearing such a stern expression: you would have thought he had just been informed that our child had five chambers in her heart. He peered down at Maria's head. Turning to Ophelia, he said, "I need better light." He crouched down to Maria's level and said, "Hey, little honey, have you ever seen my fish tank?" Taking her by the hand, he led her into the office. Twenty seconds later, he poked his head out the door and said, "Yup. She sure does."

He was speaking to the nurse, but it was his wife who responded. "Righteo," said Ophelia grimly. She asked me to follow her into her office, sat me down, sat herself down and then, with a heavy sigh, said, "I'm afraid we have another problem."

That is how I found out that Maria had nits.

Ophelia did her professional best to reassure me. It was a worldwide epidemic. It did not imply that Maria was dirty or even that I didn't wash her hair enough. It was, however, a serious problem that required urgent action. Eva Braun was one of the pioneers of the No Nits Policy, which was, Ophelia informed me, the only policy that worked. After I had washed Maria's hair with the prescription shampoo, I was to remove all the dead nits from her hair with a nit comb. As she wrote out the prescription, she told me I would also have to wash all my linens in boiling water and bleach, as well as vacuum all unwashable surfaces.

As Charlotte drove me to the drugstore, I made the mistake of saying that I felt like I was being force-marched into a religious crusade. To my horror, Charlotte nodded. "I know several people who felt like that at the beginning. But it's the only method that works. Also, you don't want to depend on that shampoo too much because it destroys the enzyme balance if you use it more than twice a year. Listen. I'll tell you what. I'll see if I can get you a copy of the latest issue of *World Head Lice News*. It tells you how to implement prophylactic measures that don't harm the enzyme balance, and so far they've worked for me one hundred percent."

Failing to interpret the horror on my face, she continued talking helpful hints. By the time we got home, I felt as numb as if I had been dropped into a vat of cement.

I made lunch with the élan of a robot. It was all I could do to put the dishes into the sink. But I forced myself to keep on going. I ran a bath. I put Maria into it. I applied the shampoo. The shampoo stank. I rinsed the shampoo off. I put Maria in front of *Sesame Street*. I stripped the beds. I scoured the apartment for hair implements, threw them into the sink, doused them with boiling water. I got out the nit comb. I tried to run it through Maria's hair. It was too tangled to receive a comb. I spent the next hour getting the tangles out. Maria was as good as could be expected.

Mister Rogers was just putting his sneakers on when I began to run the nit comb through Maria's hair. He was taking them off when I picked up the phone to tell Ophelia that she had given me a defective nit comb.

She told me I was probably using it the wrong way. The teeth were supposed to run through the hair with the sharp edge going first. I followed her instructions, but I was still not able to remove a single nit.

I called her up again. She told me I could try the Thumbnail Method. She described it to me in confident detail. I followed her instructions to the letter. I found that I was taking five minutes to slide a single nit down a single hair shaft.

I called up Ophelia and told her I was never going to get the nits out. She said she was sorry but she didn't know what else to say. She explained that the nit shampoo was only ninety-seven per cent effective. Nit removal was therefore extremely important. I told her I felt like taking Maria to the barber and cutting all her hair off. She said this was impossible as it was against the law for barbers and hairdressers to cut hair if they detected the presence of nits or head lice.

By the time I got off the phone, we were halfway through the second showing of *Sesame Street*. Maria was tired of sitting still. She started to giggle. I told her to pipe down. She started crying. By the time we had made peace, the light was beginning to fail. As I tried to remove my second nit with my nonexistent thumbnails in inadequate light, I began to ask myself how I had landed in this nightmare.

I got to work on the third nit. As I slid it down the hair shaft, I decided that it had come to this because you had made it come to this. Why were you making it so hard for me to do my job? I decided to call and ask you. I was more indignant than annoyed when Mitchell told me you weren't there. Terrific, I said to myself. As I got to work on the fourth nit, I began to imagine, one by one, the places where you might be. After the sixth nit, I called the office again. This time I got the machine.

By now we were on to the second showing of *Mister Rogers*. I got to work on the seventh nit, but my hands were so shaky that I lost the strand. I picked up another one. The same thing happened. I decided to give my hands a rest. By the time they had recovered, the light had gone altogether. I turned on the overhead. It didn't work. I went to look for a new bulb. There weren't any. I tried to take the one out of the bathroom. I burned my fingers.

This meant that removing the next nit was not just frustrating and time-consuming: it was also painful. I ran my wounded fingers through my daughter's hair: there were hundreds more.

I called up Ophelia again. She said try tweezers. I tried them. They didn't work. I called her up again. She said try olive oil, and then the nit comb. I did, to no avail. I called her up again. She said why didn't I just comb the oil through Maria's hair nonstop for fifteen minutes and then see if I dislodged any. After five minutes, I could see nothing was happening. I turned off the light in the hope that darkness would help me keep my patience.

This was how Becky found me. To understand what happened next, it is important for you to know how bright she looked to me after sitting in darkness for God only knows how long. "Those idiots!" she said when she saw Maria's oily hair and the discarded nit comb. "Didn't they look at this girl's hair before they told you what to do? That Ophelia drives me nuts sometimes. She is all goddamn theory. She has never even seen a nit in real life. And that Charlotte. She is so damned supercilious about her so-called prophylactic methods, when in fact they count for nothing. The fact is, some kids are prone to nits and others aren't. The day she has to pick her kids up from school because of nits . . . I'm being terrible, I know, but between you and me I'll be overjoyed."

She took Maria into the living room and seated her under the spotlight lamp. "I can't tell you how many times I've been through this," she said. I remember she was wearing a suit with a slip for a blouse.

"I'll take this side, and you start on that side, and we'll see who gets to the parting first." She showed me how to do the thumbnail method correctly. We got to work. As her hands flew from strand to strand, she told me her repertoire of nit-nightmare stories. It was while she was telling me about the bomb scare in the drugstore that her hand and my hand accidentally grazed against each other.

I looked up more out of surprise than curiosity. She gave me back the exact same look. We continued working as if nothing had happened. But something had. I don't know what, but I found myself talking about some childhood memory I had from Princeton.

"*You* lived in Princeton? I didn't know *that!*"

It was, I think, when we established that we had both—albeit at different times—lived on Linden Lane that she made a comment about destiny. Or was it parallel lives?

Whatever it was, it made me look up again. She looked up at the same time. There was a moment of awkward silence. Then we went back to Maria's hair. "Do you think your parents knew my father?" She launched into a story about her father and his definition of love, but I was no longer listening to her. I was thinking to myself: My God. Why didn't I ever see it? *She's the one.* And then I thought: What if it's too late to do anything about it? What if I've missed out on my only chance for happiness?

Oh my regret! Why hadn't I seen it before? Five whole years of missed opportunities. Five years and she was drifting away from me!

I forced myself to return my attention to what she was saying. And what she was saying was that she had just about had it with all things Californian. In my unnatural state, I took this to mean that my chances were already used up. She was moving on, this apparition of overlooked potential, this last ticket to fulfillment. She was leaving me.

This thought made me feel as if I were drowning. I think that is why, when she completed work on the left side of Maria's head and joined forces with me on the right side, and her hand grazed against mine for the second time, I grabbed it.

When she blushed, I thought it was because she was feeling the same way I was feeling.

Then she let it drop on Maria's head in such a way as to make me falter.

"What did you do that for?" she hissed. "Huh? What did you do that for?"

"I don't know," I said. I took a step back.

"You don't *know?*" she said. "You don't *know?* What the hell is that supposed to mean?"

"I don't know," I said. "I just thought . . ."

"You just *thought,* did you? You just fucking *thought?* Well, think about this for a while."

And then she slapped me across the face.

Then she said, "I'm sorry, but I had to do that."

"That's all right," I said, even though it wasn't at all.

We continued working.

Chapter 31

You may remember that I was quiet when you got home that evening. You may also remember that I chose to spend a second night on the children's floor.

The next morning I woke up at 6:11 precisely. I had the children fed, dressed and armed with acceptable lunches by 8:03. We took the bus to the Marina, arriving at the school at 8:27. Vampyra was waiting for us in the cloakroom.

I handed her my pile of certificates and forms. I informed her that I had received a special dispensation with regard to the TB test. She nodded to something behind my left shoulder.

She got out a red pen. While she checked through my forms, Maria and I watched Jesse march over to his cubby. Hang up his jacket. Roll up his blanket. Park his lunch. Having accomplished these tasks, he reported to Vampyra. She put her pen down and ran her fingers over his bowed head. This time I knew what she was looking for.

Maria was trembling when it was her turn to be checked. But she passed the test. "Righteo," said Vampyra. "We're ready to roll here." Looking up again at that indefinable something hovering just above my left shoulder, she said, "You are free to go now."

"What?"

"You are free to go now."

"Oh," I said. I was so surprised I forgot to say goodbye to Maria.

It was a sunny day for a change. I sat down on the wall and watched the Volvos and the Peugeots and the BMWs and the space wagons come and go.

First came a man in a suit and in a hurry. He herded his charges into school without registering my presence and then ran out again, glancing at his watch.

Then came a woman in a suit. She had to drag her daughter screaming from the car.

Then came a car-pool robot who dropped her children off at

the curb. She looked like she spent her whole life driving around in circles.

Then came an au pair who was reading a romance in her left hand while she guided two frowning girls with her right.

Two station wagons drew up next to me. Two identicute mothers emerged to greet each other. They had shiny straight blond ponytails, freshly laundered pastel-colored T-shirts with Aran sweaters thrown over their shoulders, and jeans, and teeth that matched their new Reeboks. Together they got their respective three-year-olds out of their car seats. Then one woman took them into the school while the other guarded the infants who were asleep in pristine car seats facing backward in the front seats of both cars.

Like me, these women were doing their most important outside job of the day. Once they had gotten their girls to school on time, they could switch gears and take it slow. One of the identicute mothers had brought a catalogue of children's clothing. As the other woman leafed through it, she kept saying, "And you're sure it's all natural fiber?"

The first woman nodded vigorously. "That was the founding concept," she said. "I know because I know someone who knows the women who started it."

"Oh wow," said her friend. Turning a page in the catalogue, she leaned against a car and set off the burglar alarm. She shrieked. "Oh God. How embarrassing!"

They both put their hands over their ears as a man came out of a nearby apartment house to turn it off. They both giggled as they peered into their respective car windows to check on their sleeping infants.

"Amazing what they can sleep through at this age, isn't it?" said the one in the pink T-shirt.

"It doesn't last, though," said Blue T-shirt. "This sleeping-through-noises syndrome, I mean."

They both smiled at me in a way that indicated they were expecting an answer. So I said, "No, it certainly doesn't."

"Do you have yours in school here?" asked Pink.

"Yes," I said, "both of them."

"Oh wow," said Blue—as if this were an amazing feat. "Oh wow, that's really great."

I lit up a cigarette so that they wouldn't invite me to stand closer to them.

And while I sit there blowing smoke at the women and their Volvos, I imagine . . .

Trey sitting in his newly repainted office, sitting in front of his computer screen which he has moved so that it is framed by the window, framed by the outer edges of a view that had—for so many years—sucked his attention away from his work. Nevermore:

He has before him on the bright green screen a sea of figures, figures only he can understand. Technically, he shouldn't have access to them. Technically, he shouldn't have walked out of Mitchell's house on Sunday with all those discs. But he's sure that Mitchell won't be missing them. After all, Trey had located them under a carpet of dust. That is the one thing Trey won't be able to duplicate—the dust on the discs so that they look like no one has touched them. But so what. He is fifty-four percent positive Mitchell won't notice anything amiss, ninety-five percent positive he'll be able to sneak them back into that study before anyone even notices they're gone. Either he'll drop by the house on a pretext with a prearranged diversion designed to give him sixty seconds of unsupervised time. Or else he'll just wait until they're all out and climb up to the kitchen from the back.

It's all coming together now. Finally he has a project that requires every one of his disparate skills. Even rock climbing, if he has to stage a break-in! Although maybe he should start looking for a new word. Break-in implies a broken law—and Trey has a right to these discs. Unless you are going to be technical. You could almost go so far as to say he was the wronged party. After all, he had been Mitchell's accountant for the tax year in question. And Mitchell had lied to him about his personal investments. And jeopardized Trey's professional reputation by getting him to put his signature to a tax return that was, because of the suppressed information, a hundred and one percent bogus.

Of course Trey had had a hunch all along. His mistake had been to be up-front. He had asked Mitchell point-blank: Are you a Freemason? Dumb question; he ought to have stuck to specific questions about specific claims and expenditures. By exposing his suspicions before acquiring the information to back them up, he had given Mitchell and company a golden opportunity to ruin Trey's burgeoning business.

No doubt about it; he had given Mitchell and Co. a chance to consolidate their interests. It is no accident, thinks Trey, that Mitchell had managed to swindle me, Mike, out of his operations and replace me with Kiki. It all fits into the scheme Trey now thinks he is close to unearthing.

And how neat it all is, too! There he goes again, counting his chickens . . . He returns his attention to the bright green screen. He presses a button. A new set of figures appears before him. He scans it, scratches his neck, gets up from his desk, goes to sit down on his couch, fiddles for a few minutes with his son's Rubik's Cube, looks up at the screen again, tries to determine the message in the pattern. And while he does this, I imagine . . .

The clock radio going off next to Kiki's head. It makes him startle; it is on "buzz," not "music." It is not Kiki's first morning on the office couch, but the experience of waking up here is still new enough so that it takes him a moment to remember why he's here. When he does remember, it's like he stuck his head into a garbage compactor. Ouch! Jesus and Mary! Why, oh why, did he ever think he was going to get off the hook by telling the truth?

He checks the time: 8:50. He is cutting it close. His first choice of the day is, should he get on his feet now, or should he lounge around here on this sofa for a few more minutes luxuriating in the absence of female voices?

Of course he can always count on Filly to make up for lost time during counseling sessions. What's today again? Wednesday? Great, that means two days of peace until the next one. On that happy note . . .

He sits up, looks around, surveys the damage.

The desk will pass. It sure is cluttered, now that Ophelia has decided to make it home for all his family pictures—this leaves little room for the executive puzzle, the silver paperweights, the gold golf ball she got him for Christmas—but what the hell. It's worth it. The fish tank looks sort of weird now that he has had to flush its last two inhabitants down the toilet—must pay a visit to the pet store sometime, and ditto for the liquor store. He can't keep filling the bottles in that cabinet with water, especially not the bourbon bottles. His main problem is the wastepaper basket, which contains the remains of last night's Korean take-out (never again) not to mention beer cans (at least six of them, maybe more).

Not the end of the world, he says to himself, if Filly catches this wastepaper basket looking like this. But better to get it out before she arrives.

So. Here goes. He gets himself standing. He pushes the sofa bed back into its daytime position. He looks at his clock: 8:55. He has five more minutes. Into the kitchen to the coffeemaker. Fill it with water from the dispenser. Find the coffee can behind the urine samples. Make sure it contains coffee! Into the office closet for his clothes. Oh no! Mom has not dropped off the new consignment of socks and underwear! Does this mean that she is opting out of her last remaining personal service? Did Filly talk to her about the things he said about her in counseling? Or has Filly banned men's apparel in her washing machine?

In the meantime . . . what to do about underwear?

He is about to look for those paper things the rep gave him the other day when he remembers . . . saved by the bell, his sports bag. Which smells like shoes, but which contains the items he needs.

And so. On with them. And now, what next? The Bachelor's Shower! Whoopee!

Time to push those urine samples manfully to one side. And then—careful with that pink soap from the dispenser. A little goes a long way. In fact, a little goes too far. Skip over into the bathroom for a roll of paper towels and wouldn't that be the time one of the women in his life would choose to come into the office.

He pauses behind the door and tries to figure out which one it is. He hears noises behind the reception desk. Then the easy-listening station comes on. Then Mom on the phone, complaining about a headache to her only friend. He prances back into the kitchenette with his arms over his head in the style of Prince except with his armpits all soaped up.

By the time he has them rinsed, the floor is practically a swimming pool. But the coffee is ready.

He tiptoes back into his office, locks his door, gets out a fresh pair of pants and a shirt, puts them on, gets his shoes on, checks the closet for something to hide the wastepaper basket in. The best he can do is a dry cleaner's bag. But it doesn't matter. He can still access the back door.

After he has unlocked his own door, he pauses with his load and sniffs, and makes a mental note to turn up the air conditioner.

He turns around. There, smiling at him, is the new, sensationally virile-looking nurse. God, Ophelia went overtime tracking down this one. "Can I help you there?" she asks. She looks like she could help him move a house. While he pauses in front of her, I imagine . . .

Mitchell, standing in *his* office, pausing in a similar pose in front of you.

Chapter 32

You are at the front desk. "Did you find them?"

"Not yet," he says. He picks up a box he has already gone through three times and begins to check the names of each and every disc. But he has begun to lose hope of ever finding those missing tax records.

When the phone rings, he jumps. He watches you pick up the receiver, watches your smile disappear as you listen to the voice on the other end of the line. Who is it? Bruno? If so, what is Bruno saying? More to the point, why has Mitchell let it go so far?

You put the phone down. He doesn't even know if he should ask. He is still thinking it over when who should appear but Becky and the ecumenical baby. "I couldn't find those tax records," she says. "But I did find *this* inside a phone book."

Aagh! Has she found the document in which she signed her life away, which he had hidden in that phone book only this morning? No, it's some old letter from the university-loan people. What a relief.

"I have some good news," Becky tells you. "Maria finally made the grade this morning. She's in."

"Oh," you say. Which in Becky's opinion is just not good enough.

She turns to Mitchell and says, "Some weirdo called Bruno left a message on the machine."

"Oh God, yes, that reminds me!" Mitchell almost screams as he runs into his office.

"Do you have to call him now?"

"I think it would be for the best," he says brightly. "Do you mind?"

"No. I'll just wait out here with Laura until you're ready to show me that space."

"Oh honey," he says. "I don't think I have time to do that for you today. And anyway, don't you think it would be better for you to do this on your own?"

"But I don't know where to start," she says.

"What you do is you go South of Market, and drive up and down, and look for signs, and take down the numbers, and make appointments and go look at these spaces and see if they're right for you—is that so complicated?"

The phone rings. "Bruno on the line for you."

"Right! I'll take it in here!" He slams the door.

"What's with him?" Becky asks you. All she gets in the way of an answer is a weak smile and a shrug. Of which she is supposed to make what?

So this is how you start a business, she says to herself fifteen minutes later as she cruises South of Market. You get some money-making ideas together and see which one gels. OK now, so let's see. Since we're South of Market, let's rule out any idea that involves middle-class kids. Let's go with the graphic design concept or, failing that, the Japanese underwear import-export scheme. What kind of space will she need? How is she supposed to find it cruising around these streets with Baby Roo squealing in the backseat?

She sees a sign for a space that would work for the Japanese underwear idea. But she just can't see herself spending her whole day processing Japanese underwear orders. So she drives around some more until she sees a sign for a larger space with big windows, perfect for the graphic design concept. But does she have the nerve to set up on her own like that? Is she ready to go to the trouble of leaving Baby Roo with a sitter to come down here and hang out in an empty office waiting for work that might never come?

She pulls into a space across from a purple nightclub, and that is when she has her first fantasy.

It is a replay of yesterday's nitpicking incident. But this time, instead of slapping me, she pulls me closer to her, runs her tongue over my lips, and . . .

"Don't be ridiculous!" She jolts her eyes open and returns herself to the purple reality of the nightclub entrance, tries to sober herself up by looking at the drunks. She looks at her watch. Thank God! Time for Baby Roo's DPT.

The ride to Ophelia's office is uneventful, if somewhat faster than usual. It is not until she is circling the block looking for a parking space that she has another erotic interlude. This time I pull her close to me and give her a forceful kiss. Which is fucking ridiculous. Because she has never ever thought of me that way. Why is she having these fantasies? As she finds a place for herself and Baby Roo in the crowded waiting room, she decides she must be having them in order to avoid thinking about her career, her inner contradictions and her dismal life.

This is how she sees it: a third baby fine, a third course of DPTs not fine. She looks at the other women in the waiting room. Ms. Self-sufficient in the corner with her three-week-old *número uno.* Talk to her? She could write the script. Ditto for Ms. Distracted Mother of Two Under Two in the toy corner. That voice she uses, the genuine interest she shows in *Goodnight Moon!* And even worse—Ms. Earth Shoe-who-is-about-to-reach-term, who-gave-up-coffee-six-months-before-conceiving-and-thinks-you-can-determine-the-sex-of-the-child-by-eating-a-surfeit-of-either-lettuce-or-dairy-products. Keep me away from her, Becky thinks.

Ms. Earth Shoe has begun to talk to Baby Roo when Ophelia comes through. Becky is sure that the lookers-on don't appreciate the preferential treatment, but she doesn't give a flying fuck.

Ophelia is acting strange today, too, Becky notices. She has no time for Baby Roo, sends her off as fast as she can with the strange new nurse, then sits down on the edge of the examination bed and looks at Becky as if she is about to break some important news to her. Except that she doesn't.

So Becky says, "I think I should be there when Baby Roo gets her shot."

"Oh yes, right," says Ophelia. Instead of calling the nurse back, she hoists herself up on the examination table and stretches herself out in the manner of an odalisque. She has one foot propped on a stirrup. "I'm having a hard time pulling off my doctor act today."

You can say that again, Becky feels like saying. Instead she listens politely to Ophelia as she tells her the newest hospital-horror story. This one has to do with a drain some underling accidentally drove into an old man's heart. Usually she tells these things deadpan but today she is agitated. She has not drawn the story to a close yet when she reaches into a drawer and pulls out a box of chocolate truffles. She offers the box to Becky, then takes one herself.

"I wonder what people in the waiting room would say if they saw us now," says Ophelia.

"They would say we were acting immature."

"I wish someone had told me how much fun it was. I would have started acting immature a lot sooner."

"Me too. In fact, I would have passed up the ballet years altogether."

"Too late now," says Ophelia, reaching for another truffle.

"Oh, I don't know. I can do what I like now. Nobody can stop me. I'm too big."

"The problem is what to do about it," says Ophelia.

"Maybe the best thing is to take it to the limit," says Becky, and then she brings up the story of the nits and the straying hand. In this telling, she notices, she is a shocked victim, while I become more and more mysterious as she questions my motives.

And Ophelia's reaction is . . . jealousy? She looks at herself—fleetingly—in the mirror over the sink as she lolls on the examination table, licking the chocolate off her fingers, and is relieved to see that she looks only distantly interested. When, in fact, this story hits Ophelia right where it hurts most.

Her first thought is: Why Becky and not Dr. Ophelia Mendoza? After all, hadn't she spent the entire previous afternoon on the phone with me? Hadn't she been kind and understanding and helpful? Yes, she had been, but there had not been a single moment that had contained the slightest hint of a misunderstanding developing. Had she ceased to come across as a sexual being? If so, why? Was it her body? Her body language? The way she talked? Her attitude? Her clothes? The shape and/or age of her breasts?

This has been the worst thing about living with Kiki's confessions: this sudden and total absence of self-image. She has no idea what she looks like to others, no idea even how she wants to look. She feels like an empty train on a circular track. She has no past, because her version of events has been blotted out forever by Kiki's secret life.

How many encounters had he admitted to? How many affairs? He said he didn't want to live that way anymore. He had even agreed with her suggestion that all three of them, in other words, Mom too, take the AIDS test. But in the meantime, how was she supposed to live with these apparitions Kiki had bequeathed her? Where was she supposed to take the questions he hadn't answered? Which nurses? is what she wants to know. Which patients? More to the point, why?

The counselor had told her that at least she was in touch with her feelings again. But she doesn't see how her feelings are helping things at all. She can't even look at Kiki now without being overcome with memories of questionable nurses and friends and patients. It isn't so much jealousy as a virulent form of curiosity. That is the worst thing, she now decides as she doodles on the truffle box, half listening to Becky half tell her about a man who had half made a pass at her. She sees the world through Kiki's eyes now, because her own have been proven wrong.

Here she is with her dear friend Becky, but she is hardly able to talk to her because all she can think is how did Kiki size up Becky? Was Becky more desirable than Ophelia because of her height? Her manner? Her jokes? Her clothing? The mixed signals she might or might not be sending out?

There is a moment when she almost breaks her vow, when she is on the verge of telling Becky the truth. Then she reminds herself. It wouldn't be professional to confide in friends who are also Kiki's patients. On the other hand, how is she supposed to get through this ordeal without discussing it with her friends?

It is almost a betrayal *not* to tell Becky. But say she told Becky this morning here in this examination room, within earshot of the other involved parties, where would she begin? What angle would she take? How would she keep herself from bursting into tears? What would she say to the nurse?

So she keeps the tone light. Before long, Baby Roo is brought back crying, Becky picks her up and leaves, Ophelia is left alone again and suddenly she feels as if she is dying, or will die unless she says something, it doesn't matter how little, about what she's going through. So she calls up Charlotte to tell her about this new counselor. This is a safe choice since Charlotte is the one who originally recommended her.

But Charlotte decides not to answer the phone. She is chairing a brown-bag talk that has turned out to be more of an event than she expected.

The speaker is a highflier Charlotte neither trusts nor likes. They were in grad school together. This woman was ambitious even then. Now, although she has only one publication to her credit, she has managed to get herself a split appointment and a salary even a Nobel Prize winner would lust after.

One thing Charlotte will concede—she *is* a good speaker. Her subject is Lacanian/feminist Juliet Mitchell and without lowering her tone she has been able to make her theories comprehensible to a group that is not exactly on the ball. But they are eager and not afraid to admit to ignorance. Not afraid to say "Um" or "You know" or "I mean" a thousand times as they do so. Not even afraid to pop gum in the speaker's face. Caution! Charlotte tries to catch herself before she goes too far with her little snobberies. At least these semiliterate women in the audience are bringing enthusiasm to what is threatening to become a tired subject. At least they are feminists at the gut level if nowhere else. And the biggest miracle of all, at least they are not all women! There are two men (!) sitting in the back row and, although they are asking obnoxious leading questions, they do, by way of compensation, break up that air of solidarity that can make these lunchtime events so dire.

One thing sticks in her mind as she drives home afterward. Something the speaker said during the question-and-answer period. She said that the war between the sexes had grown more subtle now that men, particularly educated men, could no longer stand up and present themselves as male supremacists. This had prompted some backtalk from the men in the back row, and even Charlotte had privately cheered them. How did Ms. Highflier know what men were really like when you had to live with them? Here she was with her megasalary and her split appointment and her singles life and *she* thought the world was sexist?

Some women didn't realize how easy they had it. That is the thought that keeps returning to her as she pushes her cart through the supermarket, as she puts her groceries away, as she cooks the supper, as she tries to correct the children's manners but can do nothing to stop her husband from staring into the middle distance. As she hunts through the papers Trey had promised to sort out weeks ago for the latest issue of *World Head Lice News.* Why is she the one who is always doing favors for people? Why do the lucky ones spend so much time feeling sorry for themselves?

When she gets to 2238 at 7:00 p.m., dinner isn't even on the table. She finds you sobbing on the leather couch. When she asks you what's wrong, you say, "We can't cooperate anymore. We can't even buy a chicken together without arguing about the sell-by date."

She advises you to go easy on me: I have had a hellish week, she informs you. You do not seem impressed. "What kind of week do you think *I* had?"

The chicken that seems to have caused the argument is in the oven. Charlotte is still reasoning with you—and standing accused of taking my side—when I emerge from the bedroom to put it on the table.

It makes Charlotte sad. To see a man trying so hard to do things right, a man who cares so deeply about every aspect of his children's welfare having to put up with this kind of shoddy treatment from his overcoddled wife. It's so unfair! Can't you just forget whatever problems you're having at work and give your husband the pat on the back he deserves?

Since you are not about to do so, Charlotte is glad when you are called to the phone. This gives her a chance to tell me what a wonderful job I'm doing. She produces the famous copy of the *World Head Lice News.* She sets about instructing me in the art of nit avoidance.

Chapter 33

I remember how clearly Charlotte enunciated her words. She made each important point three times, varying her sentence structure, and supporting her deathly boring claims with theatrical gestures. I can see now that Charlotte was only trying to be helpful. But I can't tell you how humiliating it was to have to sit there while she addressed me in a voice a three-year-old dog would find insulting.

Then, after she left, to have to slave through dinner and dishes without a word of thanks from you. To watch you ignore the children. To listen to you sigh deeply as you stepped into your bath, as you stepped into your nightgown even though it was only nine o'clock, as you pointedly turned off the light. To try and escape into the television screen but to be brought back by your impatient tossing and turning. To try and get into bed and discover a Walkman, a hairbrush, two books and a box of tissues under the covers.

And then, to have you confuse things by seeming to come on to me. Do you have any idea what it was like for me to discover you were sound asleep? I suppose it is impossible. Impossible for a woman to know what it feels like to ejaculate when losing an erection.

I can't tell you how bitter I felt. I had thought we were doing this, at least this, together. Laura, I am telling you. I have never felt so lonely as I did that night. Why bother? I asked myself. I could have been anyone fucking you, anyone at all. I was only useful to you so long as I agreed to clean your house for you and feed your children. I would be visible to you only if I fucked up. Even then you would notice the empty refrigerator and unbrushed hair and unmade beds before you noticed me.

I was expendable. I was in pain. I wanted to end the pain. Most of all I wanted to escape those thoughts. They were so fucking boring. I considered taking a sleeping pill. But it was so late. I would be a zombie the next day. Better to take all fifteen of them and end it.

Then I heard Maria singing.

I found her crouching next to the baby stroller at the foot of her bed.

"Something wonderful is going to happen," she told me. "Jesus is going to have a baby." She cupped her chubby hands around my ear. "Chickens aren't the only ones."

She put her hands on my cheeks and looked me straight in the eye. "It's a secret. But you have to be very quiet."

She picked up Jesus from the stroller to reveal an egg. "I took it from school, from that box where they're hatching them. Isn't it beautiful?" she said.

And it was beautiful, it really was. It was the most beautiful, most improbable, most defiant thing I had ever seen in my life.

No need now to go into the problems the egg affair created for us at school the next day. I knew what I wanted now. School didn't matter. I went through the motions, and allowed the women who had taken charge of my life think they were taming me. I let them drive me wherever they felt like driving me. Didn't notice where, didn't care. I let them talk. I nodded obediently at their moving mouths but did not hear a thing.

I remember that you called at six that night and said you wouldn't be home until late, but for once I didn't care because all that mattered to me now was the time I got to spend alone with Jesse and Maria. I wanted to sit at home and watch them eat their toast upside down. Listen to them tell me about alien statues from outer space and pictures that could move beyond the confines of their frames. So long as we were inside the confines of our apartment, we were safe. Safe, so long as no woman was watching us, to play whatever games we wanted.

They fell asleep happy that night. And I was glad, once they were asleep, that I had the house to myself. I didn't care where you were or who you were fucking. You couldn't hurt me. I had my TV, my books, my music and my private thoughts . . .

And my games.

This is the one I liked the most: I did everything your friends told me to do. But nothing more. I remember that Charlotte had lent me *Children: The Challenge*. I had stayed up all night reading it. I gave it back to her outside school the next morning, and said, "Thanks, that was interesting." That was *all* I said. When Charlotte asked me, "What did you think about Point X or Point Y?" I would say, "They're probably valid under certain circumstances." When Charlotte said, "I'm not so sure," I said, "There are probably two ways of looking at it." She never caught on.

Another game I played: to see just how little I could get away with doing without raising the alarms. How small could I make the cookies for the bake sale? How close could I get to falling asleep at the parent seminar without actually closing my eyes? I made a point of being almost late for Circle every morning. Five seconds, four seconds, two . . . I enjoyed watching Fatso's face.

I deliberately set out to worry them. They would ask me, "Where did you get your new CD player?" I would say, "I don't know if I remember." "But you only got it last week," they would say, and then look at each other, as if to say, Is this guy losing it? I would spin it out for as long as I could and then say, "Oh yes. Now I remember. I got it at blank for blank dollars." I would be correct to the last penny.

I let them organize my schedule for me. I went through the whole kindergarten application nightmare without a single untoward remark. And little by little I became my mask.

Chapter 34

When did they turn on you? What did they say? Whatever they blamed you for, I want you to know I had nothing to do with it. I was too miserable to care.

I don't know if you ever saw the video of the four husbands taking three Princess Leias, two Spider-Men and one ET out for half a city block of safe trick-or-treating. So let me describe it for you:

> First Mitchell walking ahead toward a porch that has a pumpkin on it. Then Mitchell looking up and straight into the camera as Trey the cameraman calls him back. Mitchell coming back. Trey telling him, "Now you hold this and record me leading the group."
>
> Mitchell asking, "Why?"
>
> Trey (still behind the camcorder) saying, "I hope you realize that everything you say will be part of the finished product."
>
> Mitchell saying, "OK, OK, just show me how to hold it," and then holding it upside down. Trey showing him how to hold it correctly.
>
> Trey leading the group of George Lucas and Steven Spielberg characters down the street toward the porch that has the pumpkin on it. Trey leading the characters up the steps, only to be stopped by Mitchell from behind the camcorder. "Wait a minute. That's a designer pumpkin." Shot of designer pumpkin. "This can't be the right address. Let me check the list."
>
> Trey coming down, reaching out for the camcorder, then straightening it out to get a shot of Kiki standing on the corner, gazing absentmindedly into a second- or third-story window while all three Princess Leias chase ET around his legs. Trey, still behind the camcorder, shouting, "Don't let them run into the street!"
>
> Kiki still gazing up at that window. ET and the three Princess Leias running into the frame and then out of it. "Stop them!"

> This is Trey. He gets no reaction. "Oh, for Christ's sake." Now the picture becomes jerky, now it is sideways, now it is upside down. Children's screams. "Could you come and restrain these girls of yours?" Trey says to Mitchell (who is still inspecting Becky's list).
>
> Finally Mitchell says, "Honestly, I don't see the point of all this vigilance. It's not as if Becky's going to let them keep any of the candy anyway."
>
> Pan to me at the top of the porch, next to the designer pumpkin. I am bending over it, using its candle to light up a cigarette.

I can imagine Trey playing back the recording for Charlotte in his study. I can see her standing in the doorway while he keeps up a steady pace on a treadmill set six feet away from the TV. "See what I mean?" Trey is saying.

Charlotte says, "I could tell from his cough he was still smoking, but I didn't realize he was doing it this openly."

"You should see his muscle tone," says Trey. "And his complexion. Not to mention his posture. Or the way he stoops his shoulders when he walks. You'd think he was carrying the world's biggest backpack," he says.

She says, "Oh Lord," and goes up and puts her arm on his shoulder. He cringes, then leans over to turn up the speed of the treadmill.

While, at the Mendozas', Kiki and Ophelia are sitting in the Jacuzzi. The plan is to try again tonight to see if they can make love instead of having the kind of bambam sex she has claimed in counseling she finds so distasteful. The idea is that the Jacuzzi might help relax her. What it is supposed to do for him Kiki doesn't quite know. He's not in any hurry, though, that's for sure. If he shows her the kind of affection she says she wants, the odds against his getting it up are considerable. If, by some miracle, he gets excited, she'll accuse him (in front of the counselor) of attacking her like a jungle beast.

He's glad to have something to criticize her about.

"I'm surprised you didn't notice it," he says to Ophelia. "Seeing as you have daily contact with him. It should have been obvious just by looking at his eyes." He is talking about me. "Which one did you say you were giving him?"

She names a tranquilizer. "Honestly, Filly. There was a scare about that one, when? Two years ago? He may be too far gone for us to help him. What dosage were you giving him?"

"Ten milligrams," she says.

"You must be joking," he says. "Why so high?"

"I don't know," Ophelia says miserably. "I thought you knew about it and agreed with me."

He sinks down into the water and turns up the jet—

While Mitchell follows Becky into what used to be his storeroom and is now her changing room. Sitting down on another box of unfiled correspondence (the very one Trey rifled through while pretending to be looking for the upstairs bathroom), Mitchell stretches his arms and then says, "Mike always had a strong self-destructive streak. So when you ask me did I see this crisis coming, I have to say yes."

He watches Becky step out of her dress. Make the best of it, boy! "Because, you see, Mike has zero money sense. He refuses to see opportunities even when they're staring him in the face."

"He sounds like me," says Becky as she slips into bed. Mitchell chuckles as he follows her. He thinks she's joking, but in fact she is not.

In fact, I am the only fantasy that works tonight—although she conscientiously tries out all the others first. They don't do a thing, not even the one in which she pretends to be an au pair undressing at a bedroom window across the street from a primary school, because one of the fathers waiting outside the school gates assumes a face—my face.

She switches to pretending to be a waitress wearing no panties at an all-weekend card game. Until—again!—I become one of the players.

Desperate now, she scans her memory for a better, more effective fantasy that will allow her to come before her husband gets creative. She pretends to be working in a peep show. She tries not to imagine the men who are watching her, because she doesn't want any of them to have the chance to become me.

She ends up having to pretend to come.

Even then, she can't stop thinking of me. The real me. The one who has all the same faults she does. Why is Mitchell so eager to knock me down? What is it about men that makes them incapable of helping each other?

The hours pass. Soon the clock says five and Ophelia is sitting in traffic on her way home from a false-alarm birth management, asking herself the same question—

While Charlotte sits on the side of her bed, next to a pile of self-help books. She puts on her sneakers, then takes them off, puts on her boots, then takes them off, puts on her running shoes, and stares at them—

While I lie on my living-room couch. I have my earphones on. The sky is beginning to get light.

By six o'clock I had given up hope of the pills working. I was not as desolate as I might have been: I had an appointment with Ophelia that morning. I was planning to ask her for a higher dosage.

So it was just a question of getting through the next few hours. I knew the drill. I could float through it. First: stand up. Brush away the records and earphones and ashtrays. Plunge toward the windows. Use one expansive gesture to open them. Do not fall out, and then use the equal and opposite reaction to swish down the corridor to the children's bedroom. Circle in on the chest of drawers, retrieve clothes, paddle back into the living room, lay the clothes out on the armchairs that remind me of rocks in a shallow sea. And drift with the current into the kitchen.

The first pot of coffee did nothing for me that morning. I was on to my second when the doorbell rang, but I was too tired to be surprised it was Charlotte.

"Get your shoes on," she told me. "We're going for a run."

I told her she might be, but I wasn't.

"I'm not taking no for an answer, actually," she said.

"I have to get the children up in five minutes."

"We'll only be gone half an hour," Charlotte insisted. "Can't *she* stand in for you for once?"

I was too tired to resist her when she pulled me in front of the mirror. "Look at yourself! You have to get out there. You can't just stop exercising because the people you live with don't take your needs seriously."

I told her that first I had to start feeling awake enough to put one foot in front of the other.

And she said, "That's what I mean. If you exercised on a regular basis, I guarantee you, you'd sleep better."

I told her that might be true but that it didn't solve my immediate problem, which was how to get my children to school when I'd gone for two weeks without sleep.

"Listen, I'm here to help." She insisted on staying, which made everything twice as difficult. She didn't think I had used the right socks for Maria. She wanted to know why Jesse blinked so much—did he have defective eyesight? It was like dancing with someone who kept stepping on your feet. "And what do *you* eat for breakfast?" she asked me. I told her nothing much and she made a face. "I'm going to have to get you some new cookbooks."

I couldn't get rid of her. We ended up going to school in her car. Then she force-drove me to Ophelia's office. I had been sitting there at least an hour by the time the nurse came up to me. "Dr. Mendoza is waiting for you in her car."

"In her *car?*"

"Out that door, turn left, and you'll see two spaces marked 'Doctor.' "

She already had the engine running. "We're late," she said. "So don't ask me what's going on until we get there."

She parked outside a building I had always assumed was a bank. She marched me to the back entrance, up an elevator to the fifth floor, and into an office marked "Dr. White, Psychiatrist."

There were two black teenage girls giggling in the waiting room. Ophelia waited until they had left before turning to me to inform me (without looking me in the eyes) that she had been wrong to prescribe me tranquilizers. I was probably addicted. But she assured me that Dr. White, a friend, would help.

It was hard to see how. Hard also to imagine this overweight man in his late forties as her friend.

Fixing me with an unfriendly stare, he said, "I am going to subject you to a list of questions that may appear unrelated." He went on to ask me if I liked the color green, and what I thought about when the word "rodent" came up in conversation, and if I had ever traveled or made a purchase on the spur of the moment.

"You don't seem to understand. I was brought up to do this," I protested.

"How long have you had trouble sleeping?" was his response.

I did my best to describe my pattern.

"You have a mood disorder," he informed me. He prescribed me a course of antidepressants. I was too tired to protest. Ophelia picked the pills up for me. She made sure I took my first one in front of her.

It did the trick all right. I was sound asleep on the couch when the phone rang at six that evening. Where were my kids? I didn't even know. It was all I could do to remember that Charlotte was coming to pick me up. I had no idea why or where she was taking me.

My legs almost buckled while I was waiting on the street corner. They almost buckled again as I was walking into the JCC.

She said, "OK now. We have forty-five minutes. I'll meet you outside the men's room."

I stared at her.

"On the poolside. We're going swimming. Whether you like it or not."

I told her I couldn't. I had not brought my suit.

She tossed me a bag and told me to look inside it. Inside it were my trunks. "I picked them up this morning."

I told her I couldn't use the pool, because I was not a member.

"You are now," she said. She led me to the changing room.

I took one look at the lockers and turned around. Charlotte was lying in wait. "I *thought* you'd try that," she said. "Now for God's sake, you piece of lardy cake, get in there!"

She was waiting for me at the side of the pool. The lanes were marked for speed and all six of them full. "When was the last time you swam?" asked Charlotte.

I told her I couldn't remember.

"Then you had better start out here," she said, pointing at the grandmother lane.

I balked. I chose one of the fast lanes. But at the end of the first lap I was out of breath. I had to rest. A burly swimmer swam into my chest. He informed me that all resting had to take place at the shallow end. And so I tried to do all my resting from then on at the shallow end. But even though I did every time I managed to get there, I could hardly make it back to the deep end. The burly swimmer ran into me again. He rose out of the water like a sea monster. He called the lifeguard, who demoted me to the grandmother lane. Even they were faster.

Charlotte was grotesquely sympathetic at the coffee place afterward. She told me you had to start somewhere. She handed me my membership card and the adult swimming schedule. I told her I didn't know if I was going to come back. "Nonsense!" she said, and then she told me the story of her own swimming success. "Trey, too!" she said. It was while she was describing his amazing progress that I lit up a cigarette.

"Put that out," she said.

I exhaled into her face.

"No," she said. "This will not do. I said put that out. I can't let you kill yourself. I'm going to get you healthy if it's the last thing I do. Listen," she said. "Three months from now, when you've renewed your cardiovascular system, you'll thank me for it.

"Just think how Trey used to be," she continued, "and compare that to the Trey of today."

I did. Then I put out my cigarette.

I decided to demolish her.

Chapter 35

That night I got my old bike out of the storage locker. All it needed was some oil. The next morning I got up at 5:30 and rode to the JCC. The first thing I saw when I walked into the locker room was Poseidon West standing in front of a mirror adjusting his bathing cap. I almost turned around and walked out, but then I decided, fuck it. I wasn't going to let this man intimidate me.

There was a new lifeguard on duty. As I surveyed the pool, trying to decide which lane to use, he stared at me as if he knew which lane his colleague had demoted me to the previous evening. But I was not about to join the little old ladies in the slow lane. Instead I went into the lane marked "medium slow." The only other person in it was a smiling, heavily made up woman about my age who was trying to do the breaststroke without getting her hair wet.

I began with a paddle: I was going for strength, not time or distance. But when Poseidon West emerged from the changing room to do his pre-swim warm-ups at the side of the pool, I switched to the crawl. I went too fast and overtaxed my lungs, but I took care not to act in such a way that would advertise to him or anyone else that I was out of breath.

I kept count of the laps. Twenty was all I could manage that day, but the following morning I did twenty-four. On the bike ride home I had an unprecedented rush of well-being. This more than made up for the wave of fatigue that hit me in the afternoon. By the end of the week I was managing thirty-two laps with only four rest periods. Already that Sunday I felt cheated that I could not make it to the pool for my daily fix.

The object had originally been to build up my strength in private and without sacrificing cigarettes. My plan was to light up one day in front of Charlotte and provoke her into giving me a repeat of that lecture. I would then allow her to coax me into the pool, and get her to time me, and proceed to do a mile in under thirty minutes. And then light up another one, right there in the pool. Unfortunately, I had to revise my plan when halfway through my second week I began to find smoking unpleasant. By the time I had graduated to the medium lane, all I could manage was the token cigarette to keep them thinking I was still smoking.

My companions in the medium lane were pregnant career women and men recovering from operations. It was hard to do the crawl in this lane without bumping into people, so I varied my strokes according to how much space I had. I was up to forty-six laps when Charlotte happened to come in for a swim during the evening session. She stood at the shallow end with a fixed smile and folded arms while I crawled to the deep end and backstroked back.

"Wowee," she said. "You're really coming along, aren't you?"

I told her I was still working up to it.

She assumed a pensive stance. "And how long have you been doing this now?"

I told her.

"And you've been coming how many times a week?"

I told her this, too.

She made a silent calculation. "Well, that's not too bad considering you're still smoking."

I made the mistake of telling her I had cut way down.

"That goes without saying," she replied. "You could not be doing what you're doing if you were. Of course if you gave up altogether the sky would be the limit."

I told her that that was my business.

She agreed vigorously. "The time will come when you make that decision by yourself," she said. "In the meantime, maybe I could give you some correctives to your backstroke."

She hopped into the pool. "You have to arch your back more," she said. "And also pay some attention to your right arm. You're not keeping it straight. Look at how I do it." She went a quarter length down the lane and then walked back to me. "Now let's see *you* try it." I protested. She insisted. When I finally went along with it, I did so halfheartedly and therefore incorrectly. She called me back. "Really watch that arm this time."

To keep myself from throttling her I took her instructions to the limit, annoying the man in the medium-fast lane who was swimming with a floater between his legs. Everyone in the pool heard *him* put *me* down, *me* put *him* down, and Charlotte tell us both not to act like babies. My only comfort was that Poseidon West was not in the pool.

I had no sleep, no sleep at all that night. All I could think was what I could have said to Charlotte. What makes you think you can run my life? or, What makes you think *you* don't bend your arms when you backstroke? or, Why the hell do you think you have all the answers? But by the time I got to the pool the next morning, I had convinced myself that I would achieve nothing by trying to reason with this woman. Action, I thought, not words. Which meant that, from now on, the hell with the backstroke. I wanted speed. I wanted distance. From that point on I confined myself to the crawl. It was only a matter of days before I reached the one-mile mark.

But I didn't stop to celebrate. I immediately set myself new goals. A mile and one eighth. A mile and one quarter. A mile and one third. Every day I strained myself to the limit. Soon I was good enough for the medium-fast lane. And it was here that I hit the mile-and-a-half mark, and set my sights on two miles before Thanksgiving. And as I swam back and forth, daily exceeding even my own expectations, I thought about you, and the ever-increasing ways in which you were abandoning me. Why were you not listening to my cries for help? What had made you so hard? I swam through your life, marking each year of your childhood, remembering the day I met you, trying to locate the turning point. Was it the unheated house in Molivos? Was it when we came back to America? Was it law school? Was it that the pregnancy had come at a bad time? Was it that I had ignored you? But if it was, why were you so insensitive to my problems now that we had changed places, now that you were the one who was ignoring *me?* Why had you belittled me when I pleaded with you to give me more of your time? Why had you left the room when I complained that we never did anything together anymore? Why—when you knew what they were like—had you abandoned me to your friends?

Outside the pool, their initiatives were continuing. They were still doing all my driving for me. They were still organizing every detail of my schedule. They even took responsibility for the weekends, arranging play dates of which they only saw fit to inform me at the last minute. It was like having my own personal public-relations office. Because, as you know, they took it upon themselves to sort out the kindergarten fiasco. *They* were the ones who took Jesse to his second interview—not me. I didn't even hear about it until afterward.

When I did, I was livid. My harsh words didn't faze them. They just told me it was healthy to feel angry. Just work your way through it, Charlotte advised me. That wasn't all she advised me. Hardly a day passed without an interesting new ethnic cookbook, a list of Adult Children of Alcoholics meetings, an article about a sensitive man breaking gender barriers, or a suffocatingly thoughtful little treat—a soap in the shape of a citrus fruit, a barrel of popcorn from Neiman Marcus, a funny article about a bizarre occurrence in South Dakota, a ham from Vermont. When she guessed I was having earthquake worries, she provided a geological survey map to show me that the kindergarten Jesse and the others were supposed to go to was on bedrock. When she figured out that the burned-milk stains you were leaving on the stove were bugging me, she looked into specials for espresso machines. When I did not act on her information, she went so far as to offer to drive me to the store. I said no, it was too much trouble for a luxury, but for all the discussion that ensued it would have taken less effort to go.

I had to argue every point with Ophelia, too. I had to prove to her that the shrink was incompetent. I had to do research on antidepressants to convince her they were not my only option. I still had insomnia. Although she did give me something light to help me, she insisted on monitoring me closely. Had I tried taking a walk, a bath, a hot milky drink at bedtime? Had I considered herbal remedies? Analysis? Short-term, group or family therapy? TA? She lectured me on the dangers of addiction to tranquilizers. It was exhausting, and so was talking Becky out of this business she suddenly wanted to start with me. Because she wouldn't take no for an answer, I had to come up with concrete reasons—why it wasn't the right personality mix, what we could reasonably expect from doing import-export with only one product, why she was naïve about Mitchell's promises about backing.

It was bad enough not to be able to warn her about her husband, bad enough to figure out she didn't know he was using her money, but on top of all that to have her *condescend* to me . . .

Who did she think I was? That was the question that kept me going lap after lap after lap, until the week after Thanksgiving, when I hit the two-mile mark.

I was glad Charlotte was in the pool that Tuesday evening, glad to watch the puzzled look on her face when I walked over to the fast lane, glad to see Poseidon West already in there pounding his way toward the deep end. I had not seen him in weeks. He did not know how far I had come. I waited until he was pounding up to the shallow end. Then I plunged in. I was glad to see him rise out of the water to confront me. I kept on going and did not look back. I did not notice that Charlotte had left the pool. I was glad when I saw her walking down the bleachers—followed by Becky and Ophelia.

They wanted to see me fit? Well, how fit was I now? And had they had anything to do with it? Not a single thing. As I pounded my way through the second mile, I overreached myself and almost had to stop. I kept going by imagining what it was doing to these women to see their favorite pet outsmart them.

I was shocked, therefore, when they began to cheer me. The lifeguard blew his whistle. They whistled back and shouted, "Get there! Get there!" to me. I was mortified to see Poseidon West rise out of the water to look at them. I was short of two miles but no way was I going to swim with this kind of attention. I got out of the pool.

"Mike! Mike!" Becky shouted. It killed me to have to look up, but I knew if I didn't everyone would see how embarrassed I was. Horror of horrors, Becky now blew me a kiss. "I knew the mountains would make you well!" she shouted.

I could not help but say, "What?"

"Don't you remember?" she bellowed. "It's a line from *Heidi.*"

The lifeguard blew his whistle again. I moved toward the changing room. "Wait a minute!" Becky jumped over the railing and ran up to embrace me. The other two followed. I extricated myself as fast as I could, but fifteen minutes later I was still hiding in the shower. How was I going to face them outside? What if they made another scene?

When Poseidon West came into the showers, I turned my back to him. But he came right up and tapped me on the shoulder. "Way to go," he said. He gave the thumbs up.

He asked, "Which one's your girlfriend?"

I said, "None of them."

"They sure think *you're* hot stuff," he said.

I discouraged the conversation from going any further. When he said, "Keep up the good work," I pretended to ignore him. But for all my embarrassment his words had their effect. It was the first time it occurred to me that there might be some people in the world who thought of these women as sex objects.

How dare they? I remember looking across the foyer and seeing

Charlotte, Becky and Ophelia leaning against the front desk. I remember they were dressed in tracksuits. And I remember thinking yes, they did look good, all three of them. They were, yes, all three of them, attractive. And yes, perhaps, if I were unattached and had never met them before, I might be attracted to them myself. I might catch a glimpse of them laughing among themselves as they leaned against the front desk, and maybe even do a double take, and maybe even find a place, an unobtrusive place, at the other side of the foyer, and take out a newspaper and check them out more carefully, while pretending to read the sports section. Because that's how men were, always putting the body before the head—and how unfair that was, how crude it was to assume that just because a woman smiled at you she was coming on to you, how wrong it was of Poseidon West to think that just because they were paying me attention that meant they thought I was *hot stuff*. They didn't think I was *hot stuff*. They just wanted me to be . . .

They were glad for me. Glad for me! They had no idea that I had reached the two-mile mark fueled by hateful thoughts. That's why they hugged me and kissed my cheeks. Not because they thought I was *hot stuff*. But because they wanted to let me know they were with me all the way, because they knew how hard I was trying, because they wanted me to . . .

They wanted me to go with them to the café on Sacramento. They all had a lot to do that night. They said they could use some caffeine. They were sure I could use some, too. I saw the bemused look Poseidon West gave me as we headed for the door. One of them had put her arms around me. I can't remember which.

I pretended not to notice Poseidon West when he gave me a knowing wink as he overtook us and said, "Way to go!"

One of the women, I think it was Ophelia, said, "Who's he?"

And I said, "Oh, just some idiot from the pool. Pay no attention to him."

I was mortified when we walked into the café to see him standing at the cash register.

The first thing he did when he got to his table was to open up his sports bag and take out a newspaper. But I watched the slippery way his eyes slid off the sports page and on to the women's unsuspecting backs. God damn it, men were dogs. His eyes went straight to Becky's panty line. They flickered with interest, then took in the larger concept of her legs. Her hair rated another two seconds. Then it was Charlotte's hair, Charlotte's body, Ophelia's ankles, Ophelia's bra strap, and then, as Ophelia turned to look for me, a quick once-over of her chest, and, finding it not full enough, growing bored with the floorshow, returning his full attention to the paper, as I myself had done so many times before.

As if that was all they were there for!

He had found an article that interested him now. He did not even look up, did not even glance after them as they carried their trays to the table. For some reason, his dismissal of them made me even angrier than his roving eyes. What right did he have to rate them that way? What was so special about *him?*

They wouldn't let me pay for my coffee. You can do it next time, they said. This was the easy way it was between them. Why had I never noticed? Why had I thought they were trying to smother me when all they were trying to do was help me out, the way they all helped each other out? I watched Ophelia tear open a sugar packet and pour half the sugar into her cup, half into Becky's. I watched Charlotte reach over and flick an eyelash off Ophelia's cheek. I listened to Becky ask Ophelia if she'd managed to get a full night's sleep for a change and then watched her eyes register sorrow as Ophelia tried to make light of an accident she had passed by on her way back from a birth. A head-on collision on the corner of Geary and Fillmore. Both drivers looked dead but she sent them off in an ambulance anyway, because there was always a chance, she said. And when Charlotte said how awful, Ophelia said it could be worse and then went on to tell about the time when she was working as a locum in England for the summer and had had to go in an ambulance with a corpse that was still twitching. "You don't know how hard it is sometimes to write a death certificate." The other two said they didn't know how she did it and she said the main problem was numbness. "Because, you know, when I got up this morning, was my first thought, What happened to those guys in the accident? No, it wasn't. It was, How am I going to pick up my kid if my office hours run over? I mean, it's a relief to have Mom gone, but the logistics of childcare are almost impossible without her."

Charlotte said, "You should have told me. I could have helped you out."

"You've got to get backup," Becky said.

"Well, in theory, I ought to be able to count on Kiki, although of course, when it comes down to it, there's always something urgent he has got to give priority to."

"The point to remember is that neither of you is used to the daily wear and tear of childcare."

"Well, we will be soon!" she said.

They all laughed, and then Becky said to me, "Just stop us if we're boring you."

And all I could think was what an asshole I was. Here they were, three women who were just barely managing to fulfill their responsibilities, and still they found time to worry about me.

I reviewed their many kindnesses. I reviewed my unkind suspicions and hostile acts. Why hadn't they just given up on me? What had I ever done for them?

I looked at Becky. I thought about her financial problems and those hyperactive girls and that albatross of a house, and I said to myself, who was I to ridicule her for these plans she had for businesses and services and community work? At least she cared.

At least she was trying, I said to myself, and then I looked at Charlotte, and I thought about *her* problems: Trey the millstone, those two disturbed kids, the demanding job, the slowly sinking star of academic glory, and still she managed to accentuate the positive. Who was I to look down on her for sometimes oversimplifying?

And Ophelia—I tried to imagine having to get up in the middle of the night to find a surgeon to do a C-section, having to write a death certificate for a twitching corpse. And, as if that weren't enough, she had to worry about who was going to pick up her kid on Tuesdays, who was going to watch him on Thursday night.

She wasn't going to get the help she deserved, not if I knew Kiki. But instead of telling him to go to hell, here she was discussing how to get around him, some other solution that wouldn't cause so much domestic friction. And her friends were going along with her. They didn't think to question her premise.

It killed me, Laura, it killed me to see how cheerfully they were stretching themselves to the limit while their husbands did fuck-all and all other men judged them and dismissed them solely on the basis of their bodies, and how could I honestly say I was any better, sitting here taking their money from them for coffee so that they could thank me for an accomplishment I had intended as an act of war?

A woman came rushing into the café loaded down with shopping bags. She dropped one and let out a soft curse. Poseidon West looked up, looked through her, looked at his watch, folded up his paper, put it back into his bag, slowly and luxuriantly, as she scurried to pick up the things she had dropped. She joined him at the table with an apology. He said, "Well, I hope at least you didn't spend all our money."

She was too busy rearranging bags to object to his tone. "I got some food, too!" she said apologetically.

He gave her a disparaging look.

Why did women put up with us? I was overcome with self-disgust. By now Charlotte had brought the car-pool graph out. They were discussing how to adjust it to help out Ophelia more now that Mom was gone. I couldn't bear it anymore. "Please," I said. "Please. Let me help too."

Chapter 36

When I say it was a mistake to enter into the babysitting labyrinth, I do not mean to imply that I didn't get anything out of it. I liked seeing how much better the car pool worked after I had redesigned it—and how quickly their children responded to my way of doing things.

They seemed relieved to have rules to follow. I know you will have a hard time believing this, but they didn't even mind watching less TV.

It turned out they preferred adult attention. I can't tell you the games I found in Seb's playroom that had never once been touched by human hands, or how grateful he was when I taught him how to play them. I think that is why he ate for me. And if Lara and Paloma were more careful about other people's property, and would, on occasion, even clean up after themselves, it was because I noticed who had been playing with what and held them accountable.

I did not—I repeat, I did not—set out to present myself as a supernatural being. They thought that up themselves. When they asked me leading questions—if I really wanted to lift a car, could I do it? Which was better, having X-ray eyes or the power to walk through barriers? How old was I when I had first traveled back in time? One day, if they were really, really good, and picked up everything, and ate all their food, could I change myself into a goat?—I was quick to set them straight.

My mistake was not to detect a common thread. So, for example, when I was at Charlotte's one night with all the Stork Club kids except for Baby Roo, and I told them that if they didn't go straight to sleep I would turn them into pumpkins, I thought nothing of it when Jesse turned to Patten and said, "See? I told you he was a demigod." Because by now I had accepted the women's view that children's fantasies were like snowflakes, appearing fully formed out of nowhere, sailing magnificently to the ground and then melting on impact. Today I was a demigod, tomorrow I would be a tooth fairy, the next day I would be a thirty-seven-year-old man who made them say please and thank you and wanted to know why they couldn't draw a house or a car or a ship without making it look like a monster.

You may think it was wrong of me to interfere in their artwork. All I can say is that they liked me having opinions. They drew and painted and made clay figures for *me.* And their mothers, who were perhaps not aware of the extent of my involvement, were happy—and in Charlotte's case, relieved—with the results.

Their refrain was, what was my secret? No one had ever managed to get Seb to eat a vegetable, to get Lara and Paloma to sit at a table without fidgeting, to get Patten to include flowers and smiling faces in his panoramas of hell. The burst of creativity was amazing, they told me. Dottie had even stopped her timid scribblings at the corners of her drawing pad. Now she was scribbling in the center, and this, they informed me, was an important developmental step. The children were also so much easier to handle after an afternoon with me. This, their mothers told me, was partly due to the fact that they *themselves* felt less stressed. They couldn't remember a more relaxed December.

After the kind of treatment I had been getting from you at home, it was gratifying to get some credit. It did not stop there. Because, unlike you, these women actually wanted to talk to me! The feeling was mutual, if for no other reason in the beginning than because I craved adult company after so many hours with children. And not just any adults, but adults who cared as much as I did whether the rash on Maria's cheek was impetigo, if Dottie's shyness was a result of trauma or a subclinical hearing impairment, if Mister Rogers was having an affair.

I remember how surprised I was at myself during those first meals they made for me—the intensity with which I pursued the topics they introduced. What *was* this American phobia about contagion? I remember asking once. Did we perhaps take our obsession too far? Would the day arrive when mothers-to-be would reject all babies that weren't genetically perfect? Was it possible to provide a childhood free of trauma? Did TV make it less or more difficult for four-year-olds to distinguish between fantasy and reality? Why, when we were so intolerant of politicians' sexual proclivities, did we have such different standards when it came to people who did children's TV programs? Where did this new puritanism come from? Did it have anything to do with the American phobia about contagion? These were the conversations that formed the basis of our new intimacy. I came to look forward to them the way I looked forward to swimming.

But the husbands were a problem.

If I were to sum up their response to my budding friendships with their wives, it would be a massive effort to deny that anything had changed. I remember how, when Mitchell walked through the door, he would try to act like it was like old times when I'd drop by to discuss work. He would make some comment about a difficult tenant or an interesting conversation he had had with a redneck client over lunch. Then he'd make some reference to you, and what you were up to, and when to expect you home—this would be followed by some condescending comment about what a hard worker you were. *He* would flop in front of the TV, *I* would keep cutting vegetables for Becky, *he* would ask Becky what she had been up to, *she* would tell him, *he* would say something like, "So I guess you guys spent the day together," and *she* would say, "Well, just about, although I managed to slip off at one point and fit in a few biker bars." He would pretend to find this funny, but I could see it made him nervous.

Kiki had to be grateful for my assistance, because, with Mom gone, they could not have managed without me. When Ophelia invited me for supper, I was the one to do the cooking, but, while Kiki liked eating the meals I made, he did not enjoy eating them in my presence. At first he tried to pass his discomfort on to me. He would play Superdoctor, ask me if I had ever considered going to a doctor specializing in sports medicine before launching into a fitness program. He would quote coronary statistics at me and useless facts about pulse rates and high blood pressure, until one day Ophelia just told him to shut up.

After that he went sullen at the sight of me. As Ophelia and I sat there discussing the issue of the day, he would wander around like a bored teenager looking for a can to kick. This was, however, preferable to Trey, who pretended he just didn't have any time for me. He rarely came out of his study when supper was on the table. He claimed to be too caught up in his work. He would make Charlotte heat it up for him hours later and then pretend to be following our conversation as he ate. If he spoke it was to ask sophomoric questions about Society and the Establishment. Once he even asked me if it had ever occurred to me that life was like a game of chess.

I remember Charlotte's anxious eyes as I paused before answering. I remember that after Trey left us to Return to His Work, she tried to cover for him. "What a card he is sometimes," she said. "It's like looking at someone without any skin." It was clear from her strained smile that she was saying not what she believed but what she wanted to believe and that this was a feat that was becoming more and more difficult.

I remember occasions when his failure to take down messages or remember grocery items stretched her patience to the limit, and she would say, "Men!" while gazing heavenward, or, "Now I am going to sit down and count to ten." I remember also the edge in her voice that day when she and I were getting ready to go off with Becky to look at office furniture, and all Charlotte had to do was get Trey to agree to heat up the supper *I* had cooked while *I* was looking after his kids and *he* was God only knows where. The apologetic way she approached him! The way he dragged his feet! The praise with which she larded her requests! And the way she rolled her eyes for us when his back was turned! "God, what a baby he is!" she said.

It was the first time any of them had been openly contemptuous of their husbands in front of me. Because I didn't stop them, they gradually became more comfortable about sharing what they called their little annoyances. I remember, for example, how comfortable Ophelia was about showing her exasperation on that night when Kiki was going nuts trying to find the channel changer that the new maid had misplaced. And how, on the morning the world stopped because Mitchell couldn't find a pair of matching socks, and Becky went upstairs to help him, she turned to me and said, "Count the number of times I have to say darling to him."

I had no trouble acting complicit. I agreed with them. These men were babies. The time their wives had to waste in order to humor them! There was no doubt that they were coming to prefer me to these useless hunks. I took comfort in this—their attention being an antidote to your continuing coldness. The time arrived when I began to feel more comfortable in their houses than I did in ours.

And yet, the more time I spent in their houses, the more apparent it was that there were areas of their lives about which I knew nothing.

Chapter 37

I remember spending an entire evening going through Becky's kitchen drawers, trying—and failing—to understand the logic behind her classification system. I wondered, for the first time, why she only painted still lifes. Looking at them in chronological order, I saw a worrying progression. I watched the flowers turn into vegetables, the vegetables turn surreal and gradually take on a grotesque third dimension as they doubled over in stunted growth and finally burst out of their frames. Why?

Every object withheld a story. What did it say about Charlotte that she had not once in ten years thrown away a shampoo bottle, that she also collected cookie tins, that, for all the evidence of good taste elsewhere in the house, the only object she had on her mantelpiece was a porcelain corncob with a mouse's head sticking out of it? Why, when there were more than eight wedding pictures hanging on the wall, were they all of Charlotte holding her father's arm?

It was, I think, Charlotte's strange wedding pictures that made me look at Ophelia's walls. And it was, I think, after a counseling session that I first asked her about a picture of herself as a young girl.

She told me it was taken on South Beach not long after her family left Havana. They were living in a hotel. Her mother never got out of bed. Her father worked double time. Even when they moved out to Southwest Miami, he had kept his poor patients. He had died of undiagnosed hepatitis. Her mother was at the movies when it happened.

She pointed to a photo of a parrot. "And that was JoJo. Another of Mom's casualties. She's never forgiven me for it. Although to be fair, I've never forgiven her either."

I waited for an explanation, but instead I got, "To think I let her in here to take over *my* life and try the same trick on *me*. She ruins everything she touches. If I'd stuck it out on my own maybe I wouldn't have lost him."

Lost whom? I didn't dare ask her because now she was crying. I did my best to comfort her. It was the first time I had ever touched her like that, but it didn't seem like I had crossed over a line. It seemed the most natural thing for her to put her head against my chest. What seemed unnatural was the way she jerked it up again when she heard Kiki's key in the lock.

I was haunted that night by the story she had half told me. I think it was to find a different and safer way to satisfy my growing curiosity about these women that prompted me to go through Charlotte's photo albums several days later.

Here I found another fifties childhood, another sixties adolescence, the same props I had used—a comfort to rediscover them. When Charlotte came home that night, we stayed up until all hours talking about the kind of candy we used to eat, and the songs we had sung, and when exactly adolescence had begun and how.

She pointed to a photo of herself at thirteen or fourteen. "That year I was deeply disappointed in any friend who even contemplated wearing pumps or stockings. And then a year later," she flipped the page, "here I am with my Mary Quant hairstyle and my miniskirt. What happened? Was it a record or some article in *Seventeen* or was it hormones?" She leafed ahead. "And then here. Editor of the high school yearbook. My most desperate wish was to be a Girl Friday to a foreign correspondent. And then a year later . . ." She moved ahead to show me a picture of herself in jeans and a red bandanna. "My first mescaline trip. But if you really want to see something amazing, it's this guy here." She got out her high school yearbook, and pointed out a Mr. Ultra Straight. "He went to Harvard. You may have known him. In fact you may remember this article." She took out an old copy of *Psychology Today*. It had an article about campus sex. There was a spread of a muscular naked long-haired man reclining with a blonde, also naked. "Do you recognize him?" I said I didn't. She examined the picture carefully and then said, "The woman was me."

"It *was?*" Before I could get a closer look, she slammed the magazine shut. I tried to get it back from her. She wouldn't let me. It was an embarrassing photo, she said, her stomach stuck out. "Anyway," she said, "it's not the stupidest thing I ever did." She wouldn't tell me what that was, and so I ended up asking Becky and Ophelia.

"Oh, she probably means that time she believed that guy in Harvard Square who told her he was a producer. She actually stripped for him for a so-called audition."

That's what Becky said, but Ophelia said, "No, actually, what she's most ashamed of is the topless bar. Or maybe that belly-dancing class she took? Did she ever work as one?" Ophelia asked Becky.

And Becky said, "Yes, of course, she did."

I don't know what shook me more, the information or the dead-pan tone in which it was delivered. This motherly figure who was standing next to me boiling chick-peas had actually worked as a belly dancer in a Middle Eastern restaurant? Posed nude for magazines? Served drinks topless? How could she read *Sexual Politics* at lunchtime and then spend the evening working in a peep show? And how did she dare to allude to this strange past of hers in such a matter-of-fact voice and within earshot of her children?

Then there were the weird phone messages always waiting for her on her machine, and her alarming stories about students, some of whom came on to her, one of whom she had once almost made it with. None of this fitted in with my picture of these women, and neither did the underwear I found in the middle of Ophelia's den not long afterward.

It just wasn't the type of thing I expected Ophelia to choose, but when I looked in her chest of drawers, I found even more elaborate items. Even a G-string! They had nothing in common with the clothes she wore over them. Another indication that I didn't understand this woman. Another invitation to look further. I tried to fight the urge to look into Becky and Charlotte's underwear drawers. But I could not control myself. For a day or two, all I did was look through bathrooms, closets and forbidding cabinets, until I got my comeuppance under a copy of *My Mother, Myself* in Ophelia's bathroom bookshelf.

It was a dildo shaped like a grotesque orange penis. It gave me a terrible fright. That night I had a dream? fantasy? that you were using it on me. I woke up in a sweat. But then the idea returned to me. I wanted you to use it on me, really use it on me. Why did I want that? What did it say about me?

I don't know if you know what it's like to be battling with the ghost of a dildo and have your spouse wake up and act like nothing is happening. I knew I had to talk to someone. But when I was with Becky the next morning, I was at a loss as to how to broach the subject. I asked her first what she thought of those self-help books. She gave the reasonable, middle-of-the-road, effete answer. And so then I asked her if she thought Ophelia was upset about something. And Becky said well of course she's in counseling and that's always upsetting. What did she think their problem was? I asked Becky. And Becky said, "Well, she's been cagey about it. Which is her way. But it's clear they've always had problems and it's hard to tell if he fucks around because of these problems or if whatever he's done is the source of the problems. I think her main problem is she never had a chance to be young. And so she's looking into it now. I'm glad it's not me! Do I want to be young again? Forget it!"

"Sometimes I want to be a woman," I now blurted out. She didn't skip a beat.

"Well, there was a time I wanted to be a man. Then I found out what it was like and decided no way."

She went on to tell me about a brief and distant lesbian affair. She told me not to tell Mitchell, who didn't "know all the details."

"Sometimes I feel so passive," I said to her.

Unfazed, she told me it came with the job of looking after children. "Not that I regret it," she said. She reminded me that Erich Fromm had said that having children was the ultimate sign of maturity. That made me feel better, but the next day when I was back at her house, I couldn't help wanting to take another look at *The Art of Loving*.

Although it was highlighted in strange places, it seemed like the most natural thing to lie on Becky's bed and read it. That was where she found me. "God!" she said as she kicked off her shoes. "It's just like being back in Cambridge."

I had, of course, forgotten she had ever lived in Cambridge. Now all the references flew out at once. The house she had shared with Mitchell. The house she had lived in unofficially with the previous boyfriend. We must have known each other, even sat next to one another at Tommy's Lunch. We established that neither of us had ever seen *The King of Hearts*. "But how about *this* for a blast from the past?" she said, fishing into a box and coming out with an old and familiar album.

It was the most natural thing in the world to be lying together on her bed listening to "We're All Bozos on This Bus."

But when Mitchell walked in, he did not seem to think so. Not that he could put his feelings into words. He, too, pretended it was just like the old days in Cambridge. "Except that my shoes won't be as smelly," he said as he took them off. He flopped onto the bed with a stupid grin on his face. I resented the proprietorial way he set about massaging Becky's feet.

I don't know, looking back, whether it was his attitude to me that changed that day or mine to him. All I know is that I bitterly resented his presence in his own house from that day on.

Even his shaving equipment was offensive to me.

I suppose that is why I started paying more attention to his so-called home office. What was this screenplay on the floor? Who was this Bruno who left weird messages on the machine? What were these final-warning letters from out-of-state banks I had never heard of? Since when did he have shares in a condo complex in Portland? I can see now how Becky might have been annoyed at my questions. But the more cursory her responses, the more alarmed I became.

The big bells went off one afternoon in the Caffè Roma when we were talking about her trust fund. She told me that it was very important for her to have control over it, and that one of the things she respected Mitchell for was that he had never touched it except when they were buying the house.

"You're joking, of course," I could not help saying.

"No, I'm serious," she said. "I mean, I've guaranteed loans and stuff like that, but nothing more."

"Becky! that's a lie and you know it," I said.

"No, honestly, this is an area where we don't have problems. I have sole control over my money."

When we got back to her house, she showed me a document to prove this to me. It was the one Mitchell had gotten her to sign in August. I explained what this made her liable for. She told me I must be mistaken. I advised her to talk to Mitchell about it. After she did, the first thing Mitchell did was get on the phone to me.

"What are you doing to me?" were his first hysterical words. "Do you want to bring the whole house down or what?" He admitted that yes, he was, at least technically speaking, putting one over on Becky, but that he had been breaking his balls to straighten things out, and although the situation was delicate right now, in a matter of weeks he would be on safe ground, and I had to realize his intentions were serious because hadn't he kept up his payments to me? Hadn't he been a good employer to my wife? "Just give me two weeks, or to be on the safe side till Easter. Then you can tell her anything you want."

I hope you can understand now why his words compelled me to ask you what was going on at the office. The fact that you refused to tell me made it that much harder for me to play along with Becky when she called me the next day to tell me that according to Mitchell

I had misread the telltale document. "Don't you think you should take a brush-up course on the law before you look for a new job? Mitchell thought it might be advisable."

I'm sure you can understand now how difficult that was to swallow.

It was at this point that I began to see who really ran the show in this and the other houses, and the lies these men were willing to tell, and the people they were willing to put into danger.

My suspicions were only reinforced by the scene I witnessed at Ophelia's.

I had been babysitting. Ophelia had been at the hospital, Kiki had been due home hours earlier. I was standing at the window watching out for him when both their cars pulled up to the curb. They both got out of their cars to discuss something. Their conference ended with Kiki kicking a garbage can and getting into his car and driving off.

When Ophelia came in, I asked her what was wrong.

She said that if she told me I would probably not believe her. I promised that I would believe her.

She said it was too horrible to even talk about. I said maybe it was important for her to talk about it.

She said no, that if she told me I would never be able to use Kiki as my doctor again. "But how am I going to go on living, with these wounds he's inflicted on me refusing to heal!" She started to cry. "What he did to me is the worst thing any man could do to a woman. The all-time worst!"

Her wailing scared me. There was, I can say this even in retrospect, nothing sexual in the way I undressed her to get her into the shower. After I got her into bed, I told her she was worth a lot more than she thought she was. If Kiki was making her that miserable, she should kick him out.

Before I left, I made her promise to call me first thing in the morning.

Chapter 38

This was the Wednesday after you went away, allegedly to Los Angeles. Where you really were, whether or not the trip had any true business motive, only you know. I remember that, when you called up that next morning, I was in the middle of reading *There's a Monster in My Closet* to Maria. And that's how I felt when I heard the phone—as if there were a monster lurking only one closed door away that would take over my life if I so much as mentioned it by name.

I remember that when I asked you when we could expect you back you snapped at me. "Do you think I'm enjoying this? I'll be home as soon as I can."

I got the same tone from Ophelia when I called up to check on her. "I'm with a patient. I'll call you back when I have a free moment." She didn't call me back, and when I saw her in front of the school that lunchtime, she pretended to be too busy to talk to me.

You may remember that school ended at noon that Thursday—it was their last day before Christmas. Charlotte had wanted to stay late at the office so that she could go to the department Christmas party, and so she had arranged for me to pick up her kids as well as mine. The plan was for me to take them all to her house: Trey was to relieve me at four so that I could do my swim.

When I got to Charlotte's house, I found Becky and her girls waiting outside it. "Listen," she said. "I have to go to Marin. I just spoke to Charlotte and she said it would be fine by her if you had my three this afternoon too."

She smiled. It was the first time she had been at all friendly to me since the disagreement about the document—and maybe this was genuine, maybe she had decided to forget our differences. But because of the way you had treated me on the phone, and because of the way Ophelia had manipulated my sympathies only to discard me a few hours later, I decided that Becky had to be using me, too.

And so I told her that she was free to use me. Everyone else was!

She wasn't to think for a second that I had anything better to do than wait on her, hand and foot.

"Good," she said. "I'll be back at three."

At 3:30 she called to say she would be back at 4:30. At 4:30 she called to say her car radiator wasn't working. "Do you think Trey could keep the girls for the night?" I told her that Trey had not made an appearance yet. "Well, maybe he's in traffic."

At 5:00, there was still no Trey. I tried Charlotte's office: no answer. At 5:30 the doorbell rang. It was Ophelia, all dressed up, with Seb, in pajamas. "You're supposed to be Trey," she said.

"Well, fortunately, I'm not."

"Do you know when he's due back?"

"I haven't the faintest idea."

"Well, I hope you don't mind if I leave Seb here as planned, because Kiki really wants me to go to this thing with him."

I think I just stared at her.

"Am I to deduce from your silence it's not OK?"

"No, come right in. Walk all over me."

"She *did* say it was OK," Ophelia informed me sternly. "And I *was* led to believe it would be Trey here. Let's keep our perspective."

"Fine," I said. "I'll do that."

"I'm not trying to say I'm not thankful for everything you did for me last night," Ophelia said. "It was very helpful to have a different point of view. But I'm sure I distorted things because I was so upset, and I shouldn't have involved you. That's why I didn't call this morning. Also Kiki and I had a long talk, and I think we've resolved some important issues. It's just a question of having the right attitude, don't you think?"

What about her attitude to me? That's what I wanted to ask her about, but in the end I just nodded.

"I knew you'd understand." Off she went.

The children picked up on my mood. This made them hyperactive: the game of Candyland they had after supper was one of the worst I have ever witnessed. The arguments about cheating became especially vicious after I discovered that Dottie had hidden Ice Cream Float. I made a big stink about it; and then I shouted at them some more while we were cleaning up and a few more of the cards turned out to be missing, too.

When Patten asked me what was the use of being a demigod if I couldn't see through simple household surfaces to find the missing Candyland cards, I blew my top. "What is this fucking shit?" I yelled.

Patten burst into tears. "OK, OK, I'll tell you. But please. Don't zap me."

"Don't zap you with what?" I asked.

"With your special powers," he whimpered.

"I do not have special powers. I am just a man."

"But that's what they all say," Patten wailed.

"That's what WHO all say?" I bellowed. I stepped back into the Christmas tree and accidentally knocked it over. This made me even angrier. "Why?" I said to them. "Why don't people ever secure their trees properly?" Unfortunately I was able to put it back up as easily as I had first knocked it down.

I can see now that this made them only more impressed with my strength.

As for getting the decorations back where they belonged, this was another matter. And the peanut gallery didn't help. The children were upset when I told them it was going to be an earlier than usual bedtime. "Please," they cried. "Don't send us upstairs yet!" Upstairs, they added, "If it comes out of the radiator, would you promise you're going to destroy it even if you're still angry at us?"

"If what comes out of the radiator?" I asked.

They said, "The Son of Diadoumenos."

"The *what?*"

I can't tell you how it sickened me to think that the children thought of me as some cartoon version of a demigod, when here I was, sitting in another woman's house doing the babysitting her husband was supposed to be doing, trying to resurrect a tree I had kicked down in a fit of hopeless anger.

Charlotte did not come home when she was supposed to either. By the time I heard the key in the lock, it was long, long past swimming time. I was not in the mood to appreciate her high spirits.

She danced into the room with two colleagues, both of whom were as high as she was. "What's buzzin', cousin?" she asked me. Her companions roared with laughter. "Do you know what?" she told me. "I've been working with these guys for eight years and they never told me they knew all the words from *South Pacific.*" They roared again. I did not. "Aw, come on, cheer up," she said, lurching toward me. "It's Christmas!"

She turned to the other two. "I think this man needs cheering up. I think he needs me to make him a Manhattan. But first . . ." She sailed to the middle of the floor. "You guys are going to have to help me," she said. "I don't know if I know all the words. So. Here goes." She took off a glove and threw it on the floor. " 'Take off my gloves!' " she sang, and then she threw the second glove onto the floor.

" '. . . Take off my overcoat!' " She did the same.

" 'I can't remember, A worse December, To see those icicles fall . . .' "

I couldn't take it anymore. I brought my fist down on the table. "Shut the fuck up!" I yelled.

"It's bad enough," I said to their three frozen faces. "It's bad enough to sit here watching Becky letting Mitchell squander all her money, and Ophelia letting Kiki fuck anyone he feels like and YOU keeping up your own fucking ridiculous charade, it's bad enough to watch you bending over backward to make life easy for Trey when all he fucking wants to do is fuck you over. It's bad enough to have to listen to you guys prepare your own funerals and know that if I make a word of protest it will always rebound on me—that's bad enough. But on top of it all, to have the whole charade be at my expense! Do you know how many hours I have been here today? Do you know the last time I had a free night or, for that matter, a swim?"

Charlotte sat down. "You mean Trey didn't call."

"No, he did not fucking call. And you know why? Because he is a total fuck-off. The way he presses your buttons. And you're supposed to be smart!"

Charlotte stayed seated at the table. Bleary-eyed, she said, "I really am sorry, Mike. Do you mean to tell me that all the kids are here?"

"They sure as hell are."

"Oh Mike, I'm sorry. I had no idea. What can I do to make up for it?"

"Not a fucking thing except maybe leave me alone."

"Is that what you want?"

I said yes, it was. And then, to my surprise, I burst into tears. And while her colleagues try to back out of the house without drawing attention to themselves, while she puts her arms around me and tells me again how sorry she is, I can imagine . . .

* * *

Ophelia sitting alone at the guest-of-honor table at Kiki's car dealer's Christmas party, watching Kiki flirt with the dealer's new fluffette fiancée. All that talk last night. And what has changed? He still can't stand her company. He still goes straight to the cutest, youngest, preferably underage chickhead in the place and does his number on her, and the thing that kills her is, he is enjoying himself. After months of stiff self-help bills, what has changed?

She surveys—without sympathy—the other guests, and the bandleader, who sings first "Chicago," then "New York, New York," and then "I Left My Heart in San Francisco." She can't stand it anymore. He is *making* her act like a hag. She goes into the bathroom (which is *still marked "Ladies"*) and looks at herself and asks herself, how long has she been running off like this, hiding her tears and her disgust?

It doesn't have to be this way.

How many years does she have left?

As she watches herself in the mirror, as she brushes her teeth, I imagine . . .

Becky grabbing for a damp towel as she tries to see through her fogged-up window as she drives onto the Golden Gate Bridge. Her heater is still broken, and her patience is about to snap. San Francisco, when it emerges, is bright, but blurred.

She braces herself for the lecture that is awaiting her at home about how it is too expensive these days to celebrate both Christmas and Hanukkah. And while she does, I imagine . . .

Charlotte, standing in front of a steamed-up bathroom mirror, holding a spring-coil diaphragm she is too drunk to insert. It keeps on bouncing out of her hands, landing on Trey's shaving kit, in the shower stall, on the (thankfully closed) toilet seat. Every time it springs away, she asks, how did this happen?

As I lay in Charlotte's bed, I asked myself the same question. What had happened to turn a compassionate gesture into such frantic groping? Whose idea had it been to come upstairs? Why, after so many years, did I suddenly want this so desperately?

THEREFORE

Chapter 39

The word we liked to use was "natural." Our affair had begun—we both agreed—without either of us willing it. It had continued in spite of serious efforts to bring it to a close. If we kept ending up in bed together, it was probably because this was the only thing we did in the course of a normal day for no other reason than that it gave us pleasure.

If it created such a strong sense of well-being—how could it be bad? It didn't take us long to decide that our affair was necessary.

What was our working goal? I remember Charlotte asking me as she rolled onto her side to trace her finger down my back, carelessly allowing her loose-fitting Chinese robe to slip off her shoulder. What we both wanted was a happy equilibrium. Had either of us been able to achieve it within the bounds of marriage? The answer—given the people involved, the "baggage" we had all brought with us, the resulting deadlocks and aggravating circumstances—was no.

It was only since our affair had begun that she had been able to be a good wife. The role of a wife was just that—a role. It did not serve all her needs. No one person could be everything to any one other person.

However.

We still had our commitments. No matter what we did in private, we had to make sure we didn't hurt the people who depended on us.

Therefore.

Our affair was a good thing so long as it helped us do right by our families.

And so far—well, just look at Trey, she said. For the first time ever, he was thriving! Before, there had always been a part of her that wanted to believe Trey was everything she told him he was. Now, thanks to me, she could see he was basically a fuckup. But, she was stuck with him. Or rather, she had decided his disappointing performance was no basis for divorce. In this day and age it was unacceptable to abandon a husband just because he was not a good breadwinner. Anyone could be a breadwinner. But only Trey could be the children's father. It was therefore a question of accepting him as he was—a liability, a drain on her resources, a social embarrassment, but in other, less easily measured ways, a terrific guy. It was a question of learning how to live with him. The obvious answer was to lie.

If he put his shoes on the right feet, she had to act like he had won the Nobel Peace Prize. If he put them on the wrong feet, she had to switch them when he wasn't looking and still act like he had won the Nobel Peace Prize. If he then forgot to tie his laces and proceeded to trip on them, she had to be there to catch him, and tell him what great progress he was making and assure him that the Nobel Peace Prize was only a baby step away.

Paradoxically!

It had worked. Now that she didn't believe in him, now that she was so good at pretending to believe in him, he was actually working.

And the children! They didn't talk back anymore. They ate the food she cooked for them, even scraped their plates sometimes, sometimes even conducted civilized conversations with her, as well as with each other. This was because she insisted on higher standards now. Because she had higher self-esteem, because of the support and approval she got from me.

She only hoped she was giving me something back.

It didn't take her long to figure out that all she had to do was massage me. And didn't she know how. She would spend half an hour on the backs of my legs, talking all the while in a desultory way about Jacques Lacan the thinker. Then she would roll me over and spend another half an hour on the fronts of my legs and the soles of my feet, while feeding me strange, sometimes even inexplicable tidbits about Jacques Lacan the man. Before pausing to give me half a hand-job, just enough to make me want to suckle her. And after I had fallen sated onto my back, while she was tactfully working her way up my torso, she would ask me if I needed body oil. Wine? Coffee? Chocolate? To which I would say no! No! Just keep doing what you're doing. She would roll me over again and say how tense your upper back is, you poor thing, did you pull a muscle while you were swimming? I would say yes, and she would ask how. I would tell her I wasn't sure, and she would say, "It's stress, it must be. It's tension. This will help." While she kneaded my shoulders and my upper arms, she would say in a gentle but no-nonsense voice, "So. Tell me. What's the state of play at home today?"

I would tell her everything she wanted to hear. I remember lying there with my eyes half closed while she worked my arms and my chest, her hands occasionally straying downward but never for long, always returning just in time to my thighs or my shoulders—while I told her what you had said and how I had felt about it, how late you had come home, how I had handled it, how I had felt guilty at breakfast, worthless at lunch, and angry by supper because of whatever detail it was that day you hadn't picked up on.

"Oh, I don't know," she would say. "I can see Laura's side, too." She would then explain to me what it was like to be finding one's way as a newly independent woman and discuss the importance of respecting new boundaries. She would support her ideas with little stories from the early days of her own career, and suggest, always indirectly, that some good things could happen if I could manage to "let go" and/or "turn away" so that the "drama" could "play itself out."

She had to work harder to get the lowdown on Becky, but little by little she drew the story out of me. She took it with amazing breeziness. The nitpicking episode even made her laugh. "You men," she said. "You think everything is a come-on." Having kneaded out of me a full account of the tensions between me and Mitchell, she suggested that perhaps a little of it was projection on my part? This would be only natural, because Becky was attractive, and I was a man. Perhaps more important, the boundaries were unclear—this type of confusion often provided the spark. That said, she could understand my rage when I figured out how Mitchell was using Becky's money.

But. There was nothing I could do about it. Becky was the only one who could get herself out of that mess. So long as Becky continued in what Charlotte called her child-bride mode, there was no reaching her. The best any of us could do was make it hard for her to lie to herself. In the meantime, she advised me to call Becky up and make peace with her.

I followed her advice—and yes, after so many weeks of Charlotte's graveness, it was a relief to have a few jokes with Becky again. It was a relief to know that these would not lead me, as they always did with Charlotte, into a deep discussion about human nature.

I remember the first time Charlotte drove up to the school gates and saw Becky and me laughing together again. Her smile was grave and approving, her wave, as she declined to join us, was almost maternal. "I'm so glad to see I'm helping to make your life richer," was what she told me later on the phone. And that was the line she continued to hold even when it had to have become clear to her that she had helped to do far more than that.

Occasionally she asked a polite question. Had the ice cream I had shared with Becky been good? Was the movie we had gone to together worth seeing? That article Becky and I had been chuckling over—was the story funny enough to bear repeating? I think there were times, when the three of us were together, when she wondered what the joke was, but her better nature had a horrible way of prevailing. She did not intrude.

Becky, on the other hand, was unashamedly curious. She had noticed a change in Charlotte's behavior. She wanted to know what had caused it, and why Charlotte hadn't told her about it. Didn't Charlotte trust her anymore? Hadn't she, Becky, always told Charlotte everything? What could Becky have done to break this trust? The more I deflected Becky's questions, the more pointed and mischievous they got, and the more they scared me. And this is why, while I enjoyed Becky's company far more than I enjoyed Charlotte's, I found it exhausting. After a few hours of Becky, all I wanted was to collapse on Charlotte's bed and let her take care of me.

I have never felt so safe with a woman as I did with Charlotte during those early months of our involvement. Whatever duplicity or perversity I admitted to, she responded by saying that my behavior seemed to her to be typical of all men. For example, fidelity. How she wished men took it as seriously as women! But the fact was, they didn't. What did she stand to gain by evading the facts?

It got to the point where I thought I could tell her anything, and that is why I told her too much about Ophelia.

As usual, even though I gave her the story in snatches, it did not take her long to put two and two together.

That should have been a tip-off.

Chapter 40

You may have a vague memory of Ophelia calling you one morning from the Creative Learning Center. It was the day of the Valentine party: she had organized it. I was supposed to be helping her. I was late and so she freaked and called you at the office. I don't know if she alarmed you, but she certainly got everyone at the school worried: when I finally turned up, Lara—or was it Paloma?—went into hysterics because she thought I had risen from the dead.

Ophelia's behavior had been strange all winter. Some days she was friendly, others hostile. Sometimes she acted as if a simple greeting were the prelude to rape, other times she would be calling me up to find out if there was anything good on cable, or if I knew a way of cooking pork to make it taste like chicken.

Once she asked me to babysit so that she could go to hear a natural-childbirth expert. She returned after less than an hour, saying (in an unnaturally breathy voice) that she preferred to listen to me. I remember feeling uncomfortable. I left as soon as it was polite. At the door, she offered me the spare room, bristling just slightly when I turned her down. Then, when I was in her office for the physical for my new life insurance—it was either the following day or soon thereafter—she could hardly bring herself to look at me. I asked her what was wrong. She collapsed into giggles, which ended abruptly when she ran her eyes down my form.

I had put myself down as a nonsmoker. In her opinion, I hadn't stopped for long enough to qualify as such. We had a disagreement, which ended with my tearing up the form and leaving. When I walked into Charlotte's house fifteen minutes later, Charlotte had her on the phone.

"No, he's not trying to take advantage of your friendship," Charlotte was saying. "Honestly, Ophelia, it's simply a question of definitions and boundaries."

When she got off the phone, she told me that, although I was technically in the right, I had aggravated the situation by acting confrontational with someone I already knew to be unstable. She urged me to go to Ophelia's and apologize before things got worse.

Ophelia was in tears when I got there. In a surge of shame, I tried to pat her on the back. She told me to get my "mitts" off her. I told her—before realizing the implications of what I was saying—that it was all very well to call it a question of definitions and boundaries, but the fact was, she was being overemotional. Her reaction was, "You've discussed this with *Charlotte?*"

I said yes but so what?

"So *what?*" Ophelia shrieked. "She promised me she wouldn't tell a soul! And then she goes broadcasting it to everyone in sight! What's wrong with her? What's wrong with all of you? Isn't a secret sacred anymore?"

She then made things worse by calling up Charlotte. She was still blasting her when Kiki walked in. "What's the problem?" he asked me. I told him about the life insurance form. "*She* classified you as a *smoker?* What a bitch!" Before I could explain to Kiki that it was already too complicated and better left alone, Ophelia had slammed down the phone and Kiki had said to her, "Babes, you can't be so literal about these forms. I mean you have got to remember that these insurance guys are ripping us *all* off."

"Don't you dare talk to me in that tone of voice," said Ophelia in a disturbing growl.

"I wouldn't have to, hon, if you didn't act so ornery."

"Apologize to me immediately for talking to me in that tone of voice."

Kiki turned to me with outstretched arms. "Do you see what I have to put up with? It's never-ending. But you know what, babes," he said, turning back to his wife, "it takes more than that."

"Apologize to me now," said Ophelia. "Or I'll throw this phone at your head."

"Oh, we're back to phone throwing, are we?" Before I knew it, he had grabbed the phone out of her hand, pushed her into their bedroom, and locked the door. She began to kick and pound on it, screaming that she was going to call the police. Turning to me, he said, "I'm sorry, but it's the only thing that works.

"Listen," he said. "Come by the office tomorrow morning, I'll doctor those forms for you."

"Oh, no you won't," shouted Ophelia through the door.

"Oh, yes I will."

"Oh, no you won't. I already sent them in, so there."

"Jesus fucking Christ," he was saying as I let myself out.

Now I had to go to Charlotte's. She was still upset about the things Ophelia had said to her on the phone. But she had already given "considerable thought" to the best way of handling the incident. She was going to put off talking to Ophelia again until she felt more collected. She advised me to do the same.

But then, a few days later, when I saw Ophelia parked in front of the school clutching her steering wheel as if she were about to expire, I had to go over and make sure she was all right. She said yes, but as she was hyperventilating I didn't believe her. So I asked her to tell me honestly how she was feeling. She said she felt like jamming her head through the windshield or maybe driving through a wall. "But don't worry," she said. "I'll get through it somehow. If not the depression, then the windshield or the wall."

When I told Charlotte about that, she decided to classify it as a call for help. At her suggestion, I asked Ophelia out for lunch to, in Charlotte's words, "talk things out."

I was alarmed when Ophelia turned up looking like a Cuban. She was as agitated as if we were having a secret assignation. She kept tittering, and saying things like, "I guess it's only right to have the man choose the wine." Every time there was a silence, she sighed deeply and looked straight into my eyes. It seemed like a dangerous idea to ask her how she was feeling. I spent the whole lunch struggling to bring the conversation back to neutral topics—only to be chastised by Charlotte afterward.

She told me I was overreacting. Ophelia was exhibiting what she liked to call the sunflower syndrome—an irrational movement in the direction of warmth.

"The *what?*" Becky said when I told her on the phone that evening. As we laughed over Charlotte's terminology, I felt another surge of shame for my disloyalty. But I couldn't help myself. Before long it was not just Charlotte's terminology Becky and I were laughing at, but a lot of her other little habits, too. "Now don't get me wrong," Becky would say, "I love her like my own sister. It's just that she takes things so seriously."

I still felt bad. The boundaries of my conscience had receded, but there was enough of it left to make me wonder why I had allowed myself to drift into the conspiratorial mode with Becky. To make things worse, Charlotte seemed to know I was holding something back from her, because as the weeks passed and I spent more and more time joking around with Becky, Charlotte's sad moments and reproachful smiles multiplied.

On that day of the children's Valentine party, Charlotte seemed particularly low, although she would not tell me why, and that was why I had lingered at her house and made myself late for Ophelia.

You did not know then, but will correctly guess now, that, when you called up Charlotte to tell her that Ophelia was frantically trying to find me, I was lying next to Charlotte in her bed. I remember the calmness of Charlotte's voice as she talked to you, the frantic gestures with which she tried to communicate the urgent message to me. Which Charlotte was the real Charlotte? Which was the real me?

And which was the real Becky? The one who met me at the door of the Creative Learning Center, and said, "Watch out. Dial-a-Mood is totally but totally out of control"? Or the Becky who went up to Ophelia and put her arms around her and said, "You can calm down now, because we'll take care of everything, everything is going to be OK"?

It wasn't as if I were in a position to condemn anyone for hypocrisy. But the demands were beginning to get to me. There were too many roles to keep track of. There was the person I was when I was alone with Charlotte. The person I was with Charlotte when we were together in public pretending to be just friends. There was the person I was alone with Becky, and the person I was with Becky in public when we were pretending that we didn't spend our time alone together badmouthing Charlotte and Ophelia. There was the person I had once been with Ophelia when she could trust me as a confidant, and the person I was to her now that she knew I had discussed her with Charlotte. My confusion on this particular day was augmented by the fact that Ophelia had, in her innocence, arranged for each of the thirty-five children in the school to bring Valentines for every other child. We were talking about more than a thousand Valentines. These she now proposed to distribute all by herself. Naturally, the children got impatient. When she tried to keep them at a distance of ten feet, they turned first restive, then disobedient, then uncontrollable—breaking through the human chain Fatso and Becky and I had created to keep them from the bench where Ophelia was stacking up their Valentine bags. It was like the night of the living dead.

Becky wanted me to go over to her house afterward and cool off with a joint. But because I had promised Charlotte I would go back right after the party I talked Becky into going over to Charlotte's with me. The moment we walked in, I knew I had made a mistake.

Charlotte was still dressed in her Chinese robe. There was a lunch for two on the table. A shooting pain crossed Charlotte's face when she saw Becky.

We had brought all the children with us. They were in a state after that exhilarating nightmare of a party. Charlotte was gracious about having to feed nine more mouths than she had expected. Having made cheese and cress sandwiches for all the little ones, she proceeded to divide the adult food into thirds.

While the children mistreated their sandwiches in the background, Becky filled Charlotte in on Ophelia's mismanagement of the Valentine party. "She was *sooo* bossy," Becky said. "I don't know what's come over her. She needs to be whipped. Those pouting lips! She reminds me of what's her name, in that leather movie about the fascists?" She didn't catch on that neither Charlotte nor I wanted to discuss Ophelia. Our reticence made her all the more indiscreet.

Eventually Becky remembered she had an appointment. Charlotte offered to watch the girls.

"And before you go," Charlotte said. "There's something of Mitchell's that I found in Trey's office that you should probably take back to him. It seems to be mostly records, and I have no idea why it's here. If and when I find out I'll certainly tell you. In the meantime, I thought I should get it back to you."

Becky seemed puzzled, but she agreed to take it. When she left, I asked Charlotte what all that was about, but she said she didn't want to talk about it. "Until I've heard Trey's side of the story. It's something between me and him. But yes, I found it depressing to think he may have been rifling things from my friends' houses." She paused and then added, "I also think she smells a rat."

"Who? Becky?"

Another pained look. "No," she said. "Not Becky. Your wife." It was the first time she had ever referred to you as my wife and I found this shift ominous.

I asked her why she thought you smelled a rat.

She shrugged her shoulders. "It may just have been projected guilt, but the truth is, when she called up looking for you this morning, I resented her tone of voice." She tossed me an anguished look. "What has she done to me that I haven't canceled out a thousand times over every time I touch your body?"

She was talking almost loud enough for the children to hear. I gestured at her to lower her voice. She apologized. "I don't know what's come over me. I seem to be losing my self-control."

That sounded ominous, too. But as I did not want her to know I thought that sounded ominous, I tried to muster a smile. It wasn't good enough.

Throwing me a pained smile, she said, "You find the prospect of my losing control ominous, don't you?"

I must have cringed, because she held out her hand and squeezed my hand. I did not like her doing this in front of the children, but I knew that, if I objected, I would lay myself open either to another hand squeeze or a long, gentle, inescapable interrogation about the source of my embarrassment. It would end, I now told myself, with an unconditional pardon which would make me glad to get away from her but also unbearably guilty, and it was to avoid all that that I made a point of not withdrawing my hand when she squeezed it—but instead allowed it to hang there limply inside hers.

Even that wasn't good enough. Because now she said, with a harsh note in her voice, "Don't worry. I'm not *that* out of control. I am aware of the limits! Although," and here she looked regretfully at our linked hands. "This is probably no way to act in front of the children."

She withdrew her hand and made a big deal about trying not to sigh. As she began to clear the table, she said, "I can tell you prefer things at this distance at the moment, which is fair enough."

At this point an argument flared up among the boys. Because I dealt with it effectively, I laid myself open to regretful praise, which was a lead-in to some free association on her part about role models, Trey's shortcomings in this area, the mystery that was his mind, not to mention his libido, and how sometimes she wondered if they were even living in the same house; how, for example, he hadn't even commented on the condom wrapper I had accidentally left behind me a few days earlier that he had actually stepped on when getting out of bed this morning, "And what does that tell you about our relationship?"

I found that worse than ominous.

"Please don't get me wrong. I'm not even considering changing the boundaries between you and me. It's just that . . . sometimes I feel like *killing* him."

I must have looked terrified, because now she apologized. "I suppose what I'm trying to say is that the subterfuge is taking its toll. So many suppressed needs. So much suppressed hostility. Not to mention the unexpected casualties." She looked me straight in the eyes and said, "I blame myself for Ophelia."

I told her it was hardly her fault.

"Now I've lost her sympathy, I can't help her."

"It works both ways," I said.

"I suppose you're right. I always ask for too little. It's my pattern, isn't it?"

Another dangerous subject. Scared that it might be a lead-in to a request for me to give her what, in all fairness, I owed her, I desperately wanted to distract her with a safer topic. But equally, I didn't want her to know I wanted to change the subject. So I said nothing. This turned out to be a bad tactic, because the next thing she said was, "Sometimes I think I give myself no ground to stand on because I am so busy considering the other person's side of the story. Where does that leave me?"

I decided not to risk a comment.

"For God's sake, relax! I'm not going to bite your head off."

"I didn't say a thing," I said.

"No," she said. "But you thought it. You men! I just don't know about you sometimes. All you think about is power, power, power. Control, control, control. Who has more? Who has less? And you know? The very people you have stripped of power, and I mean the gender I happen to belong to, are the ones you see as omnipotent. But it's all in the mind, OK? I'm *not* powerful. I am as easy as hell to manipulate, and you know it. I don't even control my own kitchen!"

"I'm sorry." I jumped to my feet and grabbed some plates. "I should have been helping you." Pushing me back down into my chair, she said, "Sit down, that's not what I meant. I'm sorry. I'm out of sorts. I probably shouldn't be talking to you when I'm in this mood. You don't deserve it."

"But . . ." I protested.

"For God's sake, stop feeling so *inadequate!*"

I felt as if I had been X-rayed.

"Listen," she said. "I can tell you need some breathing space."

"Don't worry, I'm fine," I gasped.

"Or is it something else you need? How about if I put the kids in front of the video and then we can, you know, go upstairs and relax."

"RELAX?" I could not help but shout. "With the children in the house?"

"Oh, we would hear them coming. It's no big deal but I certainly could manage to . . . but if you don't want to, don't let me . . ." Her voice trailed off.

"No, it's too risky—even though"—I tried to smile—"there is nothing I'd rather be doing."

I could tell she didn't believe me. I felt myself shrinking under her sad, serene gaze. "Well, maybe part of you does, anyway," she said.

"What could I do to make *you* happier?" I asked.

"Go talk to Ophelia and find out what's wrong. Then come back here and let me know."

I almost knocked over a chair in my eagerness to get out. An excuse to leave!

"Or you know what? Instead of coming right back—maybe you should take Becky to that movie you were talking about. You probably need a night off. I'm the first to admit I'm not very good company at the moment."

"But Charlotte, I didn't . . . I mean . . . you need . . ."

"Don't worry about me. I can take care of this end for the time being. Honest."

Chapter 41

When I got to Ophelia's sometime after nine that night, I found her lighting up a pipe. I told her this came as a surprise after her lectures about smoking.

"What I do is my business," was her slurred response.

I asked her if she had been drinking.

She said, "Yes, and while you're up, get me a Grant."

I asked her what her problem was.

She explained she was on call even though she didn't want to be on "fucking call" ever again in her life and was thinking of becoming a beachcomber in Hawaii.

I asked where Kiki was.

She laughed. "You want to know what I think or do you want to know his alibi?"

"I guess what you think."

"Oh, yeah, right. So I'll tell you what I think. I think you've taken this game as far as it can go."

"What game?"

She snorted, took another toke, knocked back the rest of her drink. "You really are the pits, aren't you? What does it take for you to drop your mask?"

"What mask?" I asked.

"God!" she yelled. She knocked her head on the table. "God! You are driving me insane! I mean, do I have to write it on the wall or what? It's bad enough to be putting me through this hell, but then to deny it's even happening!"

"Deny *what* is happening?"

"Our relationship."

"What relationship?"

She gazed heavenward. "See? That's what I mean. See?" She hobbled into the kitchen, took a swig from an open bottle of Scotch.

"Are you sure you should be drinking that if you're on call?" I said.

"That is typical. *Typical!* First you drive me haywire, then you go high and mighty on me."

"Ophelia. I don't know what you're talking about."

I reached out to remove the bottle from her hands.

"You stay away from me. I've had it with you. If you're going to insist on denying what's going on, then you know what? I'm going to start denying it, too."

"Ophelia, you're not making sense. Don't you think you . . ."

"Just shut the fuck up!" she yelled. She picked up the bottle, smashed the neck off, and held it at me.

That was when her bleeper went off.

She didn't answer it.

"Didn't you say you were on call?"

No answer.

"Don't you think you should answer it?"

No answer.

"Better yet, seeing as you're in no shape to do anything but go to bed, don't you think you should get someone else to answer it?"

No answer.

"How about if I try and track down Kiki and . . ."

"Don't you dare breathe the name of my husband, he's not my goddamn keeper—how dare you."

"Ophelia," I said, as she backed me into a corner. "I am beginning to be annoyed."

"*You're* annoyed. What a joke!" She glared at me. "You think you can have things all your way, don't you. You just think it's play, play, play. Is *that* your idea of adulthood? Do you honestly think you can go through life without paying the piper? Well, guess what. You can't. Maybe you can have your way now, maybe you can just take take take without ever offering let alone giving anything in return, but let me tell you. One day, you'll wake up. Hah! And find out that *all your playmates are gone.*"

"I still don't know what you're talking about."

"Then you tell me what a woman is supposed to do these days. Meet you at the door with a bimbo smile and a sign on her panties that says 'My brain is down here'? Is this what feminism has come to? To a society of men so cowed by real women that they refuse to co-operate unless a woman totally degrades herself?"

I took a step backward.

"If this is your idea of a come-on, Ophelia, it is not very funny."

"It is not a come-on! It is an urgent request for you to get the hell out of here!"

She brandished her broken bottle at me. "I am not going to stand for your teasing anymore!" She smashed the bottle against the counter, breaking the rest of the neck off. "I have had it with men! I am switching to women!"

"Just like that, huh?"

"Right. Just like that. I can pick up the phone and call up just about any woman I know and say let's do it, let's explore that option. Let's not waste our time waiting for men who can't get it up anyway."

"You watch what you say," I said.

"So is *that* what your problem is?"

"I am not going to dignify that question with an answer," I said. "I am going to put you to bed, get someone to cover for you because you're in no shape to drive, let alone deliver a baby, and then we'll meet tomorrow when you've calmed down."

I picked up the phone. "Where can I find Kiki?"

"Don't you dare pick up that phone!"

"Will your answering service bleep him?"

She threw the bottle at me. It missed. She came at me, but I was ready with a karate lock. When I had her pinned to the floor, I called up the office, and left a message for Kiki to call home, and, as I did so, Ophelia tried to bite my foot.

I dragged her into her bedroom. "I hate you! I hate you!" she yelled. "Take your hands off me!"

I got her into bed. I told her I was going to wait to talk to Kiki and that then I was going to split.

She looked up at me and said, "You're just afraid of me, aren't you?"

"I am not afraid of you. I am just pissed off."

"You're afraid of my power," she said.

I said, "Don't make me laugh."

"Does this make you laugh? Does it?" she said. She unzipped her jeans and put her hand down them. She began to gyrate. "Is this what you've wanted all along? To watch?"

"Cut it out," I said. "Seb might wake up."

"Or maybe I should call up Becky and have her come over and you can watch us explore that option. Huh? Or maybe you want to see what color pubic hair I have. Maybe you can't leave anything to your imagination. Maybe you can't get hard unless you see me take my pants off and utterly degrade myself."

She took off her jeans. I turned away so as not to look. It was from the far corner of my eye that I saw her reach under her bed. I buried my head in my arms. Now there was a vibrating sound.

I looked, and to my horror, it was what I thought it would be. "Ophelia," I said. "This is not fair. Your husband is going to be calling at any minute. Your child is in the next room."

"And you want it bad," she said. "I can tell from your voice. You want it bad but you can't get it up."

"This isn't fair," I said. "This should be against the law. This is female rape."

"Oh it is, is it? Well then, how about this? I dare you to look at me." I didn't. "I dare you." I did. She was rubbing herself with that horrifying vibrator with one hand and rubbing her breasts with the other. "See?" she said. "I don't need you. I'm doing fine without you. I can't tell you how good I feel. And I can tell you're dying for it. But you know, if you make one move in my direction, I'll call the police and accuse you of rape."

"Like hell you will." She reached for the phone. I lunged over to stop her. At that moment, the phone began to ring. She struggled to answer it. I threw myself on top of her to block her, and after that it was no contest. I gave her what she had convinced me she wanted. I wish I could say that I was in control of my actions but I wasn't. All I felt was anger, all I wanted was to shut her up.

I succeeded: Ophelia was already asleep by the time the phone rang again, so I answered it. It was Kiki. I told him Ophelia was in a state and that I had put her to bed. There was a long pause before he thanked me. I suggested putting someone else on call. He said he would.

"I guess she told you things have been strained lately," he said.

"Well," I said, "I've seen you two at it with my own two eyes."

He said, "Well, thanks for filling in for me. I have my hands full as it is."

His choice of words left me feeling unreal.

I began to pick up my clothes. As I was buttoning my shirt, the phone rang again. It was Becky. "What are you doing *there?*" she asked. "I thought you were sitting at Charlotte's."

I told her it was a long story.

"To do with what?" she asked.

"Oh, some worries she has about Trey's sanity."

"Oh, that's encouraging," said Becky.

"So don't mention to Charlotte that I was here," I said. "In fact—you wouldn't mind pretending you'd been to the movies with me, would you? That's what I told Charlotte I was going to do."

"That sounds highly irregular," she said. "But I suppose I've asked you to do worse?" That was how it all started.

Chapter 42

I was surprised at the ease with which I walked through the breakfast routine the next day. After my first night with Charlotte, I had been afraid that the smallest gesture might give me away. But now I had learned that all I had to do to play my part well was to believe in it. I was a family man, I was wearing my robe and slippers, I was sitting at the table with my wife and children, I was reading the paper. There was nothing more to me than met the eye.

Except . . . I was beginning to miss my cues.

"So tell me again how it happened," you said to me. You were still in your nightdress.

"What?" I had to ask.

"When Charlotte brought out the Telltale Disc."

"I already told you," I said. "Charlotte found it in Trey's office, identified it as Mitchell's, and so gave it back to Becky, and that was that."

"But what would Trey be doing wanting to look at Mitchell's records in the first place?"

"Probably he forgot to give them back after we stopped using him," I said.

"Mitchell thinks he's planning to turn us in to the IRS."

"Well, that's just Mitchell being paranoid. According to Charlotte, these were records from two years ago."

"Then why did she speak to me so coldly?" you asked.

"Who?" I had to ask. "When?"

"On the phone just now. You know, when I called her up to ask her." I nodded, although I had no idea if she meant Becky or Charlotte or even Ophelia. "She is acting so strange. It's as if there was a third person on the line. As if she knew everything I was telling her already. You haven't been talking to her about this, have you?"

"No, of course not," I said, still not sure which friend she meant. On the way to school, one sentence kept coming back to me. "She was the only one I still felt comfortable with." Which one was that?

Becky was waiting for me at the Creative Learning Center. "So what's this about Trey?" she asked.

"Oh," I said, "nothing you didn't already know."

"So why do you think he stole Mitchell's disc?"

"Well, obviously, he has some grudge against him. But you can tell Mitchell from me that if they were records from two years ago like Charlotte said, I can vouch for them."

"So what did Ophelia say to you about it?"

"About what?"

"About putting him away or getting him checked. Wasn't that what you were there talking to her about last night?"

I realized my mistake. "Oh right," I said. "Well, we decided to keep a close eye on him as Charlotte doesn't seem to realize how bad he is."

"How serious *is* it? Is he having paranoid delusions? Was Kiki there too? What did *he* think?" I was just about to make up some lie about what Kiki thought when he himself appeared at my side.

My first worry was that he would ruin my alibi. That was why I asked to talk to him in his car. When Becky called after me, "I'll wait here so we can decide which movie we went to," I had no idea what she was talking about. I gave her an ambiguous wave. Then I was in Kiki's car. And sorry to be there.

Suddenly he seemed very big.

"I guess I should thank you for filling in for me," he said. He gave me a creepy smile. I felt my lower lip begin to tremble.

"Oh," I said. "It was nothing."

"It's all my fault. I should never have left her like that, I mean in that shape. But as you may know, I have a lot on my hands right now." He gave me a knowing look.

"I don't know how much she's told you. But as you have gathered probably from what you've witnessed, we're sort of on the rocks."

"I'm sorry to hear that," I said insincerely.

"Have you ever been to counseling?" he asked.

"No," I said. "Not that kind."

"Well, let me tell you. There are some things people don't say. Some things I have to take care of myself. But the strain is killing me. So sometimes I just have to go outside and, you know? take a walk."

I tried for a nod that might indicate sympathy without a request for more information. Fortunately, at this point Becky beckoned for me. I said I had to go.

"OK," he said. "But in the meantime. Listen. I owe you one."

"Right!" I said. Squeaked.

"One of these nights maybe you and I should go out for a beer or something."

"That sounds great," I said.

"So it's that bad, is it?" Becky said after he had driven off.

"What?"

"You know, Trey. So how bad is it? Are they thinking of committing him?"

I shrugged my shoulders. "I guess we'll know by tomorrow." Wouldn't Trey find this moment to arrive with his kids. I felt terrible when I thought of the things I had been saying about him, just to provide myself with a cover story.

Becky wanted to talk about it over coffee. But I wasn't up to it; every time I opened my mouth I seemed to incriminate someone. So instead I went home and just sat there. I remember that when the bell rang I considered not answering it. But then stupidly I did.

It was Charlotte.

Just the sight of her made me want to crawl under the bed. "Caught you!" she said. She sat herself down. "So. I hear you had a nice night out."

"Who told you that?" I almost screamed.

"Who do you think?" She put her grocery bag on the table and began to take out lunch. "I *thought* that would turn out to be a movie worth seeing."

My mind ran through the clues. Then I got it. She had talked to Becky, who had said I had gone out to the movies with her, and who when pressed had given a name. So long as I didn't refer to the wrong name, I was OK.

Except . . .

I didn't have the energy to keep the conversation away from forbidden topics. There were so many of them! I told Charlotte I had to lie down. Unfortunately, she read this to mean I needed a massage.

"I can tell you're tense about something. Well, this ought to make it better." Except that with each touch, I felt . . .

"Why don't you let me take the kids this afternoon?" she said. "I have to go to the office but they can come with me."

The idea of her adding another favor to the mountain I already owed her was so terrifying I jumped out of bed and buttoned up my shirt again. I insisted on our going to school together—a move I regretted when I saw Becky and Ophelia sitting together.

Becky looked puzzled. Ophelia looked bruised. Charlotte, sensing tension, tried to introduce what she had to think was a safe topic. Hadn't the children enjoyed that Valentine party yesterday, she said, hoping to please Ophelia, but Ophelia bristled and left our group as soon as her son emerged from school. I thought I was going to die when Becky and Charlotte said she looked like she had been gangbanged.

I died again not long after the kids and I got home, when Ophelia's nurse called to remind me that Maria was expected in for a checkup. I considered asking someone else to take her for me, but just then Mitchell turned up to talk to me about the disc.

I really didn't want to talk to him, so I told him I was on my way to the doctor's office. He gave us a lift. As we drove across town, he shared with me his worries about Trey. I assured Mitchell that Trey was unhinged but that he couldn't do anything to us with the records he had stolen because we had nothing to hide. I don't remember making any date to see him later that day, although it is possible that I did promise to meet him and promptly forgot about it.

Ophelia was nothing but correct during Maria's checkup. She was going to pretend it had never happened! We never had to talk about it ever again!

Now all I had to do was find out what movie I was supposed to have gone to with Becky the night before. When I called her up, she told me which one it was, and suggested that we really go to it tonight. "I'm sure Laura won't mind," said Becky.

"Yes," I said. "But what if she tells Charlotte?"

"Just say you're going to the movies by yourself, for God's sake! Why do you have to make everything so complicated?"

That thought carried me through the evening routine. Becky was right. Things were simpler than I pretended. I was a family man, at home with my kids, supervising their bath while watching the local news on TV. There was nothing more to it than that. But as the evening progressed, I began to remember how bad Ophelia looked, and to wonder if she was OK. So while you were in your shower, I called her. I was alarmed when she didn't answer.

I decided to stop by her house on my way to the movies, just to rid myself of my anxieties. When I saw there were no lights on in her apartment, I flipped. I ran the four blocks to her office. I found her sitting outside it in her car.

Why I was suddenly swamped by affection and tenderness for her, I do not exactly know. I am just reporting the sequence of events as I remember them. When she said, "It's just so hard to watch a marriage crumble," and I replied, "Well, I'll be there for you," I meant it.

When it got too cold to sit outside, and we went into the office and began to grope each other in the dark, and I told her that she was beautiful and I loved her—I meant that too.

I was too swept up to notice how violently my emotions were shifting. It seemed like the most natural thing in the world to be embracing our family doctor, stripping off her clothes, and fucking her on her examination table. Not even the crackling of the paper cover reminded me where I was, or warned me how I would feel about this office next time I tried to enter it as an ordinary patient. I had this idea, as I bit her neck and her ear and rammed into her more violently than I had ever done with any woman in my life, that I was making her strong again, but when her knees buckled on our way out to the car, and she put her arms around me, and gasped, I felt almost proud that I had ended up making her even weaker.

I went into her apartment with her—just to be sure she made it into bed.

This was a mistake.

Chapter 43

I was not up to much—I even had my clothes on—when we heard Kiki's key in the lock. But my shoes were off, and I only had time to find one of them before I had to take cover under the bed.

The first thing Kiki did when he got in was turn the overhead light on. The first thing Ophelia said to him was to turn it off. "Still working on that hangover, huh?" he said as he obliged her. I couldn't quite make out his tone of voice. Mocking? Familiar? Just a little bit affectionate? And I couldn't make out hers. Cold for my benefit? Noncommittal to hide her fear? Triumphant because she had me where she wanted me? A tiny bit petulant?

"I'm tired," she told him as he threw himself onto the bed. "Tired and hungry."

"Well, that makes two of us," he said.

"Call up Mai's," she said. "Let's do take-out."

"Bad idea," he said. "I'm shot. I don't want to move. Let's do pizza. Someplace that delivers."

"OK then. There's that place we have the menu from in the kitchen."

"Bad idea," he said. "I told you. If it involves moving, I'm not doing it. What do I need a menu for? I'll just ask them."

"I'm not having you eat pizza in bed," she said.

"Then you know what, babes? You can take it into the kitchen and eat the whole damn thing yourself. Because me and my cooler have plans here."

I watched his hand pat his cooler, then grope for the channel changer. He turned on the TV. It was when I heard the noise of a basketball game that I knew I was in for a long wait.

If I told you that this was where I first asked myself things like, What did I do to end up here? and, What has my life become? Where did I go wrong? do not think that they were questions strong enough to qualify as pangs of conscience. I was preoccupied by my shoe, which

I couldn't reach without making my presence known. After Ophelia had kicked it under the bed for me, after the strangeness of the eavesdropping had worn off, after I stopped tensing myself for quick action every time Ophelia tried to spirit him out of the bedroom ("I really want to eat this pizza with you *at the table.*" "Didn't you say you were on call tonight?" "Couldn't you drive out for ice cream for me just this *once?")*, after I had run through all the other, more desperate courses of action that were open to me (crawling out and running, crawling out and presenting myself, crawling out and getting shot), what I began to think about was my alibi.

How was I going to explain this absence to you? To Charlotte? And—oh for God's sake, by now she would be waiting for me at the movie house—Becky? I couldn't see my watch. I could only guess what time it was. All I could do was count the commercial breaks and revise my story for each woman accordingly.

It was only when it got to the point that I could not remember what my own cover story was that I began to ask harsher questions. Except that these were offset and interrupted by the bizarre turns that were taking place just above me. Because by now the hang-up calls had begun. Or were they hang-up calls? It was only when Ophelia was out of the room that Kiki would answer the caller. He would answer in a weird combination of Spanish and English, from which I gathered that he did not want to talk to this person, did not think there was anything to discuss, in fact, did not want to meet her anywhere else either, although, if she put it that way, he guessed he would have to.

And so that's how I got out. "Filly," he said. "You're right. I'm on call. Catch you later."

Ophelia told me I didn't have to rush now that he was gone because he wouldn't be back for three hours at least. But I made my apologies. (I now realize, too abruptly.)

I caught Becky just as she was leaving the movie house. "Where were you?" she said.

I made the mistake of saying home.

"I just called your home," she told me reprovingly. "And so did Mitchell. Did you realize you'd agreed to see him at six?"

"Fuck!" I said. "I did?"

"Well, it's too late now, but you know what they say about a stitch in time! Now that you didn't turn up, he's *really* paranoid, so thanks a lot."

"God. I'm sorry. Things have been so crazy lately I don't know when I'm supposed to be where, let alone where I was an hour ago."

"So where were you?"

"Where was I when?"

"Just now."

"I'm sorry but it's a secret."

"Don't be ridiculous."

"No, honestly. It's too complicated."

"Why?"

"Just because."

We went into a café. "Believe me," I said. "If I could tell you I would. In fact, I will tell you someday. If I can."

"What's to stop you from telling me now? Is it about Mitchell? Is it about my money? What is going on? Why am I the only one in the dark?"

At that moment, as if on cue, Kiki walked by with—I did a double take—Mom. Mom was crying. Kiki looked irritated. After they had passed, I could not help laughing, could not help saying this was too bizarre. I suppose it was the strain of not being able to share the joke with anyone, the longing for someone to share my bizarre day with, that made me relent and say to Becky, "OK, I'll tell you what kind of day I've had. In fact, I'll start with yesterday. I guarantee you: you will not believe it."

"Why aren't you laughing?" I asked when I had reached the end of my story.

"Because it's not very funny," she said.

"You've got to admit it's a good story."

"It is one of the most disturbing stories I have ever heard. If you think that running around seducing helpless and impressionable women under the guise of friendship is *funny*, then you are the biggest fucking asshole I have ever met."

"Oh come on," I said. "You can't blame it all on me. They came more than halfway."

"They came more than halfway because you conned them, my dear. It was easy. They were desperate. I call that totally immoral. It offends me on every imaginable level."

"But Becky . . ." I reached out.

"Don't you lay a fucking hand on me."

"But Becky. You wanted to know."

She picked up her handbag and left. I was still sitting there, too shocked even to notice who at the neighboring tables was watching and who was not, when I looked up and saw her standing over me, short of breath and furious.

"If you get to the school and I'm standing outside," she said, "I want you to wait until I'm gone. If I'm at Charlotte's house when you get there, I want you to leave. The same goes for Ophelia's and everywhere else. I don't want to see you. I don't want to hear from you. I don't want your name mentioned in my presence."

"But Becky. How am I going to explain that to the others?"

"I'm sure you'll think of something, as alibis are all you care about."

On the way home, I stopped to sit on a bench. I couldn't bear the thought of facing you: I knew I was going to have to make up some story, but after what Becky had just said to me I didn't have the heart to lie to you.

You may remember that I was worried unnecessarily: when I got home you were giving Jesse a sponge bath. He had come down with a fever while I was out. And as soon as we got him settled, it was Maria up with her cough. I remember that I spent the night on the floor in their room. When I woke up the next morning, I felt as if I had been plunged down a tunnel with no light at the end of it. I had lost my only friend! How could I live without her?

Chapter 44

I don't know if you found out about this, but shortly after you left for work the next day, Mitchell turned up. He was, as you can imagine, the last person I wanted to see. The last thing I wanted to hear was his confession.

Another day, part of me would have been disgusted to hear the risks he had taken. Part of me would have felt vindicated: I had been right to get our money out, right to predict that you would not, even with the best of intentions, be able to handle him.

Another day, I probably would not have laughed when he told me that he had received an anonymous telephone call from someone who sounded like a field auditor. I would probably have tried to point out to him that the IRS only operated like that when they thought their targets were involved in the Mafia.

"But I *am* involved in the Mafia."

Another day, I might have thrown something at him, screamed at him for his stupidity. But by then I didn't care. He might as well have been telling me the plot of *The Maltese Falcon*. It was easy for me to tell him what his only option was—although I must make this clear: when I told him to destroy all incriminating records both at home and at the office, I had no idea how large a job this would be, or that this would mean your having to stay at the office all night.

Laura, I don't know if you have ever been in a situation like the one I am describing. But if you have, you'll know what I mean about air pockets. To go from one part of your secret life to another, you need time to be alone, to be nobody. To sit as still as a statue and gaze blankly out the window and think about nothing. If you don't have that time, then you lose control of your mind, and the people you are lying to start taking over your life. You become the lie you have been telling them. You forget everything about yourself that does not fit in with their idea of you.

That is what happened to me on the night you stayed at the office.

Because you were not there, I did not have the luxury of an air pocket. Ophelia was in the apartment, ostensibly to check Jesse's and Maria's temperatures, when you called to say you weren't coming home. After that, I had no excuse to get her to leave. The children had not been asleep for two seconds before she had whipped her clothes off. I think I still had my earphones on when she sat on me.

The only reason she left was because the doorbell rang. As she went down the service elevator, Charlotte came through the front door.

I can't say I wasn't content to lie there on the couch while Charlotte tried to give me a blow-job. I knew it was a lost cause. Ophelia had worn me out. But I knew that my limpness would only make Charlotte more indulgent. And wasn't I right? She wouldn't even let me change the music. She wouldn't let me pour my own wine. She refused to leave until I was "feeling myself" again. I did feel fine as I kissed her goodbye. But then, after she had gone, the plunge again. Instant darkness. I looked at this couch where I had been serviced by two women in as many hours. Then I thought about the woman I loved.

I reviewed my mistakes with her. How could I have expected Becky to think my treachery was funny? How could she have done anything else except reject me forever? How was I going to live without her? Imagine my surprise when I opened the door not five minutes later to find Becky sobbing in the hallway. She threw herself into my arms. "I'm going to lose my house!"

As I stood there holding her, I couldn't believe it was happening. I thought she was a vision, come to save me. And that's how it was for the rest of the night. It was the strangest sex I have ever had. I had to come inside her to make sure she was there.

When I told her I loved her, I believed myself. When she said she knew, I believed her. As we looked at the dawn, it was clear that we were meant for each other, and that being together forever and ever was simply a case of removing obstacles gracefully.

I told her so. Far from disagreeing, she wrapped her arms around me and sighed. I asked her if she would give me time. In a voice so sweet that I could hardly believe it belonged to Becky, she said yes.

It was only after she left that I began to feel unequal to the promise I had made to her.

I got three calls within ten minutes of plugging the phone back in.

The first was from Charlotte. The second was from Ophelia. The third was from you. Somehow I spoke to Charlotte in such a way as to solicit unconditional sympathy. I spoke to Ophelia in such a way as to provoke that edge in her voice. I spoke to you in such a way as to convince myself that I was just a family man, reporting back the facts to his wife who has been detained at the office.

Then Becky called, just to make sure I was OK. Hearing her voice, all the pleasure of the night together came back to me. Even after I hung up, the mood lingered. Looking out the window at the city spread before me, I tried to keep it alive, but it faded. I knew I had to hear her voice again.

I dialed her number. She picked it up on the first ring. "Telepathy," she said. "I was about to call you. I needed to hear your voice."

"Same here," I said. She laughed. That was when I realized with horror that I had finally made a life for myself. I had everything a man could want. But to keep my privileges I was going to have to live in hell.

Chapter 45

With the coming of the light, I began to notice what a mess the apartment was in. There were the remnants of three different parties—three sets of glasses and ashtrays, three sets of records recalling three different moods—and there were the mementos. Charlotte had forgotten her gradebook, Ophelia her stethoscope . . . I assumed that the pacifiers I kept finding every time I took two steps had arrived and neglected to leave with Becky. I put all these items on the filing cabinet in the entryway. Then I asked myself how I would explain them to you. Then I reminded myself that these women did not come to this house only in the capacity of lovers. There was nothing suspicious in a stethoscope per se or a pacifier or a gradebook. The problem was inside my head.

I was the one who couldn't bear to look at them sitting all together in a row. I was the one who understood what they said, as a group, about me. It was for my own peace of mind that I threw them all into the bottom of the laundry basket, which I then covered up with telltale sheets—along with the bra and the single lacy pink sock that flew up into the air as if out of a volcano when I stripped the bed. Along with . . .

A purple stud. A purple stud with a spider's-web design on it. It caused me a moment of panic as I couldn't remember to whom it belonged. Then I remembered I could always pretend I had never found it, or conveniently forget I had found it until the rightful owner asked me if I had happened to see a purple stud lying around. At which point I would pat my pocket and say, "Oh right, I was meaning to tell you . . . I've been carrying this around for days . . ."

I put the purple stud into my pocket.

I went in to check the children. Their foreheads were moist. Their fevers had broken.

I went into the kitchen to pour myself a cup of coffee. As I did so, I noticed that my hands were shaking. What was making me nervous—the design on the stud? The fact that I couldn't remember who it belonged to? The possibility of there being another stud lying around waiting to incriminate me? This last thought made my hands shake so much that I had to carry my coffee into the bedroom using both hands.

I told myself that it was only a stud. If its twin were still in the bedroom, I would have seen it already on the white carpet. I still had plenty of time to search for it. And even if I didn't find it, I had to remember I was the only one who knew why it was here—aside from the rightful owner, whoever she might be. Having managed to stop my hands from shaking, I decided to take a nice long shower. It was while I was examining my torso in the mirror for love bites that I noticed a home pregnancy test nestled behind your perfume bottles.

It was still in its box, but the cellophane was of a shape that indicated it had come as a twin pack. Where was the other one? Who had used it? If it was you—why? Who had you been sleeping with? When?

It took only this one question to bring all my tormenting fantasies back. Because, even if you had only been sleeping with me, I had no idea when the last time was that we had had sex. I couldn't even remember when the last time was I had checked out your diaphragm case. With a schedule like mine, there was no time to worry about contraception. Which reminded me—did I have any idea, had I taken any interest in, what kind of contraception the others had been using? I realized, as I stood under the shower, that they could all be pregnant.

I remember that, at the exact same moment as I thought this thought, the water in the shower turned cold. I turned it off. I stepped out of the stall . . . to find my two children standing in the doorway beaming at me.

Jesse was holding the test tube stand from the home pregnancy test. "Isn't it wonderful?" he said. "Maria's going to have a baby."

"Cheers!" said Maria, and she picked up the test tube and lifted it to her lips.

I can't tell you how fast I grabbed it from her.

In so doing, I stepped on something sharp.

It was a stud.

A green stud.

As I scream in pain and anger as well as fear, as I send the kids to the kitchen for paper towels, as I kneel down to pick up the test tube and examine the damp spot on the carpet, I imagine that . . .

* * *

Mitchell is sitting at his desk, pretending to go through his drawers and looking up with a strained polite smile to watch you push the vacuum cleaner back and forth across the carpet in the foyer.

"Anything I can do to help?" he shouts.

You don't hear him, so you turn off the vacuum cleaner. "You were saying?" Just looking at your pursed lips is like receiving electric shock therapy.

He says, "Tell me if you want me to take over."

"Actually, I find it soothing," is what you say back.

"OK!" he says, putting up his hand as if to fend off a punch. "Let me know when you need me!"

"Right," you say, in such a way as to indicate that you are not going to lighten up no matter what.

You turn the vacuum cleaner back on. As your gaze returns to the carpet, your expression softens. Huh. He runs his fingers through the contents of his top drawer. Then, when you turn the vacuum cleaner in the direction of the storeroom, he quickly shuts the top drawer and opens the middle drawer, which contains a box of matches, a joint, already rolled, and an ashtray—the kind that eats up smoke.

He glances into the foyer. You are in view again, but your back is turned. He lights the joint, takes a heavy-duty toke all the way in and holds it, slouches down in the chair, and practically French-kisses the ashtray so that it can eat up that smoke.

Next time he is going to remember to stay away from modern offices with windows you can't open.

In the meantime, he thinks, just enough time for one more toke, and that's right, doesn't everything look that much better with the edges taken off.

His desk top, for example. What a switch! Up until a few hours ago he'd had this wild and wonderful collection of postcards and clippings under the glass: the memorabilia from other people's travels in the Third World, off-color photographs and sexist cartoons. Yes, you were right to send them south. No, the IRS would possibly not take kindly to them. Yes, the magnolias you had bought will alter the auditor's first impressions. Ditto for the air fresheners. You've been super resourceful. He ought to feel grateful.

And yet . . . even as he looks at the row of Hefty Bags along the far wall, even as he tells himself that it was always going to come to this and that all things considered he is lucky to have an assistant so determined to clean up his act—an inner voice says it's not so simple. There are things you can't understand because you're a woman, because you became a player too late in the game. There are things you cannot see.

Now that the initial panic is over, now that he is stoned enough to think laterally, it is all coming back to him. He thinks back to his cowboy days when details didn't matter, discipline didn't matter, streamlined schedules didn't matter, when he and I would sit around whole afternoons just thinking up wild ideas and smoking enough to stay mellow.

True, we had had our differences, some of them serious, but deep down there had been an understanding. For example, if it'd been me around when this shit was going down, he could guarantee it that I would have done the following: I would have picked up my briefcase and said, "You asshole, don't expect me to dig you out of this one," and he could have related to that. What he could not relate to, what he had to take another heavy-duty toke before he could even begin to tolerate, were your accusing looks and terse constructive suggestions and the horrible thoroughness of this all-night cleanup operation—it is almost as bad, he tells himself as he takes the smoke to the bottom of his lungs, almost as bad as . . .

The vacuum cleaner turns off. You poke your head in through the door just as he is getting ready to exhale into the middle drawer. He pushes it shut again, and tries to smile without opening his mouth.

"Everything OK?" you say.

He nods, he hopes supportively.

"Are you sure?"

He makes a grunting noise that he hopes is not too gruff.

"When do you think we should dispose of the Hefty Bags?"

Why is it, he asks himself as he shrugs his shoulders, he hopes pleasantly, that the main point of conversation between men and women in the late twentieth century always ends up being garbage?

"Would it be too much to ask you to do it?" you now ask.

No, of course not, except that he can't hold this smoke in much longer. His lungs are about to explode.

"So I can count on you to do it," you say.

He nods. He wonders if his face is turning purple.

"I'm going out for breakfast. What do you want?"

Anything, he hopes he is telling her as he frantically waves his arms. Anything you fucking want me to want! This is worse than being married! He is going to pass out! He slouches in his chair, covers his mouth to obscure his face and, he hopes, contain the smoke.

"Are you OK?" he hears you ask with a note of tenderness in your voice.

Yes, he thinks, definitely worse than being married. As he begins to cough in earnest, he throws open the middle drawer, dives down, does another French kiss on the ashtray, slams the drawer closed, doubles up to finish his coughing fit and sits up straight.

"I was just looking for my inhaler."

"I was just looking for my personal tachometer," Trey tells Charlotte as he hurries back to his exercise bicycle.

"If you can find anything in that closet," says Charlotte, "you deserve a prize."

Trey assumes a look he hopes is blank as he increases his speed. Charlotte continues to look at the closet. "It looks like you just took all the boxes and upended them." Which is exactly what he has done. How did she know?

What she doesn't seem to know is that a man in the building opposite almost certainly has his binoculars trained on her, that the framed poster over the settee has been shifted during the night, proving that this same man or an associate has inserted a micro-listening device behind the nail in the wall. When she sits down on the windowsill, she doesn't even check for poison dust. When she pushes the curtains aside, she doesn't see the handle of his knife.

All she wants to do is talk about chores and schedules. As if there were no scheme of things larger than a house, no insidious conspiracy, no Satan, no God. What good is it going to do, Charlotte telling him that he has to be in front of the school at 3:15 precisely, if by 3:15 they could all be dead? She doesn't seem to realize that the people they are up against are not going to listen to him when he pleads childcare commitments. They are not likely to accord him much sympathy when he asks that they not spray him with bullets until he has managed to track down all the ingredients for trail mix.

"You do *know* what goes into trail mix," she says now. "And you do know it has to be delivered to the CLC this afternoon at the very latest, even though, as you ought to know anyway but probably haven't bothered to put into your diary, the bake sale itself is not until tomorrow. And you do know also, right? that if you don't comply, the kids will be suspended. Last but not least: I want the children dressed and ready for school when I get back from the pool. You do know what time that means, don't you?"

Yes, this he knows. What he does not know is why she casts a smile over her shoulder in the direction of Mr. Binoculars. Why she looks so closely at the pile of tapes that have yet to be erased, why, when she backs out of the driveway on her way to the pool, she pauses, looks up at the same sinister window, and displays three fingers.

She is not going to protect him—

While at the same moment Kiki tells himself that Ophelia is going to keep pretending he isn't watching her. Pretending that he's not wondering why the new underwear, why the new underwear paraded in front of him when she says she doesn't care if she turns him on anymore.

Every day is new and different with the human chameleon! Kiki wonders, almost affectionately, what her game is this morning, and what has caused her to change her tack since yesterday. He wonders, also, why she has made such an issue about Seb's lunch. Sure! What the hell! He's glad to make it! The only reason he didn't offer is because he didn't know it was an issue, and in fact, he's happy to make it every morning if that's what she wants. Hey—anything but to have to discuss it in counseling!

He is not feeling too hot this morning. He guesses he drank too much. It's strange, being able to come and go as he likes, and last night, for example, going out drinking without having to justify it to anyone . . . just looking at jailbait made him tired. So much work! His body just wasn't up to it, and then to have to talk to them . . . The big mysteries lately are here in this house: why the underwear, why the game about the lunch, why . . .

"Why not ham for a change?" he asks his son as he takes out the bread and the mayonnaise.

His son explains that ham is a forbidden food.

"How about peanut butter and jelly then?"

His son explains that jelly has too much sugar.

"Cheese?"

He had it yesterday.

"Just peanut butter. How about that?"

OK, says his son, but not on bread. It has too many additives.

"I guess I'd better check this apple for pesticide residues," he says, meaning it as a joke.

His son nods and then says, "Can I ask you a question, though?"

"That's what I'm here for, *mijo*."

"Why did you have to talk to Mommy in the middle of the night?"

"I didn't have to."

"Why did you then?"

"I told you. I didn't."

"But that's what she told me."

"Told you when?"

"When she came back."

He notices his wife's back freezing.

"What's this, Filly?"

"Oh, nothing, I just stepped out for a minute."

"You didn't leave the little guy alone, did you?"

"Only for ten minutes, but it just so happened he woke up while I wasn't here, but don't worry, it was fine, really."

"What did you have to go out for?"

"It's a long story. I'll tell you later."

"But . . ."

"I said I'd tell you later, OK?"

He stares at her back, suddenly aware that he is running out of time and chances.

Chapter 46

The same thought occurs to us all at the same time. To me as I hunt the apartment inch by telltale inch for the missing studs. To the children as they watch and misunderstand me. To Mitchell as he recalculates his home office floor plan and finds he is twenty-eight percent off. To Trey as he hears his wife, his enemy, return from her morning swim.

To Charlotte, as she packs her briefcase for work, while supervising the children's hunt for shoes and socks, and discovers that her gradebook is missing.

To Becky as she herds her daughters into the car and then looks down and sees she is missing one pink sock.

To Ophelia as she feels her husband's eyes on her back and so nervously fondles the stud in her left ear and then the stud in . . .

The stud in her left ear is missing.

The next half hour is unbearable. She can't get a second alone. She tries to take her own car to work so that she can stop off and make a phone call, but Kiki objects, saying it makes no sense, as they are both going to the office and then off, together, to the counselor. When she says she needs some space, he says, "Why?" When they get to the office, he continues to trail her—

Which is unbearable.

As unbearable as Becky's drive to school, as bad even as Charlotte's hunt on her drive to school for a backstreet phone booth. She is the first to get through to me. Ophelia is next and Becky last. All three are taken aback by the hostility in my voice when I answer their questions.

"Yes, of course I do." . . . "I'm sure I do, yes, but you're going to have to tell me the color." . . . "No, I'm *not* going to look now. You seem to forget I have two children with temperatures."

Imagine what it was like for me on the receiving end. Imagine me sitting on our bed, trying to get Jesse and Maria to take their

Tylenol. Imagine them squirming and bursting into tears because it was so painful to swallow, imagine me picking up Maria to console her only to have Jesse ask me why I loved her best. Then imagine the phone ringing. Imagine me picking up the phone to hear Charlotte's voice and then the call-waiting bleep, changing over to the incoming call, hearing Ophelia's voice, asking her to hold, going back to Charlotte, telling her to call later, going back to Ophelia, asking her what's up, and then hearing the call-waiting bleep again and so asking Ophelia to hold again, taking the new incoming call, hearing Becky's voice, asking her to hold, going back to Ophelia, dealing with Ophelia, going back to Becky, only to have our conversation interrupted by another incoming call, which turned out to be you.

You may remember that I shouted at you and accused you of leaving me stranded. Perhaps now you can—without actually forgiving me—understand why.

It was only after I hung up the phone that I realized I was acting insane.

What had you been doing? You had been doing your job. What had I been doing? Fucking your three best friends and then, surprise! blaming it on you.

I don't know if I would go so far as to call this an insight. Rather, it was a case of holding together in my mind several facts that I had been going to great lengths to keep apart. Even this small step in the direction of honesty was too much for me. The facts repelled each other like magnets. That is why I sounded so strange when you called back. In case you can't remember this call in detail—it took me two or three minutes to identify your voice.

After I put the phone down again, I actually had to repeat to myself all the things you had said to me so that I wouldn't forget them. You were sorry. You had agreed that you had been asking a lot of me. You felt guilty about neglecting the children. You could see that I needed some time off. You offered to be back by noon so that you could give me the afternoon off. Which left me . . . how much time to find the studs?

I went to the kitchen. Staring into the garbage at the remains of the home pregnancy test, I told myself I had to stop.

Stop fucking Charlotte. Stop fucking Ophelia. Stop fucking Becky. But how? It is an indication of my state of mind that I really had to apply myself to come up with the obvious answer: I had to tell them

I was stopping. That I couldn't take the strain anymore, either physical or mental.

How would they take it, though? This was my next thought. I ran through the three scenarios, the three hurt and howling faces receiving the news. After which they . . . went where? Confided in whom? Discovered what? Sent whom to tell me what for? It did not take me long to figure out that it might not be wise to tell any of them point-blank that it was over. Better to tell them I was exhausted and so wanted to put everything on hold while I took a break.

While I took a break and thought things over. While I went away for two weeks with my family and tried to get some perspective on things. Could I get them to buy that? Yes, I could.

The next question was, when? When was I going to tell them I needed a break? And in what order?

I thought this over while I tied up the garbage bag. Again, it took me superhuman effort to arrive at the obvious answer. Face to face, in order of appearance, and as soon as possible.

Which was why, when Charlotte called up again, I asked her if she was free for lunch.

This, of course, is when the real trouble began. Because I had a standing lunch date with Ophelia. I might have remembered this if I had had a moment to think peacefully while Charlotte checked her diary, but unfortunately I got an incoming call while Charlotte was away from the phone. This second call was from Becky. Who was upset. Who wanted to know why I was angry at her. "Something has happened to you since I left you," she said. "I have a sixth sense for this kind of thing, and so you might as well tell me."

"Listen. I can't talk now," I said. "I have someone on the other line. Listen, are you home this afternoon? I'll come by and talk to you then."

"Who are you talking to *now?*" she asked.

I lied without even thinking. "To my wife, of course! OK?" I shouted. "Are you satisfied?"

"OK," she said in a small voice.

"I think we should stop this conversation until both of us are calmer and I don't have Laura on hold. Don't you think?"

No answer.

"OK?" I asked again.

I got her to say OK back and then I went back to the original call. Confused by my own lie, I expected it to be you and so was thrown to hear Charlotte. When she said, "So listen. I have a student on the other line so I'll see you later," I had no recollection of our having made a definitive date.

All I could think, after I hung up the phone, was: Becky. What, exactly, had I done to upset her? I decided to call her to find out. I was relieved when I heard her say how glad she was to hear my voice.

"I'm just so stretched today. Do you know what Mitchell is making me do? He is making me rearrange the whole house because of this auditor panic. And even though this is hardly a real problem compared to the others, I'm telling you, it's really getting to me. I mean, it's touching on something deep inside me, some childhood memory I've repressed, something that happened maybe when my father . . ."

This time it was her call-waiting that interrupted our conversation. We both agreed, bitterly but laughing, that it was impossible to continue with these interruptions. "Let me call you back," she said. I said fine, and while I sit there on the bed watching Jesse and Maria watching the children's programs, I imagine . . .

Becky, standing in the middle of a suddenly unfamiliar kitchen, taking the other call, which is from Mitchell.

"Are they there yet?" he asks.

"No, of course not."

"Oh good. That means you can check some things out for me."

"Like what?"

"Basically the wastepaper baskets."

"Listen, Mitchell, the IRS doesn't go through wastepaper baskets."

"Actually, they do. And we can't be too careful."

"OK, I'll go through them."

"Thanks, hon. And . . . Becky? When the person gets there, I mean it, be careful. Let *her* do the talking."

"Of course I will," Becky says.

She hangs up. She goes through the house. Which reminds her more than ever this morning of a stage set. Because nothing is where it used to be. Every time she goes into a room, she still expects one thing, and is shocked, even though she is the one who ended up doing most of the arranging last night, to find another.

She walks down the stairs, stops in front of the landing window. She looks into the next house, where she sees—for the millionth time—the landing so much like her landing she could be looking into a mirror. Except that, as always, she's not there. Except this time it's not so funny.

Where is she?

Her heart begins to pound.

I'm here, she tells herself, I'm here. It isn't a reflection. It's a copycat house.

How long will I be in this house, though? How long can we get away without paying the balloon payment? What is the IRS going to do to us?

How long will I be permitted to continue to exist?

Where is my bedroom today? Where will it be tomorrow? What is the point of watering the plants, fixing the shelves, ironing the clothes, if I'm not here tomorrow?

She leafs through her calendar. It's full of fictitious business appointments. Lunches that never were. Doodles designed to look if she had been doing them all year when in fact they were the product of one night. Last night. Next to the phone is a phone log, also the product of last night. It is full of fictitious calls that Mitchell has skillfully mixed in with the real ones. Which ones are real? she asks herself—and then the phone rings.

"Hi." It's Mitchell.

"Did you do the baskets?" he asks.

"Yes, I did."

"Good," he says. "Thanks." He pauses. "I hope you didn't take *everything* out."

"Of course I did! That's what you told me to do."

"Oh shit."

"Mitchell, this is crazy," Becky informs him.

"I know," he says. "I know. It's crazy. But everything we own is riding on it." Another long pause. Then he says, "I've got it. This is what you can do for me. Go into the study and put yourself in front of the computer and print out a few files. And then crumple them up and put them into the basket next to the door—no—the basket next to the desk. We have to make sure things look casual. OK, honey?"

She feels flames flaring out of her nostrils. "I really think that's unnecessary."

"Well, do it for me," Mitchell tells her. "And while you're at it, double-check those files, OK?"

"About what in particular?"

Pause. "I'm not sure. But I'll get back to you when or if I remember."

He hangs up. She goes into the study—except that it's not the study anymore. Now the study is next door. She goes next door and selects some files at random. She prints them out.

What she sees on the printouts is not funny at all.

What she sees are early plans for projects that never came off. The marina, the windfarm, the complex in Petaluma. The import/export scheme. The early optimistic letters clogging up menu after menu. Followed by another new idea and another slew of optimistic early letters. Where will it end?

While the printer clatters on, she wanders to the window. What does an IRS field auditor look like? Is she already there on the street? Why did she, Becky, agree to this? If Mitchell has so many ideas about how the house should look when she arrives, then why the hell isn't he here arranging things instead of issuing her instructions from his office?

The phone rings again.

"Have you fixed the baskets?" he asks.

"Yes. And now that I have, I want you to stop calling me."

"OK, but there's just one thing you have to check for me first."

She taps her foot.

"Pretty please?"

She lets out a sigh.

"Thanks, hon. Now here's what I want you to do. Go into the study."

"Which one?"

"What do you mean, which one?"

"The real one or the fake one?"

"Don't even say that, Becky. Don't even think that. Until that woman walks out of our house, you have to believe from the bottom of your heart that our office has always been where it is today."

"So what do you want me to do?" she says.

"Take out a ruler and measure your foot."

"What's up? Thinking of putting a bid on a shoe factory?"

"Just do what I say. I'll hold."

"It's ten and a half inches," she informs him.

"OK, good. Now go into the study—the study where the desk is NOW—and get me the dimensions."

"In foot measurements?"

"That's right. Using *your* foot. Make sure you walk in a straight line. I mean as straight as you can."

"God! Did you think I was going to do zigzags? I mean, I went to fourth grade, too, you know!"

"Becky, please. Go do this last thing for me?"

She obeys him, thinking really, she is doing it for herself, isn't she? It's her money.

Returning to the phone, she tells him, "It's twenty footsteps by thirty-one and a half footsteps. Excluding the bay window area, which is eight footsteps wide with each of the three windows just under four footsteps."

"Thanks. Now freeze until I get back to you."

Time passes. She considers making coffee but is afraid to touch anything. She pours herself a glass of water but no ice will come out of the icemaker. Then she remembers why. She opens the freezer. It is defrosting. Shards of green glass are floating around in three inches of water. There is a horrible smell. She closes the freezer door. She drinks her water without ice and then opens the dishwasher to stack the glass, but it is full of clean dishes and she doesn't have the energy to put them away—or the courage, because one of the cabinets is full of rogue files and she can't remember which. This is not her kitchen anymore. It is a stage set.

Before she can pursue this thought, the phone rings. It is Mitchell! Again! Hooray!

He sounds hesitant. "We have a little problem."

"What?" she asks.

"First things first. Measure your foot again."

She does.

"Now, you're absolutely sure you're measuring it correctly? From heel to toe, I mean."

"God, you're condescending!"

"Make sure both feet are the same size."

She does. They are.

"That's unbelievably rare, you know."

"Mitchell, believe me."

"In that case, one of us did the original measurements wrong."

"You're the one who did those, Mitchell dearest."

"That's not how I remember it, but I'm not going to argue about it now. I think we're going to have to go with the two-room concept."

"The WHAT?"

"Listen, Becky. We have got to act fast. Go into the living room and do a footstep measurement. Now."

She obeys him. Comes back to the phone. Gives him the measurements. "Hold on," he says. "Let me work that out on my calculator." There is a pause followed by some unattractive mumbling. Then he says, "Terrific. It works out to a little more than one fifth of our total floor space. We're going to come out of this baby looking clean. All you have to do, hon, is move around some furniture."

"Which furniture?" she asks.

"You have to get the desk back into the living room."

"How am I supposed to do that alone?" she asks.

"Tape cardboard shoes to the legs and then slide it. And don't forget to put the basket in there too."

"Not the real living room, I take it. The current living room. Right?"

"Right. Then take the old living-room stuff and put it into the kitchen."

"It's going to look gross in there."

"It doesn't matter. OK, then take the kitchen couch and put it into the present study, which from now on will be our waiting room. We'll keep the table as is in there. And maybe set up the old coffeemaker?"

"Mitchell. This is going to take hours."

"Not if you start now," he says.

She puts down the phone and goes into the fake/present/soon-to-be-a-waiting room/was-until-yesterday-the-living room/study. She looks at the heavy oak desk. She tells herself she can't possibly move that desk by herself. That cardboard-shoe idea. What could be more ridiculous? Men! she screams internally.

Then she thinks about what will happen if Mitchell gets what's coming to him and what she'll lose. She has a change of heart, goes into the kitchen, makes cardboard shoes for the desk legs. She puts them underneath the desk legs, wraps them around them as best she can and starts pushing the fucker into the ex–living room. Halfway there one of the shoes falls off. The exposed leg makes a long, deep scratch on the parquet floor.

Great! she thinks. Eight hundred dollars' worth of floor sanding and two weeks of disruption down the drain! Terrific! What's even more terrific is that the field auditor will see the scratch and know right off what's going on. So. She's going to have to cover the scratch up with the living room rug.

And she does. But it looks like shit. But what can you do. Beggars can't be interior decorators. Soon everything is in its appointed place except for Becky. And Becky does not have the faintest where that is.

The phone rings. Where is the phone? She hunts for it, finds it on the fifth ring. She picks it up, and surprise, surprise, it's Mitchell.

"I did everything you told me to do, OK?"

"Oh, I'm sorry to hear that. Because I've been mulling it over. And I don't think it will work."

"If it doesn't work it's too fucking bad. I've had it, do you hear?"

"Becky, now let's be reasonable."

"I can't be reasonable! I've flipped my lid. And you've done it to me, you asshole! You know how to handle this woman, you say? Then *you* handle her."

"Honey, I think, when you calm down, you'll see it's *our* problem." But he is not saying it to Becky. He is saying it to the walls and the open door. Becky is already backing out of the driveway. Becky and Baby are going for a drive.

Her car heads like a homing device for 2238 Hyde. And while it does, I imagine . . .

Chapter 47

Charlotte, standing in her doorway, waving goodbye to the policewoman, who had been a treasure, and not the only one: everything a person would want to happen in a situation like this had happened. A neighbor—imagine!—had noticed their front door flapping on its hinges and reported a suspected burglary to the police. Policewoman O'Riley had been standing in the kitchen addressing her walkie-talkie when Charlotte had arrived back from taking the kids to school. As there was nothing missing, Charlotte had had to conclude that Trey had left the house in a hurry and forgotten to lock up . . .

"God! Men!" was the policewoman's response. She couldn't have realized, when Charlotte echoed her, that Charlotte was fed up not with one man but with two. Nor could she have known that the last thing Charlotte wanted to do at that point was sit down with Police Officer O'Riley and have a heart-to-heart. Since six that morning, she had been wading through obligations and more obligations, all to get to her office for two hours of peace, and then along came Policewoman June to eat up all her free time.

Not that she meant any harm. Policewoman June had been nice to the point of being a feminist pinup fantasy—professional in the male sense of the word, caring in the female sense of the word . . . you would have thought she had walked off the set of *Sesame Street!* Charlotte is ashamed of herself for the surge of joy she feels when Policewoman O'Riley stands up to go.

Charlotte looks at her watch and sees eleven fucking o'clock. Perfect, she says. Morning almost gone. If she cancels her lunch with me, she can still salvage it, get some work done before her seminar. But that would mean breaking a rule.

I have asked to see her, it sounds urgent, she has committed herself to being there for me in this type of crisis no matter how fucking annoyed she feels, and so she'll go.

She spends the tail end of her free morning clearing the fridge and the tables and the dishwasher and the bulletin board and the answering machine, and sweeping the floor, and mopping the floor, and watering the plants that were still, due to some miracle, Trey-resistant and alive, and discarding the plants that had withered under his simulated desert conditions. After which there is only just enough time to gather her books and her papers and position a few vital messages before she has to get into the car.

The downstairs door to 2238 is open. The elevator is waiting. When she gets to the seventh floor, she stops to compose herself, and this is when she hears Becky say, "I don't know who I am anymore. I don't trust my feelings. Not even my feelings for you."

Then she hears me say, "Oh darling. Please."

Oh darling? Please?

As Charlotte's finger hovers next to the doorbell, and as a surge of what she can only call unadulterated panic passes through her, she is tempted to stand there and listen and find out. Is this why I have been distant and irritable lately?

Now Becky says, "He's the one who loused things up. He's the one who should speak to the auditor."

And I say, "I couldn't agree more."

Which means? Which means that she, Charlotte, is reading extra meanings into everything today. Becky and I aren't lovers. We're just friends, and friends in a way that she had despaired might never be possible between a man and a woman. We are talking about the auditor, for God's sake. And here she, Charlotte, is experiencing sexual jealousy. What can it mean, this sudden surge of what she has to concede is unjustified possessiveness? Is she being dishonest with herself about my importance in her life? Or does it mean that she has been picking up confusing signals from me and therefore feels insecure?

Another topic to raise over lunch, she tells herself. But then, as her finger still hovers over the bell, she asks herself if it is going to be possible to go out to lunch at all now that Becky is there. What will I have told Becky about this lunch date? A lie or the truth, or, worst of all, a half-truth?

She tells herself she is overintellectualizing. She rings the bell. No answer. She tries the door. It's open. She walks into the foyer, turns to look into the living room.

Blomp. Two terrified stares.

The first thing she notices is an angry red mark on my neck. The second thing she notices—it can't be, she must be seeing things, hallucinating clichés!—is some lipstick on my collar. And what else? Some lipstick on my lips. Which is the same color as Becky's lipstick. She feels hysteria rising through her like mercury. Every little thing she sees now, the lipstick still in Becky's hand, the fact that Becky has no shoes on, the way she is sitting, the way I am acting—looks suspicious.

"What can I do for you?" I ask.

"What can you do for me?" Charlotte exclaims. "That's a good one."

I scratch my head. "Oh, now I remember." I dive into my pocket and fish out a stud. A red stud. I give it to her. She stares at it. "What is this supposed to be?"

"Isn't this what you left behind?"

"No, it isn't," says Charlotte.

"Actually," says Becky, "that's mine."

"Oh," I say. I give it to Becky. Then I turn back to Charlotte.

"Just tell me what color it is," I say.

"As you know full well, it's green."

I give her the green stud.

"That isn't it either," she says.

I give her the purple stud. Handing it back to me, she says, "What I forgot was a gradebook."

"Oh," I say, and then I dig into the laundry basket and bring out her gradebook.

She says, "I guess this is your way of telling me you don't have time for lunch."

"What lunch?" I say.

Several things continue to puzzle Charlotte when she sits herself down in her office half an hour later.

One is why, when she knew for sure she wasn't seeing things, that she had definitely walked into a tryst, she felt no emotion, felt compelled instead to go and get herself a glass of water.

Why, when she said so listen, it's just as well, I have a thousand things to do this afternoon, she actually meant it.

Why, as she drove to work, she suddenly found herself laughing about it, actually imagined herself sitting down with Policewoman O'Riley and saying, Now top this one.

Why, when she went to deal with the secretaries, she was so unbelievably up: *Any messages? Oh, thank you! And oh, I love your scarf!*

Why, when she saw a student approaching her in the corridor, she backed into the women's room and hid.

But most of all why, after she had decided not to go to her office, because she knew I would be trying to reach her, she then went straight to her office, in fact ran, in fact grabbed the phone the moment it rang.

Chapter 48

Leave her with her hand on the receiver and spare a thought for me. I knew that I had handled Charlotte badly, and I knew she deserved better from me. The question was, what? I wasn't sure, from her cool behavior, how upset she was. But I didn't want her to think I had been involved with Becky all along. That was why I thought it was important for her to know it had only started the night before.

Of course this did not make her feel better. She wanted to know why last night, when last night, and exactly what? That was when I started redesigning my story. I am afraid that before long I was telling her that all we had done was heavy petting.

This was when Charlotte's tone turned from confused to accusatory. She was saying, "What you're trying to tell me is that you don't consider this important because you didn't actually ejaculate inside her?"

Imagine also that while I was carrying on this conversation I was trying to feed our kids their lunch. They resented having to share my attention and acted accordingly. Add to this confusion not one, not two, but three other incoming phone calls.

The first was from Ophelia. She wanted to know if I was going to make it to Green's for lunch at one. I said yes, that you were arriving to relieve me any moment. I terminated this call somewhat abruptly.

I had only just returned to Charlotte when I got the second incoming call, which was from you. You wanted to know if I needed any groceries. I said no, again somewhat abruptly, and had just returned to Charlotte, just taken in the fact that she was crying, when a call came in from Becky, whom I mistook for Ophelia. Which is why I (tragically) told her to meet me at Green's at one.

She then said something that puzzled me, about getting Mitchell to babysit for Roo. Why was Ophelia talking about Mitchell and Roo? It was only after I went back to Charlotte and her broken sobs that I realized I had been talking to Becky, not Ophelia, that I now had two women meeting me for lunch at Green's. And on top of it all, I had

Charlotte demanding a blow-by-blow account of a sexual encounter I myself could only remember in the vaguest terms. "Listen," I told her. "We can't do this over the phone." I tried my best to reassure her that what had happened was an aberration, thereby compounding my lies. Even this took too long; by the time I got her off the line and phoned Becky, she was gone.

I sat down, looked at my watch: 12:35. That left twenty-five minutes to figure out how to deal with, explain to, Becky and Ophelia the mix-up over lunch. First I had to do my final cleanup check before you came back.

I went from room to room, trying to look at each one as you would look at it (standing in your shoes, just as you had asked me to do so many times!). Then I would look at it again, through my eyes, and ask myself, What is wrong with this picture?

When I got to the children's room (I had put them down for naps) I must have given Jesse a very strange look.

Because now he said, "You look like a poltergeist."

To which I stupidly said, "I *feel* like a poltergeist."

To which he said, "Is that what you were watching last night?"

I asked him what he meant, and he said, "I heard you screaming."

"You did?" I screamed.

"Actually, I heard *them* screaming."

"Who?"

"Seb's mom and Patten's mom and Lara's mom, too."

I went cold, said nothing.

Jesse gave me a warm smile.

"It must have been a really good movie for you to watch it three times."

I tried to nod, tried but probably did not manage to walk out of the room as if nothing he had said had alarmed me.

How much had he seen? How could I find out how much he had seen? How could I prevent him from passing classified information on to you? How could I even think, for a split second, of asking this poor boy to lie to his mother? I broke into a sweat. I thought it through again. I realized I was going to have to have a serious talk with him, a serious talk which I had neither the time nor the space to have with him now. All I could do now was ask him not to mention the events of the evening to anyone until he talked to me about them, but before I had a chance to make this request, I heard your key in the door.

The moment I saw you, I knew I couldn't leave the apartment

without talking to Jesse. That's why I lied to you and said I was waiting for a phone call, and that's also why I encouraged you to take a nap. But you took such a long time getting settled, and trying to find out why, for example, I had changed our sheets, that, by the time you had closed the bedroom door, it was too late to talk to Jesse because he, too, had fallen asleep.

I looked at my watch. It was five past one. In five minutes I would receive two angry phone calls. I could not handle even the idea of talking to these women now. So the first thing I did was take the living-room phone off the hook.

Then I sit down to imagine the scene I am missing . . .

Ophelia, first trying not to notice Becky, then going to the parking lot to warn me, bumping into Becky, lying to her, Becky pretending to believe her . . . here my imagination failed me. Here was where I realized that events had moved beyond my control. I could only make things worse by interfering. It was better, if only marginally so, to let them come to me. The important thing was to isolate myself until I could think clearly. When I was sure you were asleep, I tiptoed into the bedroom, pulled the phone cord out of the jack, returned to the living room, did the same to that phone, got out the earphones, put on "Blue Train," sat back . . . only to remember. The sheets!

As I take them down to the laundry room, I imagine . . .

Ophelia, at Green's with Becky, who has accepted everything she said, even when it directly contradicted what came before and after. Has their friendship always been this superficial? Could Becky have been carrying on a secret life for years and years without Ophelia picking up on a thing? The idea chills her.

She returns her eyes to the menu. She can hardly read it. She can't stop wondering what could have become of me. Am I waiting at another restaurant? Or did I walk in, see her sitting with Becky, decide not to risk it, and split? What if Kiki has been tracking me? What if Kiki has become violent?

He had followed her to Green's, she was sure of it. Where was he now? What if he had prevented me from entering the restaurant? What if he was sitting with me at 2238 trying to force a confession out of me? Should she get up now and try and find me? But what if she did find me, and what if I was with Kiki? How would she explain her presence? It was when she realized that anything she did could be used against her that she knew the situation to be beyond her control.

So why was she carrying on this fake conversation? Better to tell Becky straight out. If the bond was as strong as she believed it to be, it would survive the scandal.

Ophelia clears her throat. "I have something to tell you. Mike and I are in love. Let me tell you how it happened."

The more Becky listens, the more she has to struggle to keep her face a friendly mask.

What could this story she is hearing have in common with the one she heard from the other party, me?

According to me, this thing with Ophelia began accidentally two weeks ago. According to Ophelia, it was always "there," growing both stronger and harder to deny the more time she and I spent together. Until one night, neither of us could resist anymore.

According to me, it was just sex and going nowhere. According to Ophelia, it was such a powerful union of the souls that it was going to destroy both marriages. The outcome was clear according to Ophelia. She knew in her bones that I was "the one." The question was, how much would we have to go through before we reached that happy resolution?

She wants to know if Becky will forgive her. But the question is, how is Becky going to forgive herself for believing my story with so few reservations? As she stands in the bathroom throwing water on her face, she counts the lies.

Why does she feel compelled to protect one man's mismanaged business and another's multiple infidelities? Because she believes that Mitchell is doing it all for the family? Because she is willing to shaft her three dearest friends just because I have told her she is the only one I really love? There is only one explanation: she is lying to herself.

Chapter 49

It must have been about three o'clock when you came out to the living room to ask me why the phones were unplugged. I didn't have an excuse ready, so instead I reconnected the one sitting next to me. It rang almost immediately.

It was Becky. She said, "I'm sort of precarious, so I want you to keep quiet while I bring you up to date. Ophelia told me her side of the story, and it had zero and I mean zero in common with what you told me. This leaves me fucking flattened and has me seriously questioning my own motivations as well as yours. But don't worry because I know what I have to do now, and that is level with everyone I've lied to, and that includes Ophelia, to whom I was kind enough, incidentally, to say nothing, by which I mean nothing yet. I'm going to level with your wife, too, and make sure you level with her, too, and I'm not going to forget about Charlotte either, and I'm not going to lie to the auditor and what's more I'm going to tell Mitchell why I'm not going to lie and so the choice I'm giving you is are you going to come in on this with me or are you going to make me do it alone?"

Pause. It was a lot to take in, especially with you standing there looking at me. Finally I said, "Becky, listen. That's an awful lot to unload on me over the phone."

"Well then, let's meet."

"I'll be right over." I put down the phone.

At which point you asked me, "Why are you still here?"

"Why shouldn't I be here? It's my home, too."

"You were supposed to be going out."

"I decided against it."

"Why?"

"Palpitations."

"Not again! Did you talk to Kiki about them?"

"He said he would see me later but that in the meantime I should rest."

"So what was this phone call about?"

"Oh, just the usual lecture."

"I don't mean Kiki. I mean Becky on the phone just now. So what was she so upset about?"

"Oh," I said. "You know. The auditor."

"The *auditor?* The auditor's *there* already?"

"No," I said. "But she does seem to have decided that, when the auditor does arrive, she should tell her the truth."

I had forgotten how deeply you yourself were implicated. I was rudely reminded when you screeched, "The *truth?* To the auditor? You must be joking!" As you talked, you were already dialing. As you may remember, I cut the connection.

"You're not telling Mitchell, are you?" is what I said.

And you said, "Of course I'm telling Mitchell! He has got to straighten that woman out!"

To which I said, "I think I can do that without involving Mitchell. He's hysterical as it is."

But I wasn't going to leave the apartment without talking to my son. That was why I pushed you, somewhat unceremoniously, into the shower.

I did not like having to wake the poor boy up, but I didn't see what choice I had. As he struggled to keep his eyes open, I told him I had to go out for a while. I am afraid that when he said, "Off on a mission, are you?" I said yes. How was I to know what he really meant?

"Listen," I said. "There is something I am going to ask you to do for me until I get back. Keep a secret for me, just for the time being, about the movie I was watching last night."

"You mean not to tell Mom," he said.

"Just until I've had a chance to talk to her myself."

"I don't think you should tell her. She won't understand."

"What won't she understand?"

"That supermen are different."

"But I'm not Superman! How many times do I have to tell you?" At this point the phone rang.

"I bet that's one of your girlfriends," said Jesse. "Go answer it before Mom gets out of the shower."

It was Charlotte. "Have you seen Trey?"

"Why would I have seen Trey?"

"He didn't pick up the children. They had to call me out of my seminar, can you believe it?"

I heard a bleep on the line. "Can you hold?" I asked Charlotte. "I have a call coming in."

The other caller turned out to be Mitchell. He wanted to know where Becky was.

"Oh no," I said. "Where are you calling from?"

"Home," he said.

"Oh no," I said again. "She's supposed to be waiting there for me."

"Well, guess what," said Mitchell. "She's gone."

"Oh no," I said. "This is serious. Can you hold?"

I went back to Charlotte on the other line. I told her I would have to get back to her.

"Why?" she asked. "Who's on the other line?"

I told her it was none of her business. She began to sob. "I'm sorry," I said. "I didn't mean to hurt you. We'll sort it all out later. I'll come over and see you later after I've sorted all this other stuff out."

"Is that what you call me when you're talking to *her?* Stuff?"

"I'm not going to even talk to you if you take that tone," I said, and I slammed down the phone. Stupidly forgetting that Mitchell was on hold. When the phone started ringing, I picked it up, but not fast enough to keep you from hearing it.

You jumped out of the shower. "Is that a call for me?"

I had no idea. When I said, "Can you hold?" to the caller, I didn't even know who I was talking to. I told you the first lie that came into my head. "It's Kiki to say he's phoned in my heart prescription."

You seemed to buy it, but you kept the bathroom door open. I went back to my phone call. "Why did you say I was Kiki?" Mitchell asked.

I told him it was a long story.

"You'll have to tell me sometime. In the meantime, could I please talk to your wife?"

"Under the circumstances," I said, "that would not be too wise."

"Fuck you, Mike. Say it was call-waiting."

I could not think of a better idea. So I called you to the phone. When you had finished talking to him, you turned to me. "So anyway. Mitchell wants me to go over and talk to Becky."

"But she isn't there!"

"She is now," you told me. "I'd better catch her before she disappears again. Why don't I pick up that prescription for you on the way back? Where did he phone it to?"

"Who? Phone what?"

"Kiki! Your medicine! Which drugstore did he phone the prescription to?"

"I can't remember."

"What? Are you serious?"

"It's not important anyway, because the palpitations have stopped," I said, but already you were dialing. I couldn't bear listening to you talking to Kiki's receptionist. I was at the window, I remember, when you came to tell me that Kiki had been out of his office since lunchtime. "That's right," I lied. "I got him on his car phone at the golf course." I can't tell you how relieved I was that you were unable to get through to him on his mobile phone.

The first thing I did when you had left to go talk to Becky was to talk to Becky myself. It took a few tries to get past Mitchell, which was why I was abrupt when I finally got through. "Laura is on her way to see you," I said. "So if you want to speak to me alone, here's your chance."

Pause. Then Becky said, "Maybe I should just speak to her and get it over with."

"You promised you would talk to me first."

"Well, I just don't happen to be available right now. I'm sorry. I'm in the middle of asking my husband for a divorce."

"Calm down, for God's sake."

"For God's sake, why don't you start taking some of your own advice. Listen," she said in her harshest voice, "I meant what I said. I'll see you at Vesuvio's at eight."

By now the children were awake, but I was far too distracted to deal with them. I sat them in front of the TV. No sooner had I tuned in to *Mister Rogers* than the doorbell rang.

It was Ophelia. In a state.

"Is he here yet?" she hissed.

"Is *who* here?"

"My husband. I gave him the slip."

At that, the doorbell rang.

"That must be him. Quick. Let me out the back."

I'd just managed to get her into the service elevator when the inside doorbell rang. It wasn't Kiki, though. It was Trey. Trey in camouflage fatigues, carrying a tennis racket. He entered stealthily, then made a request in crude sign language for writing materials. When I got them for him, he wrote, "Pretend you have a tennis date with me."

"What?" I said.

He put his hands to his lips, then circled his finger the way they do in movies when they want to indicate a room is bugged.

"This is important," he wrote. "Say it."

So I did. No sooner had I done that than the doorbell rang again. Trey commanded, "Quick!" and gestured to the service elevator. I got him into it just as you walked through the door.

"Sorry," you said. "I forgot my keys."

"And, oh, by the way," you said. "I finally got hold of Kiki. He said he knew nothing about this prescription. He sounded strange. Is he OK? Anyway, I told him what you needed and he phoned it in to Walgreen's, so after I gave up on Becky and Mitchell, I stopped off there and got it."

You handed me a bottle of pills. "He'll be around later to check on you."

Oh great, I thought. "When will that be?"

"As soon as he can, he said. And also, I ran into Charlotte at Walgreen's. She was hysterical. Her kids have nits and they made her cut her seminar short because they needed to have her pick them up at once. Trey should have done this but she can't find him."

"Actually," I said, "he's here."

"Where?"

"Here. I mean, down in the laundry room."

"What's he doing in our laundry room?"

"He wants me to play tennis."

"You're not playing tennis, Mike! Not if you've just had palpitations!"

"To tell you the truth, I don't think he really wants to play tennis. I think he wants to talk to me."

"Well, if he wants to talk the first person he should talk to is Charlotte because she's frantic."

At this point, you called the service elevator.

"Where are you going?"

"Downstairs to get our sheets."

"No! No!" I shrieked. "Let me get them."

"Why?"

Up came the elevator. In it was Ophelia. She was shaking. So much so that, when you asked her what she was doing in our service elevator, she just ignored you. "There is something seriously wrong with Trey," she said to me. "I am really worried."

You said, "So is Charlotte."

Ophelia said, "Trey just told me to tell you he'd be waiting on the tennis court across the street."

Turning to me, you said, "I'm not letting you go unless you take your medicine."

Ophelia said, "What medicine?"

After you had gone down to get the laundry, I explained to her that Kiki had phoned in a prescription for me because I had been having palpitations.

"For God's sake, don't take *anything* Kiki prescribed for you. It could be cyanide!"

She grabbed the container, ran into the bathroom, and flushed the pills down the toilet. "Here," she said, fishing another bottle out of her bag. "Take these."

Then you came back. "I don't understand," you said. "The sheets weren't even in the dryer."

"It's been that kind of afternoon," I explained.

"Why?" you asked.

"Ophelia needs to hide from Kiki," I explained. "They've had a fight."

"Oh, I'm sorry to hear that," you said. You seemed to buy it. And so off I went to play tennis with Trey—but not before you had made me try to reach Charlotte (I couldn't, her machine was on) and take my pill. ("It's just a Valium," Ophelia whispered to me afterward. "It won't kill you.")

Trey was nowhere to be seen when I got to the court. I waited five minutes and was on my way back to the apartment when he jumped out of the bushes.

"Gotcha!" he said.

Here followed the strangest tennis match I have ever had.

Remember first of all that Trey was wearing his camouflage suit, not to mention his knife belt, complete with knife. His only concession to convention was his footwear. He deliberately lost some sets and also made a habit of hitting balls over the fence and then delving into some new pocket and saying, "I fooled you, didn't I?" or, "Win at cards, lose at love."

At one point, when I was way ahead, he hit me over the head with his racket, only to say, in response to my yell of pain, "Oh, you poor little baby-pooh. Do you want me to kiss it and make it better?"

Did he know about me and Charlotte? I asked myself. Or was he finally losing his mind? Did I dare to win the match? Or would victory put my life in danger?

Chapter 50

Leave me floundering on the tennis court as the tranquilizer kicks in, and imagine . . .

Charlotte, in her kitchen, with her autobiography students, who have reshuffled all their afternoon plans and trekked halfway across the city so that they can prove themselves flexible to the needs of a working mother.

God! The humiliation! She ought to have just told them. What is there to be ashamed of, anyway? It's not her fault! *She's* not the infesting party! She always checks her children's hair! She could—if she were that sort of person—tell that bitch headmistress where to look for the culprit. If she were a tattletale. But she is not going to get Becky into trouble. No, siree. Charlotte covers for her friends, even when they let her down. It's her nature.

The person she is really angry at now is herself. Why had she suggested having her students over to her house? How had she thought it would be possible to conduct a class in such chaotic circumstances?

One of her students—Doris—has left the group and is out in the backyard smoking a cigarette. Or rather, jabbing it at her lips, pacing back and forth, exhaling through all her orifices. Now she is coming up to the window and shouting at it. What, is she angry? Charlotte doesn't know.

I ought never to have let them see me here, she says to herself as she surveys her other students' faces, as she sees how hard they are trying not to look at the lunchboxes and jackets strewn all over the floor. What had they made of her? This woman who screamed at her children, and then threw them two boxes of fruit roll-ups, commanding them to go into the den and "just watch anything." This woman who said excuse me, there is something I have to do before we sit down, and then proceeded to open the washing-machine door and let water pour all over the floor and cry, "God damn you, Trey!" This woman, who then called up Trey at a gym to leave him a clipped Hitlerian message—not about the washing machine, but about his "contractual obligation" to buy trail mix, or else—can this woman be their serene, eternally patient and composed teacher?

Charlotte knows they all know why she had to abandon her class for the nursery school. If they didn't pick up the allusion from Dottie herself—"How old are you, honey?" "I have animals in my hair"—then all they had to do was look at the bottle of head-lice shampoo standing on the stove, with the printed assurance: REMOVES HEAD LICE AND THEIR EGGS.

Charlotte's eyes wander from the washing machine—what is in there?—to the answering machine clicking on and off—who is trying to reach her?—to the unacceptable game show the children are watching on TV. She can just see them squirming on their beanbags. They have begun to accuse each other's heads of blocking the screen. Their squeals are muffled by the washing machine, which has gone into its spin cycle. It sounds as if there's nothing in there but a sneaker and a double sheet.

Somehow this reminds her of Becky. Becky, who never has to try. Why is it that men only care about looks?

She can't allow herself to continue thinking in this vein. She has to attend to her class. To practicalities. Like supper, and head lice, and trail mix.

How can she be sure Trey will even remember to go shopping? What if he buys things that contain preservatives? When is she going to shampoo the children's hair, and wash their brushes and sheets and clothes and prepare for tomorrow's 10:30 class? What if Trey has forgotten what trail mix is? What if that's him on the phone? What if Ophelia is trying to get through to her? What if it's important? These are the questions that whirl around in Charlotte's head as she watches a raisin do a slow circular dance on top of her washing machine.

She is interrupted by a sharp rap on the plate-glass window. It's Doris, saying something hostile but inaudible. How is Charlotte going to find out what went wrong? She looks around the table, hoping her other students will give her some clues. They are all smiling at her. Sadly.

"I guess I should try to speak to Doris alone," Charlotte says.

"Again?" says one student.

Again?

What is happening to her? Before she can ask anyone, Doris comes inside. "Let me tell you what I canceled FOR THIS," she yells. "I was supposed to visit my sister in the hospital and take her this present. I was supposed to meet my husband at the Embarcadero Center. Instead, I come here to listen to you say nasty nothings and . . . well, all I can say is the hell with you."

"But Doris, maybe if you . . ."

"There is no excuse for anti-Semitism," she says.

Anti-Semitism?

"Doris. Please. Sit down. Let's talk." But Doris is out the door.

Doris is halfway down the block when Charlotte sees she has forgotten her Macy's bag.

She throws open the door. "Doris! Doris!"

Charlotte starts running after her. Until she realizes she can't leave the children alone in the house.

How can one person do it all? The head lice, the trail mix, the doctor, the lover, the husband, the children, the job . . . and now, as if that weren't enough, there's Becky. Her lipstick! Her carelessness. And the stud! The gradebook! And she called this *liberation?* When was the last time she had done something for herself?

She goes back inside. Throws the Macy's bag across the room. Picks up the phone. Dials Becky's number, and tells the bitch what she thinks of her.

Chapter 51

When Trey informed me, after calling the tennis match to an abrupt end, that he was afraid to go home because Charlotte was plotting to kill him, naturally I burst out laughing. "You can't be serious," I said, but he insisted, so in the end I offered to go back to his house with him so that I could see what he meant.

We found Charlotte at the kitchen counter chopping vegetables. She swung around, knife glinting, as we walked into the room. She screeched, "You bastard, you miserable bastard! Where the hell have you been?"

Trey dived under the table.

"You fucking coward!" Charlotte shrieked. "You get out from under there and tell me like a man!" I had never seen her like this before. She was still brandishing her knife. "Do you know what I've been through today?"

Here I made the mistake of trying to intervene. She turned on me, knife still brandished. "And you! How do you even have the nerve to set foot in this house?" I backed into the corner. "Why did you lie to me?" she screamed. "What twisted kind of pleasure did you get out of making a fool of me?"

I asked her to put her knife down.

"What knife?" she said, surprised. "Oh, OK. Sure." She walked over to the counter and set it on the chopping board, then hung her head and burst into tears. I bounded over to comfort her.

I don't know how long it was before I remembered I was speaking in the presence of Trey—until I looked under the table and realized that I wasn't.

I didn't see the point of looking for him. I told Charlotte he had probably run away. "He thinks you're trying to kill him, and now you've confirmed his suspicions," I told her. "You may never see him again."

But she said she knew he had to be in the house because she hadn't heard a door open.

We found him in his study, on his exercise bicycle. As Charlotte abased herself with apologies ("I didn't even know I had a knife in my hand, darling!") I convinced myself that fright had had a salutary effect on him.

Even so, I thought it was a bad idea for Charlotte to drive me home. But she wouldn't take no for an answer.

The reason she wanted to drive me home—and I ought to have been able to see this coming, too—is that she had some questions to ask me. The barrage began as she stopped for the first set of lights. "I know we don't have time to go into this in any depth," she said, "but . . ."

Then she winged them at me, one after the other. Why hadn't I told her I was in love with Becky? If I wasn't in love with Becky, why had I told Becky such a dangerous lie? There had to be some strong feeling involved even if I chose to label it differently—so when had it begun? And why had it begun? And exactly how?

"I don't even know myself, for fuck's sake!" I finally shouted. This made her break down again. She sobbed all the way to Hyde Street, parked, and buried her head inside the wheel in a way that made me think she was going to strangle herself. Naturally, I put my arms around her and begged her to pull herself together.

How could I have predicted that she would now launch into an even more excruciating program of self-recrimination? And how do you think it made me feel to hear her blame herself for things I knew to be my fault?

"You wouldn't have done this unless there was something wrong with our relationship," she wailed. "There must be some urgent need you have that I've been unable to fill. What is it? I need to know!"

"Don't flagellate yourself. Please! You're a wonderful person. Why are you so down on yourself?"

It was out of compassion, not lust, that I put her head down on my shoulder. It was out of guilt, not desire, that I let her unzip my fly.

Here began the longest blow-job of my life. It was, as you can imagine, the last thing I wanted or needed. I was worn out—and raw—and it had been days since I had slept.

This was the last place I wanted to be—sitting in a car on a dark street corner, trying not to cry out in pain as this woman tried to make me happy. It will not surprise you to hear that I had a hard time getting it up, or that, when I did finally manage it, I had an even harder time keeping it up. The knowledge that I was stuck there until I came made me even more frantic every time my erection lessened.

Charlotte's response was to try even harder. Meanwhile, I watched the hands on the car clock go round and round and round and round, multiplying my troubles with every minute. A quarter of an hour was too long to leave Trey in charge of the children. But then it was twenty minutes, twenty-five, thirty . . . And oh God, now it was eight o'clock. I was supposed to be meeting Becky at this very minute. If I started now I would be late enough—but I hadn't even come yet! How long would Becky wait?

8:05. 8:10. 8:11. 8:12. What if Becky called home? It was all I could do to imagine enough Nubian slaves to release myself.

But it was too late.

By the time I got to Vesuvio's, Becky was gone.

Chapter 52

When I got home—it must have been about nine—you met me at the door. You looked upset. I did not dare ask who had come by or called in my absence, so I sat down and waited for you to tell me.

"Jesse's acting strange," you finally said. "He's scared of me. Why? I put them to bed at seven-thirty, but then he kept getting up. And every time I went into the room to check him, he made me tap the radiators. Do you know anything about this? Has he told you there's an infant alien hiding somewhere in the house?"

"Oh no, not the alien again," I said.

"Have you been criticizing me in front of him?"

I said I hadn't.

"Then why is he afraid to go to sleep unless you're in the house protecting him?"

I told you I had no idea.

"Well, he's waiting for you now," you said. "You'd better go in there. But first there's something else."

I sat and waited. "Charlotte called," you finally said. "She was looking for Trey. I told her he was out somewhere with you. She asked to speak to you. I said you hadn't come home yet. She said that was impossible as she had just driven you home. I said I didn't know what to make of that, as you were definitely not in the house. This was when she hung up.

"Then, a few minutes later, Becky called—also asking for you. When I asked her for a message, she said to tell you that she was at the hospital helping Ophelia commit Trey and that they needed Charlotte for a signature but couldn't find her anywhere. What is going on?"

You may remember that I was out the door before I could answer you. It is a sign of how far gone I was that I forgot to say goodnight to my boy.

* * *

It took me a good fifteen minutes to find a taxi. I didn't get to the hospital until after ten. Walking into the foyer, I caught a glimpse of Becky with her kids and Charlotte's kids and also, I think, Seb. Before I could get to them, they had disappeared into an elevator.

I raced up the stairs, and down corridors, finally winging around a corner to come face-to-face with Kiki.

"I suppose you're here about Trey," he said.

"Yes," I said. "What happened?"

"Well, it's actually sort of sinister. Trey called up Filly and told her he had lost his mind and asked to be committed. This is not the usual way people ask for help. When she got him here, he changed his mind and said he had made it up to get out of the clutches of these people who were after him—I mean, super nuts. When he asked to be released again, the people here said, Wait a minute! Not so fast! And so . . ."

Here Kiki broke down. "Oh God oh God oh God, I never thought it would hurt like this." He made an effort to collect himself. "I'm sorry. To drag you into someone else's business. But Filly just told me a few hours ago that she's leaving me. She's found someone else!" He let the tears roll down his cheeks. "I didn't know I cared that much. But now when I think . . . about all the things we did together . . . our child . . . our work . . ."

We were joined here by an ashen Charlotte.

"I've committed Trey for the night," she said, as expressionlessly as if she had said she had bought an extra jar of mayonnaise. "So I hope that's all right. Thank you for everything you've done, Kiki."

"That's my job. Don't thank me."

"I guess I'll go home."

"Becky's keeping the kids overnight," Kiki told her. "The only person you have to worry about tonight is yourself."

She offered me a lift. On our way out the hospital gates, she informed me that she had had a good cry on Ophelia's shoulder after committing Trey.

"I told her everything," Charlotte continued. "I hope you don't mind. But I had to talk to someone."

It took a long time before I dared to ask, "So what did Ophelia make of it all?"

Charlotte said, "Nothing."

Leave us sitting in silence at a four-way stop sign, and imagine . . .

Ophelia in the hospital cafeteria. She is drawing on a prescription pad—black-edged shapes which she then covers with a spider's web, which she makes into an even more intricate spider's web, which she then fills in inch by inky inch. At the next table is Kiki with their son. Kiki's swollen face has the fresh, cool look of skin splashed with ice water. He is explaining to Seb what manufacturing methods are used in the production of carbonated drinks.

Reviewing her own condition, Ophelia notes that she doesn't feel all that bad, considering that she has just discovered that the man she was willing to change her life for does not really exist. It doesn't matter that she has disgraced herself, because no one can tell.

She still knows how to fool people.

She jabs the prescription pad with her pen and punctures it. And that makes her feel good, because she never wanted to spend her life stuck in a hospital. She never wanted a child. She never wanted to be a doctor, ever. She did it for him.

Chapter 53

It was approaching eleven when Charlotte dropped me off in front of 2238 for the second time that evening. I waited, just as I had done the first time, until her car disappeared over the crest of the hill. Then I raced down to the corner of Hyde and Union, hailed another cab, and directed it to Becky and Mitchell's.

I could see lights burning in the kitchen as I walked up the front steps. The front door was open. As I swung it shut I heard Mitchell's voice rising out of the darkness. "Don't let it . . . don't let it . . . fuck, oh well, you did."

I could only just make out his silhouette. He was sitting with his back against the inner door. Apparently Becky had bolted the inner front door. "To make a long story short, we're locked in.

"We're in the middle of a fight," he explained. "Don't bother to ask me what it's about either because I've lost track. But listen, what do you think of this part?" he said. He lit a match. I had a glimpse of his face as he leaned forward to light a joint. He inhaled. As he exhaled and handed the joint to me, he said, "So anyway, listen to this. How long have we lived in this neighborhood? How many words have I exchanged with the people next door? Well, here's what just went down."

I took a toke, handed the joint back to him. He said, "OK. So listen. Becky and I are having a serious shouting match about the future of our marriage. And so finally I say I'm leaving. Becky tries a karate chop on me. To protect my balls, I catch her foot. She falls on her ass, but not badly, it looks like, and so I split. I'm backing out of the drive when she pulls herself to the door moaning that she's injured. So I go back. Right? And of course she's really OK. Then there's a ring at the door. It's Mister Man Next Door. He says, 'I heard your wife and she sounded like she was in pain. I thought maybe I could help because I'm a doctor.' And so I say thanks but she's actually OK. I tell him we were just having an argument. And he says, 'Well then, maybe my wife can help. She's a psychiatrist.'"

Mitchell snorted.

"Great place to bring up kids, huh? And while I'm on the subject—I hope you're not here on urgent business because, when she locked me up in here, she sounded like she meant business. I'm easy, though. The way I look at it, it's practice."

"Maybe you'll get lucky," I said. "Maybe the Mafia will get to you before the IRS does and you can avoid a long and expensive trial. Or maybe when you tell Kiki where his money's gone, maybe *he'll* kill you."

Mitchell chuckled. "Hey, it's good to talk to you again." He paused, then added, "It's been great having Laura there, don't get me wrong. But . . ." He let out a deep sob. "How did we end up on this porch? Do you realize what day it is in less than an hour?" He waved his phosphorescent watch at me. "It's my fortieth birthday!

"I'm forty in less than an hour," he sobbed. "And I have nothing to show for it! And I don't know why! My ideas were always ace! Maybe if I had spent less time with my kids . . . but now, God, I'm so close to them how could I live apart from them?"

At this Becky appeared at the inner door. "Would you two stop being so fucking maudlin! Get practical. Start thinking about what we have to do to stay out of jail!"

Unlocking the outer door, she ran down the stairs. Both Mitchell and I sprang to our feet and followed her to the car. Mitchell tripped and fell as we chased her to the corner. I managed to get into the backseat of the car.

At first she refused to talk to me. Then, when she got to Julius Kahn and parked, she turned around and said, "We have nothing to discuss.

"It's over," she explained as I climbed into the front seat. "So go home. Deal with Laura. Don't pause for a second to think about me. For all I know, I'll have to go to jail as that idiot's accomplice."

"No, you won't. I'll testify against him for you."

"Oh, stop sounding so sincere. You of all people. I'm telling you. I have had enough earnest conversations today to last me a lifetime. I've had to listen to Ophelia tell me about this wonderful guy she's going to run off with—and say nothing. I've had to listen to Charlotte blame me for the world head-lice epidemic. I've had to lie to Laura. I've had to change around my furniture three fucking times to suit my paranoid crook of a husband, and to top it all off, I think he's run through every penny. I don't know what I'm going to do. So I have nothing to say to you."

"Oh Becky," I said. I was so filled with remorse I couldn't stop myself from putting my arms around her. I could feel her body going lax as she sighed. "Oh Mike," she sobbed. We had been sitting like that for two or three minutes when suddenly she said, "Fuck!"

I sat up. "What?" Then I saw a man's form through the fogged-up window. A man's hand, knocking.

It was Mitchell. He showed us his arms. "Look."

Becky rolled down the window.

"Shit. He's slit his wrists."

He got into the car without protest. Becky sat in the back and did what she could to stop the flow of blood while I drove straight to Ophelia and Kiki's.

I had forgotten the state of play between me and Ophelia. I was therefore taken aback by her stony expression when she met me at the door, and I was not at all prepared when she said, "Could I talk to you in private for a second?" She stepped out into the hallway, carefully closing the door behind her. Then she whacked me across the face.

After that she was all business. I was impressed by the cool with which she handled Mitchell, who, even as she was bandaging him, was telling her and Kiki, in a child's voice, that they were not going to get even a fraction of their investment back.

"Let's worry about all that some other time," Kiki said.

When Mitchell tried to tell Ophelia that he had slit his wrists because he had found Becky and me necking in the front seat of his car, she just said, "Everything's going to look better when you've had some sleep."

Eventually I remembered that there were five unattended children at Becky and Mitchell's, and I drove Becky home. It was the first time I had sat behind the wheel of a car since my accident.

After I left Becky, I took the long cut home. I remember that when I got there I looked up at our bedroom window from the other side of the street. I remember how tall the building looked, and how narrow our window. I remember stopping to count the lines of light filtering through our venetian blinds. I remember wondering what kind of nightmare was waiting for me up there. What kinds of questions you would hurl at me, what kinds of answers you had already gotten from Charlotte or Becky or Ophelia or even Kiki or Mitchell. One thing was sure, I told myself—even if I sat down on this curb until dawn, I would not be able to think up a lie elaborate enough to explain away the events of this evening. My only option was to go upstairs and face you like the man I had once pretended to be.

And so I went up. I remember that the entryway was dark when I walked in, and that the laundry basket standing in front of the service elevator was half lit by the light coming in from the kitchen, and half in black shadow. A single lamp was burning in the living room. Reflected in the window, it hovered in the sky between Coit Tower and the Pyramid Building. There were books and puzzle pieces strewn across the carpet—even all these years later, I can still remember what color they were, and what shape, and the haphazard pattern they made without even meaning to. I can look at the same rug, now clean and bare, and imagine those exact same pieces and books strewn across it. I remember that, while I was standing there looking at them, you came up behind me and said, "You're home at last!"

I could tell from your tone of voice that nothing had happened in my absence to prepare you for the things I was going to have to tell you. That was the hardest part—to see you come out of the darkness into the circle of light, to understand suddenly but too late that it didn't matter where you had been all those months, and that I ought to have known you would come back, that I ought to have trusted you . . . That was the hard part—to look past you into the children's bedroom and know that, even though I couldn't see them, they were tucked in their beds. To know that this, my home, my refuge, would only continue to exist for as long as I could keep up the pretense that nothing beyond the walls of this apartment existed. That even if I sat down and said nothing, even if I pulled out the phone jacks and barred the doors, even if I went to bed with you now and put my head under the pillow, it was only a matter of time before you found out what I had done. That is why I broke down when I saw you—not because I was trying to play on your sympathies but because I knew what I was about to lose.

I still don't understand why I did some of the things I have told you about. I have no idea how much was me, how much the situation. Now that you have read this, maybe you can tell me. And even if you can't or don't want to, I hope that you will accept my story as the explanation I owed you, and that, when you have inspected it for faults and congratulated yourself for having gotten out of a bad marriage to a difficult and misguided man, you will go back and read between the lines and see that this man loved you and loves you still, and that there are no longer any conditions attached to this love, and that you can take it and cherish it without cherishing me, and use it to heal the things I broke in you, and make yourself whole again.

ALWAYS

Chapter 54

As I write this, the stars are beginning to fade away, and the first light is showing beyond the Financial District. As I watch the hills change from black to gray, I keep thinking how strange it is that the hills you can see from your window are about to do the opposite.

Has it been a long day in that villa of yours? Is the heat finally lifting? Is the wind pushing the smog back down the hill into Athens? Is the sprinkler on in the impossible fairy-tale rose garden? Is your cook making coffee for your chauffeur in the kitchen while you stand, regretfully, with your back to the window, and survey your perfect dollhouse life?

Are you happy?

Are you going out this evening? Is there a wedding on at the Hilton? A reception at the Grande Bretagne? Are you looking forward to it, or are you playing for time as you sit at your antique table toying with your expensive French makeup? Now that you have adjusted the strap of your new Dior gown, now that your hair is just so, now that you have found the earrings that go with that necklace, are you beginning to think of wafting down a perfumed corridor to the nursery to say goodnight to the children?

Our children, in a nursery.

I can't imagine them in that room you showed me. And I can't imagine him. There is no room for him in this picture. He has to be out—in his car, at his office, at the home of a friend whose name you don't care to know. What reason did he give you for staying in town, or didn't you even listen when he called to tell you? Is that what you always wanted—an invisible man with a bottomless bank account? Were you in touch with him, were you secretly in love with him, all the years we were together?

Do the children ever ask about me? Did they tell you about our trip? I am sending under separate cover the photos we took on Naxos. There's one in particular I think you'll like. It's of Jesse and Maria standing in the temple, in the marble archway you always used to tell me about, the one going nowhere. I can't tell you what it did to me to see it there, framed against the sky just as you always described it, and to think that you once stood exactly where the children were standing when I took their picture. And then—to go down and see the rockpools you always talked about, to sit next to them the way you said you used to do whenever you felt upset, to look out and imagine the color of the water, imagine the walls of the old town through your eyes . . .

I'm surprised that after all these years you've been in Greece you never found the time to take the children to Naxos yourself. You used to say it would be the first thing you'd show them. Have you drifted so far away that you can't even remember your old daydreams?

Did they tell you that I tried to take them to see the *Diadoumenos* that last morning? We went straight from Piraeus to the archaeological museum, but it was closed. So maybe next time—although it may have been a mistake to take Jesse so close without giving him the chance to see it. If his nightmares come back, you may want to take him down there yourself to reassure him.

Or is it too late? Laura, could it be possible? Is our child afraid of art?

When we were having ice creams in that café next to the steps, I saw him glance up at the museum's bolted door—and then shudder, just the way he used to do when he was little. It almost killed me to see those old expressions pass over his face. And to see you in Maria, to see her laugh like you, and wrinkle her nose like you, and sit in the same café where you and I once sat and order the same kind of ice cream and draw the same line across the top of it with her spoon. To be sitting in the shadow of the Parthenon one day, and the next day to travel to the other side of the earth and see the Palace of Fine Arts, and hate it for not being marble, hate it for reminding me of what may be beyond my reach forever, hate it most of all for what it is: a concrete imitation of a ruin, sitting on the edge of a man-made duck pond.

It almost killed me, Laura, to say goodbye to them just as we were beginning to be comfortable with one another. To see them stand there on the front steps blowing kisses and then turning away and running into the arms of another man.

Do they miss me? Did they even know what to make of me? That look they both have in the picture I took of them in front of the Parthenon, with the Parthenon slanting so unnaturally into the hot white light behind them—are they squinting because of the sun or are they puzzled about this man who keeps telling them he is their father? Those ravaged eyes . . .

I hope they weren't upset that I snapped at them for not smiling when I was taking their picture in front of the Acropolis. I was feeling tense, because I knew how few hours I had left with them, because I could feel my father's pitying eyes boring into my back as he watched me repeating his mistakes. I am not complaining. I was happy we could have that trip together, three generations. I'm glad he's there in Athens to keep up regular contact with them.

Laura, I know I fucked you over. I know I am an asshole, but the children were the center of my life, and seeing them a week at a time twice a year is just not enough. Never being able to have them here in San Francisco makes it even harder. Wouldn't you let them come here sometime if I accompanied them both ways on the plane? Don't you think this is something you and I should be deciding instead of Stavros? Don't you know how it destroys me to see another man play father to my children? Don't you see, now that you have read this, that one of the reasons we ended up like this was because I put the children first?

I saw their old playmates today. It was Lara's birthday. I didn't want to go to the party, but Becky insisted. Imagine what it did to me to see those children, those same children still together, but not to see ours . . .

The entire Stork Club (except for you, that is) had turned up for the occasion. I don't know how long it had been since I'd last seen the men. Mitchell came down from Petaluma, which is where he has been living ever since he got out of the clinker. His new girlfriend runs a mail-order clothing business out of a converted chicken farm up there. She grossed seventeen million last year—she wears the pants, all right, but to tell you the truth, he looks relieved. He's running a bookstore-cum-bar and managing an exercise studio next door that recoups the bcb's losses. The girlfriend—she's no bimbo—does the books.

Trey has filled out a little, and seems content. He still has a hint of that old crazy look in his eyes, but you wouldn't see it unless you had known him in the old days. He has a nine-to-five accountant's job in the Financial District and lives in Redwood City, in a tract house, I hear, with a woman who works in the same office and who, I hear, looks so much like him she could be his sister—he didn't bring her.

I don't know if anyone told you what happened to Kiki and Ophelia. I'm sure you heard that they kept the joint practice going even after the divorce. After what Mitchell did with their money, they didn't really have much choice. For a while it was looking like they might be getting back together. Then Ophelia went to Cuba for a month and, while she was there, Kiki linked up with the first woman he met in front of Seb's school. By the time Ophelia got back, this woman already had her voice on the answering machine. This did wonders for Ophelia's ego. For a while, she was talking about moving to the country, but today she said she had gone off the idea. She and the new wife (who is an RN) spent most of the party discussing a fertility clinic they want to set up even though Kiki insists it's not financially viable.

Becky—as you may know—has just bought that studio that used to belong to that jazz dancer who died of AIDS. This is for profit to pay for her other projects while she waits for them to break even. She leads a fragmented life—there is a boyfriend she keeps way, way in the background. He lives on the East Coast; they meet once a month. She spent half the party talking to him on the phone. She has two formerly delinquent and now evolving teenagers living with her, and spends a good deal of time with a cluster of Russian refugee families whose daughters do babysitting for her. Those Central American priests are back in the picture, as well as a half-brother . . . it looks chaotic to me but it seems to work.

The big surprise is Charlotte. I don't know how much you hear, but in case you didn't—after she got rid of Trey she went into a fury of ideologically correct but unbearable selfishness. This resulted in her head of department firing her. She is suing him for unfair dismissal. The case is pending. Meanwhile, she is pursuing what she calls her outside interests. First she set herself up as a cartoonist—but not a funny one. Then she had a brief and embarrassing phase as a mime. We were all worried when she tried out as a folksinger, but, to our surprise, she's not as bad as we expected. She had a big success in Nevada City a week or two ago—and turned up at Becky's with another folksinger she met while she was up there. It's not clear what their relationship is: he's presentable, but I don't know how far I'd trust him.

She also brought Mona. Mona says she recognized me right off, but of course she was expecting to see me. It took me an hour or more to figure out why she was giving me those curious looks. Do you remember how slight she used to be? How lightfooted? Not anymore: she is sunburned and muscular and her hair is hennaed. She has a three-year-old boy whose name is Conor—she knows who the father is but she can't remember his name.

I liked the boy. He reminds me a lot of Jesse at that age. It's strange to see the child of a woman you used to be married to. I had to keep reminding myself that, if we had stayed married, this child standing in front of me would not exist. I invited them both back to the apartment after the party. For the first time in four years, a child actually played with the toys in the baskets. "You've kept all your kids' old things?" Mona asked. She thoughtfully did not add, Even though they have long since outgrown them. I explained to her that I wanted to keep something in the apartment that was familiar to them, so that when they come back they'll think of it as home.

"That's nice," said Mona. This is not something she would have said in her previous incarnation. In fact, she is a much gentler person now than she was when we were married. She's had a knockabout life over the past twenty years. Some would say it has been one false start after another, but to hear her talk there was always a logic, always some important lesson to draw from her year in a mobile home, from her ill-fated decision to go to Hawaii with someone she had met at a yoga class, from the thousand and one bars she had to work in when she turned up in strange towns without any money. She told me she had only ever had one job that was worthy of her degree and her brain. It was working for a charity organization in Colorado. She left after three weeks, she told me, because "the challenge" scared her. It was strange hearing her say this—it was just the sort of thing that would have driven me wild when we were together. I would have been furious about the stupid risks she took, the way she was trashing herself—but now I could look at her and think, almost with affection: This is who this woman is. These are her limitations, and so what? We talked until way past midnight, and that gives me hope. That makes me think that one day you and I will be able to sit down together and talk like that, too.

She wanted to know about the stack of notebooks on my desk. So I told her this story. She listened quietly and, I thought, sympathetically, but afterward she told me that she was more in the dark about what kind of person you were than she had been at the beginning. "You don't know this woman at all, do you?" she said. We argued about it—in a friendly enough way—but I couldn't convince her. "You never understood her. That's obvious. But don't worry," she said as she stood up to go, "I never understood you, either. Talk about dark continents!"

As she slipped her son into her backpack, she told me she was about to go to Singapore to work for a couple who own a gallery in Santa Fe. I told her it sounded suspect to me, and she said it did to her, too. "But hell, it's more exciting that way." She said she liked being a pioneer.

She kissed me on both cheeks—a new affectation—and then off she went. As I watched her emerge from the building with her son on her back and saunter down the street, I felt like there was nothing left of me except her opinion. I thought: This is the way things are these days. The women and children go off on adventures. The man stays and waits in what soon becomes a museum of discarded toys. He doesn't throw them away, because even though his children have outgrown them, he doesn't want them to forget, and that is his job, to make sure they don't. As I watched her disappear around the corner, I asked myself, Is this what it means these days to be a man?

Then I told myself, No, that's her version, not mine. I felt this empty before. Walking like an automaton through the museum, past the tired vases and statues and friezes, with no idea of what was waiting for me on the other side of the door . . . how can she claim to know me, Laura, if she doesn't know what happened next? How can it be that I don't understand you, if I can't even wake up in the morning without seeing you there next to me, if I can't even go into the shower without imagining you in it with me, imagining you right down to the last detail, right down to the way you rub the soap up and down your back?

How can she say I don't want to understand you, I who have spent the past four years going through your books and your letters and your pictures? Who has tried harder to look for the missing links? Who else can remember exactly how your food tasted, or how you put your lips on a glass, or how you grimaced when you were trying to string two disparate thoughts together, how you laughed with your friends in the days when they were still your friends, how you put your arms around me when you half woke in the middle of the night, what you said to me when you first saw Jesse in the hospital, how you looked when I carried Maria in to you? How can she say I don't know you when you are so much in my mind that I can't even walk to answer the door without hoping that when I open it, I'll find you standing there waiting to forgive me?

A Note About the Author

Maureen Freely is a free-lance writer and critic, and the author of two previous novels, *Mother's Helper* and *The Life of the Party.*

A Note on the Type

The text of this book was set in a typeface named Perpetua, designed by the British artist Eric Gill (1882–1940) and cut by The Monotype Corporation, London, in 1928–1930. Perpetua is a contemporary letter of original design, without any direct historical antecedents. The shapes of the roman letters basically derive from stonecutting, a form of lettering in which Gill was eminent. The italic is essentially an inclined roman. The general effect of the typeface in reading sizes is one of lightness and grace. The larger display sizes of the type are extremely elegant and form what is probably the most distinguished series of inscriptional letters cut in the present century.

Composed by Creative Graphics,
Allentown, Pennsylvania

Printed and bound by The Haddon Craftsmen,
Scranton, Pennsylvania

Designed by Cassandra J. Pappas